Benjamin Heim Shepard

Illuminations
on Market Street

a story about sex and estrangement,
AIDS and loss, and other preoccupations
in San Francisco

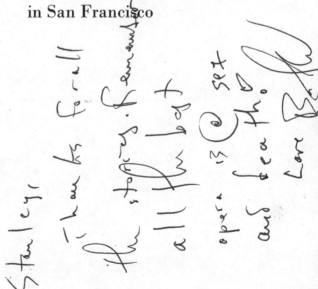

Benjamin Heim Shepard

ILLUMINATIONS ON MARKET STREET

a story about sex and estrangement,
AIDS and loss, and other preoccupations
in San Francisco

ibidem-Verlag
Stuttgart

Bibliographic information published by the Deutsche Nationalbibliothek
Die Deutsche Nationalbibliothek lists this publication in the Deutsche Nationalbibliografie;
detailed bibliographic data are available in the Internet at http://dnb.d-nb.de.

Bibliografische Information der Deutschen Nationalbibliothek
Die Deutsche Nationalbibliothek verzeichnet diese Publikation in der Deutschen
Nationalbibliografie; detaillierte bibliografische Daten sind im Internet über http://dnb.d-nb.de
abrufbar.

Cover photograph by Benjamin Shepard, design by Caroline Shepard.

ISBN-13: 978-3-8382-1211-1

© *ibidem*-Verlag / *ibidem* Press
Stuttgart, Germany 2019

Contents

Cast of Characters

Amanda — A friend of Cab's from the Inwood Theater summer job who dated one of the Peyote Cowboys and sleeps with Cab a few times

Becky — A high school friend of Cab's from English class, with whom he gets mixed up in a sex panic

Bobby — A college friend of Cab's who lives in Los Angeles but frequents San Francisco

Buck — Chloe and Charles' friend from Vassar

Phil — Becky's boyfriend, a hippy whose father works for the Dallas Cowboys

Cab — Protagonist

Charles — Cab's best friend in San Francisco

Chloe — The femme fatale of Cab's college years

Chris — A housemate with Mimi. For a brief while there, Cab dates Chris, his first girlfriend in San Francisco.

Daisy — One of Cab's friends from high school

Deg, Andy, Jade — Cab's friends from the Inwood Theater summer job of '88

David — An accountant Cab befriends in San Francisco

Elizabeth — A San Francisco sex researcher who Cab dates briefly

Grant — Cab's best friend from high school

Jasmin — A never-never girlfriend Cab keeps meeting

Jim — Cab's coworker in San Francisco

Juan — A resident at 1994 Market Street, with a dark, occasionally Christian sensibility

Julie — Cab's muse in San Francisco, who he meets at the gym

Kirk — A friend of Buck, Cab, and Charles from Vassar

Kurt — Sue's roommate in San Francisco

Lili — Cab's girlfriend senior year in high school

Louie — Friend of Cab's from high school

Lucy — A college friend who Cab dates and discusses LBJ and Queen with

Louisa — Chloe's best friend from Duncanville Tx

Marsha — Cab's girlfriend spring of freshman year in college

Marchello — Italian exchange student who lives at Cab's house in high school

Marni — An artful senior and subject of Cab's adoration freshman year in high school

Marsha — Cab's girlfriend freshman year in college

Mimi and Chris — Southern expatriots who share their home every Wednesday with Cab and their roommates Brad and Trish

Natalie — Cab's old suitemate who used to date Bobby

Pedro — A resident at 1994 Market Street, who Cab confides in and learns from

9

Peter	— Cab's younger brother
Raymond	— Cab's roommate on Page Street
Raoul	— Cab's boss at work
Rebecca	— Cab's editor at SOMA Magazine
Rick	— A high school friend from the football team, who Cabs stays in touch with
Sarah	— A bass player Cab briefly dates senior year in high school
Sue	— A waitress Cab meets in a café after a Critical Mass bike ride in San Francisco
Scudder	— Charles' roommate in San Francisco who he knows from Vassar
Ted	— Chloe's former lover who works with Cab at Massimo's
Tessa	— A friend who Cab dates a bit in college, staying in touch in San Francisco
Terri	— A resident at 1994 Market Street who owns a toaster named Frankie
Todd	— A friend of Cab's from high school
Tommy	— A high school friend of Cab's, Lili's former boyfriend
Willy	— A gay porno star living with AIDS who Cab gets to know at work

A Word to the Reader

Illuminations is a bildungsroman in four parts, built of overlapping layers of stories. Each section can be read separately or as a whole. The first and last sections, Parts I, II, and IV, take you to a world in which people are dying because they have had sex or injected drugs. They trace a story about AIDS and losses in pre-protease San Francisco. Eros still hangs in the air as hope for something good, something regenerative in the universe.

In the midst of this we find a familiar tale of a young writer, Cab, who pens his way through it all during graveyard shifts at an AIDS housing program, dashing notes about being dumped, the goings on of the people he knows, and watching the slow-motion car wreck as people live and die. Everyone has a story in San Francisco, except Cab, who feels as if he is merely a scribe to the sagas of those around him. In turn, he starts excavating his past. That story leads to the stories of similar misconduct, flirtations, losses, punk rock shows, girls with purple hair, infatuations, and indiscretions. All the while, he hears his friends tales of the city, of AIDS and death, Eros and Thanatos, and gets lost in their stories, trying to make sense of the random kindness, as well as the wreckage around him. Everyone has a story and a past, which in the times of plagues have lethal consequences. But why do some live and some die?

Parts I, II, and III trace Cab's narrative of being a young man unsuccessfully letting go of his Southern childhood, of sex, football, Texan lunacy, and a jigger of racism, mixed into a gumbo of irreconcilable memories and misgivings. Throughout this, the phobias of the past which ineffably haunt the country, linger in the way the world beyond him deals with AIDS.

So reader, if a coming of age tale holds little appeal, read Part I, parts of II, skim through III, and make your way back into the war zone of AIDS carnage in Part IV. But, if looking homeward with angels and narratives of growing up is your inclination, read from beginning to end, as the first three parts of the story lead us along a road trip from California to Texas, up to New York, by way of the Mississippi Sound and New Orleans, to Italy, back to Los Angeles, through riots, and a trip up Highway One to San Francisco as layers of this story converge and Cab searches for his story.

Part One

The Coldest Winter
Was a Summer…

Walking the Toaster

"One cannot go to war and come back normal,"
-Richard Proulx, infantryman, US Army, WWII

July 1996

I had not been in San Francisco for over a year. But the city felt different than my previous time there. Walking up Market Street, I could not place it. Hyde and Leavenworth still felt down and out, a few homeless people wandering about, the smell of pot in the air, graffiti on the walls. I hurried past Van Ness, where I had worked. Debris was still strewn about, but it felt strange. I didn't want to go back to the building, did not want to be seen or see anyone. I hurried past. I walked past an old café where I used to write, past Guerrero and Church where my friends and I drank and played pool after evening shifts at 1994 Market Street, the AIDS housing program where I'd spent those post-college years when AIDS deaths spiked and treatment eluded science. There was the Safeway where we met before leaving for the ACT UP action in Sacramento, throwing the ashes of our friends into the air and onto the steps of the Capitol so the whole world could see what we were living every day.

That felt like a long time ago, but I could still feel the ashes in my hands. Taste them. The city felt like something else was happening. There was Eros, a sex club I'd explored. Richard, one of the clients who'd lived at 1994 Market, was standing outside smoking. But he appeared odd. He looked like he'd gained weight. When I last saw him, wasting syndrome was pulling at him, seemingly squeezing the life from his body, like he was living in Auschwitz. I walked past Café Du Nord, where I had gone dancing so many times with Julie, glancing at the Baghdad Café between Sanchez Street & Noe Street, where we all met for morning coffee. A few people were walking out of Café Flore looking giddy. They strolled my way. One of them was Michelle, a transwoman who'd lived in the building. I looked at her and then away, ducking my head. Instead of the gaunt look of skin drawn into her jaw as she'd had the year prior, she seemed to have flesh on her body. She looked alive. Everyone looked alive. A line of people were getting ready to walk into Josie's Juice Joint at 16th. They were laughing. It looked like the whole city was laughing, all of Castro Street. No wheelchairs like last time, no more walking dead. I guess the treatment—highly active antiretroviral therapy for HIV—that everyone was talking about was working. People were surviving.

But things still felt peculiar.

A skinny young man wearing baggy jeans, a denim jacket, and a baseball cap walked by. Recognizing him, I started to say, "Hi Toby." When I looked again it was someone else. It was a memory. He was gone. Toby had died two years prior.

The ghosts were still walking down Castro Street.

I was supposed to meet Jim, a coworker from 1994 Market later that night. Walking past the Van Ness again, I recalled my first day at work there, years prior. I was finishing the graveyard shift. The sun was just rising along Market Street when the phone rang.

"Cab?"

"Yes," I answered.

"It's Terri."

"Morning, Terri."

"Can you come upstairs? I need to show you something."

I hung up the phone, called my supervisor Jim, who lived in the building, and walked up to the second floor. The hall smelled like rotting donated food, like decaying bodies. The building always seemed ominous, but perhaps less so in the morning. A new start.

Terri's door was open, but I knocked.

Standing with his hands on his hips, Terri was wearing a blue terrycloth robe and pink slippers. He turned around and smiled. His eyes were drawn into his face, his gums bleeding. But he didn't seem to care.

"Frankie is so demanding," Terri declared in an exasperated tone.

"Huh? Frankie?" I asked, looking around the room.

"She wants to go again."

"She?"

"She——Frankie——I'm so sorry I didn't introduce you. That's why I called you."

Jim, my supervisor, walked by and stuck his head in the door.

"Frankie wants to go again," Terri smiled, gesturing to the toaster she was pulling down the hall.

"You just went, baby," Terri was scolding the toaster, as if she was a puppy.

Jim looked at me, trying to be serious, and then cracked a smile.

"Great to meet you, Frankie," said Jim. "You need anything else, Terri?"

"No, I just wanted to introduce you guys. I found her here yesterday. She needs someone and now we have each other. But she has to go so I'm taking her out for a walk," she explained, grasping the chord like a leash, the toaster dangling behind her.

"Good to meet you, Frankie," I said. Jim and I walked down the hall. Terri was pulling the toaster talking to it.

"Dementia," Jim sighed. "It's a big part of this and no one wants to talk about it. Before people lose their bodies, their minds go. Everyone is losing their minds. Everyone."

"Me included," I said.

"You can't lose your mind. You work here," Jim responded. "You have to stay sane. And you don't have AIDS."

Terri walked the toaster outside. The sun was shining on Market Street.

"What's going on?" asked Pedro, another of the residents.

"That's Frankie," I responded, realizing I sounded as tired as I felt.

"Everyone is going bananas around here," he grumbled to himself and walked outside.

16

That was all but two years prior. Since then, it felt like everything had changed.

Later that night, Jim and I talked about it at the Motherlode, off of Polk Street.

"It's not over, but the treatment has changed everything. People are living now," he explained.

"It really works?"

"The pills work."

"I saw it today on Castro Street. People are alive again."

"But the side effects can be rough: Weight gain, weakness, nausea, diarrhea. Still, people are surviving now, those who get the meds and take them. That means insurance. But there are half the obits in the Bay Area Reporter. You remember it used to be pages and pages of obits? Now it's just five or ten, not fifty."

"So we survived it?" I asked.

"No, my roommate has it. And his life is not beer and pretzels. It's not over for everyone. But it's different now. People have a chance to live."

Walking home that night I thought about this strange moment. It had all changed since the bad days, when the Sword of Damocles hung over everyone, afraid a cough would lead to a bed, which led to an ambulance, which led to a hospital with a No Exit sign. Terri was long gone. He hadn't survived it. Most of the residents at 1994 did not make it. But a few remained. Those who lived long enough for treatment were getting better. Thank god for treatment. There'd be no more walking the toaster.

That all seemed like a long time ago—the toaster, Terri, getting to know the city, trying to forget Chloe and know Julie. It was hard to imagine any of us would look at the world with the same eyes after that. I wouldn't. A lot happened in those San Francisco years, between the plague, my friends coming and then shuffling off, and the stories reminding me of another world when I lived on Page Street. I had only moved there four short years prior. But that was enough for everything to change.

San Francisco Streets

"My whole life was a series of fade ins and fade outs..."
-Stephen Vizinczey, *In Praise of Older Women*, 1966

The first time I saw Julie, she was walking onto the elevator at the gym in the financial district. We were both going up. Leaning back against the wall, her brown eyes seemed to come right at me, connecting with mine. She paused; I glimpsed at her, and she looked down. A smile crossed her lips. In recent days, I had felt invisible. But something was happening. I looked back and she was looking straight at me. I was going through the roof. Some say eyes are a message from the soul. But I didn't know what hers were saying. It was like looking out at the sea: enigmatic, mercurial. Nonetheless, I felt warm and fuzzy. With olive skin, brunette hair, and a dizzy California demeanor, she was all I wanted. Eros whirled. I knew at that moment that I would try to figure her out. I'd spend the next year trying to know Julie.

There had been others whom I had obsessed about. But this was San Francisco. It was a place and a time to become something else, unencumbered from the past.

I loved living in San Francisco. Maybe loved is a strong word. I liked many things about the fabled town: its bawdy cinema noir feel, the wide open ethos of its hustlers strutting, making common cause with scruffy anarchists, and bohemian expats who'd just come back after hitchhiking across Cuba, telling stories about it all while hand rolling cigarettes. The city teemed with radical ecologists, lesbian novelists, Buddhists running publishing houses, runaways hanging on street corners, drag kings performing, Beatniks writing, opera goers looking glamorous, Castro clones cruising, and village people walking the streets of this peninsula separated from the rest of the country and the Pacific Ocean. Nicknamed Baghdad by the Bay, the city had famously all but ignored prohibition, serving alcohol throughout the era, becoming a home to a cavalcade of drinkers, saloon keepers, and vagabonds.

New York was money and Washington power, but as Joe Flower quipped, "freedom sips a cappuccino in a sidewalk cafe in San Francisco." The city was teeming with beauty—exquisite, never-been-so-lonely beauty. Everyone had a story, usually little to do with where they were escaping from and more about where they were going. I was ambivalent about letting go of all that had happened before I got here. There was my childhood in the South, where we'd lived for generations and generations. And like many, I romanticized the place, but needed to put it somewhere else, somewhere in the back of my mind. So I spent most of my afternoons off work sitting in my room writing about the people I'd known and going out with friends—a group of fellow Southerners I'd met my first summer in town. In between, the city felt strange, familiar, and for a little while there, like home.

Everyone reinvents themselves here, or so I'd heard. My story was certainly not in need of reinvention, at least not like that. After all, the very act of reinventing begins with creative deconstruction. The passion to destroy is a creative passion, as everyone who went to City Lights Bookstore and picked up Mikhail Bakunin's books knew.

In the years before moving to San Francisco, I romped between Los Angeles and New York, Germany and Italy, New Orleans and Princeton—as far away from the Texas where I grew up as I could get. By the time I got to San Francisco, I traded my travels for a room with a couch, a job search, roommates, and the uncertainty of the early 1990s recession, before the internet boom and bust.

I had fallen in love with the place in 1989, on a trip to Santa Cruz the weekend of the Loma Prieta earthquake. I was moved by the way people responded, offering each other cups of coffee in the wreckage. I left the trip dreaming about the Grateful Dead and the punks, the Red Woods, a couch on the beach, and the elegant gay men in tuxedos attending clandestine secret societies straight out of Christopher Isherwood novels. Over the years, I came to mythologize the secret histories of the place, its Cockettes, dropouts, free clinics, and tales of those creating an alternative to everything that was and had been in the old USA. People leaned on and listened to each other here, even as their city was crumbling. And I wrote about it all in a blue notebook. With a century of isolation and anxiety, protests and revolutions coming to an end, we were all trying to keep our heads.

"The mark of a great film is a sound that sticks with you," Dad's college roommate from 1956, Thomas, explained to me. "I first heard that sound in *Blue Angel* when I was a small boy," he said. Tom was the first person I'd known to die of AIDS, a year prior to my arrival in San Francisco. He had lived with us my sophomore year in high school in the mid-1980s. Tom was more interested in the movies than activism. "Not a day has gone by that the humiliated schoolmaster's cry has not rumbled in my head," he had said. "That's the scream of a broken man whose world had lost its absolutes. We are all the grand-children of that scream."

San Francisco was filled with such screams. But no one seemed to hear them. Tom's stories trailed through my head as I walked the streets, with signs about AIDS posted everywhere. Public health promotions read: "Safe Sex Is Hot Sex!" and "Tweaking out of control can be a drag."

I thought about the screams of the dying century: the bomb in '45; the McCarthy hearings; Stalin's terror; Mao's Great Leap Forward and the mass starvation in the '50s; what became of advisors exploring a South East Asian civil war; riots and police violence in the 1960s; Pol Pot's Killing Fields in the 1970s; Nixon resigning; the deaths of the Black Panthers in Oakland and Chicago; Gay Liberation; the White Night Riots; and then AIDS. Somehow, amidst the screams, people still found a way to be human here—to go to discos, cook meals together in communal houses, trip acid on the beach, create gender-fuck burlesque shows, and take to the streets with furious calls for something better, shouts that couldn't be quieted. I was in awe of it—all that history—that panorama of bodies, all those struggles. But the strife behind them felt like it was slipping into oblivion, being erased. Memory and amnesia seemed to plague us.

But maybe sometimes forgetting was good.

San Francisco Summers

"The coldest winter I ever spent was a summer in San Francisco," Mark Twain is said to have declared after visiting San Francisco. Those who seem to know anything about Twain dispute that he ever said it. It felt pretty cold to me.

Despite the chill, it was the summer of 1992 and a new chapter was taking shape in my life. I had a room that cost $280 a month with two roommates on Page Street, and I was trying to navigate my way through a sea of temp jobs and temptations.

The fog rolled through the city all summer long. But the coldest chill I got was with romance. Sure, there were girlfriends and a few hot streaks. Even when I did get some, warmth was elusive. I was chasing someone who was no longer there. All I had were memories (and scabies I brought from Los Angeles) that lingered, something to remember from a final rollicking month of college scenes and secret rendezvous with a girl obsessed with LBJ and Freddie Mercury.

Every Wednesday, I hung out with a colony of Southern expatriates, who converged in the cottage of my friends Mimi and Chris, and their assortment of roommates, between jobs and careers, romance and unemployment. They rented on Larkin and Polk Street and shared the space with two roommates, Trish and Brad. Brad had graduated from Berkeley (as he reminded all of us frequently). He worked at the Gap and was fired for sexually harassing one of the customers. That was an ongoing source of humor for all of us for years. He was very popular with his fans, who kept calling to ask about him long after he'd been dismissed. Mimi was an anthropology major from Florida who aspired to make movies in San Francisco. Chris was from Atlanta. We had both escaped the world of the South. Her dad went to school with my uncle at the Citadel in South Carolina, writing countless novels about the experience.

The world loved him. But they were family for me. We had all traveled to Rome, studying in Florence in college and found ourselves lost in San Francisco, watching the *Tales of the City* miniseries, as we experienced a few of our own in this upside-down city. Chris' dad gave us a glimpse into both the beauty and the cruelty of a world of toxic social relations in the south, the world our fathers endured that we somehow escaped. But that hostility toward difference never quite went away, even out here. He also showed us how much there was out there to see if we looked at the waves, remembered, and felt long enough. A continent away from the low country of South Carolina and its exquisite and sensual tidal marshes, this was a different kind of space. The beaches were cold and mysterious, like the Bergman movies where Max von Sydow played chess with death as the waves crashed around him. You could always find someone wondering about something here.

"Fuck this modern world," declared one of the Cockettes. "I'm gonna throw on a skirt, take a tab of acid, and hit the beach."

One of my first weekends in town, July 4th, 1992 my roommates and I ate mushrooms and played touch football in Mission Dolores Park. Independence was in the air. The Food Not Bombs guys were on the lower part of the park passing out free meals. The drug dealers were at the top. Others were napping on the lawn, or perched on the top of the city, looking down. A pulse filled the park. The trees, the grass, the wind, and the people breathed it in. Everywhere we looked, the world was alive. And we felt a part of it.

We played all day long, getting stoned, eating, and laughing into the night. This was new—nothing like my neighborhood in Dallas where I knew everyone, all the violent and traumatic secrets, with streets I had walked since I was a child, playing, chatting with the people down the street, feeling we were all neighbors, like Harper Lee or Truman Capote. We all grew up together. I had belonged there, until time passed, my brothers moved out, my parents divorced, sold the house and I found myself thrown into the uncertainty of San Francisco, with that past quietly pulling at me.

That July 4th we were a part of everything here. It felt like that all summer long. Walking home from work, encountering a gaggle of naked men skipping down the street, doing summersaults in the San Francisco night, dancing at Kilowatt, a bar on 16th street and Valencia Street, where a group of women bound onto the dance floor without shirts, shaking to "Dancing Queen"—for a minute there, we all were.

Some nights, we all got together at the Opera Café across from City Lights Books; others we hung out at the Casa Loma bar, making up tales, or watching movies, such as Berlin Alexanderplatz. I had been assigned the novel about lingering memories in college, reading it as I sprinted away from the south toward a new world and life. I didn't want to go back.

"Your childhood is over. Your childhood is gone," Robyn Hitchcock sang at the Great American Music Hall. I asked him to play "Rock and Roll Toilet," but he said they didn't play that one any more. There'd be many shows as I tried to find my place amidst the new sounds I was finding here, a club down the street where Don Cherry played dark foreboding cries from his horn, the sound merging jazz and world beats, pointing to a different chapter of what would be. Just walking down the street, I heard the horns, drums, and beats booming out of the Church of John Coltrane on Turk Street, dedicated to the old jazz musician. "For us the whole globe is community." That was theme of the Saint John Coltrane Church at 2097 Turk Street. And we were part of the Divine Sound Baptist's flock.

The rows of pastel Victorian homes shone a mosaic of wondrous, outlandish potential and the elusive frivolity that came with it. Arriving late at night on a road trip from Southern California, as I had, it was like taking in Fauvist painting, with a California twist. The city was a perfect postcard we could send off, asking ourselves, "Can you believe we're here?" There was a giddiness to it. Everywhere, people were escaping something and getting away with it. When I thought of San Francisco, a cosmopolitan greeting card with a chubby Buddha with his legs crossed in Chinatown came to mind. San Francisco was always a place where the colors from all those childhood memories came alive. Utopian dreams still existed here. Even decades after the heyday of the Flower Power of the Haight-Ashbury, you still felt the optimism of a decades-old experiment in living here, the myths of connection and transcendence still drifting through the air. San Francisco was like an irreverent perch at the top of the world overlooking the sea defiantly flipping off the rest of America and I loved it for that. In San Francisco, I found we could be separate and connected from the rest.

November 4th, 1992, we all danced in the Castro and sang, "Hi Ho the witch is dead" thinking for the first time in a generation we had a chance to turn things around. The joke was on us. The chances for

21

the first Democrat to sit in the White House in years to actually do something progressive meandered, dwindled, and faded.

Our best and brightest kept on taking the jobs at the expensive law firms, saying the famous last words—"Just until I get my loans paid off"—rarely to get out. We all got used to kicking the ball down the road. War raged on in Sarajevo. Every day we saw more pictures; our inaction chilled the hearts as all anyone felt they could do was watch. Sometime in the summer of 1993, Susan Sontag flew out to Sarajevo and put on a production of *Waiting for Godot*, lit by candlelight because of the lack of electricity in this city the West had left behind.

"Godot won't be coming today," the messenger announced to the audience, who were freezing to death waiting for aid. "Maybe he'll come tomorrow." I didn't know a single person who wasn't waiting on someone or something.

Still, we kept at it. We would meet at Safeway early in the morning, the sun barely rising, and drive out to Sacramento for a political funeral. Standing at the state Capitol, everyone chanted: "ACT UP!!! FIGHT BACK!!! STOP AIDS!!! ACT UP!!! FIGHT BACK!!! STOP AIDS!!!" We hurled ashes of our dead friends and cried out "Shame! Shame!" while we stood on the steps of the State House. The energy I had always loved at punk shows—the authentic emotions, tears, anger, visceral and raw—were pumped up even higher by ACT UP. Those throwing ashes would be arrested, the police declared, apparently freaked out about ash in the air. Horses rushed us as we marched in; drums sounded, and tears poured as we threw the inanimate ashes, dust that had been body parts. "That was my boyfriend," screamed one of the activists to a police officer on a horse, who proceeded to step on him. "Shame! Shame! Shame!" screamed the crowd, pushing back the cops.

Half the group was arrested that day in this opera of sex and death and activism.

After everyone got out of jail, we took our signs and headed home. The ride back may have been the best part of the whole day. Right outside of Sacramento, we stopped for gas. We bought sodas, chips, Ho-Hos, and carried them back to the bus, high on sugar and activism. Two women sat in the seat in front of me sleeping in each others' laps as the adrenaline waned.

One woman played a ghetto blaster. Others talked excitedly. I sat chatting with the woman who'd had a skeleton painted on her face during the action.

"So what brought you here?" I asked.

"My roommate is sick with this. He couldn't go. So I went for him," she explained.

"This shit scares me."

"Me too!"

"I hear an accent," she said. "Where you are from?"

"Texas."

"Wow. Me too!"

I asked what high school she had attended.

"Kincaid, in Houston" she said.

"Same conference as my school, Greenhill."

She looked at me and nodded in acknowledgement.

"We used to play you in football."

"Yes you did," she sighed.

Looking around the bus full of tired bodies, I remembered why we were there.

"I hope your roommate is okay."

"I hope so too. I'm not sure he's gonna be." She paused. "What about you? What brought you here?"

I told her about my godfather dying of AIDS the year before. For that ride we were united against a common cause. But the togetherness didn't last. ACT UP San Francisco had split in half a couple of years before, with ACT UP Golden Gate forming their own group. That was the group I was with.

After we returned, we went dancing, shaking our way through the city, and its culture of caring for the sick, praying for the dead, and partying all night.

After our night out, we parted ways at the Safeway where we'd met eighteen hours earlier. Few of us would unite again for a long time, if ever.

When I got home, I sat in my room and began to come down from the euphoria of the action, not knowing how much we had achieved beyond creating a spectacle of political theater, looking like crazy people screaming and throwing ashes of our dead friends. People were still sick and getting sicker and we hadn't changed that. I looked around my bedroom walls, the moonlight shining in, sighed, took a drink of beer, and began to crash; the same hollowness that seemed to characterize so much of life was there waiting for me.

"Here you are again old feeling," I said to myself. "Here you are again." The feeling seemed to encompass a sense of futility from decades prior when Dad was sick and there was nothing we could do about it. On one flight, they had had to pull the plane down in an emergency landing in Alaska. He'd spend weeks laid up in the hospital. Right around this time, his best friend from childhood in Thomasville, Georgia killed himself. That was back in 1975. And no one knew why. What happened? Was he gay as mom suspected, conflicted within his Catholic faith? Why not just move to San Francisco and forget out all that? Why was Dad such an alcoholic? He'd tried to run away from the south, only to be rejected by the Northeast, returning to that strange place he knew as home. And his heart exploded.

He was barely there when I was in high school, mostly working. Why was his other best friend Thomas in the closet? Why did Mom drink so much wine, pop so many pills, before she moved out? Why all these dark lives? Why were these things happening? They all came from the same place. Looking at Mom's cotillion photo from Columbus, Georgia in the mid 1950s, the only spot of black in that photo was mom's dress. She knew she needed to wear a black dress in a sea of white. That was a small rebellion. Maybe marrying dad was a rebellion. But what were they rebelling from? All those houses in Savannah in the deep south where they used to dance, built with the backs of slavery. Was Dad's best friend guilty because he was a cog in the very cultural economic system that profited from Jim Crow? That shadow was long and these were southerners who made money on it, the whole economy built on the capital from the free labor. And we never quite talked about it. The feeling just simmered away eating at us.

Sitting in San Francisco, the feeling followed me. It wasn't a sense of guilt, which I abhorred, as much as a lingering melancholy, mixed with obligation and a sense of letting everyone down. "You have a family history few people have," Dad used to remind us. "On my father's side of the family, we trace a rich Georgia heritage which goes back to colonial days," he told me. "The original Hardy's moved to Georgia in 1752 with the Midway community, which was a group of Puritans from New Dorchester, Massachusetts. We feel certain that the first Hardy in Liberty was sent to Old Midway from Boston as a minister to that church. Many ministers to Old Midway were asked down from Boston. The name was the same of the old Puritan preacher who had to slip out of England, incognito, and who made such a name for himself in Boston and New England."

Some days, Dad told us the family were related to writer Thomas Hardy, although I had no idea how. The family worked in Jonestown, his grandmother, Mama, told us. They sought freedom here, religious freedom. Then they brought slaves and killed Indians, the roots of this great nation planted its destruction. Politicians hated brown people and failed reconstruction. But we trade in myths, as Mama wrote about us in her notes about the family on the occasion of her 99th year. "We also know, from research, that the first of our family to see America came over as a helper to bring the first Jamestown Colony," she wrote. "... The first Hardys to come to Georgia rode horse-back, from——me think——Charleston, SC as among the few things he left were two law books, on the fly of which was written in a beautiful Spencerian hand, the name, 'Hardy, Charleston, SC January 1800...' That section of the state was at that time, one of the most malarial infested in the world. Hardy and his young wife, both died of soon after they were married, leaving these two small children..." Although Mama died in 1981, her life spanned the 19th and 20th centuries, with her kids growing up, serving in wars, and having their own kids with their own questions. She referred to the family's slave owning past, and their human "possessions" in the memoir without apology. Chilling. In the same text, she told the story of her uncle who, starving on his way home from the Battle of Atlanta, at the age of 16, was fed sweet potatoes by a freed slave, and condemned racism for the rest of his days. Dad refers to Mama often in the narrative of his life: "My grandmother was a brilliant, extremely powerful woman who bore five sons. One died early, three she sent to Harvard; one to West Point. The entire group——my uncles and my father among them——were a rigid, doctrinaire and severe group." ('Rigid and doctrinaire' was another way of saying they upheld rules, fought hard in wars, came home and beat their kids, who beat their kids, who screamed at their kids, who drank too much, who became lawyers, and so on.)

Over the years that 1975 feeling extended into an all-encompassing blurry feeling of loss, most recently about Chloe, my college girlfriend. She was this looming character in my life. She had dumped me, leaving me to wallow in loss. I saw her everywhere, but I could not reconnect with that optimistic part of my life that had been there before I knew her. There was a sense of oblivion like we were making our way through time, tumbling, free falling through the sky, further away from each other like the characters separated from each other in A Wrinkle in Time. In some ways, that feeling made the world of AIDS understandable. Here, everyone seemed to be losing something. My sense of feeling heartbroken, unlucky in love, and flunking in my chosen vocation as a writer drew me to the experience. The grief was an opportunity to feel a suffering as large as the world. The heartbreak offered an experience of pain that felt universal. After school, I didn't need to live abroad any more; the feeling of loss was here. I wanted to explore that sensation: the poverty of the US. I wanted to learn how others experienced and coped with it. Every tragedy is an opening for something, a space to reconsider mistakes that got us there in the first place. San Francisco seemed to offer them up in droves.

At the time, I was working at 1994 Market, a housing program for people living with HIV and AIDS. After flopping as a waiter, I found my way into the gig while temping. It was a last stop for many. Here, junkies, fags, the unlucky and forgotten all came before they died.

The day after the demonstration, I went back to work. By this point in 1993, we were nothing close to the treatment breakthroughs of 1996, which would transform the HIV landscape. People were falling like flies. Without knowing what else to do, I used to walk around exploring the Tenderloin, a raunchy neighborhood full of rough trade, trannies, sex shops, and massage parlors. One night, I found myself talking with a young woman standing outside the Motherload at Post and Polk Streets. She was dressed in black, leaning coolly against the wall, her lanky tall body comfortable with the space. She had a cigarette in her hand.

"Hello," she said.

I smiled and said hi, standing there. After a pause, she looked at me. Her tone changed. "I don't mean to sound rude, but what are you doing here?" she asked me. I didn't know her, but couldn't help feeling like I did.

"Looking around, walking," I said, taken aback.

"I'm taking notes," she offered up without me asking.

"Without a pen?"

"Mental notes," she said.

I looked around, glancing at a couple of homeless guys. "On what?"

"On you."

"What about me?"

I laughed. This was a city full of sex workers, street kids, and hustlers. Why would anyone want to take notes on me?

She shrugged. "About you walking around here. People like you and what you're looking for."

"What I'm looking for? Nothing. I'm just trying to get home."

"OK, well keep on looking. You'll find your way."

"You look like you're looking for something too," I said.

"Well, I am. I'm a lookout and a sociology graduate student. This is a better way to make money than flipping burgers. And it relates to my research."

"A lookout for what?"

"For cops. So the sex workers can do their job without being harassed or arrested."

"Really?" The ash from her cigarette was almost to the filter. It fell off. She looked down at it and dropped the butt on the ground next to her foot. "Research on what?"

"Money for sex. San Francisco is an incubator for new social policies and controls—all taking place within the streets and computer networks of the city," she said.

"That's all?" I smiled. "I guess everyone is looking for something. Tell me about it."

"The neighborhood's streets are a hotbed for the shifting meanings of a purchase, demand, and commerce of sex," she said, lighting another cigarette. She took a puff of this one, and gestured to the streets, looking around.

"I'm gonna keep on walking," I said. "Good look with your work."

She nodded. "I hope you find what you're looking for."

"You too."

She was right. Sex pulsed through these streets with their ever-present clashes between possibility and desolation, high-octane desire and bleak disappointment, pleasure and violence, closeness and isolation, and health and illness. These sensations ebbed from the sidewalks, cars, phone cables, and cultural mores of San Francisco's neighborhoods.

Part of me just wanted a girlfriend. I certainly could not get Chloe back. She seemed to be everyone here, so familiar, but still not mine. I kept exploring.

Evening after evening I walked through the Tenderloin. It was not easy to call the Tenderloin a trendy space. It had been San Francisco's first gay neighborhood. Years before speed became an East Coast public health issue, crystal fueled the thriving underground economy of the neighborhood, located just north of Market Street.

Most everyone was looking for something, trying to make something with their lives out here, families of choice expanding, with new ideas, this city sprawling around us.

Love Letters, Brief Connections

"Love does not make itself felt in the desire for copulation (a desire that extends to an infinite number of women)
but in the desire for shared sleep (a desire limited to one woman),"
-Milan Kundera, *The Unbearable Lightness of Being*

Dante only met Beatrice once or twice, but wrote *La Vita Nuova* about her. A living person and an inspiration, a projection and an idea of beauty, she connected him with a sense the divine, which lived through him forever.

I was always thinking about women. Walking down the street, riding the bus, buying groceries—my mind always trailed off to those friends who had provided solace, connection, and made me feel like maybe parts of the soul were worth sharing.

The novels I read followed a similar theme. Jaromil, the protagonist in *Life Is Elsewhere* by Milan Kundera explained that the pinnacle of his life had been the feeling of a woman's head on his shoulder. "A girl's head meant more to him than a girl's body. He didn't long for the nudity of a girl's body. He longed for a girl's face lighted by the nudity of a girl's body." There were connections and costs, the the anguish of the past dipped into the present, between successes and even more misunderstandings. It was hard to make them all feel right.

I brought a box of love letters with me from home. On the top shelf of my bookshelf, an old Hoyo de Monterray wooden cigar box of Dad's sat there, the ruins from another life, talking, reminding, pulling from where I'd been. They seemed to linger and call from their perch on the bookshelf, leaving a long shadow.

"We ought to spend the day together," Becky wrote in a postcard from Chicago years earlier, a quick affair out of nowhere. "I hope you are in town when I come home," she followed in the next card. A condom malfunction and sexually transmitted disease ended that one. And I felt guilty about it forever. There were other friends senior year.

"Cab, I am really happy with us." That was from Lili, penned in blue ink on a sheet of paper from a notebook during English class. "I have so much fun with you. I'm really happy with us. I'm looking forward to the rest of this year. We can do fun stuff together. Just what I'm looking for. Everything we've done has been superb." That didn't last too long. I dated her spring of senior year in high school, after dumping her best friend, and then that all fell apart in a messy affair. The wheel of fortune spins. What goes up, spins around, before careening down. And we don't stay on top for long. By the time I got to San Francisco I was on the downward cycle of brief love affairs. I wasn't the promising senior high school football player or the college student running around campus wearing faded jeans tucked into cowboy boots, black leather jacket, a rockabilly haircut, and a stoned, optimistic disposition.

"You are like a smart airhead," Marsha, another girlfriend described me that freshman year in college. By the time I got to San Francisco, I was a worried, chronically under-employed Generation X-er, with a meaningless bachelor's degree, roommates, a pile of dishes in the sink, and a growing existential dread. What had happened, I thought, wondering about the story of my life. Everyone had a story here, most being rewritten by the minute. But I did not know where mine was going. The feeling was with me every day, just part of the fog we navigated throughout the city.

Life was pulsing around me, but I often missed it. I'd walk by the renegade bike messengers and temp employees on my way on the way to the bus. Most nights, I worked 12 to 8 shifts. In the afternoons after I woke, I'd write or go to the gym, where sometimes I even made friends. The desolation of the AIDS world of 1993 consumed every bit of emotion I had. Death was everywhere. And it seemed to suck the life out of me. There was a public commons of the post-Harvey Milk San Francisco that I felt completely drawn to and separate from. I felt queer and straight, a part of things and disconnected from it, my assumptions about the world in pieces, trying to navigate through the wreckage. That feeling of separateness—was the primary feeling of my years in San Francisco. But every once in a while, connection offered a respite.

I couldn't stop thinking about her when I met her in the elevator.

I finally walked up to her at the gym.

"I was waiting for you to come say hi," Julie smiled, wearing her yellow lycra pants, writing her number down for me. "I saw you in your cool jeans," she smiled. "I was going to go up to you."

I called her and we arranged a date. Many dates came out of that little moment,

We laughed on our walk up from Chinatown to Russian Hill, drinking cappuccino's, chatting about the city and *The House of Spirits*, the magic realist novel she was reading. She was wearing black clunky shoes, a denim jacket, flower shirt, and black pants."

"Its one of the best novels I've ever read," she gushed, energy seemingly emanating from her Southern Italian olive skin and frizzy brown skin.

"I love it" I responded, talking about the novel and being with her. "She's a survivor. They got her dad and she lived to tell the tale."

"Who is—Clara?"

"No Isabel Allende, the author."

"They all are. We all are Cab." She looked all around, gesturing at the city. "There's this quote in there I read today during lunch, let me find it." She stopped and rummaged through her bag for the book, pulling it out of her beaten up old paperback. "Here it is," she declared, taking a drag of her cigarette and looking out at the city, before she began: "'...memory is fragile and the space of a single life is brief, passing so quickly that we never get a chance to see the relationship between events; we cannot gauge the consequences of our acts, and we believe in the fiction of past, present, and future, but it may also be true that everything happens simultaneously,' I love that," she gushed. "Its like us meeting on the elevator. Another simultaneous chance act." She paused, pulling something else out of her bag. "This for you," she looked down, bashfully passing me a card.

I was melting.

"Thank you, oh my god."

I looked at the card with the words, "Here's to chance meetings!"

"Read the quote inside," she smiled.

I read: "There are moments when you are getting to know someone, when you notice something deep and buried in you is deep and buried in them too. It feels like meeting a stranger you've known your whole life... Leah Raeder. Xo Julie." Her read lipstick kiss on the card.

We looked at each other, giggly first dates good feelings and kept on walking.

Julie made stir fry and fell asleep on the couch after dinner. I dug my nose into her shoulder and looked out the window with a view of the city. Once again spoons, the welcoming scent of her skin. The day's turmoil rose from the cricks in my shoulders, just for a little while.

Spending time with her offered a break from anxiety everywhere 1990s San Francisco. Some days we met at Cafe de Norde to listen to jazz, or we cooked at her place in Russian Hill, or stumbled into each other at the gym, or talked on the phone late into the night.

"She's got it going on," Raymond said. He had just recently come out, inspired by the openness of the city. We were bringing new people home every weekend. But Julie was different than the others. She was exquisite. Being around her, I had some idea of what Dante might have felt when he saw Beatrice. In a city gripped with Thanatos, she offered a little light. The pile of letters on the shelf stopped pulling as hard.

Julie's apartment in Russian Hill felt like the top of the city. The downtown lights below glimmered just outside of her living room window. The Transamerica building and the rest of the Financial District remained at a comfortable distance. It took two buses, three blocks, and six flights of stairs to ascend to Julie's immaculate apartment. On the #22 Fillmore I rode past the tattooed foreheads and piercings of the tired and strung out, the crusty punks staring blankly asking for change. Crystal meth and crack were everywhere. I rode past Bill Graham's revamped relic, the Fillmore West, up through the Fillmore District. I always got off at Green Street and walked up the rows of steps up the three continuous hills over to Julie's place. She lived right on top of the Broadway tunnel. I had to climb another set of steps where it seemed the street above just stopped at a wall full of flowers at the odd corner of Broadway above Green. Just getting to her apartment felt like a worth while accomplishment. Broadway meandered down back to the city, where it extended through the fish markets and dim sum restaurants of Chinatown to the old jazz corners of eras past in North Beach at the corner of Columbus, until it just trickled back to the ocean, the Bay Bridge towering above.

On Julie's 21st birthday, we stayed in and watched *Annie Hall* on VHS.

She had never seen it before.

"It's one of my favorites," I said and smiled.

So, we turned it on and sat back on the couch, the view of Russian Hill in the distance.

"I love this opening monologue," I smiled, the screen panning to the close up of Woody.
"I would hate to be a member of a club that would have me as a member," confessed Woody in his long preamble: "That's the key joke of my adult life in terms of my relationships with women."

Mine to I was thinking as I watched. Or it used to be. We didn't know who wanted to be in whose club at that point. Well, I wanted to stay in Julie's club. We both seemed to like each other a lot. But those good feelings could be elusive.

29

Looking at us, Alvy confessed that he and Annie had just broken up.

"If I were to ever write a novel I would base it on that," I gushed, imagining the notes in my blue notebook could actually turn into something. "That's the perfect lament," I told Julie, thinking about that scene that seemed to be about all of us, somehow aware that this time with her would follow a similar tragicomic pattern, like they all did, starting with infatuation and connection, giving way to giving way to estrangement. But why? That was the question I still could not figure out. And I'd be telling my own stories about Julie. Separations were part of the connections in this tapestry of friends and devotions, causes and movements somehow making the yin and yang of coming and going seem fluid. But for right now, the coming together felt sublime. Moved by all the sensations, a story was taking shape in my head as we sat there. This would be the story of my San Francisco, in between the losses, hookups, and moments on the couch with Julie, trying to find a piece of some sort of amore in a geography long influenced by a liberationist ethos, contending with a conservative backlash, the wreckage of sexual revolution and disease consuming everyone in its path, as we were coming in the midst of it all. Everyone was impacted by the backlash and queerness of it all, the stigmas of sex, disease and generativity.

From Southern California, her parents had been part of the Orange County constituency that had launched the Reagan revolution; my parents were from Southern Georgia and had helped launch the Carter revolution, until Dad voted for Reagan in the next election cycle, splitting their vote before they split up. Those years were very far past.

This night, none of the fears of turning out like my divorced parents were present. It felt good just to lay with her. Something about that strange spacy look in her eyes, that inquiring look, was endearing to me. She was the first person I had liked in a really long time, since Chloe, at least. It hadn't been going long, but enough to remind me of what was missing from my treacherous existence here. For a few weeks, everything clicked, but it felt precarious. This interplay between connection and separation was around every corner; you could see it in the conversations, the lonely strolls along Polk Street among the hustlers and street kids, in alleys across this bountiful city.

Walking home from her house, I wondered why men are so obsessed with women. Why does Dante write a book about a woman he barely met? Is it something about men? But what about women? Do women write whole books about women they've never met? Its accepted that women are seen, objects of the male gaze, they always have been. That's the history of wars, of gods fighting over Helen's face that launched a thousand ships. Men gaze and obsess. But what was I was seeking? What was it compensating for? Was it all about abandonment, a loss of mother or of feeling of being cared for, of safety, security, stability, warmth that was disappearing. In *Letters to Milena*, Kafka confessed that: "Basically it is nothing other than this fear we have so often talked about, but fear spread to everything, fear of the greatest as of the smallest, fear, paralyzing fear of pronouncing a word, although this fear may not only be fear but also a longing for something greater than all that is fearful." We were all looking for that something greater than all. When you are alone, no one validates your existence. It is like being an astronaut alone in space, as if in one of the Kurt Vonnegut stories, alone by yourself rotating above the earth in a universe without a god. But with each image of Beatrice, we find the possibly of something else, or something divine, if even for a second. Everyone was trying to find that image. The whole city seemed to be trying to connect with it.

On Fisting and Friends

"...[T]he Catacombs generated the kind of camaraderie and loyalty associated with clubs, it was not a club in the usual sense... It was about intense bodily experiences, intimate connection, male fellowship, and having a good time... People came to the Catacombs to do prodigious things to their bodies and minds, and some habitués reported having the kinds of transformational experiences more often associated with spiritual disciplines."

-Gayle Rubin

Charles's roommate screamed down at me from the fifth-floor window of his apartment at the corner of Hyde and Clay in Nob Hill to let myself in. By the time I made it up five flights of stairs and sat down in the living room, I was breathing hard. A Dinah Washington CD was playing. From the huge windows, I could see rooftops, antennas, and the tip of a cross from the church across the street. His living room had white walls with wood awning and a wood floor covered with a Persian rug. A solitary black and white photo of three preppy guys in a dorm room back in their Vassar days hung on the wall to the right. In the middle of the room there were black leather couches and a coffee table covered with copies of *The New York Times*, an ashtray from a *pensione* in Florence, and a styrofoam takeout tray from the previous evening's Chinese food. Charles's roommate Scudder pushed the tray to the side and set down two opened Henry Weinhard beers on top of the stack of papers.

"You're sweating," Scudder said when he greeted me. He had gone to Vassar with Charles and me.

"I can't believe you still won't admit that's a hill. I walked up Polk Street from work," I said.

"You couldn't catch a bus?" he asked.

"No, I just walked it. There's a lot to see along the way."

"I know. I picked up a guy when I went to the bank machine yesterday. But once I got to his apartment I called the whole thing off. He wasn't as good looking as I thought he was. Plus, as we walked up to his place I noticed he was tweaking."

"You don't feel like it's dangerous going back with people to their apartments?" I asked.

"No, it's part of the fun."

"Like climbing a mountain without ropes."

"Yeah. Risk is part of the fun."

"Guys at work hide their wallets every time they bring tricks home cause the street boys sometimes steal," I replied. "One of the tenants in our building had to replace all the locks in his apartment after a trick he brought home stole them."

He paused while we both took sips of our beer. "You know they still haven't found that guy who was killing those kids."

"I actually knew that one boy they found stabbed to death in front of the video store," Scudder said.

"Those kids come out here from Kansas or wherever, fall into bad times and start turning tricks. I wonder how many of the transients end up like that kid, having pissed off some client, only to disappear without anyone ever even knowing they were here."

"I've seen those kids wither away once they get started on the speed. They just die in the street."
We sat drinking our beers, speculating about lives right outside the door.

"Anyway, how are you?" Scudder asked, changing the subject. "How is life on the frontlines?"

"You mean work?" I smiled.

Scudder grinned and nodded.

"It's ridiculous, as always, what a story I heard today. Things were pretty quiet so I got to talk with this old Southerner from Tennessee. He just came up and started telling me this incredible story, out of nowhere. He'd been called by his priest to go see a member of the parish in the hospital. 'What could I say,' he explained. 'My priest was asking me to go. I had to go.' He went on to recall just sitting with this old friend, who had Kaposi's Sarcoma lesions all over his body—one over his left eye which was pussing up and closed shut—pneumonia... you name an infection, he had it. He was a wreck but he just would not die. He kept holding on and on. And he hadn't wanted to take the morphine or anything. He could barely move and certainly couldn't talk anymore but his eyes still reflected emotion. He was ready to die but just wouldn't." I paused to take another sip of my beer.

"Anyway, he was holding on for some reason. Everyone else went home. John, the guy telling me the story, stayed in the hospital room that night and talked to the guy because he knew he could still hear. Apparently they used to really be into fist fucking. So he said to him, 'Remember that first time you let a man's hand in and how much it hurt? How much you tightened up all your muscles and that just made it worse, but when you relaxed and just allowed the fist in how good it felt? Can you do the same now? Can you just let go and relax like you did then? Let go and let God in you.'" Scudder's eyebrows raised.

"He saw his eyes light up a little and a small smile," I continued. "Then he just sat there and watched as his breathing slowed. He was dead in five minutes. An eerie quiet filled the hospital. John walked up to the nurse's station—this was in the middle of the night—and out of nowhere slammed his hand on the counter and screamed, 'Goddamn this fucking disease!'"

"You know, Cab, in my community, sex and death have become permanently interlinked for most of us," Scudder responded with a drag of his cigarette. Outside the window, I could see fog rolling in behind him.

"Have you seen the SF AIDS Foundation, 'Partying with crystal can be a drag'. campaign?" I asked him. "It warns about putting it up your ass? I never even knew that was a thing."

"Guys like to put all sorts of things up our bums."

"Even straight guys do."

"Whatever that means," he said, leaning back on the couch.

"'Variation is a fundamental property of all life.' Gayle Rubin said it and I'm sticking with it."

"Who's Gayle Rubin?"

"She's an anthropologist who studies leather communities here. She has a study group with my boss at work. Sex Pols. I haven't been invited. You have to be super pomo sophisticated to get into the group."

"Are you going to try to go some time?" he asked.

"I think it's by invitation only. Plus, I'm kind of straight."

"Not really." Scudder vacillated between feeling protective of his gay identity and opening up a bountiful queer space for everyone, including guys like me. One part of him felt irritated, another part intrigued."

"Well, I sleep with women."

"Acts—not identification—that's a big difference, Cab. Your perspective is a little broader." It was quiet again. I had finished my beer, but Scudder wasn't paying attention. "That's what San Francisco is all about. I hope you're writing some of these stories down," he said.

"I'm starting to. Well, trying to."

"They're great stories." He swallowed the last of his beer and grabbed both our bottles to put them in the sink.

"Yeah, but crazy," I said. "I feel a part of all these stories and completely outside of them."

"Why?"

"It's like there's this whole other city that I can only look at. But can't touch."

"What?"

"Well, queer San Francisco. I feel a part of it and estranged from it."

"Don't we all?"

"You're out there in it. I'm just an observer."

"Don't be so sure. There's no neutral observation. If you're looking you're in it, even if you're a bit of a voyeur."

"I'm totally a voyeur."

"Yes, but no one gets out of this unscarred. You may not see it but you're being queered by the stigma of all this every day."

"But I just watch."

"And you feel it. Maybe not the way we feel it. But you feel it. Plus you're a complete horn dog in the city that invented sexual freedom, playing with it all."

"Just dreaming about it. Writing about it."

"So mix the two," suggested Scudder. "You're drawn to it for reason. There's something in the mix that draws you in, something to work out. Explore it a bit."

I looked at Scudder.

"Philip Roth says that to write you have to have a lot of pornography around to clear your mind, express yourself, get it all out of your system, and dream."

"Oh I practice, every day. Our regular lives are organized around work and drudgery, so its that fantasy space as a kind of resistance against the normal, the everyday."

"The prudish business as usual."

"Yeah, but it's never simple. The subject and object dance through the mind. I'm their observer. That's my meditation, wondering who I'm looking in the museum, in the porno arcade. I think about the subject looking back at me, wondering if the subject is in control of me. Who has the control?"

"Clearly, it is the object of your gaze in the picture who is in control. You're paying to watch them. But you can reverse the story."

34

"I hope I can," I said.

"Of course you can. But most straight people don't. They finally get one girl who gives them head and that's it. It's over. They've got you in control."

"We're depraved."

"Absolutely you are."

"But you don't have to be. I used to always do it with the captain of the football team. He had girlfriends. But thought I was a hot lay. He never worried about it."

"I'm not that versatile."

"It's in your head."

He brought back two more beers.

"Are you in touch with Chloe at all?" he asked, handing me one.

"Nope. She broke my heart. We don't speak anymore."

"How long has it been?"

"Almost two years. I'm still trying to get over her."

"Any progress?"

"A little with Julie. But I'm not sure. She's not quite as whips and chains Catholic reactionary as Chloe."

"Too bad. I adored her."

"Everyone did."

"Well, at least you felt something, however crazy. My tricks never last that long."

"Well, there were the kitchen guys at ACDC at Vassar," I said. "Remember walking into that big dining area on campus. There they all were."

"Yes, that was lovely," Scudder said, laughing. "You bitch."

"It's good to make new friends."

"A city of friends."

We drank our beers and then a few more bourbon and cokes. Charles never came home, but that was okay. Scudder had been there when the connection with Chloe and Vassar became more tenuous, greeting me in ways that seemed to signal he understood it was all falling apart. And that it was both hard and okay, no need to judge. He understood.

I walked home through the wet streets, thinking about the conversation, wondering what it all meant. We are the sum of the parts of our life, with stories meandering from here to there, south toward home, by way of this left coast city, full of backward glances. The Thanatos-like queer disposition which Scudder talked about had always been a part of my world view, even back in high school. Thomas pointed me toward that, showing me all those Marlene Dietrich movies, during what he called "my real education."

"It's the friends that you can call up at 4:00 a.m. that matter," he used to say, quoting from her.

I always loved this aesthetic, its a sensibility, a camp esprit de corps that only became more pronounced as the years went on. I was a fascinated with sex and art, music and bodies, but afraid people would call me a sissy. Instead, I played football, where the talk was always about body parts, gay sex,

35

smells, sweat—a seemingly unending discourse of attraction and repulsion with bodies, fixating on interchanging parts. I felt more comfortable with gay men, who understood the male id, in ways straight people did not. As outsiders, gay men had a bit more empathy. They understood without judgement at least for the most part. But that did not help me with women. It felt like I was in a desert. Julie was there, but then she wasn't, disappearing like oil in the distance. Even in the best of moments with Julie, she seemed to be a character in cavalcade, connected between Chloe and high school, and this time after as I tried to find something else, discovering social movements defending pleasure and histories of contestation. Much of the time, all I felt I had were memories and early 1980s porno magazines that reeked of cum. They still conjured up a powerful space between lust, ambition and regret. Before it all went wrong, Chloe and I used to sit up all night chatting, confessing, sharing our stories of debauchery and pain. A foxhole-type camaraderie grew out of that first becoming. But that was long past. The problem was letting it all go. Everyone else in San Francisco had a sexual story. Mine began back in those days, as sex was skewed with the taint of Thanatos and disease, compelling me to cling to affection with a desperation. Maybe it had always been that way—this struggle between being completely alone and a part of something much larger. But there was something else there that I had to figure out. I had to.

I guess, it began on a football field near the bleachers in North Dallas.

36

Part Two

A High and Lonesome Feeling

In Terms of Sex....

"I am a sick man...
However, I know nothing at all about my disease,
and do not know for certain what ails me..."
-*Notes from the Underground* by Fyodor Dostoevsky.

It began with Katie in the bleachers, directly to the right of the horn section of the band, a row below the entire Greenhill school sixth grade. She was dressed in all black smoking a cigarette. She sat and watched three hours' worth of our Friday night game, with a focused look in her eye. It was fall of 1986. Our team lost. But my best friend Grant and I were dreaming of losing something else.

"Billy Idol lost his virginity on the beach listening to 'Money, Money,'" Grant said. "He mentioned it in an interview years later." I planned to put on Coltrane's "Giant Steps," side one.

Katie had recently dyed her hair purple. She didn't want to talk with me about music because we disagreed. She was two years older. We had met in summer school years prior, when we were in grade school, spending hours writing notes, sketching pictures of each other, arguing about music, horsing around. She was smart and full of teenage pathos and irreverence. She wanted to run away to join a touring Shakespeare company in New Orleans.

Her hair color was different every time I saw her, but she always had the same punk clothes, white face paint, and black fingernails. We started dating after I stumbled into her at the Dallas Galleria, outside a smoke shop where we bought clove cigarettes. She had just seen the David Lynch movie *Blue Velvet.*

"My life will never be the same," she kept on saying over and over again. "Oh my god. My life will never be the same."

I had no idea what she was talking about. I'd never heard of David Lynch or *Blue Velvet.* It wasn't until years later that I understood. Katie always seemed to know more about the world—working in theater, seeing music, evading provincial treacheries of Texas with an absurdist humor and wanderlust. She had been part of my world for years and years—summer school study hall after summer school study hall; her friendly humor was always a respite to the tedium. We had always been friends, always picking back up that childish banter we'd begun years ago.

"What are you up to?" I asked her, standing outside the theater, others making their way for the next show.

"I wander through school, swooning at my professors, reevaluating my life decisions," she explained. She'd graduated high school the year prior and was taking classes at a local community college.

"What are you doing?" she asked.

"I'm going to see the next show."

She nodded and paused, chewed on a stray fingernail. "We have to go see music again, okay?" I said earnestly. She paused again. "Yesterday, I wore my shirt backwards and nobody noticed."

"I would have noticed."

"You always do."

"I miss you, Katie. My friends and I are going to see Joe King Carrasco next week. Wanna go?"

"No, I do that stuff all the time. I wanna watch you play football."

She was way more experienced than I was with the world, with sex. The first time we did it was after that football game. I was tired but excited to actually be doing something I had imagined doing thousands of times. I could not believe it—the proverbial *it*—was happening. I really could not believe it. John Coltrane's sax playing on the turntable, no condom even mentioned. She was on the pill and knew how to make it work. It felt like I was swimming in joy. I was alternately surprised, in awe, wondering if this was what it was all about, my body melting into an ocean; it took all of 97 seconds.

We lay in bed for a minute looking at the moon. She rolled over to kiss me again. She was tender, touching me again. I had no feeling. But I woke up. The second time—all forty-five minutes of it—was as exhausting as the ball game I had just played. Afterward, I dropped Katie off at the Valley View mall and met my friends at the 7-Eleven.

Katie and I hung out with the goth kids a few more times. We went to see industrial bands that sounded like work crews with amplified electronic hammers clanging at construction sites, Skinny Puppy shows in Deep Ellum, Dallas' live music enclave downtown. We listened to tunes in Plano with others who wore all black, smoked cloves, painted fingernails, and felt part of a counterbalance to football and monoculture. Her friends had created a world of their own, which offered a kind of antidote for the kids who were lost on the edges, or already gone. And it was certainly needed here. Plano had recently earned a footnote in the annals of cultural history as "America's Suicide Capital." Some 14 kids had killed themselves in a successive fashion over the three previous years. No one knew if it was a copycat thing or a wave of despair and ennui which grabbed the punk kids, the 11th grade nothings, who felt outside of the monoculture and monolith of football. The early departures jarred some, dislodging their foundations, as they followed their friends out of this world; others turned away as far as they could, some through drugs, others sex, or avoidance. We had all lived in this odd landscape, of cars and shopping and gas stations— ever expanding and erasing. All of America of was a part of it. Below the surface were the same historic scars, the racism always lingering, the decimation of the native people, the nukes—these were presuppositions that we did not talk about. In some way, the suicides reminded us we could question these assumptions about the world. We didn't need to live in monoculture, with a shopping mall and football field as our public commons. The givens did not have to be. Still, too few of us asked those questions. (The same Plano Wildcats went on to win their second straight Texas high school football championships and were voted the number one high school football team in America the following Fall.)

Katie knew a different Texas. These were the kids who put on radio shows and frequented the concerts downtown. I recognized the spaced-out, art school inflections of the voices from the air in calls into The Pajama Party, a legendary punk show on KNON, the alternative radio station, that ran from 11:00 p.m. to 1:00 a.m. every Saturday night. Katie was part of this scene in ways I never had been. She brought it with her wherever she went. The people she knew, the subculture was in all the places she went, cheap nail polish and a goth sensibility. Walking through the party at her friend's, it wasn't glamorous. "We're desperate, get used to it," the old punk song by X played on the radio. They seemed to speak to a sensibility. People stood smoking clove cigarettes in outfits they'd put together from thrift stores, with sad, lonely lines drawn under their eyes. There was a lot of makeup——the covering of wounds.

Katie and I didn't go out more than a few times after that. But I was ready to play. Sex was finally something attainable and I wanted more of it. This was the high. And that, of course, had its complications. Reeling from a weekend in Austin, with new friends, high spirits and lots of consensual, non-commitment contact, I brought back more than a hangover. But I didn't know what it was. Between a party, tequila shots, wanton abandon, and a sexually generous girl, something wasn't right. I hadn't known her. But she had been amazing. Not knowing her was part of the high octane feeling, going as far as we could without precautions.

By Monday, white ooze was coming out of me that didn't look like cum. And then it became painful and I was too scared to talk to anyone about it. That feeling of awe, of the oh-my-god-the-girls-are-actually-giving-it-to-me-and-some-seem-to-even-enjoy-it quickly became connected with a raw stinging sensation I was embarrassed to tell anyone about.

A couple of days of stinging peeing later, I told Grant what was going on. He knew a clinic to go to. He pestered me about it all week.

"Have you gone to the clinic yet to get it taken care of?" he asked at the end of the week, standing in the upper school

"No," I said.

"You should go today."

"I can't go today," I said, coming up with excuses to avoid the problem.

"You have to." He paused and looked at me again. "Cab, our childhood is over. Gone. No one else is going to take care of this except you." Grant looked past me, at the wall. Then he left.

I drove on the Dallas North Tollway to a clinic in a strip-mall by a bail bonds place North of Dallas in Plano. Grant told me you had to be 18 to be treated in the clinic but they weren't too rigid about checking ID.

When I got there, the receptionist gave me some papers to fill out asking me to describe my symptoms.

"Dripping, painful urination," I wrote and gave them back. I was feeling sick.

"Have a seat," she said, pointing to a couple of chairs surrounding a table with *Good Housekeeping* and *Life* magazines fanned out on it.

I sat reading *Notes from the Underground* by Dostoevsky. I hadn't really understood it in class. But it somehow made sense then, as I sat looking at people make their way to and from the clinic, all of them looking at the ground, my inner world aflutter with anxiety. I dreaded my name being called.

"Cab Callaway Hardy?" the receptionist announced after half an hour. "Cab Callaway Hardy?"

"Yes..." I replied tentatively. I was still feeling sick; I didn't want to be here.

"You'll be seeing Dr. Yoo," she told me as she escorted me through the sterile clinic. I walked into his office and stared at a pair of plastic gloves, two glass slides, long cotton swabs, and a tube of KY Jelly.

I had a feeling I knew where those were going. I felt sicker. I sat staring at the plastic gloves while I waited.

Wearing a white lab coat and glasses and huge black Sears and Roebock shoes, Dr. Yoo was bald except for four long pieces of hair he combed over his head.

"Let me see it," he said, pulling his gloves on, without greeting me.

He opened the jar and pulled out the two cotton swabs.

"Let me see it," he insisted, sounding impatient, before getting a hold, and inserting the a five-inch cotton swab into my urethra, in a circling motion with a hint of sadism. The feeling was excruciating, stinging all the way up my spine, as he moved the swab up, down and around in my urethra. It was over as quickly as it began. But that was more than enough. I couldn't imagine anyone feels very good about themselves in those kinds of moments. I went back to the waiting room while he made his diagnoses of gonorrhea, before producing a prescription for penicillin. I left, drove back to the pharmacy and then an empty house, feeling as lonely as I had ever felt. This new thing that was sex, the sensation of warm sensuality, quickly became intertwined with an ominous sense of consequences. Was sex always going to exact punishment, I wondered with a cringe, while I had been waiting for the prescription at the pharmacy. Something that had been amazing revealed a dark, painful, humiliating quality—a tint of danger and foreboding that was always going to be connected to sex for me.

On Rita, Phil, Becky, and Todd

"Every man I knew went to bed with Gilda... and woke up with me."
-Rita Hayworth

Phil, Becky, Todd and I hung out every day that spring. It was our junior year in high school. We saw as many shows, listened to as much music, and got high as much as we could. In between, we read *Betrayed by Rita Hayworth* and *Aunt Julia the Scriptwriter* and lived out some of those soap operas.

Becky and I had been in a perpetual state of flirting and chatting since freshman year. We first met in Ms. Chips' freshman English class two years prior. She had transferred to Greenhill from Frisco, a suburb an hour north of Dallas. It was hard to know if she would ever fit in as a transfer. North Dallas kids tended to be a cliquish, often insular crew, rejecting outsiders. Becky didn't even notice. Without seeming to care, Becky found a wedge at the periphery. She was tall and lanky—a bit like Olive Oyl from Popeye—with a model's frame. Each year, she became more beautiful. Her long brown hair got shorter and shorter, blacker and blacker, sexier and sexier. She talked with an accent and her outfits, out of thrift stores—many of which she wore a couple of days a week—came in stark contrast to the Bloomingdale's price tags of her peers.

During English class Becky spoke frequently, wide-eyed with interest. She responded to a comment I made during our discussion of *Gatsby*, elaborating on the point, bringing up a new angle, all the while tracing her eyes from Ms. Chips back to me. She didn't turn away from me after Ms. Chips had picked up on the topic. Her gaze continued. She didn't care if she was being obvious. She leaned over herself onto her right elbow crossed over her left on the desk, revealing a bold, inquiring pair of eyes.

Becky and I often talked at parties, my eyes trailing to her and then back around the party to see who else was there. When the Clash released their new single, "This is England" I played it for her. I think I was the only person in the world who liked it. She had a different reaction: "I don't like it," she smiled.

She was adorable. But my mind was on other things. We seemed to miss each other, neither could understand each other. I was not sure she even knew about the Clash. I didn't know a thing about Frisco but it seemed a lot different than Dallas. The cultural gap between us left me trying to explain myself and neither of us quite understanding. This was the space in which we always encountered each other. She was looking at me, amorous feelings flowing, my mind drifting, not quite connecting. I spent most of my time talking with her about everyone else I was attracted to. She always looked straight at me, like she could see through me. That was our dance. Biding her time, we chatted until Phil walked up.

The Clash broke up; she and Phil hooked up. That spring, the two of them spent most of their days reading, smoking, and sitting in class together. They seemed to find their stride.

Still, we were all friends, hanging out at Phil's house all the time.

While Becky was becoming more soulful, Phil was moving in another direction.

"SATAN, SATAN, SATAN!!!!!!" Gibby screamed as the music from the Butthole Surfers song, "Sugar Loaf," roared out of Phil's room. Phil's dad, one of the executives for the Dallas Cowboys, sat watching game films downstairs. Phil and I pulled bong hits upstairs, laughing at ourselves and the absurdity of the music. We'd cook together, watch movies, eat, and drink lots of wine. Phil was finding a way out of his father's shadow via Becky, Dallas stoner culture, and the Butthole Surfers. Like Phil, their singer Gibby Haynes was the son of an icon. Gibby's dad, Jerry Haynes, was most famous for his role as Mr. Peppermint on TV. We loved Gibby's band. Phil's mother had had the house redecorated in '70s faux art kitsch some ten years earlier. Huge yellow, brown and blue polka dots popped from every corner of the house, walls adorned with oil paintings of Cowboys players and photos of Phil with bangs parted down the middle. Wall to wall red, green and maroon carpets covered the beanbag-furnished floor. We were all trying to be our own people, outside of parents' shadows that seemed to pull us into a way of looking at the worldview few of us embraced. We were not sure what we believed in, but their old way of looking at things held little appeal.

Phil, Becky and I got stoned together almost every day that spring after school. We'd sit out on the deck by the pool listening to music, staring at the sky, the trees, and each other.

One afternoon Becky showed up before Phil got to his house. We got high without him, not wanting to wait. We sat on the swings in the front, chatting somewhat nervously. Becky talked about the satisfying—and more often the unsatisfying—dimensions of going out with Phil. She was completely unselfconscious in her Frisco, Texas intonations as we smoked. Gradually we relaxed, actually talking and even seeming to hear each other. Phil showed up an hour late. I remember the hint of regret I felt as I saw Phil's white '81 Civic pull into the round drive way. Usually I was happy to see him, but this time I was disappointed.

Summer offered a bit of a respite from the Becky dance. We didn't see each other too much. Instead, there was lots of ecstasy going around and late nights spent in the parking lots outside Target, clubs, etc. I spent the summer driving around with Todd and Grant, listening to Tears for Fears tapes, high on ecstasy, working as a waiter at Massimo's and going out almost every night after work. My friends would come by to eat and we'd go out afterwards with the staff. All our friends converged there, including the other staff members and their company. Some days, we wandered across the street to the Inwood Lounge by the Inwood Theater. Others, we just drove around, sometimes to the Stark Club, but usually nowhere in particular, just driving aimlessly through the city.

Somewhere between going out and football two-a-day practices, in the morning and later in the afternoon those last weeks of August, the summer passed into fall. A wondrous feeling accompanied me as I entered Senior year. Driving to school, the leaves changing, it all felt beautiful in ways I had a hard time imaging, as ways of living I'd only seen in movies became spaces I inhabited. Life and art collided, like the preview of black and white bodies clashing into one another in *Decline of Western Civilization* and *Moscow Does Believe in Tears* that played over and over again at the Inwood Theater. I was no longer watching or imagining I was part of a picture in a magazine or book. I part of the crowd. All my favorite bands played in my backyard, New Order, Big Audio Dynamite from England, and Hüsker Dü, by way of Saint Paul.

44

A legendary hardcore story, their final record revealed more than any of the others. I felt it watching Hüsker Dü thrash through their set. "Love and hate was in the air, like pollen from a flower," Husker Du sang, as I hurled myself across the stage into the crowd during their Dallas show that fall in 1987, Phil and Louis dancing alongside me. Over and over, I pulled myself onto the stage, then hurled backwards into the crowd, my body enveloped into their arms which held me before I made my way to the ground. On my final dive, the crowd seemed to part. No one caught me. My knee slammed to the concrete floor, pain welling up through my fragile body.

Our world was precarious in that moment at the show, with Cold Wars, estranged cultural foundations, conflicts, the throbbing noise of the music, the aching in my knees, underscoring a pain I'd made my way to as I dove, longing for an unknown. Something was out there, looming in the distance, somewhere over the cliff, descending from the coasts, beyond senior year. We all knew we were in a bubble and that it could burst at any moment, a tension between the carefree and the heaviness of becoming an adult.

And then there were the letters Becky had sent all summer long. I'd get home from morning practice and there was another one. I was never as attracted to Becky as she was to me. But there she was, tall and lovely, a Willa Cather sort of Texas country character, writing cards, sending notes from parts unknown. I could see her as one of the pioneers. She seemed to know the country, to see all of us as a part of it. One of her notes included a poem about the dynamic between us. She wrote: "As it if wasn't enough that you weren't aware what was going on with my attachment for you, I had to listen to your confessions and cravings for others almost every day. Like the elusive gasoline ahead on the highway, every time I came close to you, you disappeared like gasoline on a long strip of road." It was hard to know what to do with all the feelings she brought to me. Drawing her in happened incidentally. From the other side of the city, she brought a meaty awareness of the limitations of our world, struggling to see her way to the substance in all of us. It was not that easy. She'd found Phil. But his limitations were becoming clearer.

Early September, Phil invited us all to his house.

"I have LSD for everyone," he smiled, maniacally, laughing.

"Really?" I asked, feeling a little trepidation. That was further than I'd wanted to go. Scenes from the novel Go Ask Alice, of a kid crumbled in a closet hallucinating, covered in worms, ran through my mind.

"Do you want to try it?"

"Sure," everyone replied. I remember the sinking feeling in my stomach. I didn't say anything.

"Where did you get it?" I asked him.

"From a dealer."

"Who?"

"From Beto's apartment at Inwood and Harry Hines." Apparently, that was enough of an answer.

Before we took the acid, I trembled with anticipation. "Oh god, we're really doing this," I wondered as I put the tabs on my tongue, not sure if anyone else was as nervous as I was. Over the next few hours, we climbed in the trees in the backyard and rolled around the living room. A few of us jumped in the pool, looking at the trees and the sky above. I sat at the bottom of the pool looking at the bubbles rise from my mouth. And then realized that was not the best place to be. But I did not want to be with anyone else. Phil ruminated about the pretty, pretty sky and wondered if we should document everything. I could barely put together a coherent thought. Listening, I looked back at Grant who rightfully seemed to understand that documenting the endeavor was not that important. I was not in a place to try to come to grips with this synthesized state of consciousness. The 29 Minute Technicolor Dream played over and over again, as paranoia and otherworldly dread consumed me. I was still lost in my head and apparently my life. The drugs reminded me of this, with a surrealistic blur, taking me away from colors into an odd place where I did not seem to know myself.

In other moments, the drugs helped—MDMA for the euphoria—but LSD made me insane—a traffic jam of emotion. Sometimes the drugs added to the warmth we all felt about each other and intensified the bond we had been forming since childhood, soothing, warming myself. All the drugs blurring, my mind rushed back to another trip. We were sitting in the parking lot outside of Target, hundreds of teens outside, mulling about, completely high. "Shake the Disease" by Depeche Mode played as I sat in the back on Todd's car when the ecstasy made its way down my spinal cord the first time the year before. At first I had been vulnerable and then I felt held by the universe; a warm feeling overtook me, helping me feel a part of a loving, accepting world.

"I think it's working," I told Todd.

"You Xing Cab?" smiled Todd. We held each other by the shoulders and said how happy we had been to know each other, how wonderful it had been, as the drugs made their ways through our bodies. On the way to the Stark Club with a group of some six people, it seemed like we were part of everything as we careened through the night. Eros danced through the space. We sang along to the Prince tape blaring. "I just want your extra time and your kiss."

Alphaville followed.

"We are the high-high-high-high-high-society.

We are the jet set society

We are the jet set."

It felt like we were flying in a crescendo of feelings. Jenny and the rest of us in the car leaned into each other, and then away, in close and intimate, eyes wide, and away, out dancing all night through waves of emotional, sometimes violent, often awkward, sometimes sad, growing-up terrain.

As September eased on we had to take advantage of the final hot weekends. Around 11:30 a.m. on the last Saturday in September, I got a call from Louis, a kid in our class.

"Cab, I have so much beer here. Come over as soon as you can. Phil and Becky are already here." That summer, they had opened up their relationship, looking to other things.

By the time I got there, they were all completely stoned.

Phil had on his psychedelic secret agent man horned rim glasses. Becky, for once in a blue moon, was also drinking. She was laughing, her brown hair falling around her face as she lowered her head between her shoulders, a real laugh. Everyone was relaxed.

Todd sauntered into the backyard, setting down the Marlboro Lights from the left-hand pocket of his unbuttoned Oxford shirt, wearing Vuarnet sunglasses, and carrying a bottle of beer in his right hand. He took off the Oxford and Greenhill soccer tee shirt so all he was wearing were torn khaki shorts, and walked over to the side of the pool and stepped in. I ran from the back corner of the lawn, sprinted and hurled myself through the sunny, warm, exhilarating sky and splashed into the water. The beer that was already floating there bounced. Todd moved to place his shoulders against the side of the pool as he tilted his head onto the grass right beside the pool. Louis, with a huge smile, poured a beer straight into Todd's mouth, the whole beer as fast as it could pour straight down his throat. We all switched taking turns letting Louis pour the beer into our mouths. Todd eventually got dressed and left as he had arrived, sunglasses on, cigarette in one hand, a beer in the other hand. Phil was asleep on the lawn.

"I'm going to swim," Becky said everyone.

"That's a pretty light swimming suit," Louis observed of Becky's white one-piece.

"Well, you boys will just have to deal with seeing my body. I'm sure you can handle it." Becky got in the water. She was right. Her white suit was translucent. We did see her body under the one-piece suit. There it was, her shape, her sensuality swimming in front of us, Becky as well, her body, its own entity. Becky was being forward. She didn't mind. She swam and I lay by the pool, stoned and comfortable. Becky and I had stared at each other for so long over the past two years. Now she was a few feet away and we were at ease, relaxed from the beer and the sun.

"Becky, remember last summer before you went to Ecuador? That night when Todd, Grant, and all those guys smoked from the gravity bong in my bedroom and we sat on my bed. Do you remember that?" I asked.

"I remember. I thought we would never talk about that."

We'd been sitting in my room hanging out for hours, but she just kept looking at me and I looked back at her, as if about to make out, but it did not happen. Too many people. Phil was there, as he always was.

"Be right back," Becky smiled. She lifted herself out of the pool and sauntered inside, her bathing suit still translucent. Five minutes later, out walked Phil from the same door Becky exited. Wandering out to the pool, Phil pulled me to the side. I was nervous when he saw me, worried I was caught. But instead he was warm and gregarious.

"Don't worry Cab," Phil cautioned. "It's cool. You know Becky likes you. It's cool with me. She told me she wants you and I want to hit on Ashley, so go for it."

That night, Becky and I made out in Louis's parents' room and then drove back over to my house. Becky trusted me, but I did not really know what I was doing or why. But there she was. I liked her as a friend, but not more than. Other nights it might have just been an evening and I would have given Becky a beer and we would have sat with the awkwardness. The whole thing was taking a life of its own. Dad was out of town. We walked to the bedroom, trying to relax.

"You don't need condoms," Becky whispered. "I am already on the pill. You don't need them." I got one anyway but couldn't make it work. Later, we just lay there nude, sort of touching each other after the inglorious attempt.

"I hate condoms," I said looking at the ceiling trying to hold Becky.

"I don't know why you used one. I told you that you didn't need to." We lay in bed for a long time after that. I ran my hand across Becky's body. Becky ran her hand across my body from my thighs to my face. This time I didn't reach for the condoms.

"I can't do this," I said as I pulled away within a minute. I rushed out onto my outside patio.

"Cab, what's going on?" I told her about the trip to Plano, the gonorrhea, except that the penicillin had probably taken care of the whole thing. But I didn't know if it was all gone. The doctors had never scheduled a follow up visit. I should have used condoms. Becky stood nude out on the balcony with me in the night, her hands wrapped across her chest. Shocked, she drove home.

The next night she called. "How are you? What are you thinking?" she asked.

"Just trying to complete Dr. B's history assignment." The talk was short, tense. Becky didn't say much and got off the phone before calling back after a couple of minutes.

"Cab, I did not call to find out about the assignment for Dr. B or the records you bought today. I couldn't care less about that stuff. I wanted to talk about last night."

"Right, I know."

"What were you doing?"

I didn't respond.

The next day was one of those Mondays. I almost made it all day without seeing her. And then that afternoon, I saw exactly what I had so most feared and so much understood to be inevitable. Becky was at school wearing the expression of a person who had been stung, walking with a heavy step. When I saw her, she looked at me as someone who was no longer on her side. I had never drawn a contrast between the expression she offered me and the one she gave everyone else at school until that very moment. She looked sad; the animated expression she'd always shared before was absent, now a part of my past. I knew I'd never see that spirited side again. Now, I got what everyone else got: a dose of indifference and defense.

"Here," she said, and gave me a small note folded over many times, and walked away. On a page torn out of a notebook in her distinctive Becky scrawl, she had written:

"Cab, don't worry. I'm not going to be strange
the rest of the year. I just know I should have listened to
what people said about you, but I didn't and I have to live
with that. I told my parents and they need you to give me
results back from an AIDS test. If you do not produce results
for me within the next month they will pursue legal action.
Becky."

The note stung. I hated myself and the whole situation. Regret and anger, shame and frustration that I had let that happen in the first place coursed through me. Why had I brought her back home? Mostly I hated myself for betraying Becky. Back to the clinic I would go.

Still, Becky could have let me use a condom and taken the cue from me when it did not work. She did not have to throw me under the bus. I was coming to see the power that Eros produced and its enduring connection to Thanatos. There was a responsibility to owning that power. We were all learning about it. Our bodies were vulnerable, subject to limitations, wonderfully, fearfully made. They crumbled like my knee did at the show. Our feelings were just as precarious, maybe more so, HIV in the air, along with sexuality, linked and estranged, it was part of this life, a lingering awareness people did not talk of. We were coming to see how our innocence intertwined with darkness. I knew Becky was trying to figure out that power. I was trying to figure out what to do with all that desire that drove and consumed me.

Being confronted with the possibility of AIDS changed the landscape of our childhoods. I had to figure out what to do with that space—the limitations of my body, the expansiveness of my feelings, the leap from childhood into HIV tests and fractured friendships.

The following Saturday morning the whole football team was scheduled to watch footage of the previous evening's game. I left the house three hours before the meeting to get my first AIDS test. The receptionist at the clinic gave me a couple of forms to fill out. "We'll send your results back in this envelope. You should be receiving them back in two weeks," she explained. I signed the envelope with the name Claudius. Ten minutes later I was called back for the test. Slowly the syringe entered my skin. It drew vivid, almost velvety red liquid out of my arm into a vial with my pseudonym written on the side. I left for the game meeting.

In the following weeks things fell into a simple pattern. Becky and I stopped speaking. Phil and I stopped speaking. Todd and I pretty much stopped speaking. I didn't know if he had heard or not but I knew he was very close with Phil, who was not too pleased with the situation. He hadn't gotten anywhere with Ashley to make things worse. Sometimes non-monogamy is no better than monogamy; neither offer any guarantees of happiness. Only later did I find out that Becky had gone straight over to Phil's after she left my house that Saturday night. Phil and Becky had slept together that night. They didn't use condoms so we had all been exposed to each other and to a dose of anxiety. While my gonorrhea was long gone, the panic over who was carrying what seeped into our lives and interactions. The Phil, Becky, Louis, and Todd follies had come to an end.

None of them played football, so I navigated my way through that fall spending a lot more time with the ball team than with Phil and company. There were plenty of people on the football team to get stoned with. Soon enough, I received the HIV results—negative. I gave a copy to Becky. The panic was over. But the feeling of blame and sadness, of betrayal and disappointment, linking Eros and illness, was hard to shake. Long after the panic ended, its memories lingered.

Five years later, I'd be working with and getting to know people who had seen HIV transform their lives because of a sexual transaction. It ruined so many lives, most of them in those days, stealing them away from this world. One small moment of indiscretion or ignorance would be something they regretted their whole life. Becky was lucky she didn't have to regret that moment all her life. So was I. People with HIV had to live with the consequences. All the guys I worked with had had those same moments. They had to live with these consequences. Everyone in the culture wanted to believe they were guilty, like the *Scarlet Letter*. Sex became public because of HIV. But it had always been dangerous. Unwanted pregnancies and syphilis used to kill people. Becky got to skirt it. But the gay men, the women, the drug users did not

49

get to skirt the homophobia, the sexphobia, the drug war, and the shame. The descent from fun to the realities of danger and the consequences of sex came fast.

A Combination of the Sublime and the Apocalyptic

History seemed to move in circles here. It was almost Thanksgiving in San Francisco. Asleep in my room, noises from outside led me to think someone had broken into our apartment on Page Street. I looked up at the window in my room. The sky was yellow. Trembling, I walked across the apartment to my roommate's window where I looked out and saw flames darting out of the buildings 100 feet away. A whole block of my neighborhood was up in flames down the street at the corner of Scott and Haight.

One of our neighbors knocked on our door, asking if they could come look through our window to the street. Fire reached up into the sky. A few of us grabbed our computers, looking at the flames eating through the Victorian homes of the Lower Haight. The fire looked as if it was coming straight for us. We were all in our pajamas, just looking, talking together as neighbors do in such moments.

It was only a few years prior when I had driven out of Santa Cruz, only hours prior to the 6.9 magnitude Lomo Prieta earthquake of October 17, 1989 as it tore at the landscape, killing some 67 people, in a rush to see the Rolling Stones play in Los Angeles. But then the flames seemed to pause.

Like then, we had caught a break. The wind was blowing up the street, away from us. Our house was okay. In the end, 115 people were left without homes and 39 apartments were destroyed. Word on the street was that a crack lab had exploded, igniting the blaze.

Men stood outside the smoldering flames for much of the next day.

"I learned everything I know from living in the ghetto," a man repeated over and over again. He was sitting on the street, drinking a 40-oz bottle of Ballantine malt liquor amidst the rubble from the fire— crack viles and cigarette butts strewn across the sidewalk.

The smell of soot remained for weeks. It was everywhere.

"That's an awful way to live," said my roommate Raymond the next day, while we walked past a group standing outside, smoking cigarettes, nodding off by the ruins. One man was passed out with his needle dangling from his arm.

Someone had spray-painted a mural with the words, "San Francisco: a combination of the sublime and the apocalyptic sufficient to sharpen anyone's sense of an ending."

Looking at the words, I wondered what they meant. And what had brought me to this place? It certainly did not feel very sublime to me. What would be the ending?

Dad visited several times that fall. He talked a lot about his days almost four decades prior when he had dropped out of school to come here. "It felt just as odd in those days," he recalled. Some days we talked about poetry and writing, others he helped me try to make sense of HIV, theology, and the nature of pain. Why did some endure it while others skirted its harms? His divorce from Mom still felt very present. That compounded with his brother dying and his heart opening up after years of Jungian analysis. It all seemed to overlap. There was always a tension to the extremes of feelings.

Above all, we talked about his friend Tom. My AIDS story began with Tom. Only a couple of years earlier Tom had succumbed to HIV-related complications, including a descent into mania, hallucinations, car wrecks, dissociation, and dementia in a desert in West Texas. Dad had known Tom since college. In the years that followed, they both joined the Beat Movement, hitchhiked out to be with the poets of San Francisco before Dad went to law school and Tom worked as a bartender at Keller's in New York City— a notorious leather bar facing the westside piers, in pre-Stonewall Greenwich Village. Tom would tell me stories about his father who had known Lotte Lenya during the decadent peak of Berlin's Weimar culture after he lost his job as a U-Boat conductor during WWI.

Even with a PhD from Harvard, his queerness was never discussed as much as it remained a quiet, irrepressible defiance to bourgeoisie mores of ambition, career, or convention. "Why should I have to work?" Tom insisted defiantly in his bathrobe while he regaled me with stories in between rehearsing Chopin before the dementia from HIV-related complications set in again. I saw him in most of the guys who lived in the building where I worked. The guys would come in late after being out at the sex clubs, cruising, or running, stopping to chat about where they had been, what they had done, and what it all meant. Some lived only a few months afterward. I watched residents cringe, swagger, lose themselves, find something else, and shuffle from this life to the next.

Terri pulled the toaster for a walk almost every day, mumbling to himself.

My favorite client was Pedro. A Puerto Rican man from New York City, he used to walk down to the lobby to chat every day, sitting with his cat BooBoo. She had only three legs and a limp. "She has her disability, just as I do," he told me.

Some days, we smoked looking out at the graffiti on Market Street, reflecting on the illuminations. He was short—about five foot one—and walked hunched over, often grinding his teeth from HIV meds. He wore flannel shirts, had curly hair and a five o'clock shadow. His affect felt very New York to me; he seemed like he was from a tough, far away, transnational space, displaced from San Juan to the Bronx. He looked fragile, his frame emaciated and weak. He showed me where the drug dealers staked out the neighborhood, on lookout for the police, pointing out where people bought and sold everything.

"Did you see that fire?" I asked him at the beginning of my shift.

"Yeah, Bum's crack lab blew up."

"Bum," I said and he nodded.

"You see him walking up and down Market all the time."

"I still smell it," I said.

"Me too. The whole city is smoldering."

Other days, he walked into the building noting that the constellations were out, shining in the urban night sky.

"I don't see it," I told him.

"Just open your eyes to the lights and shapes around here," he insisted, pointing upward. "It's all there. You just have to put the pieces together with your mind and the constellations will come together."

He told me about his childhood spent in and out foster care where he was beaten, and his subsequent stays in Bellevue hospital, his teeth grinding, scratching his ear and thick head of hair. I talked with him almost every day. He coughed a lot from all the cigarettes. He shared the ins and outs of life in the building, who was doing what.

"He's mine," he told the other residents who would walk by when we were chatting. Each shift was eight hours with little to do besides buzz people into the building and ask them to sign their guests in and out. None were allowed to stay more than four nights a week. This, of course, presented a point of contention with the residents.

There was a lot to learn about the world, as I reconciled myself with what felt like a prolonged exile. Modern life was full of losses. We move for jobs and schools, leaving friends and communities behind. This was part living. But it wasn't easy. I often wondered, who was going to miss Pedro or any of the others in the building when they were gone?

I loved the beauty of the place, but it was lonely. So much of my life here was about that isolating sensation. By myself in my room, that old 1975 feeling enveloped me, wandering through my head all night long, as I looked at the ceiling. The solitude was a familiar stranger, always present, accompanying me.

My best thinking was during the small hours on Market Street, when the building was asleep. This was quite often when Pedro would come down to talk. He loved the city but told me that being here was sometimes the loneliest feeling he had ever had. I concurred, although I never told him that. Still, we talked for hours and hours. He shared secrets about what everyone really thought of the place, of living with HIV, and the social workers trying to "help" everyone.

Talking with him, I decided I would be an anthropologist here, looking at what was going on in this world of San Francisco, where everyone came from to get here—from New York or Mexico City or the south in my case; and what everyone knew about the disease that was consuming them. I wondered what had happened to Dad's old friend Tom and everyone else in the building, their lives passing by like the gas Becky used to see on the highway, disappearing in the distance. Somehow there had to be a different ending than sickness and premature death. I just knew it. This had to be telling me something. I watched the people walking all night through Market Street for signs.

Pedro and the others helped me take it all apart, unpacking everything. In between the illness, the kids in the clubs in the Mission, the weekly obits in the *Bay Area Reporter*, the people playing pool and hooking up, and my endless string of bad dates, this mix of connection with the city and separation from my childhood friends, the world had to be telling me something. What was the fire? What set it ablaze? What was burning through San Francisco, lodged in between the karma of the past and our present.

Stumbles and Separation

In San Francisco, the very lines of the city are drawn around sexual stories. Everyone had a story.

My story didn't seem to be going anywhere. At least I couldn't see it. So I fell into a routine. Every day, I found myself walking down Haight to Market and Van Ness, to work at what felt like an intersection of the epidemic transforming the city. More and more people were getting sick.

One Saturday, I arrived for the swing shift at work and asked about one of the tenants.

"He died this morning. They just took his body away," I was informed. That was the first five minutes of my shift. The next eight hours were interminable. By midnight, I walked out to smell the air and wonder about who's lucky enough to hang around, the mystery of a life in which some stay, while others disappear to god knows where just as they are getting started. Never was I more fixated with the burlesque of street life. I wandered, watching the characters, dipping in and out of sex clubs, chatting, grieving, sensing, and experiencing, perfectly aware so many were running out of time.

And then there was my on and off again girlfriend, Julie. Julie was a respite. Most nights at Julie's were a treat. We'd cook and talk, watch movies and sleep together. She listened to me try to make sense of a crazy job with more loss than I could ever imagine. The death drained me, accompanying me wherever I went. I was less the boyish character she had first come to meet. It all felt tenuous; sustaining connection was elusive.

One night when we were cooking, I made self-depreciating joke about our sex life, lamenting our occasional awkwardness when we'd make out.

"We must really like each other because the sex is terrible," I teased her.

Her body went cold as she pulled away.

She lowered her voice so her roommate didn't hear us. "I'm trying to understand what you meant by saying that."

"Nothing, I meant nothing by it. I swear to god. Come here," and I tried to pull her back to me. "It was a joke, a really bad joke, that's all. I'm sorry. I didn't mean it. I promise I didn't mean it." She pulled away, walking back to the kitchen to cook.

"Well, maybe we shouldn't be doing that then."

Her roommate came home and we all cooked for a bit. After dinner, things were just as awkward.

"Come on Julie," I said as she crawled into bed. I followed to comfort her. But she was distant.

"Do we have to talk about this? Do we have to dwell on this? Can't we just leave it be?" she asked, upset.

"I'm sorry, over-analysis is an occupational hazard in relationships. I fixate on things..."

"Cab, can't you be comfortable with not talking with me? Is that possible? Can we just lay here and be?"

"We can do that," I said. So we just lay there with an element of doom hanging over us.

"Julie, I didn't want this evening to be something serious. I am exhausted and had a crappy day. I wanted to get away from the world of conflicts at least for the evening."

"I know. I had a tiring weekend also, seeing my parents." She paused and then continued, "God, my parents, I still can't connect with them. I could barely hug my father."

"Why?" I asked.

"I don't know. I've never been able to. We just fall into the same patterns and roles and spaces we've always had."

"Does that ever get weird?"

"No we just maintain——that's it. If I understood, maybe I wouldn't be in this position with him. It's stuff we have never been able to clear up. I don't really think it's possible. Certain things can't be understood between people. They're just the way you feel. You don't go beyond them."

"Do you really think that's true?" I asked her.

"Once things go wrong between two people, they can't be repaired."

"But how can that be? What about reconciliation?"

"No, Cab...there's nothing to say——you just move on."

We were both quiet for a while.

"If countries can reconcile, don't you think you can with your family?" I said.

She sighed, exasperated. "Like the Middle East, there will always be irreconcilable differences. The more they try to work things out, the closer they both come to killing each other. They should both walk away."

"Just give up?" I replied, starting to get frustrated that we were talking about the Middle East, instead of what was happening between us. "But wait, why are we talking about the Middle East? Aren't we avoiding talking about your family? Are you trying to have a fight or to avoid one?"

"I don't know Cab. I'm upset." she wondered, pausing, "Have they gotten anything accomplished? Daily brutalities, torture, forced interrogation, and displacement. They will always hate each other." I could not tell if she was talking about us or politics.

"But Julie, they don't have the luxury of walking away from each other. They are inexplicably tied by a common history and geography. Why not just mix it up? I mean, where are they supposed to go to——an island? No, they are both in it together for the long haul and they need each other. If they can follow through on peace, everyone will better off."

"But these tribes have been through too much together. They know too much about each other."

"Is that bad? I don't know. I mean everyone has a dark side..."

"There's a point when we know too much. I know one writer, I think Dorothy Allison, who said she didn't like her girlfriend to read her stuff because the whole writing process involved bringing out memories of her past history which she never would have wanted her to hear about."

"Well, that's sad."

"I knew you'd say that."

I didn't respond, seeming to give up on us talking about her family or what had transpired. I was hoping we could diffuse it so it would lose its power. In lieu of that, a doom seemed to descend. And the more we talked the worse it got.

"I knew you'd say that because you want to know everything," she continued. "You always want to stay up all night talking and sharing. You love that stuff."

"You think that's silly?"

"No, not silly. Maybe futile, but not silly."

"I remember Chloe once said to me that it's funny how two people can be going out forever and both be having two different relationships at the same time. But I do think people can understand each other if they listen," I said.

"Cab, I need to sleep. Can we sleep now?"

"Yeah, go to sleep," I replied, feeling despondent, like she was slipping away. We both had been lying on our backs. She grabbed a pillow and turned away from me.

"Hasta la vista," I thought to myself as she fell asleep. It was like the Berlin Wall was running down the middle of the bed between the two of us, the two of us lying in bed, one set of eyes open and the other's closed. I looked over at Julie, her thoughts so completely hidden by those heavy eyelids. I remembered that first time I met her in the elevator and she stared before turning away. I wondered at the time just exactly what the limits would be for the two of us, how much she would ever show me, how much of her life's story, how much she would truly ever truly reveal to me. It was that night while Julie was dreaming and I was isolated from her thoughts that I realized I had seen all she was going to let me see.

Morning Sunrise on Market Street

Each Monday I worked the graveyard shift from midnight to 8:00 in the morning. When I arrived, I'd go through steps to make sure all was well in the building, greet a few folks, get the run of things from the previous shift and settle into late night reruns of *Columbo*, *Northern Exposure* or *MASH*, buzzing clients into the front door and chatting with those who wanted to talk. Some nights I dozed or talked with Juan or the others.

Juan was from Mexico City. He'd come to San Francisco to get treatment unavailable back home. In addition, San Francisco also offered distractions he couldn't find in Mexico City. He hadn't even made it out of the bus station when he encountered a man in a brown tweed suit staring at him in the station. They caught each other's eyes, looked around, and followed each other into the men's room.

"That was my first experience in San Francisco," Juan told me, with a devilish grin on his boyish, round face. "Only later that night did I find my pants were dirty on the knees. I was walking around San Francisco all day like that."

"I love that story," I laughed.

"Don't tell anyone," he said. I promised I wouldn't.

As Juan went up, another of our clients was just returning from a night out.

"How was the night?" I asked John, a man who had moved to San Francisco in the early 1970s and was part of the gay liberation movement years. He was in his '60s now, had a handlebar moustache, and was wearing jeans, a leather jacket and boots.

"It was a leather event. I only stayed for a little bit. I can't keep up anymore," he told me, pausing as he sat down. "I've lost so much weight from this. I don't have any padding on my butt anymore."

John told me about a party from the late '70s, one that he says set the tone for the next decade. "The party was called 'Madness Takes Its Toll,' after the Rocky Horror Picture Show. The invitation was something like: 'The master's having one of his private affairs and you are invited to a private showing of the Rocky Horror Picture Show.' People showed up in costumes from the movie.

"At that time, nobody had heard about AIDS," John continued. "But I was wondering... Would my extraordinary self-indulgence and freedom lead to some dire result, some form of madness that I had engaged in? And now in retrospect, you can see that that was true. The madness of the '70s—the 'Let's play, let's party, let's have sex'—did in fact have consequences. Even divine madness takes its toll."

"But you're not condemning it, are you?" I asked him.

"No, I wouldn't change a thing. But I'm trying to make sense of it all."

"I guess everyone is making sense of these forces," I said. "The clash between sex and death..."

"Creativity and annihilation..." John interrupted me.

"... it's everywhere here."

"But I'm not sure if I can see a resolution," John followed, before wandering off to bed.

The whole city seemed to be reeling with these sorts of questions. Was sex toxic, or a life force driving the city forward, churning creativity through destruction? The deaths kept piling up. The sick barely had anywhere to go. Hospitals were overrun with sick bodies lining the hallways. We had wait lists for our meager housing program. But people kept dying, so the rooms turned over every few months. The long-term survivors, whose bodies seemed to hold the virus in check, watched.

I dozed off some time around 4:00 a.m., before a local baker buzzed to drop off bread for the restaurant next door. I went to get it. By that time, it was 5:30. A bus zoomed down Market Street. The sun was beginning to peek over the buildings in the distance, the menacing darkness of the night passing into the hustle and bustle of the city rising.

I started to sweep the front entrance when Pedro strolled by wearing a Fedora cap and oversized tweed blazer. He put his hands in his pockets and steam came out of his mouth from the morning chill. The sun radiated off the graffiti in the lot on the other side of Market Street. A young black man with an afro stood out staring at the world of the city, the buildings now covered with light. Everything still seemed out of balance. But that was okay. The fog rolled in on the fall morning.

"You want a cigarette?" asked Pedro, offering me his pack.

"Sure," I said. "Thanks." We stood for a moment, looking out at the city as the light changed and the fog swarmed around us.

"Cab, its beautiful," Pedro said. "I left New York nine years ago and I have never regretted it."

"I love it out here. But what about your family? Do you miss them?"

"My sister and I have been talking a lot more lately. My brother still won't talk to me since I told him about..."

"Still?" I asked.

"Yes, people are still petrified. But I'm not worrying about him." He paused.

You still seeing the girl from Russian Hill?" he asked me.

"I'm not sure. We had a fight. Well, it wasn't a fight. It was a non-communication."

"I'm sorry, Cab," he said, before smiling. "Well, you always have us."

"I know," I smiled. "That's a relief."

"So what are you going to do?"

"It feels kind of over... or I'm stuck. I'm not sure. I'm kind of on a losing streak."

"Well, maybe you should write about it. You are always writing in your journal here. Why not write about what happened with her?"

"I'm not sure about her. I don't even know if she is real or not. I think there is a bigger story there."

"What is it then?"

"The whole catastrophe——the whole cavalcade of sex and failure ever crashing through my mind, colliding like the furies haunting me."

"Who are the furies?"

"Those old girlfriends."

"Yes, well, you know I haven't gotten laid since..."

"New Years, you told me."

"It was good too," he said, smirking, before he put out his cigarette.

As we stood talking, Terri walked out pulling his toaster.

"Frankie needs to get some air," she declared, walking toward the water.

We both looked down Market Street at Terri with her terrycloth robe and pink slippers, pulling the toaster down Market Street.

"What can I say?" I smiled. "I do like that Frankie."

"That's a toaster," Pedro lamented.

"Are you sure?"

"This place is getting to you Cab."

"I know it is, but you have Booboo. Now Terri has Frankie."

"But Booboo is a cat and Frankie is a toaster." Pedro paused and looked around. "Wait—what time is it?"

"A little after 6:00," I said.

"I'm going to call my sister when I go in. She'll just be getting to work in New York." He stood finishing another cigarette. I shrugged my shoulders. He threw his cigarette away and walked in while I finished mine. The door closed and I was locked out. The keys were inside on the desk. I knocked on the door, knowing I could be fired for this. Pedro turned around with a smile. Pedro had had a gleam in his eye when he opened the door as if to say, "You owe me one." We both walked inside, laughing. But it was also scary. He had done me a huge favor, even if a line had been crossed. And he had closed the door He wouldn't let me forget about that one. The power dynamic was always vexing in the building, and it just became a little odder. Residents passed me notes inviting me back to their rooms, telling me what they wanted to do with me, enacting a messy engagement/rejection/attraction/repulsion dynamic. It unfolded over and over. A feeling of sex as danger lingered in the building in this place where pleasure had led to scarlet letters and punitive dynamics of harm. I was walking that line. I didn't really know what my sexuality was. But Pedro was ready to pounce. I was the epitome of health and attraction, and unattainable. And he, like all the other residents, confronted this every night when he came into the building. It was all getting blurry. My shift was almost over.

"Go home and write that story, Cab," Pedro cajoled me as I left. "It sounds like a great harlequin romance. Everybody's got a story here. It's time for you to figure out yours."

I'd go home, sleep, and start writing. Maybe Pedro was right. Maybe it was time to write it all out, to trace the losing streak to its foundation. There was a lot to think about. I began with what mattered to me, drafting outlines of the hookups, the infatuation which began the cycle. I needed to unwrap it before I could move forward—every girl, even guy I ever adored, or adored me, who I dumped, or dumped me; I needed to look at every single one, examining the patterns of eternal returns that kept repeating themselves. It was time go back to the scene of the crime.

An image of scalding coffee flying through the kitchen, slapping me in the face, flashed through my mind; Dad standing there with the empty cup ready to fight, loud screams, parents shouting, clenched fists, slammed doors, pornography, divorce, transgressions and violence. None of it was clear. But a part seemed to have to do with losing something but I could not put my finger on it. Was it from my childhood—whatever that meant—losing a home and a way of looking at the world, trying to find another family, playing out those mistakes that they made and passed down? Trying to let go of the old world, leaving my parents' house—an alcoholic father and debutante wealthy mother, brothers who disengaged from the mess. I was looking for a Garden of Eden, an origin, a family, before it came apart. Time to face the demons of my own paradise lost. Not that it was ideal. But it was the only childhood I knew. But I needed to go back through some of the stories still lingering, my parents and grandparents flashing through my head. Origin stories are not so easy to figure out, story after story, circling through time.

Reel Around the Fountain

It's time the tale were told
Of how you took a child
And you made him old
You made him old

Reel around the fountain
Slap me on the patio
I'll take it now

"Reel around the Fountain"
-The Smiths, 1984

Freshman year, Mom fled Dad's screams and temper tantrums for graduate school in a state far far away. Dad worked out of state most of the time. My brothers moved out, off to school. So I caught rides to school and ate TV dinners on my own. Instead of going home to an empty house, I stayed out later and later, eating dinner with friends, sleeping out. Along the way, I learned where everyone lived in suburban Dallas—this football player, that senior, this disc jockey, that girl, etc. They became my everything as I reeled around town. "This is the best album you have ever heard," Carson insisted, giving me a tape of Alphaville, a clue and an invitation from someone who was worldlier wise. Laughing, we chatted about romance, dating, who was into sex, and who was not. I had to learn. Eventually I started driving myself, expanding and exploring the geography of friendships.

I first become love sick in ninth grade in 1985. Magnificent sensations exploding everywhere, bright colors connected me with beauty I saw budding everywhere I turned—the flowers growing from the cracks in the sidewalk, the cigarettes in black and white new wave movies, every chord in every song chord, every pastel painting.

Her name was Marni. She was in the high school musical with me freshman year. We were both townspeople in *The Wiz*. In between rehearsals, she organized photo shoots for her school calendar of all the alternative new wavers at the school, and drew pictures of everyone. With art school looks—short pink hair and a sunny disposition; she wore pastel colored clothes and listened to XTC, the British art band. She was like a character in a new wave French movie and; her drawings belonged in galleries. Some days, she dressed like a performance art piece. She was friends with the DJ's who ran the Pajama Party on the people's radio station. She knew Josh from Josho Mischo, a local group of students from the Arts Magnet who released their own 45 RPM single, and she was going to go to art school in Rhode Island after high school. Enlightened in ways I could never be, she was connected to a world bigger than anything I could imagine in the suburbs of Dallas.

"Fifteen minutes with you /. Well, I wouldn't say no," Morrisey sang. I listened in my room, thinking of her drinking in the feeling. Dressed in cardigan sweaters and baggy pink pants and bouffant hairdo I wandered through school, looking like a cast out from a John Hughes movie, looking forward to the occasional moments by the locker with Marni.

Eventually, I got the courage to ask her out. And to my surprise, she said yes.

We went to see *PeeWee's Big Adventure* at the Inwood Theater, a vintage art movie theater on Lovers Lane.

"Large Marge sent me," Pee Wee told Satan's helpers, playing the absurdist hero, hitch hiking a ride to find his lost bike. The room giggled, we giggled, bumped shoulders, went out for a snack afterward, hung out in Turtle Creek, and laughed all the way through it.

"It's kind of an epic narrative," I pontificated, trying not to put too much into my camp.

"Just like Odysseus," she followed.

"Exactly," I concurred. "He travels, takes an epic quest, leaves home, has adventures at the Alamo, and returns, a different man."

I knew I was stretching it to pursue her. She was a senior, few of whom showed much interest in freshman anyways. The following week she didn't respond to my calls.

There would not be another date. No more phone calls or pictures or sweet run ins. I retreated back to the Smiths, waxing melancholic, listening as I reeled around the fountain, shifting and flowing, feeling raw and exposed. One day it would be my turn to be the object of attention. But not for now. Instead, I coveted others, daydreamed, singing show tunes to myself, always wondering, what if? What if?

There was drama everywhere as we all grappled with growing, finding a place to fit, and struggling with the making and breaking of primordial bonds, omnipresent divorce, precarious new attachments, and hopes for something else of our lives.

Most of the time, people made it appear they had it together. But every once in a while cracks appeared, revealing how hard it was. We were sitting in art class in fifth grade.

"Oh, I love this song!!!" Daisy gushed, exalted as Blondies' "Rapture" began. "He's the man from Mars and now he even eats guitars. RAPTURE," Daisy rapped along. I had not known any of the students very long, having just started at Greenhill after just transitioning from a speech school for dyslexic specials need students, as well as other disabilities, cerebral palsy etc. But here, everyone seemed a little cavalier about their capacities. I was just glad to be there and reading a bit, unlike years before when I literally flunked out because I could not understand a word on the chalkboard, words dancing, letters bouncing about. Everyone was chatting, painting, and singing to Blondie.

"We had pizza again last night," Daisy quipped, kvetching.

"I'm jealous. We never have pizza," I responded to Daisy's lament about her disheveled home life.

"You wouldn't feel that way if you had to have pizza every night," Daisy replied. Out of nowhere, she began to cry, right there in the middle of the class. The mood changed, as a real feeling, something we all understood grasped the room. Divorce was a reality for many of us that fall of 1980. *Ordinary People* was my favorite movie. When the Conrad's brother died in a boating trip, he was left to pick up the pieces of his memories, grief, and guilt. But he held on. We all had to hang on, even if things were messy. The confusion was real. Like Conrad, I was lost in my head, playing football and riding my bike. I had my fears of my father getting sick again as he had, when he was hospitalized. Like the parents in *Ordinary People*, my folks were growing apart. When mom had moved out, she left me with Dad and little to no supervision. He mostly left town and me the credit card to the supermarket; abusive relationships take countless forms, including neglect. My mother was a debutante with a lot of cash and a habit of checking out when things got rough, so graduate school away felt more intriguing than staying with us. She talked about being a member of both the Daughters of the Confederacy and the Revolution. Her mother had been a founding member of the Jr. League. Her folks passed while she was in college, leaving her to navigate between Cotillion balls, her own craving for independence, and the superficial mores of Eisenhower's America— a white world of toxic social relations she abhorred and quietly concealed herself within.

"Let's not talk about that," she was fond of saying when messy questions came up. Everyone made sense of it in our own ways.

In 6th grade, purple was the color. All the girls in the know wore it. When Lili made the call for every girl in the grade to wear their purple miniskirts, they all did. Those not on the call were left on the outside, their exclusion marked with their clothes. One of the girls who never got the memo was Sarah— a cute brunette—who I shared a desk with in general science class. We also sat beside each other every day in English. I flirted with her all fall. We were supposed to diagram sentences, following *The Elements of Style*, before class and correct them during class. Sarah and I both rushed through the sentences, gabbing as we feigned working, looking at each other, smiling. It was a great way of covering the inadequacies I was feeling.

I barely retained any of that material, failing to get any sleep most of that fall. A teacher in the 1970s first identified my scattered learning habits as a form of dyslexia, as they spiraled with the years, words flipped and danced on the page. Mom had taken me to the doctor, who prescribed Ritalin and Dexedrine at the beginning of the school year. I was so high voices bounced through my brain. I told her I was hearing voices, like the backwards mumbles on "Revolution 9" from the Beatles White Album. A Chorus Line of voices mumbled, their feet tapped dancing in my head. The doctors suggested audible hallucinations reverberating inside were not worth paying notice to. Not long into eighth grade, I found that the pills had their benefits as a means to avoid sleep. They were amphetamines after all. I was not sure what the doctor who came up with the idea of giving hyperactive kids speed was thinking. But kids were getting hooked and dependent at earlier and earlier ages—a pharmacist's dream. Over time, Sarah and I started to share them. Some days she asked for some to study, even when I wasn't around. I always gave them to her. During Christmas break, ice storms put most of the streets of Dallas out of commission. I spent a couple of days at Grant's during that storm.

"Sarah is at Lili's house. Do you want to go over there?" Grant asked me.

We trudged through the ice to talk about school and music and vacation and try to make out the possibilities of visible underwear lines at Lili's.

I went over to Sarah's house a couple more times that break. The final weekend before school was to start Sarah let me know about the ninth grader she had been dating. As long as there were upper classmen around, I was out of Sarah's league. I stared at that photo of Sarah again that night, digesting that small bit of the realpolitik of dating—when someone has the upper hand, they use it. Sarah had the upper hand and other suitors. And I adored her.

63

Throughout eighth grade, she had never really wanted to be in my club. But I wanted to be in hers. Sarah formed a band that played eighties covers. In one of many backyard parties we attended, they played their first and only gig. With Susan on guitar, Lili on vocals, Daisy on drums, and Sarah on base, they played a whole set, including a cover of the Jam's "Boy about Town." With a punk tempo and harmony, Lili sang:

"See me walking around I'm the boy about town that you heard of...

"See me walking the streets I'm on top of the world that you heard of."

As most of us danced along, Mickey (who would later come out as gay) lay on the ground making out with Mandy. All the girls adored him. He wore drag every Halloween and joked about supporting gay rights. We thought he was kidding. But over the next couple of years, he would move onto queerer and queerer pastures, taking countless ambiguous hetero boys, to see what gay sex was about.

"You know guys know what other guys want and how to give it much better than girls," he reminded me when we were peaking on ecstasy a few years later. I was one of his recruits. He got on his knees to show me. I didn't mind receiving but giving was not for me.

With Sarah and company playing Jam covers on the other hand, the band offered a glimpse of something wonderful that I could not find in myself, even if they were just the popular girls following a wave. Everyone formed bands that year.

"All the pretty girls in high school, make me sick," our band sang, covering the Judy's anthem. We experimented with Clash and Judy's covers. But we were rougher. I was the lead singer, playing rhythm guitar, which the guys in the band turned down so no one could hear me as I strummed along, during our one gig at the Valentine's Dance in the cafeteria in 8th grade. With the whole class dancing and singing along, I led the band, bounding around the stage, wearing a black and white leopard skin shirt, baggy pink pants, and orange bleached hair. Dave, our guitar player rolled his eyes at our drummer Andy as they played along.

"All the pretty girls go yack, yack, yack, all the pretty girls drive new Cadillacs," everyone sang along, without anything close to the melody of Sarah and company.

Our set was a smash; at least I thought so.

"You guys are definitely the most punk band in eighth grade," noted one of our teachers.

A few weeks after the big gig, we broke up. I thought it was over philosophical differences. But a week later the rest of the band reformed without me. My fifteen minutes as a front man were up. I went back to playing the cello, unable the bridge the gap between where music had been and where it was going. But listening to Lili harmonize and Sarah play base, I knew it was taking us somewhere I had never been. I'd keep on chasing that feeling.

Music was everywhere that spring of 1984. It was at the midnight movies, with Rocky Horror Picture show, and every party. It was at the Bronco Bowl, where waves of bands dropped in from everywhere - New Order, the Alarm, the Pretenders, the Cure. Echo and the Bunnymen invited everyone to join the band performing in a moving carnival. The Alarm played there so much they were given keys to the city. On the Reckoning Tour that fall, Michael Stipe first started enunciating as well as murmuring when REM played. We pierced our ears at bar mitzvahs as punk evolved into dance music. Flux was constant. The

64

year before, my neighbor Rebecca was still wearing a "death to disco" t shirt. If disco was the catalyst for a changing landscape birthing its antithesis, the teenage spirit of punk, electronic dance music offered a kind synthesis, merging Giorgio Moroder and Manchester beats. I was still slam dancing, throwing elbows everywhere. But after Ian Curtis killed himself before Joy Division's US tour, New Order offered us a Blue Monday to a dance beat. The band's second act invited us to dance away that 1975 feeling that gripped so many of us. Frankie Goes to Hollywood, Orchestral Maneuvers in the Dark and Ultravox followed. Siouxsie and the Banshees even added a dance beat to their cover of Dear Prudence, merging beats and dispositions. But not everyone was having it. Jane's Addiction opened the show before Siouxsie played, bringing a thicker dose of androgyny and pathos. That was the first time I heard "Jane Says." I sat looking in awe as my future blurred in front of me. Everything was up for grabs in this cultural smorgasbord.

I explored it as much as I could, riding my bike through alleys, past vacant lots, where I smoked cigarettes, looking for music on the way to VVV, an underground record shop. On the way, a world opened, full of secret treasures in lost places, between Dallas' gay neighborhood, thrift shops, and subcultures. This melding of cultures in between the synthetic beats and the bars felt like an opening and an entry point into a degree of acceptance. XTC was burning with optimism's flames. We listened to Shaggy's Pajama Party on KNON. Here Texas bands, such as The 13th Floor Elevators, the Mydolls, and the Judy's shared radio time with the Clash, Charlotte Sometimes, as the Specials' ska mixed with Joe King Carrasco's jalapeno inspired Tex Mex new wave. I listened every Saturday I wasn't at a gig at the Grenada Theater on Greenville Ave or at the Bronco Bowl or in Deep Ellum or someone's party.

Within the alchemy of cigarette smoke and sweaty bodies, conceptual dancing, gyrating, crashing, and pogoing in the mosh pit, a poetry took shape with each gig. The San Francisco-based band the Avengers tapped into the urgency of this moment in a song some describe as the greatest punk song ever written. Accompanied by guitars, drums and a rolling crescendo of emotion, Penelope Houston sang about the feeling of arriving at a show in their song "Cheap Tragedies":

The doors flew open and the people crowded in
They said, we can't wait for your show to start
And their bodies flew the only way they knew
They're coming straight for the center of my heart

I see your face and I've memorized it
I see your life, I recognize all your petty jealousies
Your hidden tragedies, your bitter memories
They'll be the death of you yet, oh

My first show was in seventh grade, the Dead Kennedy's playing at Trax, a seedy club in between strip clubs on Northwest Highway. It reminded me of the sort of underworld venue Lee Harvey Oswald was fabled to frequent decades prior. A man with a mohawk haircut was screaming at himself. Watching people dance and fight, feelings flooded everywhere, bodies flying through the air into a crowd which held each of us as we leapt high off the stage into the hands of the alternately violent and supportive crowd. Jello lunged on stage as The Dead Kennedy's sped through their anthem, "Holiday in Cambodia." Over and over again, my older brother jumped into the writhing mosh pit of bodies in front of the band. They held him, he danced, and threw himself back onto the stage with the band. The show brought a combustible dose of adrenaline, feelings, the rush of bodies, music—creating an outlet for all the sensations of my life—the highs, let downs, wanderlust and disappointment of them not wanting us as much as we want them. None of us knew what to do with all the cheap tragedies the Avengers sang about that we all felt:

"Those hidden tragedies, those bitter memories
They'll be the death of you yet, oh."

They were not quite the death of me. But I was drawn to the feeling. After Sarah's gig, one of the upper classmen made an unwelcome advance at her. She pushed him away and he kept on trying. I stepped in and took him out with one self-conscious punch, watching myself as if I were in a movie. He was down on his back. I turned bright red. Sarah smiled. I was embarrassed I had shown my card and Sarah was gushing. But none of it was enough. She went back home with him.

A few weeks later, I saw her crying her eyes out sitting at the movies with Susan and Lili. We were all out watching *Valley Girl* at the mall. It seemed like the whole grade was there.

"She got dumped," Susan explained as we were walking in.

I just kept walking.

In the years to come, social dynamics shifted. By senior year, the numbers were on my side, with suitors I had little interest in who had blown me off years prior. Each year in school I had found more and more interest coming my way. It was as if everyone got together and distributed a memo that Cab was going to be popular.

Keg parties followed every Friday night football game in Dallas. Kids held them all over the city. Cashed kegs, police, and class animosities were on display here, often leading to fights outside, breaking up the parties. The football team always tried to have contingency plans for where to meet if a party went bad or ended suddenly. One Friday night I had only just arrived at a Hillcrest party and found the keg when someone called the police. Hillcrest was a public school; half my class of private school kids had crashed. The room was full of 'ropers'—those who insisted on wearing cowboy hats in our paved-over suburbia—ready for a fight. The chances of fights only increased in those liminal spaces, entrances, exists, and transitions between worlds, social gatherings and classes, especially if anyone remembered the chants between schools the week before at the games. "That's all right, that's okay, you're gonna work for us some day," we jeered. When the police showed up, everyone needed to evacuate pronto. While we did not talk about it much, class animosities simmered in Dallas. The Marcus kids, whose parents owned Neiman Marcus department stores and supported the Kennedys and the art museums, generated countless resentments. They were Jewish, supported liberal causes and flaunted cash. Raids at parties were ideal moments for a drunk in cowboy boots to take a swipe at someone in a Polo Shirt. Texas was a place where polite smiles concealed the omnipresence of a lingering violence, where people beat others for looking at them the wrong way, people of color faced mass incarceration, or were dragged through the streets, and homophobia simmered. We knew we needed to get out of there.

I stumbled into old Sarah, looking out of place, as the police arrived. Sarah had only started going to parties with members of our grade senior year. Everyone she had dated for the previous four years had graduated. Her glow had tarnished from what had become a string of ungentlemanly upperclassmen. The image of Sarah nurturing a beer struck me as odd, just the way she stood with her hand around the cup, which she held to her lips with her wrist and elbow facing me, her face partly covered. None of her friends were in sight. We looked around for a second, but they were all gone and we needed to move. She did not have a car, but I did.

"Hey Sarah, funny to see you here," I said.

"Fun to see you," she smiled.

"This is blowing up. You need a ride?" I asked.

"Sure," she smiled.

As I drove, we talked about people we had been seeing and not seeing. I put on Madonna.

"I just want to enjoy my senior year," she confessed. "Sometimes I feel like I've missed out on high school because I've been dating guys the whole time while people like you have taken advantage of high school stuff."

"It's still pretty early," I said.

"I really don't know."

"You want to go get a bite to eat? I know a great place right off Lemon Ave."

"Sounds great."

When we pulled into the restaurant parking lot, I leaned over to kiss Sarah. We made out for a couple of minutes before we went inside, sitting at the white cloth-covered tables of the very darkly lit restaurant.

Drinking red wine, we caught up with how high school had gone for the two of us—the social life, the music, the scenes, the intrigue, college applications, the dates.

"What do you want from an evening?" Sarah asked.

"To play...."

"Games?" she asked.

I nodded. We made out in the parking lot again before I took her home. We started dating that fall. Somehow, this time, I had an upper hand. Each week, we drove to and from parties, hung out, listened to Madonna, and explored in the car. We fooled around in Rick's mom's bathroom while our friend Paul was outside breaking mailboxes. Whenever I picked Sarah up I had a new mix tape to listen to as we drove around looking for the evening's parties of choice. Without it, the conversation waned. It only went so far.

"Where's Madonna when you need her?" I asked the radio a few weeks later, frustrated after my newest mix had broken. The pop music which always inspired was not working. Nothing was going to save this evening with Sarah. Eventually, we went dancing at a disco on Lemmon Avenue. Clove cigarette smoke, dry ice, and strobe lights meandered through the air in club. Sarah ordered two Sex on the Beach drinks. Too sweet. That felt like Sarah. We made out on the couches in the back and it all turned to routine.

"Cab, you said you were going to call," she scolded on the phone, when I didn't call the next day. I'd long sensed a part of her was plastic. The more I got to know of her, the more I saw it.

Sarah happened to have been the one who cared or wanted something this time around.

On New Year's Eve 1987 we all went over to Daisy's house. I wanted to be with everyone else, not with any one person. After fooling around perhaps too much in Daisy's mom's bedroom, I looked back at Sarah still laying on her stomach, nude on the floor, not even looking at me. I didn't know why we had had sex. It did not seem like something she had enjoyed. She did it partly because, as she had learned, this was something that would keep a guy involved, partly because a small part of her thought it would be something she would enjoy. But she wasn't like Katie. This wasn't comfortable or easy, although she happily initiated. But once we got going, I felt bad.

And afterwards, I left to go drink with my friends. This was the last New Year's we would have together in high school. I wasn't going to spend the evening with Sarah in a closet. We broke up the following week after a final ill-fated attempt at intimacy in Susan's parents' bathroom. Not so fun. After we had finished, she had that same look on her face she'd had on New Year's. I explained that our glorious romance was over. Right there in the bathroom, as I put my socks on. She was pissed off. I knew she was right to be.

Everybody danced to "Hungry Like the Wolf" in the kitchen that night. George Michael's "Faith" blared. I walked out with Grant to get breakfast and spent the night at his house.

"Cab, just get your shit together and come get in bed with Sarah and me," Susan said when we walked out to the car. She was probably right, but I had little interest. Sarah found me intriguing when it suited her. Tit for tat rejecting her, I told myself I was in the right, and another part felt like I should have never let it get that far. We were all reeling around the fountain.

Driving home, Grant played *Low* by David Bowie.

"I don't know this."

"It's from Bowie's post Ziggy period."

"What's this?" I asked, pulling a brick out by my feet, where I was sitting.

"They're bricks I got for mom for the back yard."

Bowie was singing, "Baby, I've been breaking glass in your room again."

We smoked a joint.

Feeling high, I asked, "You ever throw one through glass?"

"What?"

I picked up the brick gesturing.

"No."

He smiled.

"Through a piece of glass?" Grant asked.

"Want to?"

68

He pulled the car over and we both walked out, with bricks in our hands, looking at one of the suburban homes along the street. We hurled them through the night sky, directed like baseballs. *Crack!* a window in one of the homes seemed to scream. Alarms exploded. "Holy shit, let's get out of here." We ran off to the car. A man ran out and shot his gun. We drove off into the night, stopping every few miles to hurl another brick. No one called the cops. Boys will be boys, as the adage goes in Texas. White boys don't get caught. The law doesn't apply to white boys. Privilege meant we didn't have to explore the reasons why.

When I finally got home, it was sometime around 5:00 a.m.

"Stop!" a voice screamed at me as I walked in the front door.

I was jolted.

"One more move and I'll——" Dad screamed. I put my hands in the air.

"Dad, it's me!" I screamed.

He was naked pointing his twelve-gage shot gun at me, trembling.

"Sorry, I didn't know who it was."

"Dad, I live here."

"I know, son. I'm sorry."

"I didn't know you were going to be home," I said.

"Neither did I. But the trial ended early so I decided to come home."

He put his bathrobe on and we both sat in the living room and chatted about what had gone on since we last saw each other, a week or so ago. There'd been lots of late night run ins with Dad during the years. On another occasion, Grant and I had wandered to the kitchen stoned, looking for munchies, only to find Dad standing eating ice cream without a stitch of clothing.

"Hello Mr. Hardy," Grant grimaced, looking down. We all ended up chatting that night, just like this one.

"Here is a copy of William Butler Yeats' poems. I marked it up for you," he smiled, giving me a copy. "I love this poem," he said, reading from "When You are Old."

"When you are old and grey and full of sleep,

And nodding by the fire, take down this book,

And slowly read, and dream of the soft look

Your eyes had once, and of their shadows deep...."

I looked at dad and listened.

"I hope we can read these when we are old," I replied.

"Me too. I saw there is a play about Jack Kerouac at Poor David's Pub next week. I bought tickets for "us," he continued.

"Thanks Dad." It had been Dad and me against the world for three and a half years—no mom, no brothers, no one but each other.

69

The following Monday, David Nighttime gave me a note. "This is from Sarah," he said with a hint of judgment. "She would have delivered it herself but she knows you don't want to have anything to do with her. I don't know what it says, but I know she was upset."

The note was written in the same old handwriting from eighth grade, in blue ink, on notebook paper. "Cab, I know I am crazy, and annoying, and a bitch, and feel sorry for myself but I am also a damn good person to talk to, a damn good friend. Please call me if you ever want to talk." I never called. It was more interesting reeling around the fountain, waiting for someone to pick me up, as Lili had sung all those years earlier.

The Unbearable Lightness of Lili

I wasn't sure what TS Elliot was talking about. April hadn't seemed that cruel to me. It felt more like the world was awakening from a long nap.

"Lilacs out of the dead land, mixing
Memory and desire, stirring..."

I flipped through to the love poems:

"In the room the women come and go. Talking of Michelangelo...."

There was Lily, outside the classroom. While the others in Dr. Currier's advanced poetry class ruminated about the *Wasteland*, I watched Lili walk by with her black bob and Sanger Harris jumper. She reminded me of one of those women studying art history. She'd already gotten her acceptance letter to Sarah Lawrence. Lili had been the first girl in the grade who ever showed the slightest indication of interest in me (or even acknowledging my existence).

She was the most popular girl in 5th grade, eight years prior, receiving an inordinate number of fudge-o-grams during the yearly popularity contest. Friends were encouraged to buy fudge-o-grams for all their friends. Ms. Milton, our reading teacher stood up in the front of the commons pulling out the names of the fudge-o-grams from the bag.

"One more for Lili from Mindy," Ms. Milton announced.

"One for Lili from Susan... From Daisy... From Tommy..." Ms. Milton took the bags of brown, homemade fudge and threw each at Lili, adding to a heaping pile of fudge-o-grams sitting right there in front of her. With an odd expression, she was becoming aware of the uneven distribution, the fudge-o-grams imitating larger social dynamics. Most of the kids in the class did not receive one. Everyone shrugged it off. This was Texas after all. Social inequalities were long a part of the landscape.

"Hey, Cab, take a look?" Lili said in art class, and unbuttoned part of her Ralph Lauren shirt to show me her bra. A strange hum filled the room. But somewhere in middle school, she seemed to peak.

By our high school graduation year, she was hanging around more and more. I was impressed by Lili's tape collection.

"Propaganda," I commented picking up one of the tapes from the tape box in her Bronco. We were sitting in the parking lot at school. Propaganda was esoteric German synthesizer dance music I had discovered in the *Melody Maker* two years prior. I had only met two other people who had ever heard of that group. But Lili?

It was a spring day when we all got to hang out waiting for god-knows-what in terms of word from college, the final formality of the prep school education, applications having been turned in months before. Dad had tried to buck the pattern my grandmother had established of getting the kids into top schools, only so their kids could try to do the same, ad infinitum—essentially ignoring my education. Let the chips fall where they would.

It felt odd around Lili. What do you do when you peak socially in fifth grade? Somewhere, someone had labelled Lili as maternal and the label stuck. She spent the last four years going out with Matthew, her ideal-to-bring-home boyfriend. We were all essentially over it in terms of social worries. We had all seen each other through so many bad clothes experiments, or been there when so and so had lost her virginity or when Susan had given Todd head in the bathroom and on and on. There was less to hide. The eighties were about to become a thing of the past, just like our 5th through 12th grades together.

"I love this tape. I listened to it all summer two years ago," I gushed. She was sitting across from me on the other seat in her Bronco. "How did you get turned onto this?"

"I don't know. Let's put it in," she said and then lit up a Marlboro Light cigarette. I bummed one. I liked seeing her drive.

The following weekend the whole gang was over at my house, getting stoned and listening to records. My bedroom lights were out, lava lamps oozing, 25 of us, records spinning. Dad was on the road.

"Cab, you have to find 'Boom, Boom,'" Daisy screamed. "Boom, boom, boom let's go back to my room," she sang.

"Can't find it, Daisy, can't find it," I confessed digging through the piles of records. I went back to sitting. Daisy took over DJ duties. I sat on the rocking chair with Lili on my lap. Somewhere along the line, I ended up offering to go for a beer run. Lili drove. No one else was in the car. I was really high at this point. I stared at the green lights on her tape deck as she drove.

"Lili, I'm going to have to lay it on the line," the words slid out of my mouth. "I have a complete crush on you," I confessed, conflating my love for her music with her. I zoned out until I heard Lili saying something back to me.

"You're just drunk," she replied as I sat still staring at the tape deck.

"Yes, I am. So?"

"You don't mean what you're saying because you are drunk."

"Watch me, Lili. Talk to me the next time I'm sober and I'll say the same thing."

We didn't talk as much after that but it was okay. She dropped me off at my house with the beer, and then drove home. I sat in the lawn watching her drive off. I saw Lili again the next night and made sure to tell her that I had meant what I said.

The following week, I found myself at Daisy's house watching MTV. Todd had suggested we go visit her. So, on her couch I sat with Daisy to my left and Todd to my right. I was drinking Coke making sure to put my glass on the coaster. "He's so cute!!!" she gushed when Terrence Trent Darby performed "Wishing Well," flipping his dread locks to the right. "He's so adorable." The phone rang in the living room. Daisy took the call and stayed on the phone for at least half an hour while Todd and I sat.

"Cab, do you still mean what you said to Lili last weekend?" Daisy inquired.

"Yeah, I meant it," I followed nonchalantly, not giving the line of questioning much thought.

Daisy left the room and made another call.

"That was Lili," Daisy announced when she came back into the room after getting off the phone. She sat facing me with one leg crossed over the other.

"Cab, Lili is interested. Would you like to do anything with her this weekend?" Daisy sounded very intimate and serious in her scheming matchmaking.

"Totally."

"Then we should all go out for a double date this Friday night. You and Lili with Todd and me—sound good?"

"Sounds good." Never, for the rest of my days, would setting up a first date be as easy as that first date Daisy set up for Lili and me. Never again would the social network take care of things in quite the same graceful way.

Friday afternoon I brought a big jug of wine I had bought with my supermarket credit card. Lili brought some goofy, fluorescent hats for us to wear. I found the gesture very cute. We sat in the back seat as Todd drove with Daisy in the front seat on our way to Daisy's lake house. He was on mushrooms that evening, telling me later, "I looked in the rearview mirror and you kept on looking like Herman Munster."

Lili and I were taking sips from the jug with straws when Daisy screamed, "I think that was Matthew!" as we left the Shell station at Preston and LBJ. No big deal. No one reacted. He hadn't seen us. Daisy's lake house was a long drive out of town anyway. So we just buzzed along, all of us wearing those hats. "We will be forever, forever in electric dreams," Todd sang along with the Human League on the tape deck.

After an hour of driving, we turned onto a dirt road leading up to the house. Another car turned off behind us and started blinking its lights, so we pulled over. "Oh my god, its Matthew," groaned Lili.

"He followed us?" Todd asked.

"He's crazy," Lili responded.

We sat in the car like kids waiting to get scolded as Matthew walked over to the car. It felt like we had been pulled over for speeding.

His jeans were tucked inside his Air Jordans. He looked like a neat Woody Allen caricature.

"Hi Matthew," Lili feigned sincerity.

"What's going on?" he asked.

"Oh, just a beautiful evening of wine and high spirits," I said.

"Is this a date?" Matthew asked, looking down dourly at Lili and me sitting in the back seat. We were still wearing the silly hats. I took mine off.

No one said anything.

"Can I speak with you by myself?" Matthew said to Lili.

Todd and I got out of the car. I was glad to leave, laughing with Todd. We overheard Matthew ask her, "What are you doing? Just because we are having problems, I find you here with another guy?" He stood over the car. Lili never even got up. His voice grew increasingly loud as his tough guy routine continued.

"How ya doing Lili?" we asked, as Matthew stood over her.

Twenty minutes later, he drove off with a screech of the tires. Todd and I laughed. It was too much like a teenage movie.

"Will somebody please give me the jug of wine?" Lili asked in exasperation as she lit a cigarette. "Four years, such a great guy."

We sat looking at the lake at Daisy's house. Lili and I laid back, looking at the stars. "What was it like to date guys when you were in 6th grade?"

"You mean Tommy and I?"

"Yeah."

"Could you call it dating? No, we were going together, not dating. He was my first kiss."

"A real kiss?"

"Not a very graceful start. We were kissing on the lips, like usual, and all of a sudden, out of nowhere, without warning, he just stuck his tongue in my mouth. Yuck." Lili scrunched her face.

"Yuck?"

"Yuck." Lili nodded.

"I always wondered about how that stuff happened for you guys. That was such a strange period. What about that day in sixth grade, I'll never forget this, when there must have been sixteen girls all wearing purple miniskirts, just like the Go-Go's."

"We looked great, didn't we?"

"A little strange. How did that happen?"

"Well, Daisy called me telling me. Susan had called her about it. We all called each other about such matters."

"That's just it. The 'we,' what was the 'we?'—the Group? I never understood the 'we.' It was already formed by the time I got to Greenhill in fifth grade when we had that art class. I felt it from the very first day I was at the school. It was like this council or something. I'll never forget in eighth grade, I had been a nerd outside of that scene for three years. But then, first day of eighth grade. It was like all the girls had called each other the night before to tell each other that I was going to be a cool guy that year. All of a sudden, they wanted to sit by me in class. Overnight."

"The Group—that whole thing got pretty awful sometimes. Sarah had the hardest time trying to get into the group."

"Like a secret society or something."

"She really wanted to be part of it, but she came to Greenhill in 6th grade which was a little late. The Group was pretty established by fourth grade so she was asking a lot. Susan told her she had to kiss some random guy they had chosen if she wanted to be part of the Group and she did it. Then a couple of the girls said she still couldn't be a member of The Group," Lili recalled.

"Susan got hers later in seventh grade on the end of the year camp out when all the girls in the Group decided they didn't like her."

We had our first kiss that night. She broke up with Matthew the following day and we were off. She had the dating thing down to a drill. She would call and make arrangements to meet for breakfast before school and the like. Over tea and cigs, the smoke so optimistically meandering through the eight AM morning brightness, Lili explained, "Sarah is such a bitch. The stink she's making over this. I cannot believe she is going to end our friendship over this," Lili groaned.

74

"I know. Well at least you don't have a class with her," I confided.

"Really, what class?"

"Literature in Transition, five days a week."

And it wasn't just a class with Sarah——Becky, Phil and Mandy (a girl I had fooled around with Junior year in Todd's Mom's houseboat) were also in the class. I couldn't believe it the first day I had entered the room to see everyone sitting against the back wall of the classroom looking like a panel from the Last Judgement. I stared down the whole class in complete shock. Looking at all three of the women and another former friend, the class was like some absurd comical aberration, something I deserved, the universe offering me a check.

I even told Mrs. Chips, a confidant from sophomore year when I got a 44 in her class. There had been a lot of explaining to do that year. She had taught Becky, Phil and me *Gatsby* years ago.

"How much of this has to do with hormones?" Mrs. Chips inquired, quite matter-of-factly.

"Oh, none, nothing Mrs. Chips," I lied. As much as I hated to admit it, she was right.

"But Mrs. Chips, I thought we talked about this before I signed up for this class," I lamented, flab-bergasted after that first class. "I specifically asked you if either Sarah or Becky were going to be in this class."

"I know you did Cab, but I couldn't tell you they were in the class. This is material I knew you could enjoy and benefit from. I can't allow petty personal conflicts get in the way of that," Mrs. Chips replied with mock seriousness.

"But Mrs. Chips, I have had relations with girls in this class——not very positive relations."

"This'll be good for you Cab. It'll be a learning experience," she concluded, smiling and getting back to her business.

So, for the last three months of a high school experience full of girls I had fixated on who had given me the cold shoulder, I had to face three of the girls I had recklessly let down. I was assigned *The Divine Comedy* in my class rights before the Literature in Transition class. Purgatorio was my favorite part. Alliances quickly fell into place as Mrs. Chips lectured about literary influence and movies, magic realism and Faulkner. Becky and Phil took the same two seats every day for their note passing. Despite all the LSD, partner swapping and panics, they still maintained a bond. They both seemed to enjoy the questions we'd all face in the class. Mandy always sat by herself. Phil and I were fine yet estranged. Susan and Sarah took to the same seats in the back row where they both crossed their legs and defiantly ignored my presence in the back corner as did Becky and Phil.

"I love teaching this course," announced Mrs. Chips. "These are modern works in every sense. I would never assign these books to underclassmen. I wouldn't even assign these readings to first term seniors. You are only ready for this stuff in the spring of your senior year as you are about to leave having experienced so many of the things which high school seems to entail in this precocious day."

Phil and Becky listened in their distinctly Deep Ellum boots, psychedelic jewelry, paisley patterned shirts, ripped jeans, and reflective sunglasses. Mandy sat with her hand on her chin in acid washed jeans a black shirt buttoned up all the way to the top. Sarah and Susan maintained a flow of shopping mall department store Sanger Harris and Neiman Marcus up to the minute—girl about town, somewhat confident, imitation standards. The class proceeded with our undivided attention, weirdness oozing all over the room, the clothes, the books, the looks, and the lectures.

On the first day, Mrs. Chips had begun: "I want to start with *Love in the Ruins* by Walker Percy. Let's just read out loud a few pages to get a feel for the material. None of you have had an opportunity to read yet so let's all start off on the same foot. Becky, would you read starting with page one?"

And read Becky did. She straightened her back and started:

"NOW IN THESE DREAD LATTER DAYS OF THE OLD VIOLENT beloved U.S.A. and of the Christ-forgetting Christ-haunted death-dealing Western world I came to myself in a grove of young pines..."

"Cab, you're in Dr. Currier's advanced poetry class aren't you?" Mrs. Chips asked when Becky finished.

"Yes Ma'am."

"Have you started Dante yet?"

"Yes."

"Do you have your copy of *Inferno* with you?"

I nodded.

"Could you pull it out and read the first few lines of Canto One?"

"Yes ma'am." I read:

"Midway through life's journey, I went astray
from the straight road and woke to find myself
alone in a dark wood.
what wood that was! I never saw so drear,
so rank, so arduous a wilderness!
Its very memory gives a shape to fear."

"Did everyone hear that?"

"Uh huh..." Mandy lied.

"Becky, read that first paragraph again. Could you please?" Which she did.

Forests again. We were all starting sit up in our chairs.

"Cab, now read from the beginning of that first Canto again." Which I did.

"Percy came to himself in a grove of young pines, Dante in a dark wood," I found myself mumbling, thinking out loud.

"What is Percy saying about us with this allusion?" Phil inquired. I hadn't heard him talk like that for two and a half years, from back when Phil, Becky and I had our first class with Mrs. Chips studying *The First Testament* and *Gatsby* freshman year.

76

"Actually, I think there's an answer to that. I want to continue with the readings out loud. Phil, could you read from Thomas' Creed on page six?"

Phil began: "I believe in God and the whole business but I love women best, music and science next, whiskey next, God fourth..."

Listening, I knew Thomas was my guy. That could have been my creed, but I did not say so. We read the rest of the first page from *Love and the Ruins*: "Is it that God has at last removed his blessing from the USA and what we feel now is just the clank of the old historical machinery ..."

Sitting there in Dallas, Texas, where JFK spent his last breaths, it was hard to disagree. God had removed his blessing from this place built on the backs of slavery and the slaughter of the Karankawa, Caddo, Apache, Comanche, Wichita and Tonkawa peoples. While slavery was abolished in Mexico in 1829, the Republic of Texas made the practice legal in 1836, joining the confederacy in 1861, dragging its feet to abolish the practice in 1865. Even then, lynchings were common throughout the state. This history was out there for us all to see. But we didn't talk about it much. It was all just part of growing up in a part of the country that does not apologize for the cruelties of its past. We were busy trying to forget all this. The underworld Virgil led Dante through seemed to point toward a suburban wasteland, where amnesia removed us from this history.

For years we converged in vacant parking lots, listening to music, hanging out, getting high, trying to make sense of this space between the treacheries of the past and the uncertainty of the future. "It's only teenage wasteland..." The Who sang about it. And we tried to live in it. "Let's get together before we get much older." Junior year, a senior I had known for years pulled me into her bedroom at a party.

"I'm about to leave so it's now or never," she smiled. "We should have at least a taste test." She pulled me onto the bed.

Lili often came by after school and we would climb onto the roof to smoke together, look around the city, and talk about our friends. I told her about my neighbor who I made out with when we were kids. She told me about her mom's reaction to hearing she was no longer a virgin. College letters were rolling in. She was going out east and I was going west.

There were still lots of cute moments. Lili used to write notes and pass them to me before class. "I just want you to know that everything is going swimmingly. Everything you are doing is perfect—the meetings, the music, our little moments. I am so happy." I read the note in class, placing it and other notes inside my reading notebook.

Every novel we read—Kundera, Vargas Llosa, Puig, Percy—taught us to think a little bit more about the lines between these words and life, tracing meanings between unrequited love, hope, history and the questions about faith, longing and Eros that had been rumbling through our heads. Each story allowed us to make a little more sense of the sensations we had found discomforting. Kundera made body smells a driving force in his story. Ideas about morality shifted with these ideas, but so did TS Elliot's descriptions of the "Wasteland" in which we all seemed to operate.

"Oh, light and honor all over poets," Dante gushed, realizing Virgil was to be his tour guide through the inferno.

We all need tour guides through our own divine comedies. But Virgil could only take Dante so far. No one could get him to paradise, but that didn't stop him from looking, out of favor in politics, in exile from his beloved Florence, blurring his adoration with Beatrice and his hometown with a sense of the divine.

He was not unique in this way. "She ruined your life," St. Augustine warned Petrarch in *Lives*, lamenting his infatuation with his muse Laura. In lieu of some sense of the divine, we reel around, lost.

Mrs. Chips asked us to bring in quotes to class for discussion. Coding our messages to each other, we all picked quotes. I read from *The Unbearable Lightness of Being* by Kundera with a smile:

"You see how easy it is to guess where you're from? The Communist countries are awfully puritanical. 'There's nothing wrong with the naked body,' the woman said with maternal affection. 'It's normal. And everything normal is beautiful!'"

Those words became a sort of mantra that spring, a way of embracing a line between the bawdy and the sublime.

And the spring passed. One weekend after a track meet in Houston, I came back to my house with Todd to get high. As usual, Dad was on the road and the house was empty. It must have been 11:00 at night when we arrived. The den light was on but the shades were down. Walking to the door, one of the shades peeled open only enough for someone's eye to peek out. Tommy, a friend from elementary school, opened the door to the den where there were ten other people sitting around.

As we walked inside, Tommy handed me a beer. "This afternoon we didn't know what we were going to do tonight and we knew you guys were going to be getting back later, so we thought we would surprise you. I called your house and your dad wasn't here so we came over."

"But how did you get in?" I asked, delighted.

"You told me you always climb up from the balcony so I climbed up and let everyone in. I hope you don't mind?"

"Tommy, Tommy, Tommy," I shook my head, laughing.

"Plus, look who I invited." Tommy put his arm over his sixth-grade flame Lili's shoulder.

She came up and whispered in my ear, "I was wondering if I could spend the night."

Everyone stayed another hour or so, then Lili and I went to bed. We did the teenage grind, both climbing the mountain that night and then decided to really do it. There was a closeness to the feeling of the springtime, knowing time was passing. Everyone felt alive together, knowing each other's secrets, how to sneak in the back door when our parents were out, a feeling that we were all welcome and wanted, as childhood mixed with whatever we were becoming.

Lili and I went out most of the rest of the spring.

During spring break, most of us traveled to Padre Island, a barrier island in the Gulf of Mexico, in South Texas, on the border with Mexico. Lili, Susan, and Sarah had rented a beach shack. The guys from our class rented a room in a cheap hotel near the beach. I usually stayed with Lili, although at times it felt strange.

Susan and Sarah had been in Mexico one day, exploring the old beach town south of Matamoros, just 45 miles south of Padre Island. They told us about the abandoned houses crumbling where the tide came in.

"We found the ruins from the book," said Sarah. "These abandoned houses were crumbling from where the waves had been hitting. Little kids were playing in the surf with no parents or anyone else around."

"Finding their way in a wasteland," I responded.

"That's what Percy is writing about in that book," Sarah continued.

"I think you are right."

She was right. We were all part of it. Over the week we all drank too much tequila, smoked pot, and passed out on the sand along the protected beaches several times.

Lili cavorted about, looked great in her bathing suit I thought. The bartenders picked up the chairs where we were sitting and mixed cocktails straight into our mouths in the particularly grungy establishment, leaving everyone in ruins, dancing away. We were animated. Lili and I went into her room and closed the door. She put on lingerie. She was usually self-conscious, but that night in that dark cluttered room full of bathing suits, smelling like Hawaiian Tropic suntan lotion, she found the confidence, blowing and showing me what she could do when she relaxed, the rawest night we'd ever had. It went on for ages. Sarah, who was trying to sleep next door, was not happy. She was having a hard time. It was one thing to be dumped, another thing to hear your friend with the person who dumped you. The following night Lili and I came back to the room again and Susan popped her head in the door.

"You guys have got to get out of here. Sarah is freaking. Cab cannot sleep here. This is ridiculous and cruel."

Lili told me I had to leave which I was not so happy about. I asked her to come back to my room but she declined. I walked back, looking at the full moon shining over the Gulf of Mexico, past the beach, back to our suite full of people passed out amidst beer cans and couches.

The next morning, I got up, waked and baked, went to breakfast, and came back to the room by lunch time. Everyone was playing drinking games. It was raining out. All of us were there inside, chugging can after can of beer into the afternoon, trying to see if we could fill the wall with beer cans, making old jokes about *The Shining*. "Natas Slik" Todd screamed as we had as kids, triggering us with contagious silliness until we were laughing hysterically. Chuckling so much he started to wheeze, his stomach sore, Todd started feeling nauseous, pulling off his baseball hat and holding it. No one saw him at first. He started to vomit straight down, into his hat. I looked at him. He just sat there staring at the vomit in his baseball hat, without saying a word. It filled the hat and then the floor around him. But Todd wasn't moving. He looked in shock. The putrid scent enveloped room. A whiff crossed Rick's nose. Convulsing, he projectile vomited into the back wall of the room, knocking over our wall of beer cans. The smell along the puke stained beer cans, ignited a combustive reaction, as several of us followed, laughing and vomiting at the same time, stumbling into the pile of beer cans. I fell back into the cans, beer upchucking from my nose and mouth as I laughed.

And I passed out again.

I didn't wake up for hours, but when I did, I was hearing someone playing U2's album, the *Unforgettable Fire*. The sun was beginning to set out the window. I could hear my friends' voices in the background, along with the sounds of waves and seagulls. The clouds had covered the sun so everything was overcast. Slowly, I got up hearing everyone talking around me, reminiscing, remembering us as kids, Grant arguing with one of the coaches who would eventually be fired for fighting with the kids.

The passing of time from that afternoon in September of 1980 when I first arrived into this moment felt like a dream; our childhood was ending just as this moment was. There would not be many more moments like this for this group of friends. High school, like childhood, coming to an end.

Most everyone slept on the thirteen-hour drive back to Dallas. I had taken this drive many times before, the elbow of my left arm leaning outside the window, the tank filled up, the wheels turning, looking at my friends in the back, thinking about our lives here in Texas. I spent the way back, taking in the scene, the long country roads, interstates and gas stations, recalling the last time I took this ride, the year before, getting pulled over for driving 110 miles per hour, only to get the ticket reduced because my lawyer had bought the judge's daughter's pig at a pig contest that spring. Texas worked that way. I smoked Marlboros and listened to James Taylor and Peter Tosh, staring at the stables of horses, noticing the different license plates of the cars, an occasional armadillo which had not made it to the other side of the road, the signs along the interstate, the trees that seemed to bear both the beauty and reminders of the state's long messy history of war, tornados and lynchings. What had these trees seen over the years after the state officially liberated the last of the enslaved on June 19, 1865? Amidst it all, we played and figured out ways not to remember or know, cavorting about, drinking tequila. I thought about the patterns of my life, the same scenes unfolding over and over again, from infatuation to sex to expedience, Lili's bathing suit. Occasionally the violence outsiders endured crept into our worlds. Massimo, a drag queen I worked with during the ecstasy summer of 1986 was ridiculed and nearly bashed when we went dancing in Deep Ellum, the previous summer. But we got away. Others were not so lucky. James Byrd was beaten to death by white supremacists, his body dragged for miles by a pickup truck in Jasper, Texas. Somehow, we were outside of that. All these presuppositions were part of my world. Our lives were shaped by them. I thought about Mom and Dad's estrangement, not being sure what was going to happen to them, and about Tom, Dad's roommate from Harvard. They'd both dropped out, bummed around, and joined the military before going back to school. Tom had worked in the war room during the Cuban Missile Crisis, walking to the precipice before abating. When word of his life as a queer man finally got out, he was dishonorably discharged. Disgusted and ashamed, he felt like he'd lost his honor. Dad tried to console him, their friendship a tonic for a lot of pain through the years. Amidst all this, the nukes were still here pointing outward. Military industry boomed in Houston; Cold War multiple launch rocket systems funded my education. Somehow, both Dad and Tom found their way here. Tom lived in Monahans in West Texas. He first introduced me to country western music——Jerry Jeff Walker and Van Cliburn.

"They are singing about a very modern plight," he ruminated. "Of being separated from the land and the country. It's a feeling they all explore." In between being perpetually lost, never quite at home, he found music and people, writing poems on bar napkins, passing some two decades in West Texas. He helped Dad make sense of it all, giving him a copy of *Dr. Faustus* the night his father died and he drove us to his funeral in South Georgia, the place where Grandad had beaten Dad after the war, passing on a generational pattern of screams and abuses, which I inherited. Grandad's mother was from Bastrop, Texas, outside of Austin, where I was driving. She confessed a lot before she died with my grandad right by her side. Of her four boys, one died in a fight during an S & M scene turned bar fight, stumbling to the bottom of the stairs, his neck broken. But no one knew why. No one really asked. That story was rarely repeated. But the sensibility remained. There was always something people were concealing here.

Only a few more weeks of high school remained. Lili never put back on that negligee. She wasn't always as passionate as she had been in Padre Island. We all drifted.

Prom was the following week. Dad didn't show up and mom was still at grad school. They were attending to their own lives. I danced with Lili's mom during the parents' dance. Said hello to the professors and other parents. I took ecstasy like I had for every formal dance in high school, all par for the course. After the formalities, we made our way to the afterparty at Daisy's house. Glad to be away, all the guys ripped off our tuxes and went sprinting through the golf course in her backyard. Someone stole Tommy's and my tuxedos so we sat out in the back yard nude drinking frozen margaritas. Eventually we just walked in and found our tuxedos in the laundry.

While I was off running with the guys, Lili sat and talked with Michael. Walking back inside, Lili told me she had decided she had not been comfortable not being with Matthew, who had come with Susan. She explained that she was having second thoughts about having broken up with Matthew and wanted to spend her last few months in Dallas before college with him. She came back to my house that night, but nothing came of it. I couldn't sleep so I drove her back home. On the way, we listened to one of those mix tapes from Padre Island.

"This music will always remind me of you," Lili said before I dropped her off. My novelty had worn off. It was not the last time I would feel that way after a breakup. But I knew I deserved it; bad karma coming my way.

Lili lived right by Marni's old house where I rode by all those times freshman year. I remembered the feeling after we had worked on *The Wiz*; the whole thing felt both comic and earnest. Music bound from us that spring, the optimism of the moment opening me to new people and possibilities: the DJ's who were in the musical, Marni's friends, her world, when everyone was about to graduate. It all flowed back, even the sweet, sad feeling after our big date to *PeeWee's Big Adventure*, driving through the neighborhood on that North Dallas Morning. Marni's spirit was hard to replace, even by Katie, Becky, Sarah, Lili or any of the others. It was reeling around, an incessant pattern, through stages, sadness, and an inability to make sense of the loss at the core, driving back home to an empty home, with a family that seemed to have vanished. Instead, that 1975 feeling accompanied me. I thought of sitting with Tom watching Fritz Lang's Weimar era film, *The Testament of Dr. Mabuse*, two years prior when he helped me get through history. "The whole population is hypnotized by Mabuse," Tom chimed in, pointing to a culpability of the people. I felt like I was right there.

We had one more week of classes before graduation. I would only have to face my makers in that god-forsaken Literature in Translation class three more times. In class that last day, Sarah was wearing all black, including the pair of black boots she had bought that day in Mexico from spring break. Her jeans were tucked inside the boots. Mrs. Chips asked Becky to read a favorite passage of hers to start off the class. Becky thought for a second. "Do you mind if I read something from a book we read earlier in the term?" she asked.

"Not at all," Mrs. Chips replied. "What book is it from?"

"Unbearable Lightness again."

"Great, do you want to explain the scene?" Mrs. Chips asked.

"Okay, well this is my favorite passage from *Unbearable Lightness*. It's from Sabrina when she was sleeping with that young guy."

"Oh, I think I know the paragraph you are talking about," Sarah added with a smile. Becky read with animation:

> "In fact, it was his closed eyes that made Sabina turn out the light. She could not stand those lowered eyelids a moment longer. The eyes, as the saying goes, are windows to the soul. Franz's body, which thrashed about on top of hers with closed eyes, was therefore a body without a soul. It was like a newborn animal, still blind and whimpering ... No, she would never again see his body moving desperately over hers...today was the last time, irrevocably the last time!"

"That was it," Sarah replied with a smile. "I really loved that part." She glanced over at me, as did Becky. It was the last time any of us would be together. High school was over.

Part Three

Southwest Towards Home

Tabula Rasa in San Francisco

"It had taken six chance happenings to push Tomas towards Tereza, as if he had little inclination to get to her on his own. He had gone back to Prague because of her. So fateful a decision resting on a so fortuitous a love... And that women, that personification of absolute fortuity, now again lay asleep beside him, breathing deeply..."
-Milan Kundera, *The Unbearable Lightness of Being*. 1984

A tabula rasa—that's what life becomes like in San Francisco. We all come here fresh and new, ready to start over. Still, past lives—the parts of who we have been—remain, just beneath the surface. They are the people we see as we walk through the rain, shimmering in the reflections in the water on the sidewalk, the ghosts who linger, lurking in boxes of old letters. They are in all the usual places; you see them in the familiar places Billie Holiday sang about. They help us navigate and sometimes they take the lead. Along the way, we look for clues—in chance encounters, clothes, movies, novels, the outline of a stranger.

Julie wore a faded tee shirt and maroon sweats at our gym off Union Square. She worked out two hours a day, five days a week: an hour on the treadmill before her high impact aerobics class. She maintained a diet of pasta, stir fry (with only veggies), red wine, *90210* and *Melrose Place* on Wednesdays. When she looked down after a brief glance in the elevator, I encountered both a person and a spirit, a feeling of a soul, a body and a spirit. With God out of the picture, she remained the closest thing to divinity I could find. Julie would never know who and what had come before. But it didn't matter. I wasn't even sure she was real. She was like an apparition, disappearing as I came close to her, her elusiveness forever reminding me that there was something I needed to figure out.

Pedro had suggested I write about it.

"How is the writing Cab?" asked Pedro at work.

"All I write is crap," I kvetched.

"Why? What are you writing about?"

"Trying to write about social activism and AIDS in San Francisco."

"I thought you were writing about your depraved sex life, trying to find your story."

"I was, I am. But I don't know what to say. My life seems too boring compared to everyone else so I'm doing my oral histories."

"But that's what makes it real. Not many of us are actually getting what we want. It's the myth of this place that everyone is feeling groovy, getting laid and doing great. But no one really is," he said.

"Well, there are the guys in Ringold Alley."

"Yeah, but that's not your story."

"I guess so."

"Aren't writers supposed to write that they know?"

"Yeah." I couldn't believe he was lecturing me like this.

"So, write about what got you stuck...."

"Lost in a dark wood..." I mumbled, recalling the old literature in transition class.

"Huh?"

"With the women and my life."

"Begin with the women. All of them. And then everything else will grow from there. That's a book I would read."

"It has to be fiction, not truth. I can't just write about me."

"Why not?" he asked.

"Because I'm not sure what's there."

"That's the problem."

"I know."

"Write your sentimental education."

"It would be fun to write it all out."

"Every girl, every fuck."

"There were even a couple of guys," I said.

"Now that's a story to write about," he replied as he started to walk upstairs. "You're the expert."

I'd spent weeks after that conversation puzzled, writing, categorizing the whole affair, interviewing people with HIV about their lives, tracing their stories and mine. Theirs seemed immanently more fascinating. I'd written notes about girlfriends. But I wasn't sure what was my story. It began with the Chloe debacle. Julie was the first girl after the demise—the AD Period—to make a difference. Marni, Becky, Sarah, Lili, Marsha, Amanda and the other girls of freshman year in college made up the BC (the Before Chloe) Period, before she drove her proverbial spiked high heel into my consciousness. As a therapist had observed, "Chloe was the whole shebang." She was all about peaks and valleys, the risky sex, Southern stories, and emotional crescendos; between writing and music and an experiment in living and feeling, she had left me in pieces. We met on a few breaks from school back in Texas, forgetting everything else that came before, as it all became lost. Between the Southwest and home—the road to the crescendo that became Chloe—back when Eros and attraction intersected, and neuroses were problems other people faced up to, before the tabula rasa got dirty—that was a territory I couldn't shake. It seemed to paralyze me. So I wrote about what happened.

Summer 1988

In the weeks after graduation from high school, everybody found summer jobs. Lili got a job as a waitress at a uniform-required, faux authentic, Victorian themed, suburban sports bar. They served everything from fettucini alfreddo to burgers to chili, extra bland. I worked down the street at the corner of Inwood and Lovers Lane, tearing tickets for foreign movies at the Inwood Theatre. Lili only came by once the whole summer. And that was fine.

Other friends from the ecstasy summer of '86 were around. Our manager Charlotte, a lanky, trying-to-be avant-garde, 37-year-old brunette, perused and scolded each of the summer hires (Andy who was 19, Deg who was 20 and myself, 18) at one time or another during the summer. Andy and I bonded in our adoration for Jade, the former class president from Hockaday (the cross-town all-girls school) who also worked there with us. She spent the last two years at UC Santa Cruz in Northern California. She was two years our senior in age, but not in spirit. We worked our shifts and drank at the art deco lounge next door, drove around taking poppers, listening the B-52's, gulping cheap bear, going downtown to see shows, and dance.

Amanda had been around all summer with the gang, hovering on the periphery. Wearing a cowboy hat and ripped jeans, with long brunette hair, and a Texas stoner twang, she was an abundant personality. She loved music and the scene and had the cow-punk look down. In her sophomore year in high school, she had dated the base player of the Peyote Cowboys, a psychedelic punk band, hooking up with him after a show at the Circle A Ranch, on Commerce St. downtown.

"At their show, they invited us to sit on the stage with them," Amanda gushed, recalling their meeting, in between tearing tickets at the theater. "I was entranced, zoning out in the feedback and Jesus and Mary Chain reverb. It was a sick, sick show."

"Well, Eddie Brickell is going to have my kids," I retorted, referring to the singer for the New Bohemians, whose album was finally coming out.

"You and half of Deep Ellum."

"No, just me. She told me so with her eyes."

All summer long, we sang along when "Sweet Child of Mine" played over the radio at the theater. It was the song of the summer.

We had even planned to go to the Texas Jam together to see Guns N' Roses, but tickets were sold out. Deg went the year prior. "It was hot and wonderful. We were on the top deck, pouring the spit from the spit cups down on everyone below."

"Gross!"

"I know," he laughed.

Our plans to hang out had not quite materialized. I was too busy running around with Jade and Andy. And she had shows to go to. Katie even dropped into town from New Orleans, where she'd finally joined the traveling Shakespeare company she always talked about. We romped around, going out for food and then back to my old bedroom, as we had years before.

"You don't mind, do you?" she smiled, unzipping my pants in my room. I always adored her.

"Everything is temporary," Eddie's voice flowed over the radio at work, as the summer wound down. The New Bohemian's new album finally came out and it sounded magnificent. Deg had gone to see them every Friday night all summer long. But after this album, they were no longer our neighborhood inside secret. The world had them now. Their music was part of the fabric of a summer that felt like it couldn't end. Adventures were every week. One weeknight, Deg, Jade, Andy and I took acid after work, watching *Koyaanisqatsi* at the theater.

"It's not working," I kvetched at Andy, staring at the screen, transfixed by the cavalcade of images. The walls of the theater bulged and bobbed out, along with the music. Maybe it was working.

Another night, we drove around peaking on ecstasy, finding ourselves sitting in the parking lot of the old Twilight Room on Commerce Street that hot summer night, looking at the stars, music filling the nighttime. Summer passed and college was around the corner. But not before a final staff party at the theater.

My friends did most of the heckling after the bon voyage staff party for the summer hires. Jade and Andy went home early. Charlotte and Deg made out in the office. Amanda invited me upstairs for a cigarette. Giddy to actually be alone, we made our way up to the roof of the majestic old theater for cigs as the party continued downstairs on the theatre stage. We bumped thighs by accident stumbling up on the way to the roof. That was the first physical contact we had with each other; she giggled and did not seem to mind. In many ways it was enough, because whether intentional or not, a barrier had been broken. Once on the roof, we looked at the sky, and the lights of downtown. We chatted and started to make out, first standing, then laying on the roof. Amanda grinned as she pulled my pants off by the ends of the legs as I lay down. She talked me through a few things; she told me what she liked as I was doing it, as opposed to afterwards when there was nothing to be done about it. She let me know, in the middle with a smile, that this was good.

Three hours later and that was one that I would have to think about for the next seven or eight years—day after individual day, not a day passing without recalling an image, a sound or feeling from that dingy rooftop zooming to the present, rewind, replay over and over again. Doing so, that night with Sarah in the front seat, faded, the Padre night with Lili and the Hawaiian Tropic, forgotten. Perhaps the attention to detail, maybe the joyful revelry; life produces mysteries that intertwine through collective experiences. Certain moments come up over and over and over, to be rewound and rewound. Some memories overflow only after the switch goes off: a pastry here, an avalanche of sensations flowing. Maybe everything went right with the body's buttons. How else do you describe such moments, when companions offer everything and are willing to share, when everyone gets what they want? Life offers few such moments. Blanche DuBois depended her whole life on the kindness of strangers. Occasionally strangers don't let us down.

"My back is aching with fiberglass," Amanda declared, laughing when she walked into work the next day. The theatre roof had been covered in fiberglass shavings. We lay there playing for hours without even thinking about it. The whole shift everyone chuckled as Amanda and I groaned about the small shards in our backs, arms, and legs.

Another slight shred of glass ground into my foot the night I met Zoe the first weekend of college in Claremont, the home of five undergraduate liberal arts colleges, just east of Los Angeles on Highway Ten, where I found myself. I was on my way to one of those college parties that tended to make everyone nuts. Most of the freshmen had spent the first few days in orientation. I was one of the idiots who'd been there a week early for football practice. Songwriter Kris Kristofferson was our program's last college football star back in the mid-1950s.

Freshman orientation was mostly about ethics, college, sexual harassment, consent, and attempts to combat the patterns of abuse and rape by football and rugby players all too common on campuses. Some used the sessions as opportunities to establish their bona fides as opponents of such practices. "My tubes are not interested in your tubes," Jack, who lived one door down from me declared during one of the sessions. This was met with eye rolls from the guys and a collective, "awe" from the women on the hall.

After spilling our guts, we poured out for one the Claremont college parties, where most of the trouble took place. With loud dance music and a frat party vibe, I was ready to leave when a group of four people ran up to me and announced, "Think of the graduate school you want to go to. Our friend wants to meet you..." and they ushered me away. Zoe was 21 and a senior, articulate and busty. She wore baggy overalls, a t-shirt, and Chuck Taylors, her strawberry blond hair in a bob.

Zoe's collegiate gothic dorm room exuded an air of sophistication and frivolity. There were books strewn around the room, an overflowing trash can, an unmade bed, and a laundry bag inauspiciously standing by the door. Zoe, who wrote a column in the five-college paper on men, made no apologies for the mess when we walked in.

Zoe's friend, a closeted engineering student from Harvey-Mudd who clearly didn't know what to do with his hair, made drinks and Zoe put on some music. I surveyed her tape collection of '80s disco and gay synthesizer groups. Her collection wasn't better than Lili's, although I could tell she was proud of it. She and her friends pranced around the room to the music, reveling in a new-found autonomy and androgyny.

Conversation ensued about topical collegiate issues of the day, a homophobic economics professor from the business graduate school, competition between the five colleges, and words of encouragement for the sexually confused engineering student.

"I talked to a friend of mine at Wesleyan University," the girl who had first run up to me announced. "She told me about Harold Bloom coming to the campus last week. He was early for the lecture he was going to be giving so he went for a meal at a breakfast place off the campus and ended up falling asleep. The waiter woke him up saying, 'All right Mac, it's time to pay up and get out of here! Let's hit the road!' With his hair all mangled on one side, Bloom took offense saying, 'I am Harold Bloom.' The waiter responded, 'And I don't care.' Then Bloom says, 'I am a preeminent literary critic.' Isn't that hilarious?" She mimicked, "I am a preeminent literary critic." Blah blah blah... passing the time for something else which could only come once the time had passed. Soon everyone left for food at the coop and Zoe and I were on our own. I looked at her.

"Do you give good back rubs?" she asked. I noticed how blue her eyes were.

"Sure," I said.

"You won't be embarrassed if I take off my shirt? You can handle that?" she asked, winking. "I know you haven't been around too much," she said. "Mr. freshman football player," she continued and jabbed her elbow into my stomach. She unbuttoned her overalls, pulled them down to her waist, pulled off her striped tee shirt and lay down on her stomach. She was wearing a white bra. I started on her neck, not quite covered by her medium length hair, kneading her creamy skin and avoiding the bra straps. She asked about other women; I told her about Lili.

"Bitch," she observed, "She was just toying with you to get her old boyfriend back in step. I hate to say it my dear, but you were a pawn." I agreed that she was probably right. It wasn't the first time.

Zoe read me a few of the columns she had written for the paper during the previous academic year, all about men, critical in a good, honest way. She was able to both show that she really liked guys, found them irresistible, and that they needed to stop screwing it up with women. It wasn't long before we were fooling around a bit, rolling on the bed. Zoe cut to the chase, "What are we doing?"

"Well, a little back rub, code words, figuring a few things out..."

When she ordered me to strip, I took off my shirt, socks and pants off so I was down to my boxers. "Everything," she said.

"Including these?" I smiled.

"Including those," she pointed at the boxers with a smirk. "Off."

So, I took them off and lay on my side with my elbow on the bed and my hand on my ear, trying to tighten up my abs as much as possible.

"You are, without a doubt, the most gorgeous thing I have seen in a long time," she observed.

"Now your turn," I said. She did, but with the same sort of hesitation as Teresa in *Unbearable Lightness* when she, the fashion photographer, had the camera turned on her and was told to strip by one of her models. Her body had the same light cream color as the skin on her neck. We fooled around for a while, cautious and indecisive about where this was leading. We rolled off the bed, all over each other.

"Put it in," she whispered.

"I can't without..."

Zoe got up, put on a bathrobe, and walked to the door. "Hold your horses," she ordered. "I'm going to put in my diaphragm." Zoe had a lot more idea about what she wanted than I did, or at least a lot more about the variations. When she got what she wanted, she shared. Her columns had been so critical. But something worked about the moment. Zoe was pleased, warm, and expressive.

She asked what I wanted to get warmed up. I looked at her and smiled, nodding downward.

"That, oh, I'm so bad at that," she observed after only a minute.

"How about this then," I suggested. And we cut to the chase.

"Let's try that then." And we did. This was better for a while until... She sighed, moaned, and we started moving faster. And then "Ahh!!" her voice and her body sharply jolted, tightened up and then recoiled. Zoe lay down on her side, clutching her legs, knees pulled up to her chest.

"Zoe? Are you ok?" I said, coming back down to earth. She didn't say anything, instead she lay speechless, ignoring my questions.

90

"I had an abortion last spring and it still hurts..." she whispered. We lay for a while, sad, but not knowing what to say or think. We tried to sleep, but that didn't work. Zoe looked far away at something as we lay and she told me about the guy she had been with over the summer. Her body became cold. She was far away in that bed. We tried to fool around again but it didn't work.

"Let's just sleep for a while," Zoe suggested, crawling back under the sheets. We lay there in bed for another hour. I couldn't rest. She got up again to go to the bathroom down the hall. I got up to pick up my clothes and was leaning over the bed putting on my sneakers when she returned. "You are dressed," she observed, surprised.

"Yes," I responded.

She looked at me with an air of curiosity.

"Have you read *Unbearable Lightness of Being* by Kundera?" I asked.

"Yeah."

"Do you remember what Thomas said about one-night stands?"

"Vaguely."

"He understood sex as something acquaintances shared... Sleep—that was something a little more intimate, that was something more exclusive, something only lovers could share."

"Yeah, and?" she asked.

"That's where I am at right now."

"If you leave right now, you will never be welcome in this bed again," Zoe responded and pulled her sheets up to her chin.

"Ciao," I responded and kissed Zoe on her cheek before I left. She pulled her the sheets up over her head.

I walked out of the dorm room, down the wooded hall in the inner sanctum at the woman's college. In the next four years I would never receive another invitation to stay there, or in any other dorms at Scripps. In that moment, as I walked under the pines, I assumed there would be others. She was lovely, but it was the first weekend at school.

The moon shone clear through the empty campus on my way home in the early morning.

I always felt dirtier, more used, as if I got less from the arrangement of a one-night stand than I always hoped when it was still possibility. Sometimes I felt like I used the other person. Sometimes I felt total disgust at the idea of seeing the person again. I certainly had no interest in seeing Amanda for the swing shift after the roof escapade. How honest were we really being when we smiled and agreed that it doesn't matter?

A one-night stand can be a liberating process if you're willing to live with the consequences, including any lingering regret or embarrassment. Most of us hope that both parties are in complete agreement. But that's rare. People are expedient. All we see is a possibility. We hope in some way the experience will give us insight into ourselves, or the other person. All too often we ignore the insights of the impacts or the vulnerabilities beneath. There were smiles and flirts and kicks. But naiveté wanes and we can't pretend sometimes it doesn't feel hallow. And then we pretend it doesn't hurt when it doesn't go that way. When

91

we get older, we know. Callousness translates into neglect. One or both of the partners has been through a thing or two. At a certain point, we know exactly how many delicacies may live inside. Still, we ignore, pretending we have the ever-egalitarian complex. I couldn't imagine how it would feel to have gone through what Zoe went through last spring. I thought she was intriguing. But I didn't want to deal with all those feelings, especially on the first night.

In the colleges, flirting, meeting and hooking up was what everyone spent their days doing when they weren't studying. It happened after class and out and about. I dropped Anthropology when I found out Priya, a cute girl from India who lived across the hall from me in the Sanborn dorm, was taking Literature in Translation with Barry Sanders. With a Jerry Garcia beard and grin, he looked out of central casting. But the reading list was amazing: more Kundera, more magic realism. His class gave me my first exposure to Gabriel Garcia Marquez, with whom I fell in love. With *Love in the Time of Cholera* (which had just come out) as the first novel we'd read, the class was not to be missed, and neither was Priya. Sanders, who taught history of ideas, was tracing subversive histories of laugher. He brought out an antique encyclopedia from the year the story took place and read us its definition of cholera the first day of class, chatting with everyone and pointing to what the story suggested about a history of subversive ideas.

After class, Priya and I hung out and smoked cigarettes in her cool dorm room covered in tapestries. We talked about Marquez, cried about lost love, and read our favorite passages out loud. "It was inevitable the scent of bitter almonds always reminded him of the fate of unrequited love," declared the master in the first line of the book. We read it over and over again. I wrote about the novel. Instead of a paper full of red marks, Prof Sanders said he could see I loved writing. We could take care of the typos later. For now, I needed to write more, he advised. I had never been treated that way. Priya had lured me into something wonderful. She had other loves, but we connected through that class and the stories that grew from it. After class, we wandered around our Southern California campus in the desert.

Then there was the election. Bush beat Dukakis by a landslide that fall. People moped about, depressed, looking for company. I had never really been a liberal. Few of us from Texas were at the time. But I could see there was some concern with what had happened. Most weekend nights we all went out looking for someone to feel less alone. For the first few months at school, I was with someone new every weekend.

Some evenings, I would go out for a ride with friends. We drove through the desert, riding past cacti, porn shops, In-N-Out's, and blasting Jane's Addiction over the speakers. Some nights, we'd get on Highway 10 and drive West to Los Angeles. I would roll down the windows and take in the night air.

When I went home for the holidays that year, Dallas had taken on a whole new complexion. Everybody I had worked with at the Inwood Theater job was in town—Andy, Jade, Deg, and the rest of the crew.

One of the first nights I was back, Grant called. He was at a debutante party his mother had begged him to attend, but it was horrible, so he left and was coming over with some friends.

"Who are you bringing?"

"Buck and this girl who Buck brought but she's been flirting with me the whole night," Grant explained. He brought Chloe, a girl from Duncanville who went to Vassar, over to the house. And obnoxious!—Grant, Buck and Chloe—all three went to college in the Northeast. It was like a contest to see who could be the most outrageous in their barrage of ridicule of all things absurd about Dallas. They lampooned all things Texas: the accents, the people, the parochialism.

We went for food at Denny's. They were still all dressed in their formal garb. I ordered grilled cheese. Grant had chicken fried steak. Buck just smoked cigarettes. Chloe smoked cigs and sipped bottomless cups of coffee. We sat in a linoleum booth and the three of them pretty much worked the Coppell, Texas jokes, with stronger than ever drawls. I was dumbfounded, speechless by their sarcasm. We didn't need another loud mouth voice for the group.

At the end of the night, Chloe bought Grant a stuffed purple dinosaur and gave it to him along with her telephone number.

"I'm having a party next week. You can't forget to come," Grant reminded us. "Definitely come," he said directly to Chloe, imploring her with a prolonged gaze.

"She's not the most beautiful girl I've ever seen in my life, but there's a strong sexual quality about her. I hope she comes to the party," he said once Buck and Chloe had left. We ran into Chloe before the party at the 500 Cafe the next week, where the New Bohemians usually had a set.

"I'm seeing you everywhere this vacay," I said and smiled.

"It's because I *looooove you, man*! I *love* you!" Her voice was hoarse and I had no idea what she was talking about. She sounded as frizzed as the medium length hair she had on her head. She was bubbling over with energy and I didn't quite know what to think, but that was okay.

"I love this place. I saw the New Bo's here my junior year in high school," I said.

"Deg and I were here," Chloe gestured to her barstool and beer. "Every Friday night last summer."

"Really?" I was jealous, and I realized what a groovy chick I was dealing with here. Envy immediately turned to regret. I hadn't even thought to ask Deg what he was doing all those Friday nights that last summer. Then I felt regret about a lost opportunity to be a part of seeing the New Bohemians before their album broke, being on the party. I had seen them several nights over the past few years and loved them, collecting their bootlegs. They had made it big the following fall. Those summer shows were the last to catch them as a local act and Deg and Chloe were at all of them. I had made just one. I had some things to learn.

Everyone from the Inwood summer gang came to Grant's party. As it turned out, Chloe and Deg had been best friends from high school in Duncanville on the other side of the city.

Jade and Andy were fighting. She was more interested in one of Grant's friends. Grant, ever the consummate gentleman and host, offered to walk Chloe to her car, looking for an opening, early on.

"Cab, I need to talk to you," Jade said to me later on in the evening. She pulled me out of another conversation.

"It's about Amanda," she said. "She told me she doesn't know how to explain it, but that when she saw you, she started to have that same itch between her legs from the summer. Go, Cab!" She smiled stupidly. I walked to find Amanda, who was chatting with Deg in the kitchen. In faded, ripped jeans, a

Peyote Cowboys t-shirt, and cowboy hat, a Shiner Boch beer in hand, she looked great. We chatted a bit about music and bands, college and what was going on going on in Dallas.

I invited Amanda upstairs for a smoke, just like I had earlier in the summer. We wandered up to Grant's old childhood bedroom, attached to the same bedroom where I had seen my first real live pair of breasts—Grant's sister's by accident—that I was attracted to for the first time back in 1980. It was a place I had spent a thousand and one nights; smoked pot for the first time; read Grant's atrocious sixth grade math homework report card; talked about California; listened to 'Dirty Deeds Done Dirt Cheap' and Richard Pryer Albums; hung out with Grant during the last years before his parents' divorce back in eighth grade; woke up late and hungover for summer football workouts; and lazed around wondering what exactly the world we were coming of age into had in store for us.

Amanda and I made out under the heat lamp. I had carried a condom case around after the nights with Zoe and Amanda earlier in the year when there had been no condoms to be found. Tonight, however, they were nowhere to be found. It was another one of those nights. Condoms would have been nice but it was pretty easy to be talked out of them as necessities.

"I can't find the condom I thought I had," I confessed as we sat on the bed.

"Is that what you want?"

"The condom?"

"Yeah, well the condom and to do what you do with condoms?" she asked.

"Yes, but I can't find it, I'll run and go ask Grant."

"Cab," Amanda said, and put her hand on mine. "Have you been sleeping with any creeps?"

"No," I assured her in a half lie.

"Then don't worry about it."

And while the party ran its merry course, Grant and Chloe groped in the ally, and Deg lit his beer farts, Amanda and I worked off some calories. There wasn't any fiberglass this time around but, as in the summer before, it still felt pretty abrasive by the time we were done.

A week before I was to fly back to California, a friend was leaving Dallas for good. Massimo, the drag queen from Milan whose restaurant I had worked in during the ecstasy haze of 1986, was moving back to Italy. I had promised to go out with him before he left. The last time we'd gone out some guys had called him a "faggot" downtown, so we were going to his places. I was desperate to find one of my usual dancing buddies Olivia (who I had taken X with so many times), or Kharmi, who had graduated in my class and dated Grant the previous summer. If I didn't find someone to come along, it would be me, Massimo, and the whole male junior staff from Massimo's favorite hair salon. Just as everyone else was turning out to be seriously busy, I received a call from Chloe.

"I am so glad to hear from you!" I said. "Chloe, I am seriously in a bind. Can you do me a favor?"

"Yeah. Sure. Depends."

"Massimo is moving back to Milan and I promised him I would go out with him again before he leaves town and I can't find anybody to go with me. You know Massimo, right? Can you come along this Friday? I'll pay for everything. I just need female companionship."

"I know Massimo! I used to go out with Ted from Massimo's."

94

"You're kidding. I used to work with Teddy," I said.

"When?"

"Summer of 86."

"That was when we were going out," she said in wonderment at the chance encounters that were piling up in our history.

"Wait, I think I met you then. You came in once when we were all going out dancing with Massimo, but you were so drunk Ted had to drive you home before he went out. I remember you sitting with your head face down on the table."

"Yeah, that was me," she said.

"Alright, Chloe! He was an amazing guy, very sexual, very open. I remember how raw he was after the Bowers vs Hardwick decision. Was he bisexual? I never really knew."

"Okay, buster, we can talk about all that later. I did call for a reason. I left my jacket over there when we went to Denny's with Grant and Buck. If I go with you, will you bring it on Friday?"

"Will do."

"Also Cab, you have to tell me about Grant."

"Okay."

"We can talk about it on Friday."

"Fantastic. Chloe, I really owe you one."

Chloe came over to the house that Friday. Dad invited her in, flirting with her over cappuccinos, talking about poetry, before I pulled her away and we went over to Massimo's.

"He's a little much," she noted in the car.

"I know. He's lonely in Dallas. Mom hasn't smiled at him in years." We drove past the Inwood on the way to Massimo's house. Mannequins lurked in every corner of the place. Shadows darted from the colored lights.

It would be the last of a long series of dancing nights we had with Massimo. He was dressed the part, wearing only a long black shawl as a jacket, black boots up to his knees, a black lingerie hose body suit, a G-string underneath, and lots of blinking Christmas lights on top. "For the season—don't you love it?" he gushed when he opened the door, showing off his outfit.

"Chloe, Cab, it is so wonderful to see you! Wait, I have something for the two of you." He rustled around for a bit and produced two t-shirts with silk-screen images of himself. "I had them made for the season. They're for my new restaurant I'll be opening!" He looked like a character out of a French 18th century Revolutionary period piece. His long, curly brown hair blew through the wind on the way to the car.

We did the usual rounds of late-night spots; everywhere Massimo and his guests got in for free. He knew practically everyone, talking to every doorman for at least a couple of minutes. "It's a good way to make sure you never have to pay," he whispered after we had our jacket check comped. I had been right about Massimo's gang. Every hairdresser in the city knew Massimo and they all seemed to be at the clubs that night. Chloe disappeared on a crystal run. She showed up right as we were leaving for the Stark Club.

The coolest places in Dallas were the gay bars where hipsters, dandies, drag queens, and outsiders could share space in a non-homophobic culture. Leading them all was the Stark Club. Opened in 1984, Grace Jones was there to perform the first night. She used to hang out, perform and cavort, rubbing shoulders with Rob Lowe, Allen Ginsberg and a few of us. MDMA pills were openly sold and enjoyed there until they were made illegal in 1985. I used to sit there for hours, my eyeballs bulging out of my head, munching on ice cubes as the ecstasy pills made their way through my system. It was a space for all of us to be a little larger, a little more honest than our restricted everyday selves; camaraderie expanding, with legions of friends. When heterosexual class hierarchies offered mostly exclusion, the Stark Club opened doors. It was a part of an ever-expanding queer Dallas. Rather than cliques, here the citizenry built community through pleasure. The Stark Club was an open space for everyone to experiment with identity and sometimes to really be themselves. I was fixated with the music, the clothes, the sensibility, the underground, the pleasure, the connection to culture, and the gayness of it all.

The Stark Club had been Massimo's number one haunt for all five years he had been in Dallas. Everyone could find a bit of what they needed there——be it drugs, drag, a place to be seen, to connect with others, to be out, to dance, or just to be free.

He kissed the door person, a lady wearing black slacks, with no hair and only a bra for a top.

Grace Jones's "Pull up to the Bumper" came on as we walked into the black cavernous club designed by Philippe Stark. People sat in couches on the ground floor. A set of descending steps sprawled open, leading people toward an underground dance floor below.

Massimo pulled us by our hands and ran us down the stairs to dance with him. In our own little ways, we all acted out what pulling up to the bumper meant to us. I walked up the stairs and stood at the top of the steps of the pit, and Massimo gestured his hands as if he were pulling a rope and I was at the other end. After a bit of theatrics with Massimo, Chloe and I found a table behind the downstairs dance floor and got drinks. We yakked it up for about an hour down there before Massimo came to sit down, immediately stealing my cig to show me just how sexy and wonderful he could look if he so chose to smoke. We took turns striking a pose with our cigs.

We left sometime after 3:00 and went for pancakes. Massimo, of course, knew the waiter so we chatted with him, ate, and called it a night.

Chloe's car was at my house.

"Do you want to come in for a bit?" I asked.

"Yeah," she responded. We went into the living room, settled in and I turned on MTV. Michael Jackson's video for "Bad" was on.

"Oh, I really love this video, it's so cool," she said as we watched as a middle-aged Michael took on a street gang he ran into in a New York City subway, insisting he was the "bad" one, not them, and teaching them to dance. I leaned over to kiss Chloe. We kissed for a while until doing only that was boring, but we knew nothing else was going to happen so we stopped.

"That was a little out of nowhere," Chloe said as we lay relaxing on the couch.

"How was it out of nowhere? It's 5:00 in the morning and we're watching music videos. What did you think was going to happen?"

"That wasn't what I was talking about. I knew this was going to happen when we came in. It's your approach I was talking about."

"My approach?"

"Yes, your approach. We were just sitting there watching TV one minute, the next it was like you had taken a dive at me. It was a little abrupt, that's all."

"What was I supposed to do?"

"You're supposed to soulfully stare at the girl in the eye and then slowly make your approach."

"I can't do that."

"Here, try," she said. So I stared at her for a second, looking into her eyes, and I couldn't stop laughing. "I can't do this," I said.

"You can do it. Try again." The same thing happened. It was hard to be serious.

I put on an old copy of *American Werewolf in London* and we made out another hour until she left.

"My dad, my brothers and I are going to be watching the games tomorrow. Do you want to come over and watch with us?"

"Thanks for the invite. Buck told me you were a ball player, but nah." Chloe walked over to her car. The sun was out.

As she was about to drive off, I skipped out in the cold in my socks, "Chloe," I screamed telling her to roll her window down, "I'm going to remember this night forever." She smiled and drove off.

And with that, vacation ended and we all returned to our respective lives. The old buddies would never congeal again, never quite like that during that holiday break. During that first Christmas back, the dynamic of having left for a while, having learned a bit, and returning triumphant—chock full of new experiences of a new life—while still being a part of where we were returning held strong. Rarely, if ever, would I feel as much a part of that world again.

Freshman year in college comes but once. Both exciting and unnerving, everyone was away from home, some for the first time in their lives. The first few weeks were a feeding frenzy of people who didn't know enough about each other desperately searching and seeking, making new friends, arranging sleepovers. By the time the second semester rolled around, this was slowing down. I began to feel like my reputation was established, and not one that I wanted.

It was okay to take a break for a second. I was supposed to be working a bit anyway. I spent my afternoons between classes studying at the Honnold Library. I had a usual couch in a secluded spot on the third flood where I stretched out to read for history, skimming *Darkness at Noon*. "History had a slow pulse; man counted in years, history in generations," wrote Kessler. I marked the passage and took a break. I used to go out and take a lot of walks and lots of study breaks from claustrophobic, moldy smelling stacks. During one of my walks, I strolled by the rose bushes and noticed a girl with sandy blonde hair cut in a bob, sitting cross-legged. She was pulling a couple of the branches close, covering her eyes with leaves.

Strange, I thought and walked back into the library.

As it turned out, she played varsity soccer. My friend Steven told me about her. "She's a bit odd," he said.

"How come I haven't seen her all year long?"

"She lives in Holden."

"Not exactly a party place," I said.

"Nope, not exactly a party place."

Holden was the quiet dorm. I started having lunch with Steven more and more. Marsha often ate with Steven. I tried to talk to her at a party the following week. She didn't seem interested in chit-chat. The following week the same thing happened when I saw her at another party. None of her friends were there. She had talked to everyone else she knew so she walked up to chat. She was drunk. That helped. When she feigned tired, I feigned just as tired and walked her out. There was a two-minute window opportunity to try to distract her from her homeward walk as we headed down from the fifth floor of Mead Dorm.

"Do you want to go out to the cactus garden?" I asked as we stepped out into the night. (Later I would find out that the way to Marsha's heart was through her green thumb.) Chance of chances, she said yes. We walked. We swung on the swings. We talked the usual getting-to-know-someone nonsense.

"What are you doing? Why are you doing this?" she mumbled and pulled away as I tried to kiss her when the swings slowed. She didn't stop me but she certainly didn't reciprocate.

"Well, because..." I stammered. We stayed on those swings for a long time, me trying to make Marsha talk, until we both walked home.

Spring break was the following week. I flew to visit Mom in London. After napping all afternoon that first day, I couldn't sleep. Jetlagged and discombobulated, I felt both a fogginess and a sense of clarity about my life, pulling out a pen to write Chloe and Marni from high school, my once and future obsessions. Over the break, Mom and I went to the Tate Modern and to see the film version of *Unbearable Lightness of Being*, enthralled by the black and white scenes of Prague in the spring of 1968. History felt alive that spring. Something was brewing.

Marsha 's room was one of the first places I went when I got back to the west coast. She was sitting on the top bunk of the bed she shared with her roommate. She didn't even get down when I came by.

"How was your break?" I asked.

"Pretty good, I went back to Oregon." She paused. She didn't ask what I had done.

"I thought about you over the break," I said. "I was wondering if you were interested in going out to the cactus garden again?"

She played obtuse. "What are you saying? I don't know what you're talking about."

"Nothing, it was nothing," I said and then left.

Oh well, I thought. *So much for Marsha.*

Instead, I set my sights in other directions and the year continued with lots of rugby, some home-work, and more socializing. Weekends began on Wednesdays that year. WedNite was probably the most fun night of the week on campus. It was a party held in a dingy, mildew-infested academic basement party room at Pomona College, one of the five campuses. The walls were spray-painted black as a kind of base and topped off with layers of free speech murals: "End Apartheid!" "ACT UP!" "US out of Nicaragua!"

Ideas and music clashed and collided, with the bad college bands playing in the front, and great deals of beer from the kegs, smoke, and an omnipresent attitude from everyone. These were the most irreverent students on campus. Everyone wanted to show that. WedNite was one of the only parties that everyone at the five colleges frequented. There, in the bottom of a dark college gothic dorm, the college radio punk crowd seemed more predominant than the reggae, Deadhead prep school scene. I was chatting with some of my friends from the rugby team when Marsha showed up.

"Marsha!" I greeted her jovially while bumping into her. She looked different, wearing a black sweat jacket from soccer zipped up to the neck and tight black pants that suited her. For the first time I had ever seen, she had a smile on her face. Her grin betrayed her usual seriousness. After a few beers were in her, we were both a lot more relaxed than our previous meeting.

"Hi," she responded. That was all she said. We both stood there enjoying the moment, glad to not have the feeling of needing to immediately break the silence.

"It's great to see you here. Who did you come with?" I finally asked.

"I came with my suitemates," she said. "You sound like you're surprised."

"I just didn't expect to see you here."

"Why not?" She sighed, "Cab Hardy, you have got a lot to learn."

"Oh really?" I asked with a smile.

"Yes. There's a lot more to folks that you can find out if you stop prodding them and just let them be themselves."

"Yeah, you're probably right. I do have a few things to learn now, don't I? But at least I'm trying. Wait, your beer's empty. Can I get you a refill?"

"Sure," she said with a smile. I waded my way through the keg line, filled the two beers, and came back. She thanked me.

"When the big one comes, I'm going to be wearing my cowboy boots," screeched the lead singer for High and Outside, a college punk band playing; their music washed us in a cascade of emotions, tempo ebbing and accelerating. The band thrashed through their songs, enveloped in a cacophony of sounds, sweaty coeds lunging with the music and bumping into each other in a dark slightly sexy, mixed gender mosh pit dance moment.

Marsha was right in the middle of it.

After the music, it didn't take much effort to get her to leave the party with me. We sat on the lawn in front of the Pomona quad, surrounded by graffiti, talked some more, and then went back to my room. We both sat on my bed where, this time, I asked for permission first before the kiss.

"Yes, you can," she agreed, smiling. She hung out for an hour before she went home. We had planned to go out that following Friday night.

"She's a big drinker, Cab. She loves to tie one on," Steven advised, "I'm having friends over for drinks this Friday. You should bring her by. I'll feed her vodka shots."

"Excellent, thanks, Steve."

She met me in my room before going out. I was just getting out of the shower when she arrived and the door to the bathroom was ajar. I smiled. She looked at me. I closed the door, got dressed, and we walked outside into the Friday air. Spring filled the air as we walked to the party, both of us feeling good. Steve was right. Marsha did enjoy her vodka shots. A couple people from her high school in Oregon were there. They were a tight bunch and they drank a lot. Marsha and I had planned to go to a five-college party that night but when we saw the line, we decided not to even try. As we walked home, Marsha told me she had to pee. We were standing outside the football field.

"Be back in a second," she announced as she ran over to the bleachers. She told me about soccer and growing up in rural Oregon. We both got to talk about playing on that field and how much of a joke the whole thing felt like before walking back to my room where she spent the night.

This night, she initiated. She was on the pill and found calls for safe sex silly, so we skipped the condom. AIDS was not something people in Oregon talked about. Sex was still what kids did outside, in the woods. Marsha knew how to make it memorable. I had fumbled for the condom like usual, once we were pretty much already started and, of course, between trying to find one, fumbling with the package and trying to put it on, there was nothing left to put it on anyway. And, as was par for the course, my resolve to be safe faded at that and we just did it. I was the first guy she had slept with since her high school boyfriend. She had no hang-ups about getting what she wanted. She knew what she enjoyed in bed. The best was later in the night, with the tension out of the way, when we could really talk. The light from the field outside shone through the bedroom window into my dorm room. We lay there naked, propped against the pillows by the wall with the comforter over us.

"How about that attempt with the condom? " she joked.

"I tried. You have to at least give me credit, for that."

"Oh yeah, good job, Cab," she said sarcastically and patted me on my back.

"My friend Frannie once said that trying to do a guy with a condom was like fucking a fire hose," I concurred.

"Frannie said that?" Marsha followed.

"Yeah."

"Surprising. I wouldn't have thought. That's the first thing I have ever heard her or anyone else say about her that was half intelligent."

"Did something happen between you and Frannie?"

"No, not really, it's just that she's from New York."

"You have a problem with New York?" I asked.

"No, it's not as bad as Southern California."

"This is Southern California. What are you doing here?"

"Half my family went to the Claremont Colleges," explained Marsha. "It's a tradition."

"That's not a bad tradition."

"You're defending this place?"

"Yeah sure, why not?"

"So you're one of those weirdos who made Pitzer their first choice school?"

"Not exactly. To be honest, I came because it's the only school I got into," I confessed. "I didn't even visit. I asked my Dad for a trip out here and he said, 'Why? You're in. What else do you want?'"

"See, you didn't exactly dream about this as some wonderful destiny for yourself. I hate Southern California. When I first got here, I used to sit under the bushes at Honnold Library and put the leaves in front of my eyes, pretending I wasn't in the industrial waste zone."

"The school was built on a garbage dump. What's a little trash? You know, I actually saw you sitting there at the library. That's how you caught my eye."

"Pretty sight. You must have been like, 'Who is the freak?' To come to think of it, I remember the first time I met you."

"When?"

"You were in the Brit Lit class last semester," she said, "You were wearing jeans with cowboy boots tucked in and you had a pen in your mouth."

"You were in that class?" I asked, "I don't remember ever seeing you there."

"It was a big class." She paused. "Anyway, you came up to say something to me after class. Something about Dante, I think. You were wearing your black leather motorcycle jacket and you sounded very ditzy. But then when I listened, to my surprise, you actually had something intelligent to say."

"Wow, well that's a surprise."

"Not really," she said, still smiling. "I know about you, Cab. I've heard about you."

"What? What have you heard about me?"

"Nothing. I can't say," she teased.

"That's not fair. You can't just bring up something like that without backing it up." I turned and lay on my side, tickling her torso. Marsha shook her head and smiled even more.

She sighed. "Okay, fine. I talked to Jenn."

"Jenn? What Jenn?"

"Jenn——on the soccer team. You brought her up to your room last fall."

"Oh. What did she tell you? We didn't even do anything."

"I know you didn't do anything, but it wasn't for your lack of trying from what I hear. That wasn't it either. She also told me about ecstasy pills you took when you were in high school... No small sum."

"Then why are you here?"

"I want to be here. I think you're cute. I'm a big girl. I can take care of myself. I'm very glad. Jesus, all year without sex. It was time to get laid again."

"I know. I've had the same kind of a year," I said.

"Not really."

"You have no idea how tough it is being me," I feigned, half sarcastic.

"Oh god, I'm sure. I can tell already. I know it must be really difficult being you."

"It's better now that you're here," I said and pulled her close to me.

We had sex again the next morning.

The following weekend, my friend Melissa celebrated her 19th birthday. She lived across from me in the Sanborn dorm. Her dorm room was filled with art and kitsch——a picture of Johnny Depp from "21 Jump Street" with the words, "Fuck Me Johnny!" hung in her bathroom; and black sheets and a poster

101

for "Betty Blue," a trendy French movie, behind her bed. For hours, we sat, talking, feeling a little jittery. A bon vivant, she passed out ecstasy pills as favors to everybody who came to the party. Several people had never taken it before and were nervous. It took over an hour for everybody to start to feel high. But gradually a buzz ran down my spinal cord, a soothing warmth making its way, wrapping us in a feeling elation and euphoria. The room became higher and higher, and as joy combined with relief, we started feeling the effects; everyone was dancing around the crowded room to Melissa's new favorite tape—the Jackson 5 Greatest Hits. We blew on plastic party horns, chewed on ice cubes, ground our teeth, our pupils bulged, and we piled onto her bed. For a while, a group of ten of us lay on the bed feeling each other's bodies.

"Come on Jack," Melissa implored the only one of us who was still feeling a little shy. Gradually, he joined us in bed. Later when everybody had run off to go explore the campus, Jack, Melissa, and I stayed on the bed, lounging shoulders on the countless pillows, and we had very little motivation to leave.

"Melissa, I love you. I really do," Jack said. His pupils were huge. He gave Melissa a kiss on the cheek. "Cab, I love you too. I really do." He kissed me on the cheek too. "We've been friends all year, way before this love fest."

"Guys, you know what?" I asked emphatically.

"What?" both of them responded emphatically back, giving me a full audience.

"I have a girlfriend now."

"I know—Marsha. Cab, that's so wonderful," Jack followed.

"Where is she tonight?" Melissa asked.

"I think she's at home, probably asleep by now." I looked at my watch. It was almost 1:00 in the morning. I was feeling fuzzy and full of emotion.

"Go see her," smiled Jack.

"Yeah, you should definitely go see her!" Melissa added. "Look at you—you are so cute. It would be a really romantic gesture if you went over there now."

High, I walked over to Holden Dorm and hesitantly knocked on her door. I started to walk away but then heard a faint, "Who's there?"

"It's me. It's Cab."

"Come in," she said. Marsha was lying in bed, on the top bunk, looking at me in the dark, wiping the sleep out of her eyes.

"Can I come in?"

"You can sleep over, but I'm too tired for sex," she said.

"That would be great," I said. I felt relieved she was okay with me coming and she would have me.

Marsha was wearing pajamas. She unbuttoned the buttons to her top, took my shirt off, and pulled me to her.

"Cab..." She whispered. "What's Cab for?"

"Cab Calloway. My parents went to go hear him play in Paris the night I was conceived."

Marsha smiled and we both went to sleep.

From that night on, we spent a lot of time together. We'd go to the library together, then back to her room to hang out, always hoping her roommate had found somewhere else to sleep. Most nights, we started with missionary position, then reversed. I would lie on my back with her on top. Some nights Marsha mumbled to me, encouraging or reveling. Closing my eyes, I had to think of whatever I could not to cum, distracting myself with thoughts about World War I treaty alliances I'd been studying in history. One night, when I opened them, Marsha was smiling at me. Then we lay in bed, sharing the space, listening to Roxy Music and Pink Floyd. I was very happy, I told her.

"There's a change in the way we feel about each other," she said in a feeling of connection and vulnerability.

Lying there, "If" by Pink Floyd came on.

"If I go insane, please don't put your wires in my brain."

"I like this song," Marsha noted.

"It's all about Syd Barret, their old singer who lost his mind," I whispered.

"We all lose our minds," Marsha said.

"Sometimes the whole world does. Last week in class, we talked about the first World War. Millions dies in a battle to take over a few miles of trenches... The world went mad. It was crazy."

"Still is," she sighed.

The following Friday night, some friends had a party in the cactus field behind the campus, Mount Baldy and the desert were in the distance. Someone had started a bonfire. We spent the evening drinking from a keg. Marsha and I had a several beers and went back to my room. We were both buzzed. She was very aggressive that night, ripping my clothes off. As we did it, Marsha was breathing super hard. A minute later I looked at her and slowed down. She was crying.

"Marsha," I whispered, "What's wrong?" Tears were flowing down her face. "What's going on? Are you okay?"

She shook me off.

"Don't just let me do it without letting me in on this."

She looked away and back at me.

"What are we doing?" she asked.

"What?"

"What are we doing going home from parties and having sex like this? I don't even know you that well."

"Marsha, come here," I pleaded, and pulled her close to me for a hug. "I'm sorry. I didn't mean to take you for granted. I want this to be comfortable for you, for you to be comfortable with me. We have been spending a lot of time together. I thought things were going pretty well. You don't feel like I am holding anything back from you, do you?"

"No, but I still don't know you that well. Not like my old friends. I'm homesick."

"This isn't easy. It's never easy getting to really know people. All we can do is hang out and it'll slowly happen. I miss everybody from my old scene. I miss them so much, but they are really gone, for right now at least. They aren't part of my life anymore."

"Oh Cab, I'm sorry. I just don't know what's going on in my life right now. There are a lot of people back home I wish I was with now. It's April now and we should be together."

"April? Why should you be together in April?" I asked.

"Because of the accident."

"What accident?"

"This is the second anniversary of an accident that happened to a bunch of people from my high school class in Oregon. They all went for a hiking trip to Mt. Hood for a day hike to the top. Twenty-five were high school students, another three adults. We all had to go on these class trips. But I had family stuff to do so I missed this trip. The other people in my class were miles from anywhere, up in the mountains, and a storm started to hit. They didn't think they could make it back from where they started, so they pressed forward and things just got worse. By nightfall, they were completely snowed in and separated on either side of the pass. When they did not return that night, people started to worry. It was snowing too much to go back. The hikers found their way to a cave. The next day, two of the hikers appeared at a lodge after going to get help. Desperate, they told the story of the hikers getting snowed in. Twenty-five more were stuck inside the cave, waiting for help. The blizzard continued all day long. They were separated from anyone who could come in and get them out of there. The town sent helicopters but they were so snowed in, no one could see them. The state went into an all-out search for them.

"By the third day, a search party found three more people dead outside the caves. One had ripped off her boots, another had no parka. They had lost their minds from hypothermia. Delusional, they probably thought they were hot. One of the search parties found their dead bodies a week later, frozen, buried in snow. The hikers inside were frozen. An intravenous link could not break their skin. There were twenty-five of them. Twenty-five people from my high school class. I could have been on that trip. I *should* have been on that trip. I wish I was with them."

"But you weren't with them. You lived. Marsha, you lived."

"Those of us who didn't go, we'd have to live with the guilt of not taking part, of wondering what their last days were like, wondering why we were spared. I think we all died a bit that day," Marsha continued, crying at this point. I just held her, not sure if she was actually feeling suicidal or just missing her friends, in the throes of survivor guilt.

"For the rest of my life, I promised myself I would be with the rest of the class to remember that day. Cab, I don't know how to go on from this. If I did, I would. I can't imagine the desperation as they continued hiking, trying to beat that storm as it got worse and the sun was going down. Cab, I don't know about this life. Last spring, when I was out looking at colleges, I went to visit Boston College. There was this huge party. I asked one of the guys I was staying with if I could just go on up to his room because I wasn't in the mood at all to deal with that party. I was lying on the floor in my sleeping bag, trying to go to sleep, when this guy from the party came into the room. I told him I was trying to sleep but he wouldn't leave."

"Marsha," I said softly.

"Same old story. He wanted head. He said he would leave if I gave him head. I screamed but the party was so loud that no one heard. He came in my mouth. I thought I could taste his semen for days. I still can taste it now."

"Oh, Marsha," I said quietly, breathing in, holding her.

There were tears in both our eyes.

"What a disaster," Marsha laughed and wiped her hand across her eyes. "You must think I'm a freak, telling you about all this catastrophe and violence. I've run pretty much the whole gamut, haven't I?"

"Yeah, you have," I responded, and held her. I whispered, "You want a beer? I think I have a couple more in the fridge."

"That would be great."

Marsha and I did our best talking in bed. We spent a lot of time in her room, on that top bunk, listening to her Chuck Mangione. She was the only person in the whole world who still grooved out to that immortal horn line imbedded in all of our consciousness. I heard a lot about Oregon those nights. She told me about her brother, who she seemed to believe was addicted to fishing and showed me pictures of her hiking around the state with her friends. And of course, she talked a lot about her memories of the accident.

"The school offered a Philosophy of Love class for all of us to take to help us understand the feelings we were having. For the next year, all the classes in the grade were half empty."

With a vulnerability I had only rarely seen, Marsha offered me a glimpse of a big kind of pain that many people endure. I suspected a lot of women had similar thoughts and memories. This was the way the other half lived.

I began to think about things I'd been oblivious to before.

All of a sudden Marsha would be very far away or numbness would grasp her. Her expression blackened; her eyes stared off. We played Jane's Addiction all spring long. "Jane says, I'm gonna kick tomorrow." We listened to the tape over and over.

"It's just like the song before," Perry Farrel sang: "His sister's not a virgin anymore. Her sex is violence. SEX IS VIOLENCE! SEX IS VIOLENCE! SEX IS VIOLENCE!" The super cool girls from the X party on my hall who dressed to the hilt with lipstick, short fierce haircuts, and cigs all sung along with this chorus at parties; frivolity was a form of defiance. At first, I hadn't understood what they were talking about when they sang along. After Marsha told me her story about the party at Boston College, after I felt the blank jolt in Zoe's body when I touched her the wrong way, as I heard other similar stories, I began to understand the reality of the statistic that a quarter of undergraduate women endure a rape in college.

Some days, Marsha laughed with me. Other days, she said nothing, so we shared silences. I would try to tell her something with no reply. More often than not, sex took the place of words. I would serenade Marsha with her own specialized version of the chorus from the Elvis Costello song "Allison."

"Marsha, I know this world is killing you."

105

"Shut up," she'd respond, shaking her head, looking at me like I was an idiot, smiling underneath. We learned to trust each other.

Still, an optimism was in the air. Tens of thousands of Chinese democracy activists clogged the streets, some 50,000 in April calling for freedom of the press and improved treatment of intellectuals. And the government wasn't stopping them. By the end of the month, the crowd had swelled to 150,000, marching in defiance. The world changing, we felt the flux.

In between Marsha, school, and rugby, a few of us made our way to the desert to see the Grateful Dead and trip, wandering for hours. I'd been reading French surrealist novels, Proust, about time travel, and ingesting hallucinogens, taking me from the sky back to the earth. The rocks of Joshua Tree seemed to go on forever, taking us out of this time. Desert flowers made their way from the ground. We climbed and climbed staring at the horizon. I stayed up looking at the cacti, a coyote in the distance, the stars above.

Unable to sleep, I wondered what it would have been like for Carlos Castenada to encounter Don Juan as a young anthropology student in these same desert paths, doing field work, reflecting on that line between the terror and the wonder of living. Michele Foucault had famously come to give a talk in Claremont only to get lost in the desert with a young graduate student, doing psychedelics, missing his talk. I thought of him descending into oblivion, as we hiked, wondering what is was like to let it all go. We hiked all day. My friends meandered, eventually climbing up the rockface without ropes where the line between gravity and infinity felt very small. People love to visit the jaws of death to somehow feel alive. But I was quite happy where I was on the ground without risking too much. There had been enough pain, enough crash landings already. But the experiment was everywhere. It was a time to reimagine, to re-experience the world; what I could be, what we had been, what we should be.

Few of the insights remained the next day as I tried to pull my mind together for my Western Civilization exam back at campus. Still, I made my way to my spot in the Honnold Library. Reflecting on what was happening in China and Russia that spring of 1989, history opened up a whole new set of questions about the porous line between the newspapers and books, the library and the lived moment. I napped and slipped into deep sleep and began to dream. But even there my thoughts drifted to Marsha. I was overcome with a powerful, heart-wrenching melancholy. Sometimes just knowing her made me sad. She had been through so much pain. My life had been full of something approximating happiness. Not the stuff of great stories, but the making for a different childhood. Hers seemed to be filled with stories of despair. I felt so much for her. But her preoccupation with her past frustrated me. The summer break would offer a welcome pause. The academic year was winding down.

But not before a final rugby match of the season. Occidental came to Claremont. The hits to the body and the head seemed to loosen my mind, jarring me out of myself. The game was tied going into the final minute. Their fly ran across the field to our sideline. Time seemed to slow down as the play went on. I sprinted to across the width of the field, to the player with the ball, meeting him at sideline, hurling my body through his, without breaking stride. He fumbled the ball. We recovered and scored the winning try. The passion of the sweat, the day, the heat, the scrum of teammates, lunging for the ball, the entire game encompassed me. The season had been full of so many such moments, playing on the edge of the continent, the waves rumbling along the shore.

Like all games, we drank with the Occidental team after the game. The next day was the alumni game during the Kahoutek festival. The festival started in 1973, bringing Dead Heads and musicians to cavort with the hippies at the college. The festival was named for after Russian astronomer Lubos Kohoutek, who predicted that a comet would end the world in 1973. The students at the new college decided that if the world was ending, they should seize the day. They spent it dancing, playing music, eating acid, and contemplating the luminal space between this world and the other. One woman sat playing Sun Ra and Taj Mahal songs on her guitar. "Space is the place," she repeated. That feeling filled the air. I arrived for the alumni rugby game at noon. One of my teammates handed me a beer from the keg. The graduates were 90 minutes late. We were buzzed by the time the game started. We played the game in the sun and drank some more, before heading to the rugby party. Marsha laughed when I arrived at her room later that night. She still let me stay over.

A week before I was to go back home, I got a call from *Detour*, a Dallas magazine I loved.

"Is this Cab?" Louis, the slightly effeminate editor asked.

"Yes."

"We got the clips you sent. We love your writing. We want you to do an interview for their July/August cover story." He paused. "Can you?"

"Sure, I'll be home in a week."

"No, we want you to do it in Los Angeles. Can you do that?"

"Yes, of course." I gushed.

"Meet Billy at Chaya Venice next week for the interview."

"That's perfect."

I quickly put together the story, compiling interview questions. One of my suite mates drove me out Venice Beach for the interview, and wrote up the story the next day. The magazine would use it for the July cover story. Was it that easy to be a writer? You just get calls, interview people, write stories and they put your name on the cover of the magazine? Writing took me in any number of directions, from album and concert reviews, to free form essays, and experiments in form as the year went on. Everything felt like it was coming my way.

Arriving back at campus from the interview, I checked the mail, finding two envelopes: Chloe's response to my letter from spring break from London and Mari's letter from RISD came the same day. Marni told me about her life at Rhode Island School of Design, art, video editing, even confessing she regretted not talking with me before she left. That was okay.

I knew I was going to be seeing Chloe that summer. Her maniacal charisma bubbled off the page of her letter written on a drunken spring afternoon of her own on the grounds of Washington Square on the other coast.

"What an incredible spring," I gushed to Marsha later in the afternoon as we were drinking coffee at the Grove House, the swings where I tried to make out with her just behind us.

"Look at this headline," I said, gesturing to the LA Times: *BEIJING STUDENTS WIN CONCESSION* CHINESE OFFICIALS AGREE TO TALKS; MARCHERS SWEEP PAST POLICE LINES.

Marsha smiled.

"What a time we are living in. Gorbachev's Glasnost changing everything. Yesterday, all 110 old party members were booted and replaced with Gorbachev supporters. As we speak, thousands of kids are out in the streets in Beijing."

Finishing coffee, we walked over to the dining hall for badly needed replenishment. There was a group of people playing in a fountain in the quad. Spring in Southern California was enticing. For a brief moment, all the beauty of what Southern California could be, without the smog and pollution, revealed itself; Majestic Mount Baldy was visible in the distance.

We both joined the crowd, cleansing our parched and still clothed bodies. We never made it to the dining hall before we went back to her room and up to her bunk, soaking wet.

The year finished on a high point with Marsha, rugby, friends, and feeling a part of everything. Marsha and I spent almost every night together. Marsha's world became much lighter by the day. She smiled and seemed to trust.

"Next year will be great together," I whispered in bed on the final night of the year.

"Hopefully I'll be able to come to Texas this summer to see you," she said before I left to get the shuttle to the airport for my flight back to Dallas.

On the plane, I pulled out my journal from freshman year.

"I just said goodbye to Marsha," I wrote. "The last couple of days have been some of the best ever."

A Mysterious Domain

"He continued on his way without quickening his pace. When he came to the corner of the forest he found a lane whose entrance was marked by two white posts. He took a few steps into it and stopped, surprise and troubled by an inexplicable emotion. He went on walking with the same tired steps, and the icy wind still chapped his lips, occasionally taking his breath away, yet he was filled with an extraordinary contentment, a perfect and almost intoxicating serenity, a feeling of certainty he had reached his goal and from now on he could look forward to nothing but happiness."

-Alain-Fournier *The Wanderer of the end of Youth (Le Grand Meaulnes)*

"I met you in an earlier time. We had just one thing in common. That was the only thing in my life. I remember one spring day when we drove out in the country. Flying past houses, farms, and fields. ... I remember a summer with you when we lived out in the country, so much life and so much time..."

-Ten Hands, "Old Eyes."

I got home from the airport and called home. No one was around. No one was answering their calls, not my Dad, not my brothers, not my old neighbors, not my buddies. So I took a taxi, taking in the expansive Texas skies on my own, arriving home to an empty home. A wondrous quiet filled the house as I arrived. Looking at the message machine, Dr. B., my old history advisor, had left a message welcoming me back home.

"I studied there in the 1970s, but this is different," Dr. B. commented over dinner, reflecting on the changes taking place in the Soviet Union. "This is like nothing I've ever seen." He'd lived around the world, settling into a long-term gig teaching history. We chatted about China, poverty in the U.S. and a flux in the air. Something was happening in the world. We all felt it. I felt it playing rugby on the beach in Southern California and eating Mexican food in Texas. Something was opening up in our minds.

The next night, people started getting back to me. Several friends came over, Grant brought a case of beer, the first of several, and Phil brought an extra 100 tabs of acid. Over the next few hours, friend after friend stopped by. We sat on the patio taking in the summer night—drinking, tripping, wandering through what felt like a limitless summer evening, laughing and laughing into the night. Blue skies turned to rain, crying from the sky. Sitting in the patio chairs, we rocked back and forth and watched, listening to the patting as the raindrops landed. Eventually, we went outside into the greenway behind our house, walking out to the usual spaces. Although it was only the width of a football field, it felt like infinity. It stretched between streets, yards, the trees, bushes, past lives and secret places. We explored like it was a new land, looking at the leaves and the light rising in the morning due, the sunlight playing tricks. We walked along the inside alley by the house, a place where we'd all smoked cigarettes and wandered thousands of times before, bouncing on the rusting trampoline that had sat there for better part of a decade, the sun shining through our thoughts. Pieces of light rippled through the sky into a pattern of peacock feathers, colors flying as they swam through the dawn to greet us, painting a kaleidoscope of interweaving watercolors in the sky. Knowing and illumination danced through this morning of our minds, youthful feelings bounding everywhere.

We talked about Orwell and Huxley, TV the dope of the nation. We could give away our minds and thoughts or we could live. Grasping for something, we knew there were other ways of being if we allowed ourselves to look and see. Some felt completely alive; others seemed diminished, the lights in their eyes shining less and less. Some of us were opening; Grant was going to live in Australia to surf; Phil was planning to go on an archaeology dig in Southern Mexico. New thoughts exposed a world that we could grab for ourselves, ideas and feelings flowing everywhere, moments we shared, things we'd gone through, adventures we'd had in the spring, connecting the past and present into something exquisite that early summer dawn, a most beautiful day. Walking through the old neighborhood, we seemed to stumble upon something of an unknown that was becoming real, a domain that really mattered; for a second there, a truth in that moment between childhood and adulthood when an ideal feeling became real, discovering a domain that had always been around in which we were only just now becoming conscious.

"Dallas is a strange city," I wrote in my journal, jotting entries whenever I could. I wrote and wrote in between looking for work at local restaurants. Driving around looking for gigs, the DJs on KNON announced free tickets for music. I was broke and free music was a solution. A local jazz/funk band called Ten Hands that Todd and I had gone to see the previous summer had a show coming up. The eleventh caller would get tickets for the show. Driving down Commerce Street, I pulled the car over, ran to a pay phone, put in a quarter, and called in. I got a clear line. It was ringing.

"You are the eleventh caller," the voice answered, on the air. "You win free tickets for Ten Hands tomorrow night at Club Dada!" screamed the DJ on the other end of the phone.

"Really, I won?!"

"You won!" screamed the DJ. "You're the eleventh caller!"

I was jumping up and down with my arms in the air like Rocky.

Later that night, I met Dad for dinner.

"She's from Oregon," I told him. We were eating at an Italian restaurant off Lovers Lane. Marsha was on my mind.

"The most conservative state in the Union. Bland," Dad responded, dismissive as ever.

As we sat eating, a familiar silhouette walked in from the door.

"Chloe?" I commented unexpectedly.

"Hi," she said to me. "I went by your house and a friend of yours said the two of you were off to dinner here."

"That was Tom," Dad smiled, referring to his old college buddy, who had been staying at our house again that spring.

Chloe, who was wearing cut off jean shorts, appeared to have been drinking and paid Dad no attention. She looked right at me. "I thought I'd come say hello. So I've said it, 'Hello.' Now I'm saying, 'Goodbye.'" And she turned to walk out of the restaurant.

"Chloe, wait!" I pleaded as she walked out.

"It's okay. Have fun with your dad."

110

And she left.

"She got you," Dad laughed looking at me, stunned.

When I got home, there was a note from Chloe. "Hey Cab. I came over but your house is vacant (except for some random guy who just walked by). Anyway, call me... Chloe."

I called her the next day. We both had been dating other people all spring, but none of that seemed to matter in the whirlpool of emotions we were riding. Neither one of us were too concerned about the other people in our lives. Between infatuation and irreverence, other forces were in motion. And we felt it on the way to the Ten Hands show I won tickets for that night.

Exuberance filled the air that May. A pro-democracy student movement was expanding in China. The Poles were casting ballots for parliament; the Solidarity Movement was gaining ground. Gorbachev visited China. Deng Xiaoping and Gorbachev both danced around the issue of the 150,000 students converging in Tiananmen Square. But as soon as Gorbachev left, China imposed martial law. Many said the only reason China did not crack down earlier was because of Gorbachev's visit. Within a week, we'd all hear reports: "Chinese troops fire on protesters in Tiananmen Square," "Reign of Terror," "Massacre in Beijing."

In early June, I was still in between jobs. Chloe and I drove down to Austin to spend the weekend with Deg. We chatted all the way down, talking about our favorite classes. Russian Novel was hers, the Novel in Translation was mine. *The Wanderer* by Alain Fournier, a story about a man finding something magic in his old childhood home, had been on my mind since school ended. We only stopped once, at Carl's Corner truck stop just outside of Waco with the dancing frogs from the roof of the old Club Tango. 10 feet tall and 500 pounds each, artist Bob "Daddy-O" Wade made the six frogs for the club in 1983. The club had closed in 1985 and the human-sized frogs had found a new home at this loopy truck stop, full of yard art, nick knacks, wooden nickel sculptures, and waitresses serving chicken fried stakes. "Always served by a waitress named Mabel," Chloe chimed in. That night, we stayed at Deg's place. I was broke. But it didn't seem to matter.

"We all slum from time to time," Deg pointed out, opening a Shiner Boch beer for me. "Don't worry about it." And I didn't. I felt welcome in his arty house full of roommates, with Marti Gras beads, and beers he'd stolen from the Wheatsville food co-op where he worked. The whole place resembled something like PeeWee's playhouse, except that the front porch was filled with empty beer bottles.

The next day, we went tubing down the Brazos River, drinking most of that Shiner Boch as we floated. A long lazy day, high and outside in the sunshine, we made our way down the river for hours. Everyone was exhausted and dehydrated when we got back. I went for a shower. Washing my hair, I heard a rustling in the bathroom and the curtain opened. In came Chloe, without a stitch of clothing, inviting herself into the shower. "Shh..." she whispered. We spent the late afternoon in the bathtub, experimenting, sitting, standing, this way and that.

Chloe and Deg made us spaghetti. I assumed we'd stay in.

"No, we're not staying in," Deg scolded. "We're seeing my favorite new band."

"What band?" I asked.

"Poi Dog Pondering. They are like the New Bo's but with more sound. They've got a zeitgeist thing going on."

111

The stage was full of people at the outdoor show that night: a violin player, a man with a ukulele, a trumpet, drummers, a wall of sound filling the night with a mix of electronic and acoustic textures, horns and violins. The band opened with "Living with the Dreaming Body." Their lead singer Frank, who played a cameo as one of the village people in Richard Lanklater's film *Slacker*, an underground homage to Austin's characters, sang:

"Robin's in the metaphysical section
She's got "Living with the Dreaming Body"
She's sprawled out along the carpet floor."

Deg knew all the words. I imagined the Robin from the song was one of Deg's roommates. He'd come close to flunking out of the University of Texas that spring, when he began a new "No clouds, no class" policy, skipping class on most of the nice days. Chloe sang along with Frank and the band.

"Drunk on margaritas and full of food
She says, "It's hard to be with one when you're in love with another.""

Drunk on music and sex, a melancholic summer feeling enveloped us. Dancing after the bathtub sex romp, Chloe pressed her behind up to me as the band played, late into the evening.

We hung out all weekend and drove back to Dallas the next day with freshly fucked grins, feeling good to be alive, to be driving, listening to music. We chatted all the way, talking about Austin, Deg, music, and summer jobs.

The next night, we went to see another a Ten Hands gig in Ft. Worth. They were our favorite band. Percussion, bongos, congas, base, guitar, and lots and lots of shaking; we danced through every show, going to whenever we could. Ten Hands, Sara Hickman, the Reverend Horton Heat, New Bos—each night was different. As much as we could, we'd go see Ten Hands, who, having formed in 1986, were peaking. They played nightly most of that summer in 1989, with us in attendance whenever we could go. Railing about Reagan and political indifference, they combined a funk jazz with the irreverence of the punk, silliness, and an occasional earnest crescendo pumping through each song. The shows started around midnight and lasted well into the morning.

"The big one is coming," they sang over the sounds of bongos played by ten hands, beginning most shows with a warning of environmental apocalypse, or adventure, chaos, and hopes. We loved all their sets. Some songs, such as "Old Eyes" lamented the end of a great summer and the lost hopefulness of throwing away caution, celebrating opening up and showing someone what was inside. "If you'll handle it with care, I'll share my life with you," Paul sang. A tragicomic feeling was everywhere, at the shows, dancing, talking, gossiping, and traveling from Dallas to Ft. Worth, Austin, Denton or even Arlington to see them. Mike D., their Pan-like percussionist, maniacally danced as he performed, sang, never wearing a shirt, and inviting the audience to hold him when he dove off the stage. Gradually, we got to know the

112

members of the band. Earl and Mike were on drums. I made arrangements to interview them for *Detour Magazine*. After that, they put our names on the comp lists so we could get in to their shows for free.

I dropped by Chloe's house as much as she would have me. She still lived with her parents, who seemed to live on a constant flow of wine in a box, pouring me heaping glasses whenever I dropped by. Her mom was a former nun, her dad an East Coast transplant who had gone to Fordham. He was always smiling drunk and ready to chat whenever I came by.

"Be right there," Chloe smiled running from her bedroom through the living room to the laundry room in her underwear.

"You should spend the weekend some time," her dad gushed. "You'll see Chloe running around in her bra and underwear all weekend long," he laughed. Working class and very funny, they were a light-hearted breath of fresh air. There was a down home easygoingness to their house. I was welcome to stay over whenever I came. We'd sleep on the couch together before Chloe made it back to her bedroom before sunrise.

Driving back to my house, I looked out at the mysterious Texas sky, feeling an uplifting connection between myself and the rest of the world, the histories I'd studied, the novels—it grasped me, enveloping me in a space between the infinite and my imagination. Possibilities felt like they were everywhere. But so were forebodings, the Chinese arresting intellectuals and putting out most wanted lists for protesters, the pain of the world just beneath the surface.

We talked about high school and compared notes on our lives. She always had stories. Driving home after watching the Reverend Horton Heat, Chloe recalled a moment from grade school. But this story was different. "I'd been walking around the halls after a school dance. Alone in the hallway, one of the janitors had offered to help me find my way." She stopped talking looking off into the distance, glassy-eyed. I just sat, listening.

"He took me back to the janitor's closet, pulled out a knife, and forced my pants down," she continued. "A few hours later, a school nurse found me passed out, bleeding, and took me to get help. It took a dozen stitches and months to heal."

"Oh Chloe," I whispered. "Can we pull the car over?" She kept driving, looking forward. At the next stop-light, we both embraced. At a nearby parking lot, she stopped the car and walked to a playground in the summer night. It was hot that night. And everything was quiet. We crawled up onto the jungle gym. Sitting there looking out, her mood started to elevate. She smiled to herself.

"I am happy to be alive," she continued. "I'm happy to be alive. I'm glad I made it."

"I'm glad you're here," I replied, moved by her emotional outpouring. I had seen Chloe as a kind of a party person, out to have a good time, not someone with a tragic history, with which her smiles were forced to contend. Yet there was more I was seeing every day.

We drove home and found my little brother Peter had just gotten home from prep school. He was sleeping on the couch with the TV on.

He showed us a new kitten he had brought home.

"Her name is Puck," he told us.

"From the *Midsummer Night's Dream*," Chloe said.

Dad called the next day and invited us out for a bite. Over lunch he told us Mom had asked him for a divorce. When I tried to talk with him, he just nodded his head. He was the picture of exhaustion and disillusionment with a life falling off the tracks. It didn't surprise Peter or myself. Mom had moved out years ago. During that time, Dad initiated an on and off affair with an older woman. In his early-50's, Dad was painfully aware that time was passing and he wasn't doing what he wanted with his life.

"What about teaching, Dad?" I asked. "You can get back to it now that you are done with Mom."

"That's just another thing I won't get around to doing now or the rest of my life," Dad lamented, feeling sorry for himself, as he was prone to do.

Later that night, Peter, Chloe, her best friend Louisa, and I went out to State Bar. Louisa and Peter spent the night making out. Chloe and I sat at the bar, talking past each other. She was back to being a party girl, amped up, in a separate space from me. Some nights I had no idea where her manic energy was going. There was a bipolar part of her that sometimes eluded me.

The next day, Peter and I helped move Dad into his new apartment on Travis. The lights looked dim on his face as he moved everything. He was a complete wreck. The sweat was pouring off his forehead, his shirt unbuttoned, exposing an undershirt saturated with sweat. Every once in a while, he would make a comment like, "Do you think I'm overdoing it with the Afghanistan posters?" Later, when we finally got all his stuff into his apartment, we all felt a discernable sense of relief. His books that he'd loved were all there, smaller than the old library at the big house. But they were still there. "It's up to you to seek out this knowledge. It's your responsibility to explore these books now," he said and gestured at the books. "Let's go out," he continued. We went to Dave's Pawn Shop downtown to listen to music and then to eat some Tex-Mex just down the street. Robert Earl Keen was playing, his very humorous form of Texas country. He asked if there were any Aggie fans here. People shook their heads, moaning. "Oh no! No Aggie fans here!!!" he lamented. "No!" everyone screamed. We smiled and laughed as the music filled the night. It was going to be okay.

As the summer passed, I tried to balance my time between high school friends, Dad, Peter, and Chloe. Peter went to a few of the Ten Hands shows with us. The third Saturday in June, we went up to a party at Todd's house in North Dallas. By the time we got there, everyone was gone. The whole old world of my life there seemed to have vanished. Instead of despairing, we turned around and went back downtown to go see Ten Hands at Tommy's in Deep Ellum. Still just 19, they took my fake ID. I had never been there before. Walking in to check the place out, Chloe strolled up and gave me a hug. I was delighted to see her. It was the beginning of a turning point. We danced all night. She enjoyed so much good stuff: reading, music, life, so many ideas pouring out of her. Unlike the week before, we found ourselves on the same wavelength, enjoying being around each other.

Over the next few weeks, I came to idolize her, to romanticize her as a Texas writer who'd won journalism awards in high school, gotten a scholarship to Vassar, and loved sex, even if she sometimes recoiled from it with childhood memories that sent her into shivers. I drafted page after page about her. We started sleeping with each other daily. Sometimes we communicated about it. Sometimes, it just happened.

"We should talk about this," I whispered, thinking about the others.

Marsha's visit next week was looming.

"That's communication," she said, and leaned over to kiss me. But I didn't get much from her beyond that.

One day, when I arrived home, there was a letter from Marsha that was confusing, but made me smile. "At first I was scared to trust you," she wrote. "But now I can. I've never felt so sensual as I have with you. At first when you called sex 'making love,' it scared me. But now, it seems appropriate." By the time the letter arrived, I knew it was over. I was too caught up with the momentum of the summer.

"We should have a double date—you with Marsha, myself with John," Chloe chuckled. It was the night before Marsha was to arrive in Dallas for her week-long visit. Chloe's boyfriend John was arriving the same week.

"I don't even think I'll be able to kiss him again in good conscience. I think he'll be able to notice that I'm not used to being with him," she said.

Nothing about our past lives was off limits. We knew almost everything about virginity losses, past lovers, friends, old scenes, and hook ups. She shared the story of her courtship with our mutual pal Ted from Massimo's. I told her about my courtship with Marsha. She told me about getting together with her current boyfriend.

"He had been after me all semester long. Finally, one late night, when I had been at work all evening, I called him and invited him over to my room and we ended up doing it. I had my first orgasm a few weeks later after we'd been fucking all night. My body just caved in. I was out of my mind." Chloe's eyes looked crazy as she talked. She began laughing. I started laughing, caught up in Chloe's world.

I picked up Marsha the next day. The warmth of the spring had passed. She was back to her fish-out-of-water act. She had no comfort with urban space or going to see live music, which was the life my friends and I reveled in. I had a negative visceral reaction, wishing she had not come. I stayed at work late all week long to avoid spending time with her. I knew I was going to be spending the entire summer with Chloe and I wanted to get on with it. The feelings of loneliness that had led me to Marsha were gone. She felt like a burden. I hated the inconvenience of taking the time to spend with her instead of Chloe. I called her Chloe twice that week while we were making out. She never called me on it. We drove down to Austin that weekend and hung out with some of the high school buddies. Frat boys instead of hippies— I could not stand them and they could see it, sensing that I had a condescending view of their world. Yet, instead of stewing or ignoring it they called me on it, trying to start a fight. Seeing a fight coming, I eluded their drunken advances, escorting Marsha back to our friends' college dorm. Two of their house-mates made sex sounds Marsha and I went to bed. Fights were everywhere in Texas, repression and sex, one set of emotional outlets competing with another over and over.

"It makes me like you and respect you even more knowing what assholes you were surrounded by when you were growing up," she commented on the drive back to Dallas.

We went to Shakespeare in the park her last night in town. Mom gave me money. "Go take Marsha out for a fancy meal to thank her for coming," she said.

I took the money and bought beer and fried chicken for the festival. They were performing *Two Gentlemen of Verona, Texas*. We left after the first half.

115

"I have some other great friends I'd really like you to meet," I told Marsha after the play. "They're all hanging out downtown. Do you want to go see them?"

"Yeah, that sounds great."

She was being good-natured and still feeling the warmth from the beer. We got to Dave's Pawn Shop, the open mic joint where we were meeting Chloe, Andy and Deg. Feeling the beer, Marsha went into the bar barefoot. Amanda was performing that night.

"Not wearing shoes in Deep Ellum?" Chloe blurted out when I introduced her to Marsha. Actually, Chloe and Marsha got along very well. They talked to each other as Amanda performed. When Amanda was done, she came to sit by us.

"Cab, you have done an incredible thing, bringing together these three women you've slept with," Andy said to Deg and me after Amanda left and while Chloe and Marsha were in the bathroom. He had a huge teenager grin on his face.

"She's really nice," Marsha said when we got in the car. "I liked her and the rest of those people a lot more than your high school friends."

When we got home, we slept together, as we had every night that Marsha had been in town. And for the first time, Marsha pulled down my pants and gave me head.

I took her to the airport the next day.

"See you next September," she said. We kissed and said goodbye.

"Bye, Marsha, have a great summer."

That afternoon, not long after her plane had taken off, I wrote her a letter ending things. Not thinking about what the fall would be like without Chloe, I put it in the mail before meeting up with Chloe. I didn't feel good about it but the feelings of the spring were done. I wasn't thinking of the fall that would leave us separate. Still, breaking up in a letter was nothing to be proud about. I knew it. But I wasn't too concerned with the cowardly gesture. I didn't have to. None of that mattered. We'd both deceived friends for each other, not thinking these things spun both ways. Wheels of fortune spin. Yet, none of the blow back seemed to be coming my way, not yet at least.

Chloe was my siren. And I had to swim to her all summer long. She was more interested in sex. The stories she told were crasser. Her sister and she affectionately termed one of her old boyfriends, "Pencil Dick."

"About a week later, he tried to apologize to her for screwing her over," Chloe said laughing.

We went to see more bands that summer than I had seen in the previous ten years. She held court at shows—a cigarette in her hand, sitting at the barstool in her jeans with her legs crossed, at her helm, laughing, greeting friends, loving the world. She conveyed the fierce street smarts of the generation of kids growing up with guns in the public schools. Running around with her was a bright spot I flew to regardless of the danger.

"Cab, we must really love each other because our sex is terrible," she told me one night. She was leaning back, nude, spreading her legs, tired, unable to find a climax, chin on her hand at the opposite end of the tub after a clumsy escapade without any lubricants. I reveled in her body; her toes, her brain, her everything. We dedicated the summer to the task of improving our sex life. And through our mutual dedication, the hard work bore fruit. We talked and talked and talked in bed. I pointed out a detail, a secret or two; wow, she followed and, for perhaps the first time in my whole life, the fantasies of thousands of bored nights actually materialized. Most of it was subtle, a move to the left by a few inches, a confirmation, a vote of confidence, or affirmation. Along with it, we shared ourselves. Sometimes it is scary to let people into this part of yourself. So when someone sees it and says it is pretty neat, you don't hate that person or anything. For a moment it's a glimpse of freedom to be, of a becoming of what you really would love to be. The word epiphany gets thrown around a lot. But sometimes in life, a friend helps us to realize something we had not conceived or even consciously realized we were capable of. Sometimes, these moments offer a glimpse of a possibility of who we really are, opening up a something you never knew was there.

A few nights after the bath, we walked through the greenway in the back of the house, we'd explored that first night of the summer. The rain started to pour, drenching us with wetness like a friend, a reminder from another time. Chloe smiled at me, laughing, and we kept walking in the warm rain. Outside, someone was playing a song from an old childhood eight-track recorder—"Raindrops Keep Falling on My Head." I hadn't heard it since we'd been in Princeton in the 1970s. Listening, I started remembering being with my mom and brothers on another rainy day after driving into the city to see a movie, before divorce put wrinkles on Mom's face, before Peter was sent off to boarding school to become someone I didn't understand, sent away all too young an age. The rain brought back a car ride in which the eight-track played "Raindrops" over and over again and we chased every green light, every single one for eight miles in row. It was the same feeling. Walking in the rain with Chloe was really a coming home after never knowing I was away in the first place, allowing me to know that those days and feelings of home were not behind forever—they could come back. That's what it was like being with Chloe. It was a kind of homecoming.

In early July, we went to see a punk funk band the Daylights play at Club Clearview in the heart of Deep Ellum. A red neon light with its name etched into the sky in front of the dark theater. Inside were connected rooms of music and people, everyone shimmering in white blinking lights. The club drew people from all over the city. Inside with a beer in hand, Chloe bumped up against me as the band began to play the dark, half empty room. Ran, the singer for the Daylights, strutted, clad in his denim shorts and cowboy boots. "Punk rock is a movement that is here now!" He channeled his inner Iggy, funk thumping from the dance floor. More and more people poured inside. We all danced, lunging into each other and the stage, dislocated together and separate, more and more of us slamming into one another, with the throbbing guitar, drums and base out of the overworked, cheap speakers. We had to do something with that feeling, the yearning of those evenings we congregated together down on Elm Street. Things could be all right, but we were not sure with the pain never far behind, thrashing with the bountiful bodies in our club, sweating the beer from our veins.

After, we went out exploring the former blues and jazz district that had come to be known as Deep Ellum. "When you go down on Deep Ellum, put your money in your socks," Jerry Garcia sang about the place in "Deep Ellum Blues." We didn't have to hide our money. But we did go there as much as we could, passing the murals on Good Latimer, on our way to the shows. Monday nights, Bass Ale was free with a five-dollar cover charge. There local bands worked the funk and jazz riffs they'd learned at North Texas State University. My favorite venues were Club Dada in Deep Ellum, and Caravan of Dreams in Ft. Worth.

"Truckers treasure," Chloe whispered in my ear as she mounted me on the highway overpass while two RV's passed us to the left, on the way home from hearing Reverend Horton Heat in Ft. Worth. Close to midnight, we did it for a few minutes, as I drove, trying to avoid careening into other cars or off the side of the overpass. Finally, we pulled over fucking on the overpass.

Soon enough a siren and red-light blare behind us. A policeman walked over to us as we got dressed and looked out the window.

"Go home or get a fucking hotel room," the police officer grumbled and walked away from the scene, telling us we could not fuck on the side of Texas highway.

Outside, in the front seat, in nature, in my backyard, under the bushes in the Greenway, parked on the side of a bridge—we did it everywhere, even occasionally in bed. But that was rarely the case. Usually there was some degree of risk.

"Let me give you head," she nudged me one night on her couch in the living room, her father passed out on adjacent couch, adrenaline oozing everywhere. When I was just about to cum, we had to go in the bathroom to finish with her sitting on the sink. She slept on the top bunk in the bedroom with her sisters—a wonderful place for more of this stuff when staying late. I bit her neck as I tried to keep from making orgasm sounds. Sex injuries were common. When we were sharing an apartment a year later at Vassar, her housemate complained that she was way too familiar with our orgasm noises. We were so loud, she complained about the sounds rising through the wall. Surprising pieces intimacy grew out of these moments.

"Look at all we have," Chloe said one morning in July as the sun came up. We were sitting in a field we'd discovered off the road near her house after staying out all night. Looking at the world opening up for the day, Chloe started talking about an old house she used to live in as a kid.

"We'd roll down the hill, laughing and rolling, and getting up and doing it all again," she whispered looking out into the morning dew. "By the end, we both had itchy and irritated skin, and crushed leaves in our hair and clothes. But we didn't worry about it when we were doing it. Back inside, mom gave me a bath to soothe the itchy skin and lack of foresight. Years later we'd go back to look at that old house and the urge to roll down the hill would grasp me again. And I remembered the itchy skin and decided not to do it." Sitting there looking about, she told me she wanted to roll down the hill, and sighed with a sense of wonder in her voice. "It's funny, not knowing." She paused then said, "Holding the feeling of not knowing how things end in sorrow. We're so young." She smiled.

Driving in the country, floating down the river in Austin, seeing shows, taking showers, peaking on ecstasy, we were high on each other. On the way to Austin for another trip I jotted some notes in a fresh new journal. In between flyers and set lists for gigs, the journal began, "June 28th, Thursday, first entry to new journal. I plan on leaving for Austin in two hours... The events for the weekend as follows: Thurs arrive in Austin with Chloe and friends and go to Trash Disco, post retro club. Friday, go cliff diving in the afternoon with Deg and see Ten Hands that evening. The weekend prescription: Thursday Night—Chloe, Todd, and I—1.5 tabs of LSD each. Friday—MDMA—or as close as possible."

When we arrived in Austin, we went straight to the club. The door guard who scrutinized my fake ID for what seemed like ages before he finally stamped my arm. Inside, I dug through my pants and found the acid. "Reality, bye-bye," Chloe and I toasted each other as we dabbed the last two tabs on our tongues. A video on the screen showed monster trucks, with six-foot high wheels driving over each other, "MONSTER TRUCKS!!!! Trucks! Ucks! Ucks! Ucks!!!!" As the acid made its way through our minds, the words echoed over and over. "MONSTER TRUCKS!!!! Trucks! Ucks! Ucks! Ucks!!!!" The themes of the weekend were: extra high, extra American dream gone bad, more sex, more drinks, more music, more ridiculousness all weekend. The screen showed the trucks over and over again. We turned around and a man with a ponytail was playing with two puppets, dancing with them. Chloe was struck by just how absurd he looked—it all looked. The music roared. We had to turn away.

"All life is parody," Deg groaned when he joined us, showing up out of nowhere, at the club.

The whole weekend, we lurched between possibility and ridiculousness. Neither the LSD nor the ecstasy really hit; it didn't have to. It did not matter. Dancing at the trash disco set the tone, inspiring the whole room to shake. We met Chloe's best friend from high school, a gay boy and the head master's son. He regaled us with old high school football stories, including an interception in the state championship game.

"And the ball fell into my hands and I was like, 'I don't know what to do with it,'" he said. "'Run!' everyone screamed. So I ran for a touchdown."

"He loves to tell that story in gay bars," Chloe said. We drank margaritas late into the evening, laughing and enjoying Austin for all it was worth, connecting more and more.

Deg, Chloe and I went out to the Brazos the next day for swimming.

"You think there are rocks down there?" I asked Deg, looking down at the Brazos River, what looked like a hundred feet down. We stood at the Possom Kingdon Lake on one of the two cliffs that seemed to tower out of the river's reservoir. It's never a good thing to be the first to jump in such situations.

Chloe was looking straight down at the water.

"Only one way to find out," smiled Deg stepping off backward, falling nearly a hundred feet, splashing into the water below. I flashed back to a memory of a senior at Pitzer who died climbing without ropes and falling off the rocks in Joshua Tree, and wondered if that would be Deg's fate.

And then—nothing.

Chloe and I looked at each other.

A second later a head bobbed out of the water below.

"You okay, Deg?" I called out.

"You bet!"

"Here I come!"

I looked at Chloe, smiled and jumped.

"Holy shit!!!!" I dropped through the sky, imagining I was one of the Aztec gods learning to fly, my stomach moving into my throat as I gained speed, tumbling before crashing into the water. The earth held me, welcoming me back.

All summer I belied she would.

We swam most of the day before making it back to Deg's place where everyone napped. Deg went to work. Chloe and I hung out in the shower, on the couch, playing all weekend long before making our way home the next morning.

After the blur of it, it was nice just to just drive. "We gotta get some gas," I noted driving through downtown Austin, waving goodbye to Todd, whom we stumbled into on 6th Street.

"Remember the man dancing with the puppets?" I asked, reviewing the weekend's events, starting Thursday night when we'd arrived for Trash Disco.

"That must have been the most idiotic thing I have ever seen," Chloe laughed, slaphappy after the shower sex we'd just finished. "I swear to God."

"MONSTER TRUCKS!!!! Trucks! Ucks! Ucks! Ucks!!!!" I repeated; she declared with more and more gusto, over and over together: ""MONSTER TRUCKS!!!!"

I looked at the dashboard. "We're below a quarter tank," I said again, with Austin in our rearview window. Looking for gas, forgetting to pull over, we traced the story of our summer together: first dates, meetings, her summer the year before.

Chloe was digging through her tapes.

She put on De La Soul, a mellow hip hop soul beat carrying us out of town.

"We tried really hard too," I laughed, recalling the final sex attempt earlier in the morning before we left. It had been a full weekend it, every morning, afternoon and evening when we got home, and often in the morning.

"I was just hurting," she lamented, feeling hungover from the weekend of partying.

"I'm sorry." I looked down at the dashboard. "We need gas," I said again looking at the sign for fuel pointing to less than a quarter of a tank.

"Okay, there's a station a mile ahead," Chloe replied.

"Yeah, but I have a Mobile card from Dad."

"Is there money still left on that? We bought two cases of beer with that last week."

"Oh well."

She told me to keep my eyes peeled.

"Look," she pointed. "The cliffs of insanity!!! Hurry up and move the thing! Move it." She was refer-ring to her favorite *Princess Bride* line. "The cliffs of insanity." Of all the road trip games, strings of non-sequiturs was our favorite.

"I'd like to thank each and every one of you," I followed, referring to the old Steve Martin gag. "Thank you, thank you, thank you thank, thank you, thank you..."

"And then shower number two," Chloe interjected, adding to the narrative.

"We were like 'we'll see you guys later...' And then we had third time experiences." I groaned recalling, feeling spent. "That was hot."

"You're pretty hot."

"We're driving up 35 North. Carl's is coming up."

"No Carl's is a half an hour."

"Biggest small town in Texas."

"Smallest big town."

"Cows!" I declared, referring to Danny Devito's non sequitur from his film *Throw Mama from a Train*.

"Who's more of a Texan?" I asked.

"Me."

"Really?"

"You're more of a Georgian, especially when you eat chicken."

"You have an accent."

Chloe changed the tape and put on "Behind the Sun" by the Red Hot Chili Peppers, dancing along.

"What does this country feel like after getting back from the Northeast?" I asked, just feeling good on this road trip.

"I love it every time, every single time. I don't even mind the three-and-a-half-hour drive. Usually I drive by myself on the way back." We looked out the window at the blue sky, full of clouds, going on for what looked like forever.

"I love driving by myself."

"I was driving back from the first time I came back from Austin from the wedding reception for your brother earlier in the summer," I followed. "And I looked at the sky, into the infinite."

"That sky was with us that night when we were outside. I was just looking around," she replied. "We have so much. We're young and still able to soak it all up."

"In California it's the beach that goes on forever," I said, looking at the landscape passing. "New York's it's the mountains. And the leaves on the tress and the Gothic Architecture in the fall. And in Texas it's the highway. The road goes on forever..."

Chloe looked down at her friendship bands on her wrists.

"From Deg."

"Yeah!"

"Deg is the best. God, the only reason I would have wanted to stay tonight was for him." The practice of friendship was her everything.

"Yeah, well, we'll come again."

She turned up the music rapping along with the Chili Peppers cover of "Subterranean Homesick Blues." "... Look out kid, because it was something that you did.... Look out kid, and they keep it all hid!"

"Deg and I just loved spending time with each other," she went on. "We could have fun just doing anything together, no money—just driving around."

"But what really pulled it all together?" I asked. "What sealed the deal?"

"Oh, ACID, ACID, ACID!!!!!" she replied, simulating the monster truck echo from the TV at the Trash Disco the night before.

"MONSTER TRUCKS!!!! Trucks! Ucks! Ucks! Ucks!!!! And then you went to see the New Boh's every night and I wish I'd been with you guys."

We were always talking about us, the collective story of us growing by the mile.

"What did you think of me when you met me?" she asked.

"Last summer with Deg? I was pretty self-absorbed. I didn't think too much."

"No, over Christmas last year?"

"I saw you everywhere, ran into you with Grant, at the 500 Café...."

"We went out with Massimo," she said.

"And then I wrote you from London."

"I was sitting outside, high as a kite when your letter came."

"Remember the end?"

"It said you looked forward to trying out some more of your moves,"

Chloe replied, pausing and turning up the music. "I want to party on your pussy, baby. I want to party on, party on your pussay!" She sang along with "Special Secret Song Inside" by the Chili Peppers, reviewing the mix tapes she'd made the previous spring at Vassar.

"Are you hungry?" I asked. Chloe nodded and kept on singing. We pulled over for chicken fried steaks at Carl's Corner in Milford, Texas.

"Carl's has turned the truck stop into a work of art," I noted, looking around at the Texas ephemera: a painting here, waitress here, the frogs dancing above the eighteen-wheeler outside. She had a burger. I had a chicken fried steak. We forgot to get gas.

"One of my friends ran into Willie here. He shared a jay with him as they filled up," Chloe recalled as we drove away. On the way out, the gas light turned to yellow, meaning there was less than an eighth of a tank of gas left.

"We gotta find a Mobil," I paused. "I can't believe I forgot at Carl's."

"Road tripping with Cab, learning to be with me," gushed Chloe, switching the tape to Robin Hitchcock, and then to Vivaldi violin. "I love playing this on stressed nights when everyone is studying in the winter. That's the best time of year at school. Everyone is up. The libraries are open 24 hours. Best time of year."

"Wait, did we pass the gas station?" I asked.

"No, there is one coming up in Waxahachie."

"Right, there is a sign."

After twenty miles of driving on fumes through fields and taking in the rows of Victorian houses on our way, we pulled over for gas in Waxahachie.

"I can't believe we made it from Austin."

"This place is amazing."

"Look at this out here." I grimed, looking out at the fields in the distance. "I love this state."

"Look at all we have," she gushed. We were both in awe; that we'd found each other, that our friends adored each other, the music every night, the road trips. "Carpe diem," she repeated.

"You got that from the movie."

122

"Honey, I said it long before the movie."

Back on the road, Dallas was just thirty-five miles away. Talking about Texas, the conversation meandered back to our favorite topic: ourselves.

"I can't believe you came back after your first night hanging out with me over the summer," I said.

"Seeing Ten Hands?"

"No, when you came by my house the next day."

"Yeah."

"You just called at 2:30 in the morning a few times and then I picked up one early evening and you said give me directions, that you'd come by."

"And I talked with your dad all night," she said.

"Yeah, you were talking and talking with him. And finally I waved and said I was still here."

"And you walked up and kissed me when he left for a minute."

"And then it all got started. Next date, we ended up at my house."

"But I was scared of your room."

"You did fine in my room. That was super fun," I paused, looking at her. "Super fun."

"Yeah, but I was still with Jon. I had him in my mind."

"And we had our visitors," I said.

"Our visitors?"

"Jon and Marsha."

"Oh god!!!! The second he arrived, I wanted him gone. It was so awful."

"I know. I stayed late at work every night she was here. It wasn't so great."

"Do you know when you became my guy?" Chloe asked.

"When?"

"When we were cooking."

"Yeah? I love cooking together, watching the flavors of foods come together into something wonderful. I love that."

"And you were just making your way around the store with all that great food and then cooking away at home. I saw you and knew you were my boy."

Driving, napping, chit-chatting, slaphappy with fatigue, the drugs wading in and out of consciousness, we drove into the early evening, gossiping about who was and wasn't coming to the show that night.

"Jade won't go to Ten Hands because Andy is going with Margie so she can't go," I gossiped.

A part of Chloe wanted to be back in Austin, she confessed. She missed her high school friends there. "He wasn't trying to guilt me, but Deg observed, 'We're not growing apart. We're growing up away from each other,'" Deg told me in a quiet moment over the weekend. "That broke my heart."

"There'll be other weekends. We'll go back," I assured her. "Plus, we have friends for you to see here." We dropped by Louisa's on the way to the Ten Hands show at Tommy's downtown. They started at 11:45. The band roared through the set, everyone dancing, as if in a blur.

Still, Louisa seemed down after the show.

"What's up, Louisa?" we asked.

"Mikey ..." The week before, she'd blown Mikey back stage after the show.

"But he wasn't looking at me all show." Her voice started to slur. She passed out on our way home. The evening was ending, the apogee of the summer passing. For a while there, all the lines on the horizon intersected, stories and memories, kismet and change. That was the last day of freedom from caring.

Two days later, Chloe met me at the house for a quickie before we made our ways back to work. Leaving, she dropped me a note:

"Cab, I don't know what to say. I wrote this today at work with my new crummy editor breathing down my neck. But I wanted to give you something to show you how I feel and what I think; I want you to know how much you mean to me. I love you, Cab. It's even scarier writing that than saying it. I can't say that I know exactly what love is, but I know you've given me something I've never had before and I hope it'll go on for a long time. I'm kind of scared about going back to school... Not because of work, or friends, or John, or even because I'll miss you. But because I want to come back to Dallas every break and pick up where we left off. That's something I know by experience to be almost impossible. But I can't help but want it. I want you to look at me like you do now every time you see me; I want to pass over the uncomfortable feel of having to reacquaint ourselves so we can step back into what we have now. Maybe if we work at it, we can do that. And Cab, if you do come back and don't look at me like you do now, for whatever reason, I'll understand. I want us to be friends first and foremost, because that way, I'll know you'll always be around. I don't want to lose you. I don't know why I'm saying all this to you now; I must be getting manic again. Better take my lithium. Xo, Chloe."

Chloe and I knew we were playing with lost time. Classes in California and New York were less than a month away. So we upped the ante, going to see even more music, back to Austin more, to Poor David's Pub, to see Café Noir, Dallas' gypsy jazz band. They played sad, slow, soulful old-world music, a beautiful feeling lifting from their set.

We saw Ten Hands wherever they played all over the state of Texas. On July 22nd, we saw them at Tommy's again, then Three on a Hill the next night, and another Ten Hands set August 1st. It started like every other show. Shirtless as always, Mikey began his rap during "Amoeba," the bands absurdist anthem. Channeling his maniacal feeling into the music, it wasn't always containable. In the middle of the song, Mikey leaped from the stage in a stoned attempt at a stage dive but no one knew what he was doing. The stage dive is a collective compact between audience and performer, that has to be done with care. In this case, the crowd was more into space, dancing with their eyes closed, and he hadn't connected with them. Out of the air, he stumbled, falling hard, crashing into reality, and lying motionless, before he pulled himself away, unable to finish the set. We didn't know it at the time, but that would turn out to be Mickey's last show with the band. Later that week in Arlington at Fatsos, the band began another set. Yet, Mikey was not stage. Paul, their lead singer, offered no explanation. Earl looked down, trying to compensate for the two missing hands and starting without him on the drum intro to "The Big One is Coming." The crescendos of the beats were off tempo and empty, as if there were a hole in the set. Most of us in the audience just sat looking at the band, our jaws agape. The next day, Chloe woke up stressed about every-thing so we stayed home, had sex in the kitchen, and ran off to the museum to play. Walking through the

Kimbell Museum of Art, where I'd gone so many times as a child, we just started laughing. It was always okay not to know what was going on with Chloe.

"Bitterness over crackdown remains," reported Nicholas Kristof in the *New York Times* on August 6th, referring to events in China as the state arrested more democracy activists. Some tried to make their way out of the country. Other languished in jail.

Chloe was still working and writing me little notes from work. "It's raining," she wrote in black pen in her reporting pad. "... And I want to go home and crawl under the covers and find you there, feel your skin, smell your hair, hear your voice, and see your eyes looking back at me as we fall asleep. Then I want to wake up lazy and happy like in a dream—misty and fuzzy, but sharp, with the deep moaning and groaning feeling I get when I'm with you. It's just raining like it has before, and will again, but the gentle inviting pattering of the rain sounds like peace. And the peace is swelling inside my chest—the rhythm of your breathing, the feel of your lips on my forehead; I love you like the rain."

It was all too good to be true. And it was ending. As I wrote that August afternoon: "Really scary, lately, I've had a pit in my stomach. And there is nothing I can do about it. An ominous fatality now accompanies me. I'm going to be shattered to leave her and go back west."

Life was getting more and more manic. Some nights we connected. Others, we seemed to talk past each other's moods. She was more like that first night I'd met her with Grant and Buck. I had a harder time making sense of things.

Chloe wrote me a note after one such night in mid-August: "Oh Cab...." she wrote in a parody of herself. "...so many things, so many actions in this splendid life of ours direct me to you! All right, enough of that mushy stuff! Seriously Cab, sorry I was a bit of a 'neuro' last night. It's just hard being so vulnerable to someone. I love it and you and I get scared sometimes. I guess I think a lot of the times the reason I pick the people I pick to go out with is because I know that they'll either never depend on me, or make me depend on them enough for things to get out of hand. But here I am, writing this crummy note and knowing that I can't stop myself with you. I don't want to. Remember how I was feeling about how different we are? Well that was my evil twin Naomi speaking there. She's terribly trauma-oriented and scared all the time. She seems to be afraid those old fears and insecurities can't be reconciled with this, and she wants to stay safe. But I repressed her until last night when we met Grant for drinks. Seeing him and how he is made Naomi resurface again and badger me about not really knowing you, how different your friends are, and how different your life has been until now. She was pretty persistent, but with a lot of effort, I shut her up and told that doesn't matter. Because I love you for who you are now and for who you were then...The best part is that I (and Naomi, reluctantly enough) feel loved and appreciated for who we are, not for what other people are or have been to you. Thanks for dealing with Naomi, Cab. I know that was a silly way to put it. But I mean it and I love you and I know you'll understand. Xo, Chloe."

There were adventures every day as we flew higher and higher. I hung out and barbecued with her family, sitting outside her apartment in Duncanville watching the sun go down, looking at the stars. There were always more stories and secrets to share.

Chloe wrote me a note when we were all in Austin. I was with Rick and some of the buddies from Dallas. She was at her sister's apartment in Austin.

"Big Night Separation and I'm thinking of you so much its S-C-A-R-Y. No mincing words here, bud. I've suddenly found myself relating everything to you... I constantly think of not only how things affect me, but how they affect you. I'm drunk. I don't know what the fuck I'm saying... God, I just think about you all the time. Your face, and the talks we have and the way you're tall and have long legs and you are so beautiful to me. I apologize for my ridiculous vehemence, but I just love you, Cab Calloway."

Wandering through Deep Ellum late into the night, she consoled me over my parents' divorce, the waves of subsequent grief gripping, letting go, and reappearing all summer long. The choice we were making to care and feel as much as we possibly could juxtaposed with this separation. Sex and mystery mixed in an alchemy of living. But we didn't know how the concoction would turn out.

"I love the sex in the novel," I explained to Chloe, referring to *The Unbearable Lightness of Being*, and to an extent, something about us. "And the politics, the philosophy, the struggle against separateness, the adoration, the sacrifice, everything." I was peaking my brains out on ecstasy sitting in the parking lot outside of Club Clearview, the club's red neon lit sign shimmering in the night. We'd stopped by the club after going to the circus with Chloe's younger sister. It had not been for us.

"I always feel sad at the circus," I gushed, relieved to be away. The conductor was playing with the alligator, seemingly tormenting him.

"Sad to be watching them put through that," she followed.

"The animals look so sad and so docile, caged, unfree."

"Wanna get out of here?" she asked. I nodded. We skipped out and made our way down to Deep Ellum, happy to get away from the show.

"In Tereza's eyes, books were the symbols, inviting us into a sort of secret society. I love her," gushed Chloe, relieved to be back downtown, ecstasy flowing through her veins. "She saw novels as a 'weapon against the world of crudity surrounding her.'"

"I cannot believe Thomas went back to Prague for her," I wondered out loud, thoughts pouring out of my mind in a free association of ideas. Chloe looked at me with a worried expression on her face. The second I said it, I regretted those words.

She was holding my hand, sitting by me, knees up, our backs against the hard brick back wall across the parking lot from the entrance to the club, watching everyone enter.

"I can," Chloe lamented, looking worried. "I can. I would do that." A part of me didn't believe her. It all seemed like high talk. Usually I loved this banter between us. It was like a performance. But sometimes I wondered if it was real.

"He came back knowing he was sacrificing his career to be with her," I recalled.

"And to be true to himself. You wouldn't do that?" she asked, looking at me.

"For you I would do that." I replied, feeling cornered. It felt crazy.

Chloe saw it differently. "It may be chance that brings people—like us—together," she explained. She turned to me, grasping both my hands in hers. "But it is always will that keeps them that way. Will, says Nietzsche, is the essence of our being. And in order to affirm life, our will must say yes."

Looking at her, I saw the stars, acutely aware of an infinite, of everything around me.

"Sartre says we have to carry the weight of the burdens of the world on our shoulders. That's part of what Thomas was doing," I insisted. "And, I guess, we're doing."

"There has to be light. It can't just be weight..." she replied

"There is lightness and weight."

Two flies were dancing around a light bulb above us.

"We all fly to the light," I said, pointing to the flies diving into the light bulb. "Everyone does."

"Even if it kills us, we keep saying yes to it, to that light," she insisted, dovetailing back to Nietzche. "A nihilist says no."

"Or a nihilist embraces his fate. Even Nietzsche talks about *amor fati.*"

"The love of fate. I love Nietzsche."

"I do too," I replied. "But I can't love all of fate. It's too hard. There is too much arbitrary suffering out there."

"What I'm saying is, I say 'yes' to life, to you, to us, to our life together," she insisted. "I say it with the very essence of my being." She was looking at me with unabated earnestness, her dilated pupils bulging. I looked right back at her. She became self- conscious. "I hope that doesn't sound too obnoxious."

"It doesn't, Chloe. It's our fate, our punishment, our reward, our everything."

Talking, I started to feel worried thinking about Thomas, who could not shake his feelings for Sabina or Tereza in the novel, wondering if these feelings were not just a gift, but a strange sort of curse a double-edged blade. He always cheated on her. I wondered if the novel was some kind of foreshadowing. I flashed back to the images of the clowns and the animals at the circus earlier in the evening with Chloe's sisters. It was Chloe's sister's idea to go. Then I flashed to the Chinese activists who'd been in the streets, now sitting in jail while we were outside in the hot summer night. I started to feel really high. Finally, we walked into the club. Inside, we made our way through dark smoky corridors of fluorescently lit space with multiple doors leading in different directions. Noise and dissonance filled the frenetic space, bouncing against the walls. The Daylights were playing again, much less affirming than the fertile playful ecology of Ten Hands. Their beats were darker; dissonant amplified sound filled the dark club.

"Is everybody feeling funky?" asked Ran, their singer, strutting in his cutoff jean shorts and cowboy boots. No I thought to myself.

Listening, it was almost as though everything we had was dissipating, slipping away. Dancing, I closed my eyes letting the music move through me. I don't remember how long my eyes were closed. When I opened them, I look to my right, where Chloe had been and then at the whole dance floor. She was nowhere to be seen. None of our friends were around either. She usually would come back after wandering somewhere in a club, to get a drink or go to the bathroom. I kept dancing, completely alone. After twenty minutes, I started to look for her, winding my way through the labyrinthian club. I walked, circling from the bars, to the dancefloor, through the sitting areas, back around, over and over, asking the bartender if he'd seen her. He shook his head. She was gone.

Finally, not knowing what to do, I found a corner with a couch where I pulled out a pad of paper. Everything I had known was gone, changed. In its void, something else was here, another part of myself, in this moment, even away from her. I was more vulnerable than I ever had been.

After what seemed ages, I walked outside.

Across from the entrance, on the back end of the parking lot, under that lamp with the flies sat Chloe, staring up at the sky, just where we'd been earlier.

"Cab," she said smiling, oblivious to leaving without telling me. "I'm really glad I found you."

"Me too." A part me felt a little flustered. "I really missed you."

I walked to her and sat down. She crawled into my lap.

"Cab," she said. "While I was sitting here, I was thinking of you and us, and feeling like it could just fall apart. When the crazy intensity slows down, I was thinking you could lose interest in me. But Cab, I need you. You've helped me see myself in a way I've never seen myself before." Leaning against the wall, I felt more moved than ever before.

"Things change, and being together in regular life with you is perfect," I tried to explain.

"I see so much in you. I see a kid growing up with dyslexia and a football player and that kid who carried the cello to school and the kid whose mom moved out when he was in high school along with his brothers and dad half the time, and now even that is gone, the person who listens to so much, writes, thinks. I see so many things in you."

"What were you doing out here?" I asked.

"Just thinking about everything—the summer of love—so very young—but then a thought dropped into my head and it made me sad," she confessed, holding my hand.

"What were you thinking?"

She didn't say anything.

"What were you thinking?" I asked again.

"Sitting here, I saw a picture of life, of us being together and now... Of us all apart, saying goodbye."

"Transfigurations never last long. Soon enough we all have to walk back down."

We both looked out at the sky.

I pulled out the notes I had written inside the club.

"Can I read something to you?"

"Of course."

"I just wrote it. It's about the summer and us.

I paused and looked at the crinkled paper.

"So, there is another side of the city," I read. "Driving to your house, I pointed the car south toward 67. I'd driven around the city thousands of times, circling it, but never that way, never that route.

The city jetted out of the distance, buildings splashed across the sky, showing another angle, allowing me to see them as if for the very first time.

Between falling and growing older, driving and looking at the light reflecting on the buildings, I saw another side of the city. Looking at it, I'd stumbled upon a magic domain. Everything was clearer and brighter. A glow shown over everything. It rained in the greenway. And peacock feathers danced with the colors in the sky.

Visiting there, something changed, I changed.

I never wanted to leave.

One day everything I had ever known was gone.

So I looked around, gazing at my friends—the abundant contemporaries of my age—the music from the streets, the reflections on the buildings, the Mexican food from the border, the illuminations from the sky, and realized how precious it all was, here in the domain. The city that had always been there- that place that was always there, that I had never noticed, that I saw with you... The other part of the city, the other part of myself."

The summer was coming to an end. August 13, 1989, Todd, Rick, Chloe, Louisa, Andy, Jade and I went out to see the final Ten Hands show of the summer—a free concert in Lee Park. It was a benefit. But we did not know for what. Still, everybody was there. In between sets, Jade and I went off and talked about her long-distance boyfriend.

"Getting reacquainted is not that easy," she confessed, looking a little sad. "Sometimes it's the best time I've ever had; other times I would spend two weeks with him and feel like we weren't in love anymore, or I wasn't in love with him, and I'd fly home in a plane crying. I'd have to relax and take things with a grain of salt."

Music started to play in the distance.

"Jade, the band is starting!"

"Let's go!"

One more spastic day dancing together—Todd, Jade, Chloe, Louisa—no shoes, no shirt on me, wearing sunglasses, energy flying from all of us, shaking everything. Ten Hands played all our favorites, including "Old Eyes."

"I met you in an earlier time," Paul sang. "*We had just one thing in common. That was the only thing in my life.*" It already seemed like a long time ago that I had met Chloe and we drove through the country. Her favorite song was next.

"*Say the word/And I'll be yours /Forever and ever, say it to me, say it to me...*"

"It's so pleading and urgent," she whispered in my ear. "That's like us. That part when he says 'Are you ... with me?' I wonder and hope."

The two sets lasted hours. By the time they ended, the sun was going down. Leaving, we said goodbye to Earl.

"See you next week," he smiled.

"No, we're both off for the rest of the year."

He looked sad and walked up to say goodbye.

"I'm leaving. I'll leave my heart here and go to school, do some work."

Rick, my old high school football buddy and I spent the next day in defensive driving class. "Shoot me!" He smiled, looking up at me as the instructor droned on. And Mom, Dad, my brothers and I had a family dinner. Dad talked with the guys. Mom sat on the other side of the table, humming, not saying a word, not wanting it to feel like she left anything behind. But it was a mess. She'd left. Dad cheated. Trust was gone. And so was the quarter century of marriage. But that's what it was. So I retreated more and more into Chloe.

Later that night, we all met at the Inwood Lounge for drinks, sitting on the roof of the theater, climbing in the projection booth, running around like we owned the place, although I had only worked there one summer the year prior. But it had been my playground for years.

There, we all wrote each other notes.

"Oh, to be young, drunk, virile and reasonably indifferent to the inevitable destruction of the worm-infested fiber that our tattered corpses will become as the millennia closes without acknowledgement of our menial existence. And how about those opposable thumbs baby!" Deg scribbled in my notebook.

Louisa followed, jotting a few notes of her own. "... I wish I was eloquent enough to express here exactly how *Rimbaud* this whole three-month hiatus has been so you could look back on this or even show it to your friends and say 'yeah, yeah....' Last night definitely epitomized our summer, beer, cigarz, talking in the living room. I still think that I heard someone say John Hughes wants the rights to the Chloe / Cab summer '89 story. (Thank you for making my 'best friend'——translate: soul mate——so happy). I could go on for days about that one. I love you both so much. Ten Hands, Fever in the Funkhouse, Caravan of Dreams! Remember me backstage sucking off Mikey's dick?! Dada! Café Noir, Ethiopians, Bohemians, etc. Yay! I love it. I'll see you again before I know it."

"Whatever happened to Tiananmen?" Deg wondered. "Last month, last week, it was all anyone talked about. This week no one says a word." Fortunately, his sanctimonious sentiment never lasted. But he was onto a point. There was a larger world out there, creeping in on the rest of our lives. Of course, Deg was right. His words went right over the gang's head. Chloe and I were too busy with our own little world.

At some point, we all rumbled into the men's room at the theater, the movies playing just outside. Louisa pulled down her pants, peed in the urinal standing up, striking a pose, everyone rolling on the ground laughing, as sacrificed her dignity for the absurd. We made our way back upstairs, all of us dangling our feet off the roof. Sitting beside Chloe, I smiled.

"What's up?" she greeted me.

"Chloe! You know what's up!" We wandered down before everyone else, and sat on the hood of Deg's car. We drank a beer, talked, and reconnected. Slowly, the car started moving with us both up front on the hood. At first I thought Deg was just joking around. But then he started driving faster, taking a turn, and we both flew. I watched Chloe disappear off onto the pavement.

"Dumb bastard!" I screamed at Deg, wondering if Chloe was okay. I walked her back to my house.

Just as Deg failed to consider how we'd fly off the car, we'd neglected the pain of others else all summer. Marsha responded to my Dear John letter with a letter about dead flowers. She wrote about how she stared at the dead flowers in a vase in her room, always knowing that she could put photographs of live flowers on her walls. As in the cases with Sarah and Becky before her, I had no idea what she was talking about, and had even less interest in her ruminations. I had little time to consider their humanity. There was hubris to the entire thing, to the era of expedience——on to the bigger better thing. Sex exacted its costs. And Chloe and I were, of course, in store for a few lessons ourselves.

After a few wild days turned into a summer, the exuberance faded. "I'm still feeling sad about life," I wrote in my journal the next morning. "It's 6:00 in the morning and the birds are chirping outside...and I'm listening to Charlie Bird. But I still feel down. I should feel happy."

We had both tampered with a psychic equilibrium. Behind every breakup lived human beings with emotions of their own. Cosmic karma takes motion. The trysts, scenes, and climaxes——actions created reactions that became life histories, punishing as much as they delighted. Fantasies fulfilled sometimes stung as much as they liberated. With orgasms stretching from crotch to very bare essence of my being, emotions intertwined; pain became commonplace. I took it for granted. But it was everywhere.

The months that became years with Chloe proved the case in point.

I kept thinking about that early August show when we went to see Ten Hands when Mikey jumped off the stage and the crowd parted. But no one caught him. An equilibrium was somehow broken between Mikey and the band. And perfect summers rarely last.

Last week in August, I drove up to New York with Chloe to see her off to school. We wandered through the West Village in New York City. I loved the Village. We drank cheap beer sitting on park benches on Seventh Avenue, reveling at the people and pace of the dingy city. A man with a can of paint drafted an image of a cartoon character on the sidewalk beside us.

"Pinto Bean Man is against apartheid," he explained to me, smiling, as I looked on. This was his hustle. He was selling t-shirts of his character. I bought one for Chloe and myself.

We listened to street musicians and ate cheap Indian food on West Fourth Street before making our way uptown, through Grand Central Station that last afternoon together, chatting about the concerts we'd seen all summer, New York, and the fall. Talking, one of my evenings with Amanda came up. There had been something in June or so. Chloe was only finding out now. For the first time I saw a spark of regret, even jealousy. We had been libertines. But now we were attached and emotions became raw.

"But I loved you then," she implored, looking at me, not understanding.

"It was before us."

"But I loved you then."

"The whole thing happened in a whirlwind when the summer was starting," I explained to her.

The Inwood Theater gang had reunions all summer long that summer.

"Cab!!!!" Jade screamed into the phone two and a half months prior in early June.

"JADE!!!!!" I screamed back.

"What?!"

"You're the one who called."

"You're such a butt but I'll let you in on the hot tip anyway, just because I am that kind of girl. Andy, Rebecca, your favorite person, and myself are going to see Fever in the Funk House tonight and you have to come," Jade announced.

"My favorite person?" I asked.

"A-M-A-N-D-A," she teased. "And you have to come tonight. It wouldn't be the same without you."

"I think I'm into Chloe now. I can't."

"I *don't* care," Jade responded.

I did go along that night after buying a box of condoms on the way home. So much for self-control. We all danced, paved through the pretense of this just being a buddy-buddy night at the club.

When everyone left, Jade confessed, "Cab, I'm feeling something for both of them. What should I do?"

"Put it off before you make a decision," I replied.

"How come you get to have both?"

131

Amanda broke the moratorium on talking about what everybody was thinking with a toast: "To fiberglass asses!"

We all danced for hours before going back to Jade's place. Amanda and I were in the back of the packed car. I started to slide my hand along her leg. Her hand moved slowly and gently up to the inside of my crotch.

"Let's go back to your apartment," I whispered to her.

"Do you want to?"

"Yes."

She smiled and agreed as we continued to feel each other up.

"Jade and Rebecca kept on telling me how cute you looked all night, goading me on. 'Go on, aren't you going to sleep with him tonight?' They kept pushing." Amanda chit-chatted as we drove back to her apartment. We didn't use condoms. The sex wasn't that great. Her abandon was the turn-on. Her openness to go for it, to talk about it, to enjoy it—that was the fun part.

As usual, shame oozed afterward and I couldn't wait to get out of there.

The next day, regret coursed through my mind. "Just part of the inevitable, like death itself, sort of a self-fulfilling prophesy," I lamented, equating promiscuity with futility. "The pursuit of joy only brings death," I continued, doing my best Thomas Mann. "Passion only aids the process, like smoking to cancer. My stomach is turning, sick with disgust at myself." As I had sex that night with Amanda, I looked at her and wondered. There was that old odd feeling that she could have been anyone as she played with me. I could picture Marsha there with her hair in her face, Chloe there with guilt and memories of horror, and then Amanda. But do any of them care? Why would they? Why me—what's the appeal? Mom's downstairs talking with lawyers, ending a 25 year marriage, with all the pain in the world. Is it right that I feel joy, or is pleasure the only way to combat that feeling? Is effervescence the best way to face up to the sadness that is consuming Mom and the rest of the family?

Ring, Ring, Ring, went the phone in the kitchen again a couple of weeks later after another Inwood reunion night.

"CAB!!!!!"

"JADE!!!!!"

"What!?" Jade screamed indignantly.

"What your face, Jade?" I retorted.

She sighed. "Should I sleep with Andy?"

"What? I thought that was over."

"I did too but when I saw him last night, the second I saw him, my crotch began to itch."

"What about Duddley?" He was her present beau.

"You get to have both Amanda and Chloe. Why can't I have both Andy and Duddley?"

"I'm not sure I do. When it rains, it pours and then there is nothing. That's just the way life goes."

It seemed like it was off right then in Grand Central Station. Chloe looked at me standing by the information booth. It was before, I reminded her. And somehow we got the genie back—sort of—at least I thought so. But the story stung, drawing deep grooves into her memory. The summer ended and

Chloe and I faced the daunting decision of either breaking up or pledging loyalty. I had broken up with Marsha earlier in the summer. There was no one on the west coast to go back to. So, we promised to give long distance a go. The best summer ever and now it was over. It was time to leave the domain.

Earthquakes

A hears by chance a familiar name, and the name involves a riddle of the past.
B, in love with A, receives an unsigned letter in which the writer states that she is the mistress of A and begs B not
to take him away from her.
B, compelled by circumstances to be a companion of A in an isolated place, alters heresy views of love
-John Ashbery "by an Earthquake"

Chloe called about a month after I had returned to school. When I answered the phone, she sounded strange and insistent.

"This isn't working." Her voice came distant, hard to reach.

"Huh? What?" I asked, sitting in the pay phone in the dorm.

Talking her back from the ledge, I walked back to my room, lying back on my stained dorm mattress. There was a pile of pizza boxes in the closet by my roommate Earnie's guitar amp. He never left, just slept all the time. Years later, he would get busted for trying to hook up with preadolescent girls online. But at the time, he just seemed like a homebody.

I stared at a wall of pictures and cards from the summer I had built of Chloe, thinking about her confession of sleeping with the director of the play she was in. Brad was only the first crack in the armor of our determination to fight our way through the year apart.

I was the next to break. I spent the night with a girl from my Italian class. Then Chloe had sex with her co-star in her play.

Then I slept with my suitemate Natalie, whose old boyfriend Bobby later told me she had herpes. We had all been on a road trip to Berkeley and Santa Cruz, dancing for hours. She moved closer and closer to me on the dance floor as a blues band played. Later that night, we all slept in one room, three of us crashing in the bed, another two on the floor. And Natalie pulled me closer to her, insisting. Again, I told myself this didn't really count as much because I didn't pursue her; she pursued me all weekend long, dancing in between the wreckage on our way to Santa Cruz, escaping the Lomo Prieta earthquake of October 17, 1989 by a matter of hours on our way back.

Within a few days, warts turned up. I went to the doctor to get them removed. He suggested I inform my most recent scenes. So I told Natalie and a few of the others, which was not too much fun at all.

By Thanksgiving, I flew to New York to be with Chloe. She was wearing a turtleneck, an Irish wool sweater, and jeans when we met on Lexington Ave, outside of Grand Central. We made out right there on 42nd Street and then took the Metro North up to Poughkeepsie. Fall was alive, with red and yellow leaves blooming along the Hudson. We'd talked about this moment for weeks.

134

"I'm home. I'm home again," she smiled as she snuggled in for an embrace, as if trying to convince herself. She gradually took off her sweater and turtleneck beneath it. Her skin was pale. The suntan of summer was gone.

I felt unfamiliar to her. No one's touch felt right. She told me that she had been going to the counseling center at the school. While she was with Brad, sex stirred up a memory from that rape. Even all these years later, the memories of that seventh-grade dance lingered in her body. The body remembers even when we forget. It was a lesson learned again and again.

"I don't want to have sex again," she confessed that night in bed. A week earlier she'd written me a letter saying it wasn't working for her to be away from me. We'd been writing weekly letters, sending mix tapes. "Helpless hoping ... only to trip at the sound of goodbye," she titled hers. We had manic, two-hour phone conversations. When she got off, she was a wreck. It was ruining her life at Vassar, she told me. She needed to stop it all, dating, everything.

I had to go. This was too much, I thought. This was beyond what I could handle. Desperate, I called Grant, who was extremely stoned. I told him what happened.

"Then I'm coming to get you," he responded on the phone, agreeing to drive from Wesleyan College in Connecticut to pick me up in Poughkeepsie and take me back to his dorm.

"We gotta save my friend," I heard him telling someone in the room with him.

"Grant's picking me up in a few hours," I told Chloe.

"He's a good friend," she responded, looking hurt and disappointed. But she seemed resigned. We sat in the room for a while, silent. A depressed feeling filled the space. She broke the silence.

"Let's get out of here," she suggested. "We can borrow Wisi's car."

"Okay."

We bundled up, put jackets on, picked up a six pack of beer and walked out to jump into her housemate's old 1975 station wagon for a drive through Poughkeepsie.

"How Deep is Your Love," by the Bee Gees was on the radio. She started to change the channel.

"Keep it on. I love this song."

"Me too."

"I used to listen to this every night when it came out," I recalled, "Putting the transistor radio up to my head as I went to sleep at my grandparents' house."

We looked at each other, singing along a bit, trying to hit the high notes. Then she changed the subject.

"Are you sure?" she asked.

"What?"

She looked at me.

"That I'm leaving tonight?"

She nodded.

"I guess so. I feel like I should be asking you that. You're the one who is breaking up with me."

"I know. But it's all..."

"But how? How did it all fall apart?"

"I don't know... I'm not sure about things now. It's kind of confusing. I mean. I adore you. I love you. But I don't know if I'm in..."

"Don't say it," I mumbled, stopping her. I changed the station.

"Hey Cab..." She felt that peculiar feeling she'd had all night, like she was about to cry, but might break out in a chuckle. "I'm scared too."

"You're my best friend," I lamented, sounding almost desperate.

"I know. Let's just drive. Okay?"

We opened two beers, driving through the cold wintry night, telling ghost stories. *Children of the Corn*, Stephen King's novel about a group of children who followed a scary preacher, was the scariest book she had ever read.

"Bone chilling, never want to sleep again terrifying."

I recalled *Communion*, a book about people who had been kidnapped by aliens.

"I was up for days after just looking at it in the bookstore."

Talking, we slipped into a bit of our comfort zone, remembering where we'd been; she told me stories about dating my old co-worker at Massimo's from years prior, somehow connecting our old life with this new space in which we found ourselves.

"I love that story," I replied. "How did you meet again?"

"This is a pretty good story actually," she started. "I was friends with his sister. We were out doing ecstasy one night. We walked around downtown, grinding our teeth for hours, chatting. And went back to her place. Her brother, Ted, who also went to Vassar, was about to go jogging, although it was close to midnight when we got there. He had a funny bandana on his head. He looked at me right in the eye as he was tying his shoe. He had a really hot smile."

"I know. He was super charming. And I thought bi."

"Me too. Now mind you, I'd been on ecstasy for hours, and he was gorgeous.

And he was super flirty. I didn't know what to do. I was immobilized. Should I sit by him or blow it? Finally, I got the courage and sat by him. Just as I was sitting down, he was getting up. I blurted out, 'Don't go. I wanted to sit by you.' He had this really wide smile. And sat back down, saying 'Okay.' We talked for a while and I said, 'You can go now.' That was it."

"That wasn't completely it. It was the beginning. That brought you to Massimo's and eventually to me, on this crazy road."

We both looked down the cold road.

"Funny, it seems like a long time ago."

"It was only three years ago."

"You told me about dating Ted last Christmas when we went out with Massimo."

"A lifetime ago. And here we are." She paused, looked around, and pulled the car over. "I know a spot here."

It was a big parking lot. We traipsed out, stepping over a railing and walking along a cliff until we stopped at a spot with a view straight down to the river.

"Wow," I gushed, looking out. The fog was rolling over the river. "How did you find this place?"

Chloe was smoking a cigarette.

"It was an accident. I just drove by it one day."

"It's amazing," I mumbled, looking at the mist in the night along the river, beautiful and lonely, like a lot of the spaces we'd explored the previous summer.

"Do you remember the night we first met?"

"Yeah, you were smoking a lot."

"Bucky, Grant, and you came over. Well, I also met you with Ted two years earlier when you were passed out at Massimo's," I said.

"That doesn't count. The first night I remember meeting you, you made us those really bad screwdrivers."

"Yeah, there were a few other chance encounters."

"But I guess you are going now."

"Huh?"

"Nothing."

"It's only for a year or two, until after we graduate. After we've figured things out....Staying away will be the hardest, scariest thing," she said.

"You don't have to stay away, we can..."

"Yes, I do...." She started to cry, as if to honor the moment. It felt crazy that it was falling apart. It was getting cold out. Eventually we both got back into the car, listening to more easy listening music.

"C'mon..." she reached out for my hand. We sat for a while. I couldn't take her hand. But finally, after a pause, I put my hand in the middle of the seat, offering a kind of a détente.

"I'm gonna miss you," she replied, putting her hand on top of my hand.

I held her hand, feeling a sense of connection again, albeit a tenuous one.

We drove back to her dorm and got into her bed, holding each other, as she fell asleep. And eventually Grant, who'd been driving for hours, called the room. By the time he arrived, I regretted he'd come. His stoned gesture felt heroic. But the trip was also impulsive. He was exhausted, just coming down as he arrived. I had to honor his effort. Chloe was asleep when I left. I just needed a night to think, I told myself, but a tinge of regret hung in the air driving past the main gate at Vassar, as if I was leaving something irretrievable behind. I only stayed at Wesleyan for a night. Chloe had asked that I join her for Thanksgiving.

The next day, I took the train back to meet her for Thanksgiving on Long Island, where she'd traveled from Vassar. Her aunt and uncle, as well as great aunt were there. We drank a lot of red wine and laughed and laughed at dinner. Later, after everyone had gone to bed, we got some time to ourselves. I went to sleep in the other room. A couple of hours later, she woke up and came to me. She said, "I dreamed my dead aunt was walking through the house." She crawled into my bed, holding me. The intimacy was back. And we were back on.

The next day, we read the papers about the Germany. The Velvet Revolution was all over the news. Walls were crumbling. Eastern Europe was opening. Playwright Václav *Havel* was hailed as a national hero. Communism had collapsed like a pile of Jenga sticks, there was no more Cold War. Friends again, reconciliation was everywhere. But the foundations were still uncertain. We were not the same.

The image of Chloe and me as young libertines was over. We were full of conflicts and contradictions, on and off, connected and separated, west coast and east, Catholic or agnostic. At Thanksgiving, Chloe confessed she wanted to reembrace Catholicism. I had always loved the Madonna-whore thing she had going. But this was the first time I had seen her move back toward the other end of the pendulum.

"Have you read the Book of J?" she asked me, referring to a newly discovered book of the Old Testament which was all the literary rage. I hadn't. And neither had she, but she was interested in exploring it. I was confused, but also intrigued, with her elusive ever-evolving self, and I was more attracted to her than ever.

Reuniting for Christmas break, adventures were everywhere. But instead of just living for the moment, we were trying to hold something, even as we retraced the stories of our lives together. She gave me a copy of *The Unbearable Lightness of Being* as a Christmas gift with the following inscription:

"My dearest Cab, I've taken the liberty of marking some passages. I really think you should read this whole book again. It may be chance that brings people (like us) together. But it is the will that keeps them that way.... I love you. Xo, Chloe. P.S. Yes, I ADMIT I TOOK AN ENTIRE SEMESTER OF NIETZSCHE." And we stayed together, revolutions in the East, earthquakes in the West and long-distances in between.

We drove to Austin over spring break, dancing to bands at the South by Southwest music festival, cliff diving and exploring. I decided to take my junior year at Vassar.

But before that we had another summer of running around in Dallas together. She suggested we both get HIV tests together.

"Why are you here?" asked George, the very effeminate counselor at the gay men's health clinic on Cedar Springs, across from the WOK, the Chinese Restaurant where we'd gotten high for years.

"A little of this and that...." I mumbled, looking at my hands.

"Sex, drugs and rock and roll," he replied. "Without condoms?"

"Without condoms."

"Without condoms," he repeated, with a pause. Silence. He glared at both of us. "Do you look both ways before crossing the street?"

"Yes."

"Then what were you doing?" he asked in angry frustration.

"I don't know."

"Do you want to die? Do you know how many people I see dying every day here? Kids just like you two."

We were shaken, but I'd been through the tests before. Still, the fear was very real. It would be two weeks before the results came back. Jittery, we went back to meet George to get the news. He was smiling when we walked in to meet with him. "I have good news for you. Both your results are negative," George told us. Relief filled the room. We all chatted for a minute.

"What are you going to do now?" he asked.

"We're going to go down to JR's for a drink." We asked him to join us.

When we got to JR's, the bartender brought us two large frozen margaritas with a note from George. "You two are wonderful people. Stay safe." He reminded us we could enjoy pleasure and reduce risk, offering us a bit of courtesy stigma. Even that summer of 1990, a foxhole comradery was part of living with the fine line between promiscuity and disease.

That August, we drove east, making our way through the Gulf Coast, stopping at a dingy hotel in New Orleans that felt straight out of *Streetcar Named Desire*. We went out for gumbo at Coops, enjoying Albita beers and crawfish and made it back to our cheap hotel room, its lock barely closing. People were skylarking outside in the parking lot. It was hot and humid. We had sex for hours, watching cheap porno movies on the hotel TV. The next day, we stopped at the beach on the Mississippi Sound, swimming all afternoon in the hot empty beach on the gulf, a perfect end to the summer. The following, we drove northeast. But unlike the year before, I wasn't turning around.

This time I was on her turf. I loved the idea of being there. The fall leaves on the Hudson River, the deep engagement. That fall I took Intellectual History class, writing about jazz and magical realism. I buried myself in the library. But I was still at Vassar on Chloe's terms and Chloe and I grappled with the dynamics of control—who was in charge, who made the calls. She knew that sex was part of a package deal which could be manipulated for an advantage, as a form of coercion. As long as the Scarlet O'Harra's of the world have resented gaining a couple of inches around the waist after child birth, sex has come with a price tag. It has always been a commodity. You pay for it, or you pay for it.

We spent days together at the library, reading, cramming, studying, cooped up in the dorm in the cold of winter all weekend, reading all afternoon, sneaking off for a grope in the stacks, writing papers, comparing notes, jerking each other off, reading, eating, getting stoned, studying, drinking, having sex, reading, gossiping, repeat.

At night, we listened to the Stoned Roses, a Manchester band whose beats everyone adored. Quiet words flew from the radio.

"Every backbone and heart you break
Will come back for more
Submission ends it all..."

I got up to pee after sex.

"*Bye-bye badman, ooh bye-bye*," Chloe sang along with the chorus, lying on her back naked, her legs swaying from right to left, waving at me as I left. There were many tender moments.

When Chloe was not around, I read and poured through a collection of porn I'd carried from Dallas, taken to California, and up to Vassar. These were my initiations into a lusty imaginative world of abundance and chaos. She couldn't stand it that I'd brought my decade-old stash of sticky magazines from grade school. There was no way to cram for an exam or draft a paper without looking through the magazines. Philip Roth understood this. You can't write without a pile of giny magazines around, he explained in an interview. Honoré de Balzac took himself up to the edge over and over again when he wrote. When Thomas Wolf jerked off, ideas danced, as "the sensuous elements in every domain of life became more immediate, real, and beautiful." Words flew onto the page. I concurred and practiced, wanting to be a writer myself after all. I needed to liberate my head from its bodily notions. Ideas could not flow if I was

139

clogged up. There was a Proustian quality to the images and smell, conjuring up worlds of memories, hopes, and aspirations. We all have a relationship to the feeling we had when we first found Eros. It helped me explore, imagine, and find out a bit of who I wanted, hoped, and aspired to be. Yet, it was not without its anxieties. Like countless others, I eschewed Freud's advice to sublimate the energy flowing from it. Jerking off was intimately bound up with the power to create, the process of self-making, and cultural combat over social control. And it slowed things down with Chloe.

Sometimes we adored each other. We would order cheap pizza and get a six-pack of beer and sit together enjoying the fall leaves. On other days, Chloe could not stand that I was crowding her world and she went off to the campus pub on her own, only to return to my room a day or two later. Sometimes we met on the steps of the Metropolitan Museum of Art in the city, or had more adventures on Houston Street, hanging out at Max Fish and the East Village dive bars, or going to see jazz in the West Village.

On a bathroom break on one of those trips, I heard a knock on the door. "It's me," I heard her say. She sneaked in, sat up on the sink, and we had at it right there. When the excitement was high, we thrived. But the manic-depressive peaks and valleys were more than I could sustain. The excitement was hard to keep going. So she looked elsewhere. During a swing-themed house party, I saw her making out with a man who had come from Yale for visit as they were dancing. I walked up to her, tapped her on her should, flipped her the finger, and walked out.

"I think some of us swung a little too hard," one of her housemates commented the next day, hungover. The next day Chloe came to my room and we made up. Those were some of the best afternoons, making up, with the leaves outside, delicious together.

Delicious Intoxication

"I was filled with such delicious intoxication that I could have walked straight off into the air, climbing on the strength of my own drunkenness into the stars. And the intoxication, as I knew even then, was the recklessness of infinite possibility, of danger, the secret ugly frightening pulse of war itself, of the death that we all wanted for each other and ourselves,"

-Doris Lessing, *The Golden Notebook*

A quiet evening in December, I walked back to my room and saw a note waiting for me. At first, I thought it was from Chloe. But then I saw. "Tom Died," the note from one of the White Angels explained. The White Angels were the ladies who worked the front desks in all the Vassar College dorms. They took notes for all incoming phone calls. It had been years since I had really known Tom. We all lived at the old house after Mom moved out—Dad, Tom, and me for a year. And now a note, a little three-by-three-inch square piece of paper hanging on a rack with other notes for other students, announced in two words that his life was over. Mom told me she would call if anything changed in his condition. The death-watch hadn't been that long. That's the way it went in those days.

Dad had only told me about his AIDS diagnosis the previous summer.

On word of the news, I drove to Lubbock, Texas to visit Tom. Wearing a gimme hat, he was skinny, in blue jeans and a cowboy shirt. He played Chopin's Nocturnes on the piano. Years earlier, Dad told me he had had a chance to play with Leonard Bernstein, but it did not materialize. Like his career as an academic, it was another fumbled opportunity in a life of them. He'd refused to publish, although his Harvard dissertation had been rated one of the best in the century by his peers. He subsequently lost his job teaching in West Texas. Now all that seemed unimportant. I thumbed through the books on his shelf. He could still play Chopin with a smile.

"Isn't it nice?" he remarked, eyes sparking. For a second, I felt like I was in prewar Berlin or was listening to Liberace. He had an otherworldly presence.

I was looking at his wall of books, beat poetry, German philosophy, French novels, pulp fiction, and countless Latin American works.

"Who is this?" I asked, picking up a small volume.

"That's Jorge Luis Borges. He is a wonderful writer," Tom said. He was visibly gaunt. He got up, picked up the volume and opened it.

"I thought of a labyrinth of labyrinths, of one sinuous spreading labyrinth that would encompass the *past* and the *future* and in some way involve the *stars*," he read from Borges in his 1942 work, "The Garden of Forking Paths." Tom looked at me and kept on reading. "Sometimes, the paths of this labyrinth converge: for example, you arrive at this house, but in one of the possible pasts you are my enemy, in another, my friend."

We talked all afternoon about Latin American fiction and the metaphor of the labyrinth.

"When you look at the story of the Minotaur..." Tom began. We were eating nachos at a cheap Tex-Mex spot. "You know the story, right?"

He never lectured. But he wanted to make sure I was with him.

"Yes, the hero, Theseus, is walking through the maze being chased by a monster, the Minotaur," I recounted.

"But who is the Minotaur?" asked Tom.

I shook my head, not knowing.

"Could he be the hero?"

I interrupted, "Out to kill himself?"

"Possibly. You have to decide," Tom said, smiling. He was never didactic. But he was when telling the story of Theseus, who eludes the Minotaur with the help of Ariadne, who was in love with him. She gave him a string so he could make his way back through the maze, only to abandon her on his way out, setting off a chain of events that led to his father's death. The unintended consequences of love and vanity are many. Tom seemed to see that and wanted me to as well. I would have to figure that out.

Later in the day he told me, "If you are ever shooting up with anyone, put the syringe in bleach. It'll kill this," he explained, referring to the HIV running through his veins. "Before you use the needle. Or just use a clean one." I had never heard of syringe exchange, not until then. Tom was dropping a few clues. "We all ingest things that could hurt us," he suggested. "This was the story of Homer's attempts to elude the the sirens calling him. Our opponents are our vanities. We are always killing ourselves."

That was the last time I talked with Tom. I had a feeling he was sending me off with a map to an alternate geography, but I was not really sure where. Up at Vassar, I wrote an Intellectual History about the books Tom recommended. As a class we had to imagine ways to "convey the negative"—whatever that meant. I wasn't quite sure about Hegel. But we had to make our way out of "a general mystification," that Calvino described as the muddy haze of consciousness that we were all part of in this modern world. We had the capacity to move through the contractions, the shopping malls, arcades, and false consciousness toward a something freer. All the jazz I loved and magical realism Tom told me about were means of resistance and freedom. I was not sure what was happening to me. But like the fall leaves, between the energy of the city and its jazz, the pulse of the subways, the sounds of street musicians, and the libraries filled with books popping off the shelves, my world was changing.

"I have always imagined paradise to be a kind of library," Borges wrote, pointing me toward a way of looking at the world with irreverence and engagement. But his infidelity was toward the text and form. Fictions and nonfictions, essays and poems, encyclopedia entries and journals, they all could be places for liberating expression, unencumbered by past structures. A generation of writers was built on this thinking. Italo Calvino wrote about books talking to him as a reader, half revealing themselves to readers tasked with searching for the right endings to the books they were reading. Each reader was involved in a detective mystery. They had to find out what was going to happen, not simply sit on the couch. Who was the Minotaur chasing? We needed to get up and find out. History could be a great tale, unencumbered by picky details or quaint notions of truth, noted Peter Shaffer in *Lettice and Lovage*, a play we saw with Maggie Smith on Broadway. The news could be as compelling as a soap opera, as if there were really a difference, Mario Vargas Llosa said. I reread my old copy of *Aunt Julia the Scriptwriter* from that Literature in Translation class, seeing the love-obsessed protagonist who rewrote soap opera scripts and radio news as a kind of hero. A whole world was opening up for me in this alternative geography of the library. I was spending dozens of hours there. I read and wrote and tried to distill everything I could see—every play, every story, every book, and every jazz show into my paper.

In December, Chloe and I locked ourselves in my room for two days and edited my intellectual history on Latin American fiction and Borges' *ficciones*. Snow poured, we edited, groped, edited, explored, slept. "*Freedom is just another word for nothing left to lose,*" Janet Joplin sang. We tried to practice it. And I felt like Tom was pointing me down the labyrinth into a world of the unknown. And I was finding a voice there.

The following winter, I signed up for a class jointly taught by the History, Philosophy, Music, and German departments that was only offered once every four years. It was entitled, "German Culture at the Turn of the 20th Century." I sent Tom a copy of the syllabus. I asked if he had any suggestions as to what subject I should address for the seminar paper. He died before the letter got to Lubbuck.

By the end of the year, it was over with Chloe.

"Cab, I am only going to say this once," she lamented as we lay in bed in her room toward the end, looking at the moon through her window, "But we've been through a lot together." We had one more trip to Austin, ending things as they began, with an open-ended declaration of care that would never work. We were kids, only just beginning to create our own lives. From Texas to California to New York, two years together—that was enough to change everything. I got lost in it all.

On the way home from that bittersweet last trip in Austin, I listened to the radio, looking at the oil on the Texas road and recalled Chloe singing "Bye Bye Badman," waving as I departed. "Let's Stay Together" played on the tape machine as I watched the city grow smaller in the distance. We were not staying together, and I knew it; I wept and I smiled.

My eyes turned towards the clouds, booming through the Austin sky, thinking about the space between childhood and growing up where I found myself. The domain had disappeared, but there was still something there. I knew nothing was going to be the same.

I changed tapes and thought about my grandmother who went to college in Bastrop, Texas, outside Austin. I had no idea why she'd come. Or left. Or why we'd arrived here ten years prior, her grandkids growing up just as she was shuffling off. I thought of getting lost drinking beer on the way to Mexico with a six pack with Chloe and Deg, of Dad and everyone else from here, and that trip down from Dallas in the summer of 1989 when I had no money and everyone took care of me, telling me they didn't care if I was broke, I was welcome. They were glad I'd come. The fulcrum between childhood and adulthood left me out of balance, somewhere on the road as we floated down the Brazos, shared a shower, and talked about Russian novels all the way back to Dallas, feeling a part of everything—the sky, the music, the city, the road that went on forever and the party that never seemed to end. We were part of everything. The sky was us and we it, full of illusions, hallucinations, oil disappearing and reemerging in the distance just as we got close to it. I could never touch it. Looking at a mirage on the road, I was still chasing it. Colors

143

flashed in that sky reflecting in the Dallas skyline, talking and recalling and being. We drove back and forth, saying goodbye hello, back out west, to South by Southwest for Spring break where we played in the woods, jumped off cliffs into the water below; and back through the Gulf Coast, staying in a dingy hotel in New Orleans, listening to hot tunes, swimming on the Mississippi Sound, driving out east and back up to Poughkeepsie, observing fall on the Palisades, getting drinks at the Village Vanguard, sneaking off to the bathroom together, writing all night through the winter, and sitting on the steps of the Met. And one more trip back to Austin in 1991 to dance, drink beer, share, and say goodbye before a semester away in Italy, even if we didn't want to remember how much had happened since that first trip in 1989 when we had been driving in the country and laughing and dancing through a thousand shows. When we were still kids on the cusp of something between the city and the country, whirling across the state, back and forth between shows in Ft. Worth and back to Austin. And then it was over—that part of my life was like a mirage, disappearing in the distance. We couldn't go back.

Other adventures would have to do. The delicious intoxication of Chloe was over. The next day, I caught a flight for Rome, where I spent the rest of the year careening between Firenze, Venezia, Rome, Berlin, Siena, Nice, and back again, through California, Los Angeles, Joshua Tree, San Francisco, and another life, always lost, but learning that was okay.

Ciao Italia

io vivro' Senza te, io senza te solo continuero' e dormiro' mi svegliero', camminero' lavorero', qualche cosa faro'
qualche cosa faro', si, qualche cosa faro' qualche cosa di sicuro io faro': piangero'
-Lucio Battisti, "Io Vivrò" (Senza Te)

History and art were everywhere in Florence. Curvilinear streets weaved from markets to piazzas to churches to the Arnò and back through the city. Michelangelo's David was down the street from the pensione where we all stayed on Via Ricosole, with its rooftop garden where I read under an umbrella with my feet up after touring the city.

Each morning, we walked with our amiable tour guide, an aesthete art historian, both queer and monastic, who talked about the city like many describe lovers.

"In Florence, a great church was considered a 'project for the city'—a civil as well as a religious symbol, translating into architectural terms the moral process by which men overcome prejudices and transcend individual interests to join others in 'a single will,'" Professor Timothy Verdon declared on one of our art history tours through Florence.

We started in Rome. Unsure of things when I arrived, I wandered through the city in a daze, looking at the men standing on the corners, in the piazzas, the ladies riding their motor scooters, making their ways through the labyrinth, all part of the multitude. And I felt very, very small. I had no idea where I was going, so I let my senses lead me, exploring the history of the space. Looking at the Pantheon—once a temple to the Roman gods that had become a church, rebuilt by emperors Augustus and then Hadrian—I felt like my life and my history had little relevance to any of this. It felt like all of history stared back at me when I looked at the ceiling, a testament to order and chaos, the building's old gods still lingering around the edges in the corners.

With each day's stroll through the old streets, Verdon recalled stories of a people and their humanist aspirations for urban space. We retraced that imprint of Florence, where Verdon pointed out the lines from the old Roman walls. Every city has it layers. In Florence, they pointed to a renaissance in consciousness; Verdon's voice elevated as he told us about it, seeming to rejoice in the rebirth of ideas and the spaces of beauty in the very archeology of the city.

Early one morning, I looked at the birds make their way across the piazza in front of Santa Maria Novella, the venders just outside, people coming and going. Energy from another time pulsed from the museum and mixed within this modern locomotion of bodies passing to and from. I was completely alone. Time seemed to slow as I watched a panorama unfold in front of my eyes. Gradually, our whole group made our way inside the space where Boccaccio began his Decameron; across the room, we took in Masacio's Trinity, a fresco from 1424 creating illusions in space onto the cloisters of the dead, and Paolo Uccello's The Deluge before we went back into the church. Away from the group, I sat in the pew looking at the light pouring through the stained glass. I had never felt so alone with such exquisite beauty, hauntingly alive.

Verdon sat to join me.

"I love the lights pouring into the space," I commented to him.

"Well, Alberti and the other architects knew that we come to God through light, scent and sound," smiled Verdon.

"It's so solitary and lonely here," I commented.

"I know."

"But I am strangely touched by it. I don't know why."

"The art touches us. It reminds of us of mysteries and beauty."

I didn't know what to say or feel. But I was moved beyond anything I had ever felt. History seemed to move through me, through all of us here.

"Come, let's go outside," he said. We walked to the market.

"Vitello arrosto," I asked for my sandwich from a gruff vendor selling roast beef sandwiches. Verdon walked back to the monastery where he lived year-round. I made my way to my usual lunch spot, watching the water along the Arno. A summer of exploring took shape. I was learning to look at a city as work of art.

It felt both strange and familiar. Grandmom and Grandad had lived here in the 1960s and early 1970s. I had grown up visiting them, so the streets felt familiar, full of memories and modern ambitions. I'd played in the piazzas that I walked by every day when I was a kid.

"When they first brought David out into the piazza della Signoria, vandals threw stones at it, offended by its obscene nudity," noted Verdon, recalling the story of Michelangelo's David positioned outside in Florence. "But the Florentines pushed back, ever ready to defend the idea of civic space, keeping it open for everyone. The art reflected the character of a people and their civic aspirations."

Verdon told us about the culture wars and history, tracing battles between a reactionary Girolamo Savonarola and a civic humanism. Three-dimensional bodies, art, ideas, and monuments belong in the public square. Savonarola saw this art as a "bonfire of the vanities," while the artists suggested that body was something noble; Savonarola blamed the plague on hedonism and the artists saw it as a health calamity. A few saints tried to care for the sick. Several got sick themselves. The names of most of them were lost. Botticelli knew Venus was not perfect. None of us are. Eros has to struggle with the irrational. We all dance with Pan from time to time. Bodies were noble, glamorous and capable of bold things, if also fragile. It all sounded very familiar to me in the context of the AIDS years.

I'd made friends with a few wayward art history students who joined my afternoon walks. Verdon often left us with suggestions for other places to visit after our morning tours were over.

"We don't have time to get to the Bargello this time, but I highly suggest you give it a visit," he concluded in mid-July, standing outside the old palazzo-turned-museum on Via Del Procsolo.

"You guys want to go with me?" I asked a couple of my friends.

"Go see Donatello's David and let me know what you think of the difference between it and Michelangelo's," Verdon said.

"Is it as hot?" I replied, referring to Verdon's running commentary on all the 'pouting buttocks' one could see in the statues of Florence.

He smiled and strolled off.

I made my way upstairs with a few friends who scattered once we got inside.

Gradually, I found the room with Donatello's bronze David created from 1430-40. Certainly his buttocks pouted, but more than that, his pinky pointed outward. Nude except for a pair of knee-high boots and a wild hat with a feather, he looked more androgynous than Michelangelo's David, almost as if he were a drag queen. But the work was from 1430 and lived in the gallery at the Bargello. I was mesmerized as I stood there. He wasn't as sexual or sensual as the Sleeping Hermaphrodite sculpture we'd seen at the Galleria Borghese earlier in the day. But there was a lot of drama going on in the piece.

Looking around, I saw a beautiful African woman; she was very tall and standing with a much shorter British-looking man with one blue eye and the other a dilated black.

"That's David Bowie," my friend whispered to me.

"And Iman," I noted, taking a quick glance at the pair. "Don't say anything," I whispered. All of us were looking at the heroic David, trying not to stare at the androgynous David, who refused dominant norms, reminding us we could all be heroes.

"Just turn on with me ..."—the old lyrics passed through my mind as I looked at the light shining from the David statue, feeling touched. We'd all been together through the years, David on the stage, ourselves dancing, watching Bowie show after show in the 1980s, having sex after the shows back in my room, feelings flowing. "Nothing, nothing will keep us together. We can beat them, forever and ever..." Stealing a moment, however fleeting, and soon it was all over. Ziggy was over. The Rock and Rock Suicide had passed. And now we were looking at relics in a museum. But we were very much alive. So, it seemed, was the world. Bowie and Iman left, as did my friends who followed him. I was back alone with Donatello's semi-clothed hero, who stood staring at us in triumph, a different kind of hero than anything I had known, flaunting all his feminine and masculine power, merging in symmetry.

My mind drifted off to the Sleeping Hermaphrodite we'd seen earlier in the day in the Borghese. According to legend, Hermaphrodite was the offspring of Aphrodite and Hermes. The sleeping god reminded us we all struggle with ourselves and few of our male and female selves align at all. We were all estranged from something inside.

"The Platonic ideal," explained Verdon earlier in the day, referring to *The Symposium* and the unification of our male and female selves that only seemed to take place in such works of art.

I walked home from the museum alone. I made my way upstairs, back to the roof in the pensione, where I pulled out my copy of the *l'etranger* and watched the sun set into the hills, the Arno in the distance, reading all afternoon long. My feet were tired. It felt good to sit and stop. These were delicious moments, lovely to be alone.

But none of them lasted too long. There were other amici along the way, friends from school or the trains. We ate and drank wine late into the evening, and read the *Death of Artemnio Cruz* on the train from Rome to Florence, up to Venice where we swam in the Adriatic till dawn, the light shining over all of us making out in the water. Always trains, always novels, and new places to find.

"Siamo forte," my homestay father reminded me in Treviso as we drove through the Italian Alps listening to Verdi's requiem, music blasting from the speakers, both of us singing, no hands on the wheel.

147

We were all strong. Gravity did not matter. Italian cars could handle it. So we careened through the hills, around curves, zigging and zagging. The car seeming to jet off the road, out into the air and back.

Toward the end of the summer, I found myself on my way to Marchello's apartment in Milano. He was our exchange student with us in high school. My friends were all making their way around on the trains, to Ibiza or Paris. I wanted to pause, to get away from people for a minute to think. The long train ride, the hassles with the luggage, the friend we never met up with at the station, the image of the small boy staring at the pornography at the news stand, getting ripped off by the taxi driver—these were all par for the course. The problem was silences: the Sunday mornings alone in August.

When I arrived in Milan, I called for Marchello. Instead, a woman answered.

"Yes, I was just calling to see if anyone was there so I could get in."

"Marchello isn't here, but I am."

Okay, I thought.

"Grazi, I will see you soon. Ciao."

"Ciao."

On my way there, I wondered if this was going to turn out like I was thinking it would. The apartment complex, across from the Palazzo della Judicia, was empty. She was a black woman from New York City, squatting at various apartments as she attempted to get her import/export business off the ground, drifting between work and the summer vacation party circuit.

"It seems like we're both doing the same thing," she observed, lying back on the couch adjacent from me. We passed a hash cigarette back and forth. She would soon leave for India to buy some jewelry and was taking it easy until the trip. I had plans for Berlin and Spain. Between wine, hash and a movie on TV, we were both feeling just fine.

There was nothing going on in town. Milan was dead, so staying at home seemed the best thing to do. The movie was winding down and I was fantasizing about her wrapping her legs around me on the floor, feeling curious, ambitious and hopeful.

"What?" she said, pushing me away after I had leaned over her to make my proposition in my stoned haze. I thought about Chloe warning me that I needed to stop and look into someone's eyes soulfully before making the move. And then she was gone. She went to bed. After apologizing, I went to wash the dishes. About five minutes later, she came into the kitchen.

"How can you wash dishes now?"

"Because I'm stoned," I said. She went to sit down again for more TV.

"I can't sleep. I'm used to staying up until 5:00," she said wistfully, pointing to the TV in the dark. I went to bed up in the loft.

An hour or so later, she called up to me.

"I would climb up to the loft but I'm too fried. I was just in the bed, still awake, wondering what I was doing in bed alone." She paused. "I don't know if that offer still stands, but I was just wondering if you wanted to come down to Marchello's bedroom."

I took her up on the offer. Fooling around with her was weird and sweet. She smelled different from I was used to, but what I was used to was thousands of miles away.

148

It was fun and sensual. For hours, we were at it. I could barely see or feel. A memory of a scene from movie from the late 1970s flashed through my mind. A man who had gone away for his junior year abroad in Paris. Once in bed with a Parisian woman, they were at it for ages. After he had had all he could bear, he stammered something to the effect that beds could also be used for sleeping. The camera panned up to a sleep deprived man staring at the comforter with a body moving under it. After a while, the sex became labor.

Chloe's admonitions dashed by, and then disappeared.

Here I was, in the middle of the night, flies buzzing through the room, having a hard time keeping my head in it, but unlike with Chloe, it didn't matter. It wasn't a matter of being attracted to her, or having thoughts about others doing the same things. The window was open to let in fresh air. A mosquito buzzed close to my ear. The sheets on the bed were dirty so we tried to sleep without them, tossing and turning, a restless night in long hot summer. That first night, trying to sleep was living a lie.

We met up a few more times, passing between trains and the apartment. She was on her way to Lake Cuomo. I toured between Berlin and Austria. I was mesmerized with Vienna, looking at Egon Schiele, Gustav Klimt, Max Beckmann, and Otto Dix paintings.

After looking at art, I wandered into a place that looked like an art deco cabaret, reading about the Soviet leaders abducting Gorbachev in a coup by the last hard liners. While I sat drinking, a woman walked up to me to chat. We talked for what seemed like an hour. She told me her price was the cost of an expensive champagne bottle. At first I demurred. I wasn't there to pay anything, I explained. I had never needed to. She smiled at me and asked again, giving me a wink. And then I started to realize where I was. I found some money for champagne, which we both enjoyed, made it back to her room for a romp, then stumbled home, knowing a line had been crossed from which I could never return.

There are lonely moments—closings and openings on the road. I walked the city and hung out with a girl at the hostel. I made friends everywhere. Some wanted money, most wanted company. There was an adorable black girl from Paris who wanted to make out on the train. Exhausted, we all slept together, chatting, sharing, and recalling our voyages on the trains. A month away from seeing those I cared about, I was encountering a new sensuality, the Arno, books, daydreams, new plotlines. I wrote every day. Back at Marchello's apartment in Milan, the birds chirped outside his seventh-floor bedroom window. I sighed, paused and packed.

I went back to Rome for the next semester. Waiting to meet everyone, I sat in a café outside the Pantheon where a story was taking shape. It began somewhere between the School of Athens, where Plato pointed up and Socrates down, debating the nature of truth. Was it in the heavens or earthly paradise below or in the streets of the city? The layers of Rome unfolded in front of my eyes. Walking through Rome, we passed a busy corner called Largo D'Argentina with Etruscan ruins, Roman relics, a cat sanctuary and moderns darting about; the layers of history were overlapping. Men in lovely suits on scooters zoomed past on every street corner where kids hung out, taking in the scene, much like the Fellini movies. At night, we listened to street musicians and danced outside in the piazza at the campo. We made our way to Siena where we were to spend the rest of the term. There, we picnicked in the Tuscan countryside, lounged, hoped, and listened to jazz in a cavernous café where everyone drank carafes of wine.

Idria, an elderly woman who grew up under Mussolini hosted me, giving me a room with view of the Duomo. During the afternoons I translated all the Lucio Battisti lyrics into English to practice my Italian. At night, we talked about history and pop culture, who this prime minister was and what it was like to grow up during fascism.

"One part saint, another part a devil," she replied when I asked her about Mussolini. She'd seen a thing or two in her days. And she knew how to adapt. She saw me when I got the news from Chloe.

"Trovi un altra," Idria reminded me when Chloe's final Dear John letter arrived, with a shrug of the head. Quoting from Adrienne Rich, Chloe's letter compared men to suckling pigs. I was devastated. "Find another girl," Idria said. History was porous and messy. I was learning that.

All fall long we drank beer after beer at the spoko bar, a dirty dive bar, cats and beer bottles strewn all over the place, before wandering through medieval streets where the cobblestones cemented together hopes and grievances. We talked about a changing Italy. Faced with a tax revolt from the north, the mob had threatened to blow the Uffizi gallery with the Bottacellis. That was this summer. But the grievances ran deep, touching everyone we knew. People talked about the U.S. intervention in the Italian election of 1948 tilting the tide to the right. The Red Brigade bombed the hospital where Marchello was born on the day he left with his mom in 1969. The Communist Party of Italy reformed to the Democratic Party of the Left.

"German writer and statesman Johann Wolfgang von Goethe suggested that history is not about the past and future as much as a story about an ever-flowing present," one of our amiable tour guides pontificated, embellishing as we walked past the Forum on a burning hot day in Rome. It all felt beyond time. The stories were everywhere. I wrote about them, wondering where I would ever fit. Could I somehow be part of this pageant? Looking at the Pantheon, my pen channeled words of ideas, page after page—what would we do, where could we go, how and where the bodies of ideas might fill the public, a first novel taking shape out of the connection and separation among the ruins.

On Halloween, we all dressed up and made our way into the night in Rome, dancing and drinking as long as we could. I was high. Italy was a love affair for me. I found myself smiling in a way I had not since before the Chloe demise. There were so many stories, so much treachery here. Dante exiled from the city he loved; I read about the lives of the artists, imagining their world. Gramsci had rotted in a prison only a few blocks away at the Regina Coeli. Heretic Giordana Bruno had his tongue cut off before he was burned at the stake at Campo dei Fiore. Everyone suffered in some way.

That connection fulfilled me after the loss of Chloe. There was so much more to learn. Here in Rome, I reflected on my life in my home town that had sprung up in the desert where there was so little to no connection to the past. This was the problem back home where people have everything. But few feel a connection to all that came before—to the protests, revolutions, slavery, and genocides—that formed us. Abstracted from history, our alienation was everywhere back home. It was good to be away.

"Good artists borrow, great artists steal," advised Vernon. We are all part of vast anxiety of influence. I had found another. That night, we listened to songs, not worrying about what had happened before, or what would come next as the red holiday lights shone through the December night in Siena.

Exile and the Kingdom

"Jane says, I'm done with Sergio."
-Jane's Addiction

"...every night, when he didn't want to be alone, or to age or die... the madness seizes them and hurls them desperately toward a woman's body ...."
-Albert Camus, *Exile and the Kingdom*

AIDS ripped the life from Freddie Mercury that November, robbing his last breaths before Thanksgiving. I read the news from a tabloid in Siena, seeing his face on a news stand, walking to get a closer look, dismayed and standing in the rain. He had been my hero, his music an emblem of my childhood, playing on Solid Gold on TV right after Elvis died. Freddie inherited that mantle in a twisted, sexually ambivalent way. Years later, an unknown virus was running through his veins, his body coming apart. The paparazzi stalked him, trying to get a glimpse of his wasting body, soon to be a corpse. Reading the news report in Italy, I recalled rushing out to buy my first single ever of "We Are the Champions." It was a song about a collective feeling. We were all the champions, even as we suffered and grew. The black and white Bowie and Queen video offered a telling confession: "*It's a terror to know what this world is about, watching some good friends scream, 'let me out.'*" That once mighty life force had been unable to get out alive. I hadn't known he was singing about himself. But he was also singing about all of us. I was beginning to understand what he was feeling..

I caught a flight back to the States in December. I had thought I was going to go back east, but that didn't work out. Like Dad, after he was fired from Princeton, I felt expelled from the east. So I drove west past Duncanville where Chloe was making plans for a new year, unencumbered.

We got a coffee but she ended up running away. I got back in the car, watching as she said goodbye, turning away fast, covering her eyes. And I left, knowing I'd never live in Dallas again. Mom had sold the house with the greenway in the back. Dad was moving up to Chicago. There was no other place to be. So I drove, looking back at the city. The sun reflected off the skyscrapers of downtown as I drove past. Now, it was in the rearview mirror. Too many memories there, so I kept on driving.

I drove west to New Mexico and listened to Freddie and Queen and Jerry Jeff Walker from a tape of the record Tom had given me for my birthday six years prior. I didn't stop for hours. When I finally stepped out to go pee and light a cigarette, I stared at a silhouette of mesas looming in the distance, amidst a red sky and a pastel sunset stretching as far as I could see. All night I drove west through the desert, exploring the distance between the sky and the horizon. It was starting to feel like the most beautiful thing I could imagine. I was on my way to the other side of something. Los Angeles was only a few hours away. Exile was just beginning.

It would be a long time before it felt okay.

I arrived back at school for the final semester of college in a peculiar state. On the one hand, it felt like a new kind of homecoming. Classes and old professors were familiar and engaging. I was working on my novel and thinking about the history of ideas. But it felt strange.

There would be other friends. Still, the manic twenty-four months with Chloe cast a shadow on all my other interactions. I couldn't stop thinking of her. That would become an occupational hazard, thinking of her, being with them, connected by the body, separated by the spirit.

At night, I experimented with ways of sleeping badly. The dreams started becoming more vivid. Chloe and a Minotaur made their ways through labyrinthine subway corridors, or infinite hotel hallways, floors and bedrooms, red lights lingering in the distance, sex in a hotel room with strangers, others, sounds. I was always just an observer. I saw Theseus's father Aegeus hurling himself into the water, and Ariadne's incessant weeping. I was alone, watching as others lived—connecting, separating, falling out of windows, off buildings, enduring earthquakes, voices tumbling through the air in a word soup of nonsense, an empty bedroom, up all night awake, alone. Lying in bed, I could not move, could not say a word. I imagined I was one of the players in Fellini's *Satyricon*. Over and over I had that recurring Jorge Luis Borges dream, but there was no way out: "The road kept descending and branching off, through meadows misty in the twilight. A high-pitched and almost syllabic music kept coming and going, moving with the breeze, blurred by the leaves and by distance." Eventually, I sought a little help to navigate between the concrete jungle and the garden of forking paths.

Midway through the semester, I stumbled into a therapist's office, still reeling. The counselor listened and gave me all the usual suggestions. ("Get in touch with your anger," etc.) I was having none of it. After a few sessions, it was the young doctor's prognosis that I had not really allowed myself to let go of her, or to really say goodbye, and until I did so these problems would persist. For our last session, he suggested a role-play exercise, in which I would say everything I'd say to her if we were to permanently say goodbye.

I closed my eyes and the room became hot. Sitting there, I imagined looking at the sprawling, hot Texas sky. "Thank you for the summer," I started to mumble and then just saw myself. I was in the car, on a trip to Austin from Dallas in the summer of 1989. And then I was alone. But the car with the two of us kept fading away in the distance. I was still driving after that mirage in the distance, oil disappearing on the horizon, still unable to get close to it. I could never touch it, but I kept chasing it. Then I flashed back to our house in Dallas, images of workmen putting mom's stuff into a moving van. Mom crying and walking away from a funeral, meeting Dad, and driving with Tom through the Middle East; Dad having a stroke, his plane being pulled down and lying alone in a hospital bed with tubes coming out of his chest, nose and arms. Mom crying, years and years of pain, the two of them screaming at each other before they called it quits that summer after a quarter-century of marriage. I saw my brother walking by mumbling down the street, talking to himself. I saw him as I was driving by when I was going out. I had been so wrapped up in Chloe. I didn't begin to think about the divorce. I had other things, other music to dance to. Chloe allowed me to distract myself, at least for a bit, as I grew in another direction. When my grandma died, she'd comforted and soothed me, became my family, substituting one bond for another. And now that had passed like sand through grasping fingers. I never really talked with my brothers about what happened, to ask how they were coping, not at the time, not ever. Still it all unraveled, the wreckage of

152

a separation with my nuclear family, severed ties to a city and community, revealing themselves bit by bit. Wiping my face, I rubbed my wet eyes. The therapist was still there in the room looking at me, completely quiet. He handed me a tissue.

"You okay?" he asked.

"Yeah," I replied, wiping off my face. "I guess so."

"Good," he said and smiled.

I sighed a big sigh.

"You feel any better?"

"A little. Fuck."

I couldn't go back. I didn't want to. I had to find my own life far away from that Texas sky on this westernmost expanse of our continent.

Closings and Openings in the City of Quartz

My first weekend back in Los Angeles, someone in my dorm hosted an evening film screening of *Blade Runner* on the roof with the desert in the distance. It was maybe the most beautiful film I knew. The world seemed like Los Angeles.

"I've seen things you people wouldn't believe," Rutger Hauer mused standing in the rain in the final soliloquy. "Attack ships on fire off the shoulder of Orion. I watched C-beams glitter in the dark near the Tannhauser Gate. All those moments will be lost in time, like tears in the rain. Time to die."

But it wasn't time to die. It was time to explore this coast, its myths, and collective daydreams. I hiked through Joshua Tree, bodysurfed on Venice beach, dug into the history, and swam the cultural currents of Los Angeles.

One of my old roommates gave me a copy of *City of Quartz* that winter. It had never been that easy to be here. But that was beginning to change. Looking at the flowers growing, I grew to love the desert and its expansiveness. Driving through the freeways listening to NWA's "Straight Outta Compton," taking in the moon over the desert and the postmodern hotels, shopping malls, and corporate offices made it easy to feel both freedom and a sense of foreboding. It felt like empty space, extending hundreds of years into its Mexican past beyond anything we could know and then out into the horizon. The desert was like a church, the city like a strip mall—cut off from itself. Driving here, one automatically became a part of a clash between what the landscape had been, its skies and vistas and the exponentially expanding shopping complexes of urban sprawl, between the mythic desert and the "massively reproduced spatial apartheid" Davis saw. "The designers of malls and pseudo-public space attack the crowd by homogenizing," wrote Davis. "Architectural and semiotic barriers to filter out 'undesirables'... enclose the mass that remains, directing its circulation with behaviorist ferocity..."

With stimuli coming from all sides, the city felt both connected and ever isolated, the affluent in their sports cars and the poor on the margins rarely crossing, with freeways extended across fault lines between the Pacific and North tectonic plates.

"Don't find yourself in South Central," a senior warned us freshman year when we told him we were going dancing there. "Keep on driving."

All through college, we zoomed through, passing between the neighborhoods, to drop in for raves or parties, dancing in a crumbling warehouse with a hole in the ceiling, open to the sky, people beating

154

trash cans, high on something in the punch, as the rain poured in and our bodies shook. Everyone seemed to be drawn to that feeling. We were all dreaming, even when we were surfing, or driving, or swimming, or smoking, or exploring the desert. On the way home, we just drove. Once our car got hit by another car in South Central. We did not stop. We just kept on moving.

Driving, I thought about one of my favorite Los Angeles punk bands the Germs whose singer suffered perhaps the saddest of all rock 'n roll suicides. I had picked up their record at VVV records years before in Dallas. Their singer Darby was a Bowie fan. "Five Years" was his favorite Bowie song. Back in 1975, he started talking about that song. Darby would say he had just had five years to live, just like the song. Crash infused his life with a messianic death wish. Yet, instead of fashioning himself as Christ on a cross as Hibiscus of the Cockettes had, Crash built his life around Bowie's glam fantasy of Ziggy Stardust.

"That's how he had all those girls weeping onstage, 'cause they knew he was gonna die," Geza X, a friend and member of the Mummymen (another LA band at the time) recalled.

The final Germs gig was the first week of December, 1980. After most Germs shows, no matter how terrible, almost everyone in attendance would converge at the Oki Dog, a fast food restaurant on Santa Monica and Vista Ave. There, Germs fans hung out, sometimes sharing "Germs Burns"——putting cigarettes out on each other's arms. And this gig was supposed to be no different. But it was a rainy night and no one really made it except Darby. He despaired as he watched his scene and the connection to others seeming to fade away.

"Darby and I had been doing consistent drugs for about a month and a half," remembered Casey Cola. "We'd really been trying to put our lives together. Everything was fucking up with our plan... We looked around the courtyard of the Hong Kong and said, 'Man, fuck it, let's do it. Fuck this shit, it's not gonna ever change, it's not gonna get better. We're going to be doing this same shit next year.' We talked about whether we could get enough drugs, and that if he hit me up, would it be murder? I can't do it myself because I have a manual dexterity problem. We were each asking, 'Are you sure? Are you sure?' He didn't coerce me and I didn't talk him into it. We never talked each other into anything. I didn't make Darby die. I got water and a spoon. He wrote a note, which he didn't show me, but which I think said, 'My life, my leather, and my love goes to Bosco.' He hit me up first and said, 'Are you okay?' and I said, 'Um, yeah.' He put his hand at the small of my back and he said, 'Just hold it, just stay there, just wait for me, okay?' He held me up for a second, then he hit a vein and laid himself against the wall and pulled me into him. It was almost like he forgot what we were doing, and he goes, 'Wait a minute.' And he kissed me and said, 'Well, bye.'" Crash died the morning of December 7, 1980.

The next day, John Lennon was shot outside the Dakota in New York, a leader of the life on a fringe tumbling through an abyss, perhaps crossing paths with a man who had conceptualized political struggle as a battle between the Blue Meanies and those who hoped to sing. Crash reflected on his struggle against monoculture and jettisoned himself out of this world. The story got me through the odd winter days in Los Angeles.

I listened to Jane's Addiction a lot, daydreaming and writing my novel throughout the semester. Barry Sanders, my old prof from freshman year, was there to guide me, encouraging draft after draft.

By a strange twist of fate, Grant was in Los Angeles taking classes. He'd graduated from Wesleyan and was making plans for law school.

"It's great to see you here," he said when I dropped by the apartment he was renting with his sister. "But to be honest, I'm kind of surprised. I thought you'd be in your room writing an 'Ode to Chloe.'"

"Fuck off," I said with a smile.

Grant was right; I needed to lighten up.

I studied at Claremont and came out to Melrose to visit Grant and his sister whenever I could. He planned to go back to Austin to study at the University of Texas. His father was a lawyer. It would be the first time they were in the same state in years.

In the meantime, we were in Los Angeles together, watching the Democratic primaries and cheering for Jerry Brown, enjoying the helter-skelter of the city——its art, sushi restaurants, Mexican food, beaches, and the culture we were discovering together.

I found myself dating any number of women at any given time——one, a freshman, another a junior, and a senior graduating with me. My favorite was a lanky junior who idealized LBJ and Freddie Mercury. Her name was Lucy, and we called her LBJ Lucy, or just Lucy. She wanted to go to law school. We used to talk about Great Society social programs as foreplay. Senior year made for fun, grungy, LA terrain. A number of my classmates had traveled abroad for the previous year; some in Nepal, and many in Russia, where accidents seemed to follow them everywhere through the post-Soviet landscape. Lucy was planning to be a civil rights attorney like Thurgood Marshall, LBJ's famous pick to the courts, who had only died the year before. She had long blonde hair, and wore bell-bottom jeans and was often chain-smoking. I adored her oddball reverence for the past. We hung out drinking in her dorm room, listening to Queen and Prince tapes. Through the windows, we took in a view of the outback on the edge of the Southern California desert, full of indigenous plants and wildlife.

"Did you see the way Freddie kissed his thumb and greeted the crowd in Radio Ga-Ga at Live AID?" she asked, gesturing in awe.

"My favorite scene in the whole show."

"That thumb kiss is the epitome of not just the performance but all that is great and joyful in the world. That's always when I start crying or cheering, depending on my mood. I love when he starts singing and the crowd is singing so loud and he gets that look of 'Yep, they are going to eat out of my hand,' but it's nothing compared to the thumb kiss. The whole performance was timed down to the second, but you know that was spontaneous...."

Other days, she was in love with Prince. Her favorite song was "Darling Nikki"——an homage to masturbation. And of course, there was LBJ, from my home state.

"When Kennedy died he could have done anything in the world. So LBJ used all his political capital to pass the Civil Rights Act. Who else wields their power like that?" she said in awe.

We were on and off. But after a few nights of staying over in a row, things started getting uncomfortable. We went out for an opera, but the vibe was too weird, too much like a date. She could not stand the quiet. Sensing the discomfort, I didn't call or come back for more. She came back a few days later, a cigarette in her shaking fingers. She'd been taking pills all night. She could not get over her disgust with our odd discomfort with each other or the opera. She thought I was pushing her to the side. But I really did not care. We hung out for a bit, chatting, but she was too high on mini-thins or god knows what. We both smelled like cigarettes.

To break the tension, we started to fool around. She went to the bathroom for a second. While she was there, I decided I could not really deal with this. I had no desire or interest; there were too many problems and pills, too little communication. I did not want to be sleeping with her.

"You have to go," I said to her when she came out. "You have to go. Please." Things got a little hairy at this point. She was shocked and surprised, and said she would not leave. We went back and forth. I threatened to call campus security. That didn't go that well. And finally I walked her to her room and she became very real.

"Oh Cab, don't do this to me."

"Goodnight, Lucy."

Lucy and I got it back together, chatting again over the next few weeks, more as comrades than anything. But I never quite understood her anxiety.

There were others that semester. My old roommate Hank had just gotten back from a semester in Nepal. While we were drinking beer at a party, he introduced me to a woman, Tessa, with frizzy brown hair who had also been in his program.

"Hi, Tessa," I greeted her, chatting about Nepal and how the program compared to my Italy experience.

"How was that?" she asked.

"We had picnics in the hills of Tuscany. And got credit for drinking wine and exploring the history of Italy."

Tessa looked away.

"Excuse me," she said, walking up to greet another friend.

"She's kind of cute," I whispered to Hank when she left.

"She's not a good person. She made one of the people in our program cry for not being culturally sensitive enough. She's super, super PC," Hank said. Hank was one part Jerry Garcia wannabe, and another part anthropology Carlos Castaneda groupie, and he lost respect for anyone who did not laugh. That included Tessa.

Tessa walked back and greeted Hank. Her earthy smile and brown hair impressed me. They talked about their year in Nepal. I immediately wanted to sleep with Tessa. She went to Pomona and was active with the campus activist community.

I didn't see her again for a week until we ran into each other at the Jenny Holtzer show at the college. The gallery was filled from floor to ceiling all the way around with one-square-foot pieces with words and phrases written inside. Tessa and I ended up walking through the whole show together. "LADIES, SOMEONE WANTS TO TAKE A PAIR OF SCISSORS AND CUT A HOLE IN THE MIDDLE OF YOU," one of the squares screamed out.

"The signs and messages circling us come at you everywhere we look," I said, hoping not to sound too ridiculous while conveying my awe at the work.

Tessa and I walked, looking and chatting. I ended up getting her number afterward. She was a bit of a crunchy granola type, not much for style or fashion beyond jeans and a sweater. Her long, curly brunette hair covered her eyes and a smile just beneath. She was born in a commune in the rural Northern Californian town of Sebastopol and her father left her mother when she was four. She seemed to harbor resentment toward men but also had an interest. There was a wedge there that seemed intriguing. She has had gone to high school in Paris and had acquired a working understanding of French, Spanish, and Nepali through her travels. She seemed the perfect sort of person to help me create some distance between the present moment and the Chloe past. All the outside elements were there—the intelligence, the possibility, and perchance the willingness.

I confessed my attraction inside the library.

She looked at me for a few seconds.

"Then what should we do?" she finally responded.

I looked at her, smiled, and gestured back to the dorms.

"I'll come by your room when I'm done with work."

We said goodnight and I left the stacks of Honald Library.

She knocked on my door a quarter past midnight that night. Coltrane was playing "Giant Steps" again. She showed me past journal entries she had written over the last couple weeks of knowing me, which included a few references to myself. Both of us sat on the bed talking, thigh to thigh, thumbing through the journal not knowing what to do for the next 15 minutes. We slept together that night and a few other nights that week. Those first few nights were full of boisterous sex and connections, orgasms, and fun.

Our small affair grew out of those conversations. But, as was the pattern, it grew into something messier, including obligations to call, to say hello, to listen and talk about language.

"I don't like to use that word," she said to me over and over again, replacing feelings of connectedness with separation. During one of our chats over the following week, she corrected me when I explained something in terms of "girls" instead of "women."

"That's women," she explained. The conversation waned. My point seemed less important anyway. My crusade to present myself as a guy outside of the world of generalizations about men was not working.

Later in the week, we went to see a movie and ran into Janet Brodie, a professor who was teaching a history class I was taking. Tessa had taken a class of hers the previous semester. I had hoped to get out of her class.

"She teaches with an agenda," I kvetched. "You have to be on her side of things. It's not an open conversation." Tessa gave me one of the strangest looks and we went our separate ways. Lukewarm feelings took over.

The excitement was fading and I didn't know why. Something did not feel right. I wasn't enjoying lying close to her. She usually didn't shower much. Her clothes smelled like patchouli oil—the fragrance for the counterculture set. One night the following week after a mediocre effort at sex, I watched Tessa with a somewhat despairing expression on her face as she pulled on her dark purple cotton underwear. They kind of looked like the underwear a great aunt might wear. A light went off in my head.

I had had enough of hippies. I wanted women who would shower and occasionally shave their underarms. Did that make me a pig? Probably. If that meant that future lovers might not be Grateful Dead tour groupies or Sandinistas, so be it. I didn't have to endure the constant stench of patchouli oil or body sweat if I didn't want to. No one was making me.

"Why not just take a shower with her?" asked Grant's older sister that spring, as I kvetched about things.

"It might be the scent. But it might also be the whole package," I lamented.

As much as anything, Tessa and I were suffering from conflict of perspectives. Part of our initial dynamic involved a sharing of information and ideas in an expanding dialogue. Tessa, having lived in Guatemala and Nepal, told me about her experience and understandings of the third world while I shared my experience of the U.S., of the South, and the Northeast with her. Her experience in the world allowed her to understand the ways U.S. policy influenced developing nations, while I viewed the U.S. in terms of the wonderful people I had known throughout the country—poets in New York, farmers in Georgia, musicians in New Orleans, clubgoers in Dallas, storytellers in Tennessee. But all Tessa saw was U.S. imperialism, not a "holy America." I knew it was a wreck. But there was so much more to it.

"I remember a guy in my Political and Cultural Geography class saying he could not believe U.S.-sponsored companies would run sweatshops in the maquiladora factories in Mexico," I said sympathizing with Tessa, trying to sound down with the cause.

But I was slipping away from her, feeling less and less comfortable as the relationship metamorphosed and tiresome feelings took over.

So, I spent more and more time at Grant's. We explored more of the art and whimsy of the place. I laughed when I walked into the Los Angeles Museum of Contemporary Art and saw a mannequin with pubic hair at the exhibition, "Helter Skelter: LA Art in the 1990s." The sprawling show pointed to an ephemeral city of multiple narratives; border crossings, aesthetics of longing, brightness, a subcurrent of darkness, sexuality, pop culture, alienation, police violence, hallucinations, natural disasters, voices from the South clashing with this land of shopping malls and plastic, suicidal thoughts meandering throughout an estranged, ever-expanding geography.

"I can never drive my car over a bridge without thinking of suicide," wrote Bukowski, who traced his stories throughout the city. "I can never look at a lake or an ocean without thinking of suicide." That feeling of abyss grasped at us here. "We went up the Harbor freeway north and then we cut onto the San Diego freeway north," Bukowski said. "I hated the San Diego freeway. It's always jammed." This was everyone's angst here, kids screaming all night long when we wanted to sleep—the lunacy of sex; the isolation of people not quite able to connect. Driving, we were always stuck, cars and people, pollution, smog, consumption, rush hour after rush hour, in repetition with little momentum forward, then repeating all the joys and sorrows of our life over and over again. The city left us separate, with the same impulse toward annihilation repeating itself over and over again anew. We all lived in a bubble here. Tessa saw something else and that was more than I wanted to see. I was not moving forward. We all had stories here of taking part in an expanding capitalist shopping daydream, leaving us separate from nature and each other. But there were other stories. There were people breaking through to the other side. And people realizing this was as far as they could go; this was the end.

The Call

"This is the end, beautiful friend
This is the end, my only friend, the end
Of our elaborate plans, the end
Of everything that stands, the end
No safety or surprise, the end
I'll never look into your eyes, again"
-The Doors
"The End"

Toward the end of April, I got a call from Grant that something had happened.

Something bad had happened? Grant did not talk like that. I got in the car and drove West from Claremont to LA, thinking about our years of knowing each other, playing, and sleeping over at each other's houses. His Dad was there supporting us, taking us to the movies, cracking a joke in carpool. He was there when we lost the conference championship games freshman and sophomore years in high school, holding us after all those years of effort when we just could not win it, putting in all we had and still losing. Somehow it felt like the end.

When I arrived, Grant and his sister were sitting toasting with a bottle of champagne between them.

"What happened?"

"He killed himself," they whispered.

Their dad was gone. After a couple of divorces, he decided to let it go.

"All his paperwork was laid out there, neatly on the desk," Grant explained. "Insurance, wills, all that was left of him." They were drinking together, not too many tears, just numb. It was a chilling moment, and a prelude to a world where losing each other would be everything. It was all we would know.

"I'm losing you," people said in Los Angeles, losing contact on cell phones. We all were losing something here. We felt that anxiety every day, with wildfires and floods and a city that seemed to erect freeways separating sprawling bodies of people whirling around.

None of us knew how to react.

"Are you okay?" I asked.

"Yes," they said, looking in shock.

"Really?" I asked.

"What are we supposed to do?"

We talked about his life and theirs, his marriage to their mother and the betrayal which led to their divorce, his next marriage, and the problems which ensued.

"He used to sit up reading all night," Grant recalled.

"By the time your mother got remarried, it felt like he was on the outside," I followed.

"He was," Grant followed. "We were furious at him."

161

"Did you see him any during your college years?" I asked.

"Not really, not at all."

"We were still pissed at him," confessed Grant's sister.

"That was the plan this summer. To go back to Dallas and talk law school with him," Grant continued, his voice trailing off, looking out into the distance.

We talked about what happens when life turns sour, relationships fade, and kids move on without us.

"His life caved in on itself," Grant lamented. "And he could not get out."

"Here's to him," I looked to Grant, tears starting to well in my eyes. I looked away. We all toasted him.

They left for the funeral the next day.

While Grant and I were numb and unsure how to grieve the death of his father, news of the Rodney King verdict came crashing in on everyone. All spring, we followed the case of the police officers who had beaten Rodney King. Everyone had always told us don't drive through South Central. And so we did not. But the riots brought South Central to us, screaming out loud: "This is not okay! Rent's too much. This city is killing us! Its all too much! Fuck the police!" A divided city will burn. The racism lurking ate away at the body of the city with each day. We all saw videos of King lying face down on the pavement.

There were only a few more weeks to go in school. We'd been studying Vietnam in Brodie's U.S. History class, reflecting on people being left behind and veterans it took years to bring back. But it was hard to connect that history of racism with 1992 Los Angeles. But maybe we should have. Why were we there? Why was that policy? Why were payoffs, beatings, and brutality common practice in Los Angeles? An open and shut case, we thought at first. Yet, things started looking odd about the trial of the policemen accused of beating Rodney King. It was moved to Simi Valley in a suburban courtroom away from where King had been beaten. There, ten white people, one Hispanic, and one Filipino woman—no black jurors—found the police had done nothing wrong. The ensuing acquittals invoked a stinging sense of betrayal. Only 13 years prior in 1979, the San Francisco White Night Riots occurred when a jury that lacked a single gay person gave former policeman Dan White a slap on the wrist for the murders of Mayor George Moscone and Councilman Harvey Milk. Citizens in 1979 and 1992 in San Francisco and LA had maintained faith that criminal justice would do the right thing.

The day of the verdict, a palpable disgust filled the air. But instead of sitting with the feeling, people acted up, as they had in 1965 in Watts—lighting fires, throwing trash cans, attacking and rescuing each other. It was beautiful and horrible to watch the smoke rise in the sky in the distance after the city began to blaze.

"It's been 400 years, baby! 400 years!!!" yelled a fellow student, an African American, singing and chanting as all the dorms emptied. We hit the streets. I had never seen anything like it before. All the libraries emptied. The administrative buildings emptied. The dining hall emptied. Students from all five colleges, the grad school, the faculty and staff—everyone—walked into the streets, screaming, blocking cars, honking, chanting for justice into the sunset, whatever that meant. The cathartic plea spoke to a collective disgust and hope for something else that we could find together. Looking out, we saw a cancer

162

at the center of Los Angeles that could not be neglected without more riots. The inequality of Los Angeles could no longer be ignored. There had to be an alternative to the state-programmed default of gang life, drugs, violence, and prisons, but we did not know what it could be. There had to be more than a warfare state characterized by mass incarceration, HIV/AIDS, police corruption, and brutality.

The headline from the April 30, 1992 front page headline of the *L.A. Times* said: "All 4 in King Beating Acquitted, Violence Follows Verdicts; Guards Called Out." The headline was accompanied by photos of relieved baby-faced police officers hugging one another to the left, and rioters against a backdrop of flames to the right. We all attempted to grasp the significance of the unrest erupting across the city. Marches, rallies, riots, fires, looting, speak-outs, and more marches—it went on like that for days. After students were ripped out of their cars during the riots, the campus was quarantined. With the LA riots, America's shadow reared her ugly head. I wasn't prepared for what I saw, with people tearing at each other, beating each other, flames erupting through the streets.

We all reflected on the history. *It's been 400 hundred years, baby*, my friend's words echoed through my mind. There are moments when it's possible to actually see. All of America is built on slavery. Marching, I thought of Mom and Dad and what they became: a detached lawyer who'd never gotten to the business of social justice he said he aspired to in college, and a museum docent who did not want to talk about so many things. The cultural amnesia was everywhere. It was in LA. It was back home. The South turned away from countless inconvenient histories. They profited from the slavery; free labor built the plantations and picked the cotton that created capital that got reinvested in corporations, in the stock market, that supported the KKK while electing presidents who would decimate the Black Panthers and undermine the legacy of the first black president. That's all they wanted to do. They hated that black man. From Ramparts to Watts, LA was the festering boil of racism and it was especially apparent in South Central LA. Year in and year out, corruption rotted within the LAPD, with payoffs, cops selling drugs, planting evidence, and beating those such as King. Racism that the South never atoned for or tried to rid itself of after Reconstruction that meandered further and further west, inspiring the Chinese Exclusion Act of 1882, the Manzanar camp, one immigrant backlash after another, and festering inequality. Nope, I was not going to be a lawyer like Dad, justifying this stuff. This country was built on a sickness that we never reconciled or tried to understand or address. Looking at the flames, I knew I had to remove myself from the system that supported it, that reproduced it, somehow. I could see this thing and I could not live with it anymore. Maybe my godfather, maybe Grant's dad couldn't either. Darby couldn't.

Looking at LA, we could see people breaking windows and stealing diapers. People on the fringes don't have a right to privilege, to water, to freedom. So they riot. History felt alive as it had never felt in my life. I had always seen civil disruptions as things that happened somewhere else—in Prague in 1989, in Chicago in 1968—not on my campus, not in 1992. Something was changing in the world and in me as the riots festered.

"There are riot cops down the streets here in Beverly Hills," Grant said in awe when he got back from the funeral. Grant and his sister were in the air from LAX to Dallas when the riots started and watched the news on TV the whole week. Armed police took over as they arrived home, as the sickness of the city exploded for everyone to see.

"After burying Dad, we returned to see the aftermath. I remember making the turn in a cab back to LAX into Beverly Hills. The Chevron station a half block from our apartment was torched to the ground. Not a single sign of unrest anywhere else on the whole block. Just the gutted and blackened mess of the gas station that had been run by a very friendly and fiery patriotic family of immigrants from Iran, a surreal and poignant image."

"The riots changed Los Angeles," I said.

"And us," he responded. I nodded in agreement. Grant paused, thinking about his Dad and the Helter Skelter of that whole spring: "We just keep soldiering on, my friend. We, the Generation X, had it strange and rough from the beginning. We are used to the deconstruction and chaos of the post-World War II America unraveling. It's been happening our whole lives."

Leaving Los Angeles after graduation, I drove through Mount Baldy one more time, thinking about Grant's dad, the communities I had left behind, my friends who had already left, letting them go, the riot, fire burning on the horizon, and a world I was moving towards, catapulting me into someplace new. The exercises in loss would be many in the years to come. Driving through the desert, I saw the road as a liminal space, opening me up to experience a vast collective daydream up the road on Highway One.

Part Four

Down and Out
in San Francisco

New Cycles and a Critical Mass

"angel headed hipsters burning for the ancient heavenly connection to the starry dynamo in the machinery of night"

-Allen Ginsberg, *Howl*, 1956

Stories are always moving in San Francisco. That's what the city is all about—people arriving, disrobing the old, revising, and starting new narratives. I came to San Francisco in May of 1992 with a romance for the city that lasted about a week. The angel-headed hipsters I saw were passed out in the park. Poverty was everywhere. Most of the memoirs of the beats celebrated a down and out, oddball, eccentric feeling of the city. The myth was it was a place where you got laid, robbed, high, met your best friend, and joined a commune the first day, not necessarily in that order.

Even Allen Ginsberg admitted things could get a little messy in this experiment in living. Dating queer performer Hibiscus, then a member of the anarchist drag collective the Cockettes in the 1970s, he became all too familiar with the sticky trails. "I know his bed was a little gritty because he had a lot of it. And it was difficult to sleep on the sheets because there was this sort of like difficult glitter stuff there. And it was always in our lips and in our buttholes. You know it was always around. You couldn't quite get it out."

I had two roommates—my old buddy Andy from Texas, and his old college roommate, although he soon moved out. We lived in the Haight, only a block from the apartment where Dad had lived almost four decades prior. Temping or waiting tables, few of us took getting jobs or starting careers very seriously. There were too many adventures to be had. The city was teeming with friends, popping into town, going out for drinks, meeting for coffee, hanging out, anything but to think about career.

When I asked my Dad about his days in the city during the Beat years of the mid-1950s, he didn't have too much that he could recall. "Mostly I was broke," he confessed. Dad was part of a crowd in postwar San Francisco—poets who dropped out of school and drifted westward, inspiring a new movement of ideas. Over and over, we read through *Howl* together, taking it apart. The Beats helped Dad see that streets and minds could be filled with words, creating an alchemy of nonsensical verse to help us reject an ugly materialistic Moloch seeping the life from America, tracing another more authentic way of being. It transformed his life. But as soon as he arrived, he made his way back East, in a pattern that repeated itself anew again and again through the schizophrenia of his life story and its countless contradictions. Still, he always came back. Reading Beat poetry, driving up and down the Pacific Coast Highway, staying in cheap hotels, watching waves crash on the cliffs, and walking through the city streets of San Francisco, we talked and talked and life took a new cycle. As soon as he came, he was gone.

But the past was hard to shake.

Lucy and I had been on and off throughout the term. But one thing remained after I left L.A., the crabs I brought with me after our evenings of fun. They seemed to burrow themselves into every corner of our apartment, which I had to fumigate and clean. It took all summer to get that straightened out.

The dynamic extended beyond the physical ecosystem of the apartment. Having dumped and been dumped, a dry spell ensued and would not quit. Still, I fought the furies, struggling to avoid what felt like my fate. I went through cycle after cycle. The high school and college cycles were over but their memories lingered. The San Francisco pattern would not be much different. But other afflictions followed.

We all wanted to be writers or poets. I found my first girlfriend in San Francisco over a talk about *Anna Karenina*, between beers in the Haight, and a few nights in North Beach. The whole city was beat. Chris and I connected through a bigger story of literature and hope, linking our southern roots with this new city. She grew up reading and chatting with her father about the South. She lived in the Tenderloin with three roommates, Mimi, Trish, and Brad, who had just graduated from Berkeley. I walked by the massage parlors and hustler bars on the way to her place, wondering about everything that went on in this new town.

"Look at the pouting buttocks," our professor, Timothy Verdon, used to comment, looking at the Donatello; Chris paraphrased him, recalling our days in Florence in college, not quite overlapping, but close enough. We ran around all summer and fall. Nothing much was going to come of the romance. I was chasing Chloe and she was not it. But I kept coming around, hanging out with her and her roommates, chatting, watching *Beverly Hills 90210* episodes, and gossiping about our temp jobs.

"A legal secretary took me out last night," I confessed between commercials. "She was pretty cute at work. Her boss had given her a gift certificate for one of the swanky restaurants in the financial district, the Tadich Grill on California Street. I would never go there on my own. So, we drank a lot of wine and she took me home."

"So, what happened?" Mimi and Chris asked.

"Well, I knew she was older. And I thought it was cute. When she asked me home, I said yes to be polite. On our way there, I started having apprehensions. As soon as I walked in the door, I knew I needed to leave. The whole place smelled old. I thought I was dating Jacqueline Bisset. Once she got undressed, it turns out I was with Maude," I confessed, laughing. "Everyone loves *Harold and Maude*. But not all of us have the courage of Harold."

"Cab!" they screamed, laughing.

"I tried. I really tried. And now I can't shake the memory. Memory burn."

"Memory burn!!!" they roared.

I wouldn't live down that night for the next three years. It set the precedent. It was going to be more fun chatting with my buddies about the ridiculous dating world of San Francisco than most of the dates themselves.

The next Friday, the temp job told me they no longer needed my services. Temp jobs were like that. And it was ok. The manager of the copy center where I worked made too many dick jokes, speculating about the anatomy of several of the guys working there, including myself. "Six or seven, inches," he whispered, demonstrating with his hands to his friends. So I was unemployed once again. But this time, I was less afraid of the prospects. I wandered home through the financial district. Something like a hundred bike messengers were hanging out, their piercings and tattoos out there for everyone. I asked what was going on.

"Critical Mass!" they said, looking tough in their messenger gear.

"What's that?"

"Critical Mass is a monthly mass bicycle ride that takes place on the last Friday of each month," explained a man named Chris. "We started it a few months ago to increase the visibility of bicyclists and reclaim public space by making social use of the streets on a regular basis."

"How's it work?" I asked.

"Usually after work, we ride home, dodging the cars. But once a month, we ride together. The streets are ruled by bikes, not cars. You'll have to join us to find out."

Everyone was meeting across Market Street.

"It's an experiment in prefigurative community organizing," said Greg, a young sociology student, just out of Brown University, who was editing *Socialist Review*. "Through each ride, we create the world we want to see." He explained how it worked. "On a typical Friday evening, as work lets out, people mill about. A handful of flyers circulate proposing a route. Eventually, there's a general drift down Market Street, and two thousand or so cyclists completely occupy the major downtown street right in the middle of rush hour."

We were walking with a few of his friends, including another writer for the *Socialist Review* and *SF Weekly*.

"What do you write about?" I asked.

"I just finished a story about undercover infiltration of the religious right for the *SF Weekly*," Leslie explained. She was punk-looking but seemed super smart. "I'm writing a book about the history of the direct-action movement in the U.S. It ought to be out next year."

"Cool. I can't wait to read it," I said, trying to sound like I knew what I was talking about. I didn't even know people wrote about such things. But everyone was arriving and cheering each other. There was another cyclist who had just gotten out of a psych ward and was starting an organization for others going through that.

"You should ride with us," noted Sasha and Brad, who had just arrived after tree sitting in Oregon, gesturing to a bike share the cyclists had created.

"Really?"

"I found it in the trash and just fixed the tire. Just give the bike to someone else when you are done," noted Brad.

"Thanks."

Looking around at this group of crusty cyclists, bike messengers, scenesters, and tree sitters, I felt like I was actually part of this city, instead of hearing about how great everything was a quarter century prior, when the Grateful Dead were still the house band on the Haight. So much of the time, it felt like all we were left with were the jittery, strung out remains, with homeless kids sleeping on the sidewalks. This cavalcade of cyclists felt alive, occupying the entire street for blocks. As we rode, cars seemed impatient trying to edge into the crowd where individual cyclists might "cork" an intersection by blocking the front car with their own bike so others could go through. Most drivers waited in good humor. Some grew angry or frustrated.

The police asked where the ride was going. But no one really knew.

"This is a leaderless movement," said Chris.

"We follow a different path every month," explained Brad. "Sometimes riders split up and regroup, and end up somewhere, or drift off for a drink or an after-party."

Rather than going straight down Market Street, the cyclists turned left on a side street and stayed away from rush-hour traffic. The police started to push riders off Market Street. As people started out from the plaza, some turned left off of Market Street. But just behind them, another group did not turn off. They continued up Market Street. More followed and found themselves, exhilarated, beyond the police, with Market Street theirs.

"Whose streets? Our Streets!" cyclists screamed, in joyous defiance.

A few blocks later, the riders who'd turned left, joined the larger ride, making their way through green, then yellow, then red lights, hundreds riding, ringing their bells, few even paused. But the police stopped one straggler at the end, giving him a ticket and confiscating his bike. Cyclists surrounded them chanting: "Give it back! Give it back!" regarding the bike. The policeman called for support. We heard sirens in the distance. The police, with their lights blaring, were a few blocks away, but they could not move any closer. Cyclists were blocking them. And a few other cyclists started to grab on the confiscated bike. It was twenty to one, pulling the bike away from the police. I couldn't believe it. They had the police completely outnumbered. And the ride moved on. The police turned away, after we'd taken the bike back from the squad car and unarrested the cyclist.

"We are our own temporary autonomous zone," declared Greg, smiling, looking around at the sea of bikes filling up Market Street.

Those in cars were not too happy about the cyclists slowing down their commute. A man in a moving van tried to drive into the crowd. Screaming the cyclists blocked him. He got out, his face red, gripped with road rage, and tried to punch a cyclist. The police were nowhere to be seen. A group of cyclists started talking. Some started to sit on his truck. Others talked about taking his van. As everyone was debating, one of the cyclists got in, smiling. It looked like he was going to drive. Instead, he grabbed for the key and ran to the side of the street where he dropped it into the storm drain. While friendliness was thought to be more subversive than anger or retaliation, many quietly reveled in the moment of defiance. And the group kept biking.

The ride looped through the Haight where I dropped out by my house, and stopped to get a coffee at the Mad Dog in the Fog, a pub and coffee shop on Haight Street. The place was full of people. A young woman with a brunette bob, a nose ring, and a smile sat in a table near the front. She was staring straight at me.

"Are you a schoolboy?" she asked as I looked at her and sat down. We began to talk. I was still wearing a backpack from after work. We chatted about the ride and the city. From the East Bay, she had only just moved to the city, and was working as a waitress. We talked and talked and before I knew it, we had a date set up to see Alphabet Soup, a funk/hip hop band, at the Elbo Room, on Valencia Street in the Mission later that night.

It was all that easy. I was usually completely terrified by these moments. But there was no need. I bought her a beer when we met at the club. She was wearing a black and blue skirt, lots of black eye liner, and very red lipstick. We sat talking about music and books. She told me her favorite novel was *Demien* by Herman Hesse.

"I love that story," I said and smiled, looking at her. "I wonder if I have a doppelgänger here, or somewhere else in the city, or even the world."

"Maybe China? Who knows?" smiled Sue, lifting her hands in a gesture of wonderment. The band started playing, and we flirted and danced. Some days and moments, the city seemed to come together. Sue and I certainly did.

Eros and Thanatos in San Francisco

"My gleanings of erotica and frequent, guilt ridden masturbation were
all that kept me sane until I escaped parental supervision . . . The inner voice of
eros is arbitrary, bizarre, impeccably honest, bountiful, and so powerful as to be
cruel. It takes courage to hear its demands and follow them."
-Pat Califia, *Public Sex*, 1994 [1980]

"And I see Malcolm's spirit, his eyes burning red
Black and Green flames and crying tears of Thunderbird wine that seems to touch my lips and make me thirsty for a
taste of FREEDOM! Freedom by any means necessary
...And I begin to hate with love and love with hate
This Is Madness!"
-The Last Poets, "This is Madness"

An eerie otherworldly beauty seemed to emanate from the fog, meandering through the streets. Still, I had never been so lonely. Even in the summer, the fog trickled down from the heights, into the ethereal hills and alleys, mixing into the light. You had to be careful if you daydreamed too long or stopped paying attention. Hungry ghosts, crusty punks, and runaways roamed about, some asking for change, desperate, longing, covering themselves at night as best they could. One was stabbed in his sleep a week prior. Others just sat staring, like they were only half here. Generally friendly, they greeted you. Some guys sat selling old Last Poets tapes and incense on Haight Street. Sometimes exchanges became dark.

"Chicken shit white motherfucker," a young boy screamed at me as I wandered by the projects on the way for my 4:00-midnight shift at work.

"I'm just trying to make it through this savage life here," Brad, Chris' roommate said, laughing at what a bad day he had had looking for work. "Walking home, a guy threw trash at me on the street," he laughed. He'd been ripped off, fired, and wondered what he was doing.

I took to listening to requiems. I loved Mozart's. But Verdi's was my favorite. The chorus sounded as if the angels were crashing down to earth, violently disrupting our everyday.

My friend Caroline briefly worked on a 24-hour rape hotline. "You have no idea how dark things can get late in the night here," she said. "There's a lot going on below the surface of the city."

When we weren't working, some of us met at the Opera Café in North Beach, a dive bar with a juke box that only played opera.

"What do you want me to play?"

"How about Death of a Butterfly?" I asked Mimi and Chris as we sat drinking.

"I love that," Mimi said.

"The best opera is about sex and death."

Over drinks, a man who resembled eighties heartthrob Matt Dillon dropped by. Mimi and Chris' jaws dropped.

"Is that Matt Dillon?" I asked, nodding at Chris.

"I think it is," she whispered, starring in awe.

Chris ran over to the jukebox to get a closer look, and tried to pick a few songs. Dillon walked up to look. Chris played it cool, chatting with him for a minute before walking back to us.

"What did he say?"

"Are you going to fuck him?"

"No," she smiled. "He asked me what I played so he wouldn't play the same! I told him I played 'Nessun Dorma,' from *Turandot*. And he said he liked it." Mimi and Chris went in the bathroom and cried.

When they came back, Dillon was comparing notes on the jukebox with his friends. First they put on *Tristan und Isolde*, by Wagner, and then his friend, who looked remarkably like Joe Strummer of the Clash, put on "Bizet Toreador" from *Carmen*, and led the group in a sing-along.

The city was full of secret places, the streets seemingly alive, offering up clues. I tried to make sense of them every day. "Silence = Death," "This is madness," and "The revolution will not be televised" murals could be found all over the city, messages and philosophy on the walls. George Bataille's brash words "Truth has only one face, that of violent contradiction" were sprayed on Page Street, leaving me to wonder on the way to work. The next day, the message was more elaborate:

"Reproduction and death condition the immortal renewal of life; they condition the instant which is always new."

That one left me scratching my head. I wrote it down.

"What do you make of this one?" I asked Jim as I arrived at work.

"I think that's George Bataille again," said Jim.

"Just like last week's mural."

"Yeah, he was a French philosopher obsessed with death and sex," Jim said.

"Me too."

Take a look at this. He pulled open his bag.

"The *Diseased Pariah News* is the most popular zine in San Francisco," he explained, showing me a copy.

"'*Diseased Pariah News*?'" I noted flipping through.

"Morose AIDS humor. Very sick."

"The *Diseased Pariah News*."

"The last issue had a story about a writer inviting a trick over, the author shaving to get ready, cutting himself, and not being able to stop the bleeding because of his compromised immune system. You should read it."

"Did the date work out?"

"Yeah, but he had to use up a whole roll of toilet paper to stop bleeding."

"It's not easy is it?"

I flipped through looking at the first article on 'History of Sex, Death, and Literature.'

"Can I borrow this?" I asked.

"Sure. But you have to give it back," Jim said. "Let me know what you think." Jim paused and remembered. "You should read this too," Jim concluded, offering me a used copy of *The Plague*.

"Thanks Jim."

For periods, it was pretty routine at 1994 Market Street. Uneventful weeks on end, and then three or four deaths in a row. The job offered a glimpse of a slow-motion car wreck. I bought a blue journal to write about everything I saw.

Pedro was usually the first down, hobbling around feeding the plants, taking meals out to the homeless people outside, buying Henry packs of Kools, walking to the Safeway at all hours of the night, telling me about the graffiti artists outside, standing on the corner smoking and looking around. Henry was one of the black residents, who usually looked like he was falling apart. He had just passed.

"The last time I saw him, I was spoon-feeding him. He could see I was so upset that he was counseling *me*," noted Pedro.

"He was losing his mind."

"Not really. He just smoked crack every once in a while."

"His girlfriend really helped him out. She always came when he had diarrhea or was unable to walk. She was always there for him. A white girl, she slept by him in a sleeping bag for his final days. She wouldn't leave, except to get food."

"I didn't get to go say goodbye to him. I had been planning to last week, but I didn't." Pedro paused and looked down.

"You didn't know he was going."

"Well, I should have." Pedro paused. "I should have—another lost..." His voice trailed off. Shaking his head, Pedro mumbled. "None of us chose to be here. My parents brought me from Puerto Rico. And then I was stuck at Bellevue. The welfare department in New York put me on a bus out here. Black people were sent here in chains."

"Madness, right?"

"And people blame the poor. They blame the Henrys of the world for getting sick."

"Without asking about why, but we're still reeling from it."

"The shadow of this country is coming through with this."

"Yeah, the mean side."

Listening to Pedro I thought of all my life in the South, the churches where people wore their Sunday best, the courts and town halls. They lost the war. But their thinking won. Everyone wants to move on and forget, to forgive and forget without apologizing. Amnesia expanding and people walk like zombies, half-awake, the bankers zooming about, people sleeping in corners, out looking for a fix.

Richard came to talk with me as I settled in for my shift. He had just heard about Henry.

"I'm about the only one of us from the original people who moved in last winter," he told me. Ed and Charlie had died that week.

"I don't know what to do," I told Richard.

"There's nothing you can do," he replied.

174

It all just kept coming and coming. As we talked, Jeannie, a woman my age who lived in the building, was coming back from a bike ride.

"I tried to take a bike ride to the park, but had to turn around early. I was too exhausted to make it," she said, angry and frustrated with being constantly sick. "Riding my bike to the park on sunny days—that was one of my favorite things to do." She walked upstairs.

Everyone seemed to be dying and I couldn't react. I couldn't ignore it or say I was sorry, which sounded patronizing. On the surface, it was smiles. But the suffering was everywhere. So I just listened and wrote in my journal.

"Can you call me an ambulance," asked Carlos, who'd phoned the front desk

"I can barely move or breathe." I called 911. He trembled as he left the building in a wheelchair.

Mark, who'd lived with the disease for over ten years, was walking in as the paramedics wheeled Carlos out. He looked at me with a resigned expression.

"Whatever happens is going to happen, and worrying about it won't change a thing," he cautioned, looking at me, and walked upstairs.

I looked inside the copy of *The Plague* that Jim had given me. "Freedom is what you do with what's been done to you," someone had written on the inside. In the midst of the illness around us, the city felt alive, teeming with questions. Everyone was trying to figure out what to do with what was happening.

Of all people, Tessa from college lived down the street from me. Now that dating was over, we had become buddies and met for coffees. For my birthday, Tessa gave me a copy of *Letters to a Young Poet* by Rilke. She wrote a note on the inside. "Cab, on my search for this book I wandered into a used bookstore in the Mission. When I asked the man with his hair askew if he had any copies, his eyes widened and he said 'No, that book's nearly impossible to find used in this city.' There was an older man—clearly a regular—seated in an easy-chair, nodding his head. 'I'm surprised more people don't know how Rilke died,' he said, smiling. 'How'd he die?' I asked. 'He was picking roses in his garden for a lady friend he expected. He pricked himself with a thorn. He later died of blood poisoning...a fitting death for a truly romantic poet!' Anyhow, I thought of you while reading this book. Read it slowly and let the words seep in. I hope it will comfort and inspire you. Xo Tessa."

I perused the beaten up book at work. "[D]ear Sir, love your solitude and try to sing out with the pain it causes you. For those who are near you are far away..." Rilke advised the young poet. I tried to take in his message, just sitting with the feelings around me. But I couldn't take my mind off Carlos trembling as he left for the hospital.

After work, I walked toward the bay from Market Street and zigzagged left, into the Tenderloin. Strolling about, I looked at the hustlers, making eye contact with the trannies on the street corners, the shifting terrain of the city, its prostitutes and their patrons, negotiating, cutting deals and finding quiet corners or hotel rooms, trying to avoid the undercover police who targeted them. Public sexual culture in the Tenderloin felt immediately dangerous and edgy. Kids dropped off from the bus station, who had left the desperate conditions of their lives, survived on tricks, speed, camaraderie, and the hazards of this subterranean world. Different bars catered to different interests. The Mother Lode was a tranny bar, where guys from the East Bay who longed for male contact not associated with Castro clones dropped by to find dates. Some days, the vibe was rife with sadness, but a rambunctious hopefulness lingered in the air. Watching drag performers making a little change, hanging out there one tapped into a secret history of screaming queens who clashed with patrons at Comptons in a riot on Turk Street in 1966, and countless other myths. Outside, the story seemed to continue.

My new friend Sue and I wandered around there, drinking late into the night.

When we finally got back to her place in the Lower Haight, we made out for hours, rubbing up against each other through our jeans. We chatted about what she was reading and thinking about. A copy of *The Bell Jar* was by her bed.

"I love sad stories," she explained.

"I do too. I just hope you don't relate to the protagonist too much."

"I don't," she said, pausing. "That's sweet of you asking."

"Such a sad story. I hope there is room to move outside the situation that envelops her."

"There is. But sometimes we get caught. We all get lost sometimes. She was just a little down," Sue said.

"And she couldn't shake it. I've seen it happen so many times."

"When those demons wrap themselves around us, they don't let loose easily."

"I know. But I'm not sure. Life isn't that complicated. Sometimes a girl just needs to get laid," Sue said, looking at me.

"Sometimes," I smiled. She smiled back. Sad stories were great foreplay. So, we played, talked dirty, chatted on the couch, standing, on our knees, reading poetry, trying different chairs out, switching roles, top or bottom.

"Go for it! There is a degree of violence," she confessed at one point.

"You have to if I'm going to," she smiled, pulling out a strap-on an hour later. "Bottoms rule" she insisted. "I'll be gentle." She kneeled. I kneeled. She kneeled. This way and that. It felt wondrous, painful, bountiful and violent and ... she held me as I came. "There goes another novel," she joked after sex, usually with a smile.

"At your beck and call," she said as we sat chatting afterward. I was sore from all the jeans against jeans foreplay, the pain from rubbing, and from always being with a stranger.

"What do you want, Cab?"

"That's an embarrassing question," I said, blushing.

"Cab, we just had sex all night. You can tell me."

"I know...." I demurred and told her a little bit here and there. But not what I was really thinking. Sue eventually went to sleep.

Later, I wrote in my journal.

"When I'm in bed,

I want head.

I want to watch.

I want bright lights.

I want to be beaten.

I want to be sedated.

I want to be gender fucked.

I want to be released.

I want to be alone.

I want to be loved.

I want to be tickled.

I want to be Paris.

I want to be with Chloe.

I want to know you care.

I want anyone but the person I'm in bed with.

I want to disappear.

In bed is the only way I know ..."

I picked up a copy of a book sitting on the floor by Sue's bed, called *Public Sex*. I was thinking of all the things she had told me, the stories I was hearing and seeing here. Reading, I was slowly starting to reconcile the powerful desire and the cultural shame I had grown up associating with Eros. Instead of shying away from pleasure, Califia suggested it opened up new vistas of possibility, but only if we were honest, embraced its cruelties, messiness and let it work its way through us.

I had found a fellow traveler. This was Sue's bedtime reading. Willing to risk her dignity for connection and release, she took it to heart. Looking at her sleeping in bed by me, her short brown hair covering her face, I wondered about her. I thought about what we'd done the night before, of her watching, "Bend Over Boyfriend," an homage to women who topped men, and pulling out her strap-on. "Cab, lets play a little bit," she teased, slapping it on her hand. I looked at the book and thought about that messy space that was impossible to contain, intriguing, even if it was arbitrary, sometimes caring, sometimes thoughtless, sometimes hopeful, sometimes like oblivion.

I thought about Chloe, whom I had heard had moved a new boyfriend out from Dallas to New York, only to move out while he was at work, leaving him a note and departing. I thought about how he must have felt when he walked into that empty apartment. I thought about her anger at my porn stash and her lectures about sex. There was no need to judge each other anymore. No need for the sex panics of youth, the icky feeling senior year with Becky, the shame we felt about it all. Within the San Francisco stories enveloping me, I started to put distance between my experience and the toxic elements of sexphobia, the scolds I had gotten about being a sissy for playing the cello, the condemnations for queerness. There were other ways to live without having to pass for being what one is not, without having to divorce one's self from our body and senses. In San Francisco, the social and sexual imagination was not to be seen as a liability, but rather as a part of a lifelong excavation.

I got up a bit past 8:00 and wandered out into the crisp morning. The homeless were asleep on the street. Sunday morning church bells were ringing. I stepped into a church on Fell Street to hear what it was all about. There wasn't really a plan about this. It was just a force of habit from childhood. People were singing. It was a quiet Sunday space that felt comforting, a good place for meditating. Quilts displayed for the dead lined the walls. We prayed for someone to hear our prayers for the sick. Lord hear our prayers. I was not sure anyone was.

I grabbed a coffee in a café on Sutter Street writing notes until I got kicked out for not ordering enough. Off I meandered through Chinatown to North Beach and stumbled into the Lusty Lady, a porn arcade with nude dancers. The stench of cheap perfume, cum, and cleaning detergent filled the air. A neon light of a nude woman blinked on and off. One of my friends actually found a job mopping up the cum in the peekaboo booths I walked in to. I still had a scab from the blue jeans rubbing incident with Sue. But I worked around it, getting everything I needed, smiling at the naked woman on the other side of the glass.

"Don't cum without me," she said, smiling at me.

People connect with each other in amazing ways here.

I smiled and waved goodbye, leaving with money still in the machine, the window still open. The women at the Lusty Lady were fierce. A dancer outside handed me a flyer with the words, "No Justice, No Piece," about working conditions there, asking me not to cross the picket line if they strike.

"I would never cross the picket line," I confessed.

"You'll always get good dances here," she smiled. "The best."

Back at Market Street, Juan walked in looking cheerful.

"Perhaps jacking off is the most spiritual thing one can do," he said with a grin, oblivious to what I had been doing before work. "After all, when you jack off, you release potential life."

"I totally agree," I smiled. "I try to be very spiritual."

"Me too." He paused. "My brother used to worry about Onan, the character in the book of Genesis who spilled his on the ground before he was struck down by God. But I was never caught up with that."

"Isn't it more of an undue burden in the body? It has to get out. Otherwise I start aching."

"Me too."

"And not too many of us here worry much about continuing human life anyways."

"Its kind of inhumane."

Juan walked upstairs. I thought about the walk from the Lusty Lady to work, past the other peepshows on Market Street. There was usually a loneliness to the arcades I frequented. That feeling was everywhere in San Francisco.

Sue and I met later that night after work to watch the Broun Fellinis, a gritty local jazz quartet mixing soul and funk. With the band playing, we squeezed onto the floor a few feet away from the saxophonist and sat down. Eyes closed, my senses dancing, incense wafted through the air, sound and color swirling, zooming about blurring, like one of those kaleidoscopes we play with as kids, twirling, rolling down into the ocean into the distance, into oblivion. When I opened my eyes, I saw Sue and the other groovers, smoking and shaking, their heads and shoulders moving in time.

"This is madness," the band jammed, riffing on the old Last Poets anthem. "This is madness."

Sue had her own apartment in Hayes Valley.

Back at her place, I asked her what she wanted.

178

"Honestly," Sue explained, looking at me. "But after that mouths to my skin, to bite, to be bitten on my tattoos, on the back of my neck..." she whispered. "....to have some company, someone with me, to have some company doing it with, instead of by myself, your cock to masturbate with, your body for me to get off with..."

This 21-year-old waitress from Brisbane was growing on me. She was enthusiastic, and she had a great apartment.

"Look at me," she told me, masturbating. I was not always able to cum, but she allowed me plenty of space. Chloe led me to think jacking off was terrible. Sue was quite the opposite. For her, it was just an extension of the experience, something to share and enjoy, creating a space together, for warmth. We hung out for days and days, sharing our bodies, but oddly, the more sex we had, the more distant we became. Stories and trips to see jazz receded. It consumed everything. As the space between us grew physically, our minds separated. I had a whole world of ideas I only reluctantly shared. And when I did, we missed each other.

"That's so sad," she replied when I told her about the desolate, disappearing in time feelings I was having after sex one night. We were together all the time, but more and more, it felt like we were by ourselves.

Clubland in MacArthur Park

> "Someone left the cake out in the rain
> I don't think that I can take it
> 'cause it took so long to bake it
> And I'll never have that recipe again...
> -Adrian Drover / Jimmy Webb "MacArthur Park"

Sue and I hung out all the time. After my 4:00-midnight shifts, I'd meet her and her roommates at a gay disco called Product in a warehouse South of Market Street. Electronic beats pumped on the main floor when I arrived. The place was teeming with shirtless men. Sue was one of the few women there. She was on the second floor balcony peaking out of her mind on ecstasy. I could see it in her eyes. That was not a space I was in, feeling a little tired. It was an unfamiliar feeling to walk into a space where everyone else is high, but you. It certainly offers another perspective on things. Ecstasy was legal in Dallas growing up. The city restricted its use after July 1, 1985. But clubs found their ways of creating genetic alternatives, eve, etc. I had had bountiful times with it, munching on ice cubes, huddled on the couches with buddies at the Stark Club, crunching on ice cubes, our eyeballs bulging, night after night of zooming around the city. But this was a different time. I wandered off to the basement where 1970s disco was pumping.

Donna Summer's "MacArthur Park" played, with Giorgio Moroder's majestic synthesizer beat filling the room. I joined with the other shirtless men on the dance floor singing along. This was my San Francisco. One of the residents at the building used to talk about it all the time.

"What was the cake in the song?" Mark asked me.

"I'm not sure."

"It's the pre AIDS world we lost. We'll never have that recipe for the before-years. Some dance to remember here. Some dance to forget. 'MacArthur Park' is all of those things. When we listen to it, that hopeful period comes back for a second, especially when we're dancing together. I hope we'll survive this."

"Do you think we will?"

"Who knows? I'm just going with a feeling."

Looking at the hundreds of guys, clad in jeans, sunglasses, no shirts, looking great, I thought maybe he was right. Energy poured through me, extending out into the crowd of men, boogying to this torch song of the days when Harvey was still around. A magnificent over-the-top feeling of emotion poured through the room, as if everyone was having that same feeling.

When the song finished, I wandered back to the rave floor, where Sue was dancing with her roommates. "Thud, thud, thud," blared. Herbert Marcuse's expression "flattening out" from *One Dimensional Man* came to mind. It felt like a faceless, identity-less warehouse of mechanistic bodies, dancing on their own, staring out into the distance, nonchalant, somewhat bored, looking for something, a very different energy than the Donna Summer floor where the disco ball sparkled as we danced out of the present into a never-never land of discos past and future.

"Kiss me," Sue asked, channeling the ecstasy pouring through her. I indulged not feeling in the same head space. But she wanted me to kiss her more and more in front of everyone. It felt possessive. I didn't want to flaunt my heterosexuality. I had no desire to display loyalty to this girl, at least not here. In that moment, I realized it was going to be yet another of my string of short affairs.

The cycle begins with lust, going out, talking, kissing in the bar, going home and fucking. Repeat. See her again, fuck again, and start wondering how much we should be calling each other. Pretty soon nothing is worth the aggravation of sharing time fixating on our weaknesses and foibles. Then I find myself passing time with the people I do not want to be spending time with, and inevitably this process makes me lonelier. I wanted to write on my days off, not fiddle with this stuff. I found myself becoming very turned off, even stuffy. As the night turned into morning at Product, I was just fending for my autonomy. The more I pulled away, the more Sue pushed herself on me. By 4:30 in the morning, we were with her cute roommate Kurt, playing kissing games. Kurt was adorable, and super effeminate. Flirting with him, I didn't want to be sucking face with Sue. I found myself saying, "Let's save it for later," to Sue, as we sat in the VIP room of the desolate club. We had made out in the bed there earlier. But this was not enough. It was the final night of Product. The owner passed out t-shirts to the club's faithful, sitting there surrounded by club kids one and all. Everyone was looking for a warm bed and someone to share it with, perhaps something more than just a night. But that wasn't a requirement. The morning dew began to shimmer in the end of the night. The doorman allowed the final guests into the club.

"If you don't kiss me now, we won't be kissing later either," Sue stared at me in a drugged out haze.

So I leaned over to Sue, put my hand on Kurt's cheek and kissed him on the mouth. We went off for a drink by ourselves.

"Fuck ultimatums," I mumbled to myself.

Kurt was smiling and laughing to himself.

"Just stay with me tonight?" Kurt asked. "Stay in my bed. I promise to be good. Just a snuggle."

"Just a snuggle," I chuckled. "Not tonight, gorgeous," I replied, and wandered home as the sun rose, the morning fog rolling in down the street.

****

For brunch, I met my friend Mike from college for Bloody Mary's at Casa Loma bar and watched the Dallas vs. San Francisco football game.

"It's the best time ever in history," Mike proclaimed after the 49ers scored. A Dallas fan, I could not agree.

"Fuck that," I replied, feeling grumpy and tired. "The Cowboys are losing and the poor are left to perish, the homeless kids, everyone dealing with this fucking disease. But people don't care cause they hate the poor. No one cares that black people are getting sick. No one cares. The queers and sex workers—no one cares what happens."

"Yes, AIDS sucks. But we're making progress. Science has eradicated polio," he insisted. I hadn't gotten enough sleep. Our clash was intensifying.

"But not AIDS. They just came back from the Berlin AIDS Conference. And nothing came of it at all. A dozen years later and we can't make an inch of progress. It's because its homos, hookers, and the poor that are affected. And the left hates itself. Look at us. We're killing ourselves. We're eating ourselves up," I vented. "People hate Clinton, ACT UP split up between Golden Gate and San Francisco, and people attack each other every day in the papers. We haven't improved," I insisted, venting about AIDS politics that my old college friends did not see.

"Look, we're arguing over semantics," Mike continued. "We're splitting hairs here. There are hardships. But there is also beauty. We are moving forward."

"Really?"

"You really don't see it?"

"No, not really. I'm sure you're right. But I don't see it."

White Nights

"I need to see you naked. In your body and your thought."
-Leonard Cohen

I could see bodies, but I longed for thoughts. I wanted spirits.

The next few nights, I worked the 12AM—8 shift. For the first time in a long time, everything was quiet. No one was saying a thing. After I finished my rounds, I sat to watch *Northern Exposure* and old *Columbo* episodes while letting residents in and out of the building. I wondered if Peter Falk, the existential detective, was out there walking, as he did in *Wings of Desire*, reminding us there were angels in the streets of Berlin.

"To smoke, and have coffee," he smiled, "and if you do it together, it's fantastic."

Around 5:00 AM, the bakery delivery guy dropped off bread for the restaurant.

"This is for you," he said in a French accent, and gave me a fresh croissant.

"Thanks," I smiled, rubbing my sleepy eyes. I was touched by the gesture. The morning lights were just beginning to shine onto the street, between the buildings and the water. For a few minutes, the city felt innocent, all the drug dealers back home, most of the tweekers sleeping off the high of the night somewhere else. The streets around the building were usually ominous, especially deep in the night. During the day, people were out looking for a hustle, a way to get high, or to rip someone else off. Many of the residents in the building were scared to go outside on check day; too many people zooming about. But the moon was still out while the sky was turning a lighter blue. I could see the graffiti mural as well as the green leaves on the trees lining Market Street. A hotel across the street kept their red neon sign on all night so it glimmered as the morning fog rolled in. This moment only lasted about fifteen minutes. The foreboding feelings of the evening, and the capitalist commodity frenzy of the day were absent. The tensions of the urban ruins were elsewhere for now. Gradually cars started to zoom down Market Street, the dawn's innocence passed. But that had been enough. Maybe Mike was right? Maybe there was still beauty out there.

Pedro was out walking to and fro, up and down the street. A black man stood outside, staring. This world looked like it was falling apart with the buildings crumbling, characters zigzagging amidst the welfare hotels, amidst space that seemed to shift from primordial village to modern world by the block. Standing in front of the building, then he walked off. Another man walked by, bringing more paint to the alley across the street.

"Did you see Bum?" Pedro asked, looking out and smoking.

"He was standing here a minute ago."

"Ok, I'll find him." Pedro was looking around and then at me and smiled. His pupils were still dilated.

"You still seeing the punk rock girl?" He was referring to Sue, who he saw walking with me the week before.

"We've been on again off again."

"I love that grunge look. The grunge kids skating, I just can't resist that look. But I thought you didn't like her."

"On and off, but we might try it again."

"Why? What are you doing?" Pedro asked.

I shrugged.

He looked at me.

"I could go back to Sue. But I'm not sure. At first, whenever we went out, I looked forward to seeing her. The sex made putting up with everything, all the drug stuff worth it. But then I started getting stressed out whenever she called, and happy the rest of the week I didn't have to hang out with her."

"She's keeping you with the sex."

"I'm not sure. But I have to figure it out. If only I could find someone who connects beauty of mind and the body."

"Good luck with that."

"I gotta figure this out. But I've been stuck for a long time."

"Be careful. It's hard getting unstuck. Look at me. I got a life sentence here. But wait, I have to call my sister."

Billy, another resident, very skinny, wandered up to us. He was wearing blue jeans, a leather jacket, headband, and had a red handkerchief in his left back pocket.

"Can I bum a cigarette?" he asked Pedro.

"Sure. You want one Cab?"

"Thanks."

"What's the red hanky for again? I forget," asked Pedro, gesturing at a handkerchief in Billy's left back pocket.

"Fisting. Right cheek for receiving."

"How deep," Pedro inquired, smiling.

Billy looked at Pedro, grinned and gestured to his elbow.

"Wow," Pedro commended Billy, laughing.

I felt a little sick, having never imagined the human anatomy to be capable of such feats or for that matter that people wanted to do them.

Billy seemed pleased with himself, reveling in the effect he was having on me.

"I've been at it for almost twenty years now. I started playing at the Catacombs in the mid-1970s. That was the place to be."

"Is it still around?"

"They closed it when AIDS hit."

"What are the other hanky colors? I forget," Pedro continued.

"Well, right is always receiving. Left is topping. Hmm. Let me see." He gestured with his fingers, tapping his right on his left for effect. "Apricot is for chubby chasers and fuchsia is for spanker and spankees. Coral is for foot lickers."

184

Pedro's mischievous smile was getting wider.

"Olive drab for uniform chasers," Billy went on.

"And brown is of course for—"

"Thank you Billy," Pedro interrupted, and began to walk back inside.

"Don't lock yourself out," he reminded me as I finished my cigarette.

"I won't."

But sometimes I felt like I already was.

"I'd love to show you," Billy grinned, his rotten teeth showing in the morning. "I'd start with my tongue under your armpits...."

"I gotta go," I told him, feeling nauseous. My shift was almost over. Pedro was standing outside again when I walked out.

"What ever happened to romance?" he laughed, looking out at the city. "Don't forget my Christmas Party, Cab."

"I'll be out of town by then, at my mom's new house in Princeton."

"Well you can still drop by."

"Get some sleep, Pedro."

I started to walk. Instead of going home, I wandered the opposite way down Market toward the Civic Center.

As I was walking, I ran into one of the residents from the building, Hank, sitting on a bench.

"Hi Cab," he said.

"What's up?" I asked. "You look tired."

"Sit down." I sat by him, looking out.

"Police cars burnt right here."

"Huh?"

"May 1979, during the riots."

"What riots?"

"The White Nights riots after the verdict, Dan White getting off after killing Harvey and Mayor Moscone. I was standing here with Cleve Jones. And we all looked at each other as the police cars were burning. When the first police car was burning, symbolically gays had fought back. We weren't going to take injustice. I remember when the first rock was thrown at the first window. It felt so good, and then every time a window broke, it felt *so* good for your life accumulation of trauma. We marched to City Hall and nobody said, 'We're going to have a riot,' but I think everybody knew. I remember we got there and I remember holding back friends that wanted to go into City Hall. This was after the windows were broken. One of my friends, Jerry, he had gone mad. He had gone over the edge. We were concerned that there were dozens of police in City Hall with billy clubs and we knew that if somebody got in there alone, they would just be creamed. So we held back. And in the meantime, the people were throwing rocks and we broke a lot of windows. I still remember the first window and you could hear it and everybody cheered. I still remember that and then more windows were broken and everybody cheered. It was like a catharsis for our life oppression, breaking those windows. We fought with the cops all night."

"I heard about that," I followed. "But wow."

"After Vietnam, I ended up coming here and staying. It was the closest thing to home I ever experienced. I knew that immediately when I came in 1971. Those years before, before Harvey, they were the most important days of my life. I'm not going to be around too much longer, Cab," he spoke, looking at the distance. "But I'm not really afraid. I'm just not. But I don't have long. I know that."

"But you're alive now."

"I am here but I'm also in another place. I feel like a ghost."

I looked at Hank, the cold air coming out of his mouth, staring out into space and another time.

"The cars were right there," he gestured. "It was only a few months after the riots that people started to get sick. Just a few months really."

I kept listening. And Hank looked at me.

"Sorry, Cab. I didn't mean to keep you. Go home. Get some sleep."

I walked back, wandering up Haight Street, smoking a cigarette. Making my way up the street, a man ran up to me.

"I'll sell you this jacket for ten bucks. I really need a hit."

He looked like he hadn't slept in days.

I was going to haggle and say five. But then I looked at the guy. He didn't seem desperate as much as just strung out, smiling, and hoping, another of Allen Ginsberg's "angel-headed hipsters.... dragging themselves through the streets at dawn....I thought about my Dad and Tom hustling through these streets four decades prior. "OK ten dollars," I replied. And I actually had the cash in my pocket.

After I gave him the money, I tried on the jacket. "Look it fits you perfect man," the guy noted, as I put on his jacket, smiling.

"You look beautiful," he smiled and was off. I wore the warm jacket home.

Finally, I sat looking at the ceiling. By now it was 9:20 in the morning. And I felt more awake than anything.

I looked around the room and picked up a copy of *Giovanni's Room*, sitting by my futon, thinking about the past few weeks. The conversation with Pedro had stuck with me.

"She's keeping you with the sex," he repeated over and over. I started to read but I couldn't. I just looked around. I tried again, picking up with a conversation between David and Jacques early in the story.

"You think ... that my life is shameful because my encounters are. And they are. But you should ask yourself why they are."

"Why are they shameful?"

"Because there is no affection in them, and no joy. It's like putting an electric plug in a dead socket. Touch, but no contact. All touch, but no contact and no light."

I sat reading the paragraph over and over, thinking of Sue.

"I perhaps don't like women very much, that's true. That hasn't stopped me ... But most of the time—most of the time, I made love only with the body."

"That can make one very lonely," David followed.

186

"No kidding," I wrote in the margins, thinking about an evening with Sue after Halloween in the Castro. We'd been dancing with the hordes of people out in their various costumes. We went home, and for once, Sue did not want sex at all.

"Not tonight," she whispered. But we ended up doing it anyways, in a blurry, messy moment of sadness and ill content. She didn't really oppose me when I kept pestering until she gave in. We always had sex when we saw each other, always. Was it too much? Had she consented or were we both doing it anyways? She didn't stop me. But she didn't say yes either. There was simply the absence of the no that other girls firmly offered. No when the hands moved. No when things got more ambivalent. In later years, we'd learn more about the vocabulary of consent. The absence of a no is not a yes. Chloe and I had fought through sex. And the relationship had faded. And this one was going in the same direction. There was little else, certainly not much communication. We were not feeling good about each other or what we were doing. It wouldn't last long from there.

I finally fell asleep. But just for a little while.

We met the following week. I looked at Sue and she looked at me back. She wasn't surprised with the breakup. The Halloween sad dance hadn't left us with too much.

"I was going to say the same thing to you," she lamented, not angry, not cutting, just truthful.

"All we do is have sex."

"Really?"

"Really. We don't ever go to see music or go dancing or to the movies anymore. Just sex." It felt sad. Why was I giving up? Why were we doing this I thought as we broke up. She was so cool. I don't remember who initiated, but we had sex one more time before saying goodbye. I'd see her on the bus every once in a while but that was it.

Boy Talk

"[Y]our girlfriends want your stories told in the company of the dead,"
-Rob Magnuson Smith, *Scorper*

A few days before leaving for the holidays, I met my old college friend Bobby at Vesuvio in North Beach, just across the street from City Lights Bookstore. After college, he'd moved to Los Angeles, renting a room in Hollywood. He had dropped out of his PhD program in psychology, and was looking to break into Hollywood, writing screenplays and novels in between making rent as a personal assistant. Bobby used to visit a lot.

We never knew what would happen when he came for a visit. On one occasion he ran the bill on dinner in the Mission.

"Run," he screamed and ran out. We following him, sprinting like bank robbers.

"Your friend is not that good of a guy," Brad commented after the experience.

Usually, he just got Homerically drunk.

I visited him in Los Angeles and we hung out, talking with girls, eating sushi, running on the beach for hours and hours. When he wasn't being outrageous, he was reflective and thoughtful, talking about the books he was writing, and telling stories about friends.

"Check out Michel Houellebecq's *Whatever*," he counseled, rattling off a list of books he loved reading, including *Tropic of Capricorn*, and anything by Marilyn Robinson.

"I don't know those others. But I tried to read *Tropic of Cancer* the other night after staying up all night. I couldn't get through it."

"Keep reading it," Bobby continued. Henry Miller seems to be describing these latter days of the US. "There will be more calamities, more death, more despair," he writes. "Not the slightest indication of a change anywhere. The cancer of time is eating us away...The weather will not change."

"Not here in the USA, too much forgetting," I replied, reflecting on the prevailing reality. "Our bodies are fragile, but feelings ...." I paused. "Tell me about *Whatever*."

"It's all about that horrible feeling that we get as if losing something in ourselves in between the sex and the looking for someone, seemingly consuming the thing we want more than anything, as it's consuming us. He says that when we have too many sexual relations, it diminishes our capacity to form emotional bonds. 'Successive sexual experiences accumulated during adolescence undermine ... the possibility ...'"

"Do you agree with that?" I asked.

"Not really."

"That's a dark take on things. But there might be a grain of truth in it. But I don't want to give the prudes any ammo."

"God, I hope he's not right. Then I'm in trouble."

"Sometimes I think we're a little more fragile than we like to admit."

"Don't ever marry a poet," he counseled. "They write about the breakup. They might even plan the relationship around the breakup, preordaining it."

"Are you talking about poets in general or yourself?"

"Not sure," he said.

"We've all had our attempts at relationships and the feelings that come with them. We all have our patterns. The problem is I'm starting to fall into a tedious pattern of looking for Chloe in every person I'm with. But I feel like the furies are punishing me, like I'm Oedipus, living out my fate. This bad streak I'm in is all about that—one bad romance after another."

"Not all bad romance," Bobby said. "I remember what you told me you and Sue did last week."

"No, it's not all bad romance. She was great. I have no idea why I broke up with her. But after a while, I felt like we were talking past each other. She reads paperback novels in between shifts at the restaurant where she works. She always has one at work. She's amazing. She was all I ever wanted here. But I couldn't feel anything after a while."

"You obviously felt something."

"Yes, something. The sex was amazing. Still, the sex with Sue seemed to suck something from me. I loved it. But felt like I was disappearing. And getting off. But I stopped feeling anything."

"She might have been a vampire," Bobby chimed in with a grin. "You never know. You just don't know."

"She was not crazy. The conversation just ended. We ran out of stories. When we went to the movies, I somehow didn't like the person I was with, just like with Marsha all those years ago. Our minds were in different places. When she was high, I wanted to be with anyone but her."

"How often was she high?"

"All the time," I paused. "But she still appreciated me. I appreciated her. But I took her for granted. And stopped trying."

"The sex is just the beginning, I guess."

"It's a good beginning, middle and end. But she was not Chloe. She was not it all."

"The definition of nubile," Bobby smiled.

"I know," I replied. "But that was the crazy one. I'm still reeling from the highs and lows. I'm not sure she even knows or cares."

"That was about your feelings, not Chloe. What's inside of you. I know that story. But I still don't quite understand what happened with Sue?"

"The relationship lost any weight. Maybe it was too easy? Well, I should have never dumped Marsha to be with Chloe."

"You had to ride that wave."

"And now I'm trying to find that space that connects all those things again, the feeling of beauty and love, eros and the divine. I can have sex. But unlike with Chloe, it's harder to get a sense of that larger sensibility."

"There are only so many times you get to have that feeling," Bobby lamented. "That's probably what Houellebecq was talking about. We lose our capacity for connection."

189

"I don't know. At first, I adored her look, her touch. But after a while I couldn't feel who she was. Maybe I was losing who I was, or just getting bored? That's the mystery of it. It was all there. She was smart and gorgeous but..."

"Do you ever feel like you just want to run?" Bobby cut me off, commiserating, as he looked out of the window into the San Francisco sun, shining through the second floor window of the old pup.

"Yes."

"You have everything and you can't feel a thing."

"It's that lingering Groucho Marx relationship feeling," I said.

"Or just literally running away. I had to do that with Lucy once."

"Really? I know the feeling."

"You want another pint?" asked Bobby.

"Please."

As he was ordering, I thought about this conversation we had shared for years. It began in college, reflecting on the ways we fall in love, and then lose control. But the feeling still lingers, along the with memory. When we were in college we talked about the movies and the way they transform us. But love got in the way. And now we write and share stories.

"So what's in that blue notebook you are always carrying around?" Bobby asked.

"It's the notes for this story, 'Trying to Know Julie: A novel about love and plague... or something like that."

"Who's Julie?"

"She's everyone and no one in this ill-suited affair, all the stories, between *Sophie's Choice*, *Death in Venice* and the *Rachel Papers*," I said, reflecting on the title. "It sounds better than Beatrice right?"

"...a space for self-emulation through sex."

"Huh?"

"Killing yourself looking for that authentic feeling."

"But sometimes it's addiction or compulsion or self-destruction."

"That's the Lancelot feeling. He betrayed his absolute best friend, King Arthur, for his wife."

Bobby got up to go to the bathroom. I looked out at the bar and the view outside.

"We are all just guys," he replied when he came back.

"That was quick."

"Just peeing. There was a quote scribbled on the bathroom. I wrote it down. He read to me: 'There are mornings when all men experience with fatigue a flush of tenderness that makes them horny.'"

"That's beautiful. Who said that again?"

"Jean Genet."

"Just part of being alive, right? David Bowie wrote Jean Genie about him."

"Well, my stuff isn't that cheery." He showed me a draft of an early story he'd been working on about a girl he dated in college and their breakup. We'd all been friends and things got blurry when he went away to study in England. At some point, Natalie found her way into my bed on a long road trip to Berkeley and Santa Cruz. Bobby ruminated about their moment in college:

190

"I met Natalie in Introduction to Philosophy, first year in college," he read from the manuscript he was carrying around.

"Can I read a draft and get back to you?"

"Sure."

After we finished drinks, Bobby and I went back to City Lights Bookstore, just across from the bar. I picked up the new *Disease Pariah News* and Pat Califia's *Public Sex*. I wanted my own copy.

"Try *This Side of Paradise*," Bobby said. "It'll get you ready for Princeton."

"Really? I hate that place."

"It's a great book, all about it."

Later that night I picked up Bobby's manuscript and started to read. The characters felt so familiar. The protagonist's blond college girlfriend, their lostness, their eerie encounter that night with Natalie in Berkeley. And then a trip to the beach the next weekend, in which we all ate mushrooms, Natalie, my roommate and I, munching on them like corn chips. I forgot they were shrooms. Caught in an hallucination, I thought I could never get off the beach. Fear gripped me. Blurring a space between myself and the other, I regressed. There was someone I might have known, or a dream of who I might have been with who always was in these words and worlds. We all walk in Oedipus' shoes at some point in our lives, killing the things closest to us. The stranger stares at you and tells you stories about people you might have known amidst the soul jarring by-your-selfness of the everyday. Redemption intermingles with the petty humiliations and lost connections; it feels like stories among old friends. The cavalcade of past girlfriends reminds you of something. Our protagonist is invited for a liaison with a new friend. Yet, unexpected, unwanted visitors join. "These ghosts of old girlfriends linger about him," Bobby had written.

The next day, two days before Christmas, we had a small party in the building, with cake and catered food. The residents shared photos and cards, and we watched movies. Most everyone who could came down and took part in the party, a few in wheelchairs. For this evening at least, the usual sarcasm of the space was nowhere to be found. People seemed appreciative of just being there.

Willy, who was a former porno actor, sat and watched *Scrooged*, chuckling to himself. In his wire glasses, blond spiked hair, jean shorts, Chuck Taylor sneakers, basketball shorts, he was a sight. He rarely complained about the neuropathy that had overtaken his legs. Mostly, he hobbled, spending his days painting and showing his works at local galleries.

"Are you coming to my Christmas Eve party?" Pedro asked Gab, another resident.

"I can't. I have a plane I have to take. I plan to be out the whole holiday," Gab replied in a catty tone.

"Well, tell the others in your crew," Pedro followed, not hearing the put-down.

"What about you, Cab? You coming?" Pedro asked me again.

"I am going back to Princeton to be with my family."

"You'll still be here," Pedro followed, smiling, pointing to his heart and all around the building. "You'll still be here."

He was right.

My boss, Raoul, walked up and we chatted for a minute, always awkward. The good mood did not last.

"Look around here. Most of the people in this room won't be around next year," he said.

I just looked at him. He seemed a little too comfortable saying that.

"But maybe they will?" I replied. "But everyone might be okay."

"Don't count on it."

None of us are God, I thought to myself.

Maybe he was right, but just perhaps there was room for something else within all this. It felt that way talking with Willy and Pedro and Bobby, or walking out of City Lights, strolling the streets of the city. Maybe there was another story here, in the tales of the Catacombs, the poets at City Lights, the sex radicals, and the people at 1994 Market?

Between Princeton and Home

"Souls were rising, from the earth far below, souls of the dead, of people who had perished, from famine, from war, from the plague,"
-Tony Kushner, *Angels in America*

"...my whole life was a haunted life, the life of a ghost. I was halfway across America, at the dividing line between the East of my youth and the West of my future, and maybe that's why it happened right there and then..."
-Jack Kerouac, *On the Road*

"They slipped briskly into an intimacy from which they never recovered," -F. Scott Fitzgerald, *This Side of Paradise*

The next day I packed my bags and caught a plane to Princeton, New Jersey, where Mom had settled after the divorce went through. Wearing my freshly procured, used leather jacket, I got on the plane and pulled out *This Side of Paradise*. Bobby was right. It was so good. Princeton had been one of the happiest times of my parents' life. For a while, everything worked. We rode bikes, played, and my little brother Pete was born. It was the 1970s. Dad happily escaped being a lawyer, earning his PhD and then a job at the university. But somewhere between Nixon, Watergate hearings, and Ford, life caught up with mom and dad. A successive chain of events changed everything. First a stroke laid dad out, robbing him of his critical edge, leaving him in a hospital for a year, before returning to Princeton half himself. His performance suffered—and the university let him go. The stuffiness of the place was exhausting. Their most famous president, Woodrow Wilson, institutionalized segregation, igniting the Red Scare, exiling immigrants and dimming the US political imagination. But everyone loved him for his proximity to power; the preppy East Coast—its exclusions, prohibitions, and classism—lingered with a stench like the starch in the shirts in the Polo Store on Nassau Street.

It never felt like home. In San Francisco, no one cared where you were from or went to school. In Princeton, it seemed like this was all anyone ever talked about. Still, Mom moved back after the divorce, to take up where she left off, teaching and writing and being a socialite. We didn't talk about the divorce much. The balance was off. But nonetheless, I was coming to visit her.

I showed up in Princeton, after a long flight, catching the train from Newark, and then the dinky to the campus, walking to the house through the snow on the night of December 23rd.

"Cab, what are you wearing?" Mom asked, greeting me. "That jacket looks like it's from a homeless person."

"It's my new jacket," I said smiling. Oh boy. When was I going to get back to San Francisco?

We all went to Christmas Eve midnight mass the next night. At first I laughed at how formal the 19th century stone gothic church felt. The sermon put me to sleep. When I awoke, the lights were going out. It was close to midnight. Everyone was singing "Silent Night," holding candles lighting the church. They were the only light in the old church. I found myself thinking of Pedro and his Christmas party, which

193

was taking place at the same time a continent away on Market Street. It was odd to realize that felt like home.

We were all going to go for a stroll through campus the next day.

"You're not going to wear that jacket, are you, Cab?" Mom asked as we were walking out.

"Yes, I am. That's why I'm wearing it."

"Can you please wear something else?"

"Why?"

"What if one of my friends sees you?"

"Forget it. I'll just stay home then," I said. I was flustered and my skin was suddenly boiling.

"Then I'm not going to get you anything at the sale."

"I just thought I could come back home and not be judged by you or everyone."

"Just remember the next time you ask me for a favor, what a bad actor you have been this trip."

"I'll just stay home, Mom."

"What is wrong with wanting you to be presentable?"

"Who cares what they think?"

"I do."

I wanted to be anywhere but here. I was ready to walk home

The next day, Mom came home from seeing her therapist.

"I talked with my therapist about this. He said me telling you what to wear was taking away your dignity."

"I'm just tired of all this. Why do all the vacations have to be such dramas?"

"They don't."

"Then why do you care or comment about what I wear?"

"Cab, my parents died when I was younger than you. I have no idea how to talk with my adult children. I'm sorry, okay? Are you satisfied? I'm sorry. I'm sorry. I'm sorry."

She stormed upstairs, still the daughter of the Confederacy, the granddaughter of the Junior League. She didn't like to talk about certain things. Kids were to be presented, not heard. Surfaces were more important. But the shadows lingered, concealing a lot of collateral damage. Her parents had drunk themselves into the grave, after a divorce that mom rarely mentioned. They were still her ideal.

I walked into the living room. My older brother was sitting and looking at the fire.

"Well, I've caused a fine mess now, haven't I?" I said.

"You sure have." He stared at the fireplace. A minute later, he walked up to me.

"Just think about this. Just think about how valuable being right is. Just think about it. Is it worth it? That's all I'm going to add."

I walked out, finally going for that stroll through town to the campus, looking at the eleven-foot bronze Henry Moore statue, titled "Oval with Points." My brothers and I had crawled on it when we were kids, when Dad had worked there two decades prior. It was his dream job. He rode his bike to work, never happier until it all fell apart. He wanted to walk in front of a truck when the university let him go. That was how I felt. Our Dallas adventures had come after that fateful dismissal. The West felt like an exile from

194

this. They did not want him here. Over the years, he'd gradually come to see, he could have more fun in exile, away from the East Coast. I was coming to the same conclusion. We'd had more adventures when mom moved out, leaving Dad and me on our own. I visited Mom in London and we traipsed around the city, looking at the museums, building our own relationship over the years.

As I was walking, I strolled by the local movie theater showing a double feature of *Ordinary People* and *Kramer vs. Kramer*. Over the years, these films had come to be signposts for what life could and would be like. Throughout each, families and marriages come apart, with distant mothers, the betrayals of youth, fathers and sons becoming closer, making sense of their losses together. It was hard for me not to think of Dad and our years together in Dallas before it all fell apart. "Plastic," Dad used to say, comparing Mom and Mary Tyler Moore, perhaps unfairly. None of us choose parents. And parents do not choose their birth families. Certainly, Mom did not choose her siblings who fought with her over her parents' belongings after their premature departure. She rushed home from college, but was too late to say good-bye to her mom. It was only a few years later that she met Dad when he was stationed at Fort Benning. He was her knight in shining armor. And they began a decade long whirlwind—traveling the world, having kids, and leaving the South behind before life caught up with them in Princeton. We all form attachments and then they break apart—this is the stuff of growing up. For some, the capacity for trust erodes; for others, it expands with resilience. Some come out the other side, coping and growing together. That was the story of Dad and I. But the pain in between was very real. Early in *Ordinary People*, Dustin Hoffman tells his wife about someone in the office, whispering, "committed suicide." That was also part of the story in Princeton.

The snow was beginning again as I walked out of the movies. Walking back to the house, I thought of my godfather, who killed himself when we lived in Princeton back in 1975. The week before he left, we had been hanging out. He stayed over at the house. I idolized him, looking up to him as he shaved. He gave me a handful of shaving cream I spread on my face, shaving it off with my fingers. He was playful and sweet. A week later my parents called me into the room to tell me something had happened. They had fear in their face as they brought me in the room to deliver the bad news: he had shot himself. He was gone.

"It's not your fault," they repeated, over and over again. "It's not your fault."

I remember crying as we talked about it.

Dad and I talked about what had happened. He seemed to understand, in more ways than I could imagine.

"He felt the world close in on himself," Dad explained. They took pains to point out that none of it was because of me.

Maybe this was what they were talking about late into the night? We were a generation learning to make sense of separation and its vast impacts on all of us who survive it, as kids, young adults, and parents ourselves. Primordial bonds ever forming and breaking—as we were trying to rebuild them.

My mind drifted back to that art class in fifth grade, to Daisy who had had pizza the night before, dining by herself. I could always see her sitting there alone with that pizza box. Many came out fine; others lost themselves, overdosed, threw themselves out of windows, repeating the same patterns. And, of course, our family split apart, as did most of my friends' families. The separations extended well into the distance. That 1975 feeling would always be with me.

The next day, we all got out of Princeton, and drove into Manhattan to see Tony Kushner's *Angels in America*, parts one and two. An early scene explored the underlying messages of a 1980s AIDS diagnosis.

During the scene when Cohn was diagnosed with AIDS, I thought of Tom, who had died of AIDS only two years prior. He had always loved theater. I wondered about the ways in which he responded to his diagnosis. I hated to think of the influence such forces had had on him. He had spent decades concealing his sexuality, coping with a conduct under circumstances other than honorable discharge from the military, and even participating in "reparative therapy" for homosexuality. I came to see why Tom was not more forthcoming with me about it. How much of that message had he turned inward?

After part one, we went to lunch at the Russian Tea Room.

"Do you like the show, Mom?" I asked. "What do you think?"

"I was thinking of Tom."

"Me too."

"An epic day of theater," my older brother said.

"It's the story of our time—making meaning of illness, betrayal and history," I pontificated.

After lunch, we went back to the theater for part two of the show *Perestroika*.

It would last another three hours. I could not follow it much of the time. Drifting in and out, I found myself thinking of San Francisco. I reflected on the haunted feelings, the lonely places we know, flying back to the West, as the characters were doing in the play. As Kushner's narrators explained: "Night flight to San Francisco; chase the moon across America... Souls were rising, from the earth far below, souls of the dead, of people who had perished, from famine, from war, from the plague, and they floated up, like skydivers in reverse, limbs all akimbo, wheeling and spinning. And the souls of these departed joined hands, clasped ankles, and formed a web, a great net of souls, and the souls were three-atom oxygen molecules of the stuff of ozone, and the outer rim absorbed them and was repaired. Nothing's lost forever. In this world, there's a kind of painful progress. Longing for what we've left behind, and dreaming ahead."

Watching the play, looking at our lives, souls rising, away from home, and back, ebbing and departing, it would be like that for a long time.

Balkan Dreams

"Sarajevo is the Spanish Civil War of our time, but the difference in response is amazing...In 1937, people like Ernest Hemingway and Andre Malraux and George Orwell and Simone Weil rushed to Spain, although it was incredibly dangerous."
-Susan Sontag, August 19, 1993

"Her eyes change like the sunlight,"
-Walker Percy, *Thanatos Syndrome*

A couple of days after getting back to San Francisco, I went out with Jasmin, a woman with a European accent, brunette hair, and a sexy old-world sophistication. On our first date, we went to see Puccini's "*Turandot*" at the San Francisco opera. The palace was a cathedral of high culture, society men and women in elegant clothes with jewels. While we were sitting in the balcony seats, a commotion started bubbling from the stage.

"People are dying and you're sitting in the opera! You have blood on your hands," screamed the members of ACT UP, standing up, disrupting the show. "People are dying!" They hoisted a sign declaring "Out of the Opera into the Streets!" "Silence Equals Death."

"Let's get out of here," Jasmin whispered, and we made our way out. We chatted all the way back to her majestic apartment on Nob Hill, just across from Grace Cathedral. We spent the rest of the weekend holed up inside, barely opening the shades, escaping from the world around us. Sleeping there, I dreamt of us driving through the Italian Alps, the wind blowing across our faces.

"Have you been here before?" she asked as we drove, listening to Verdi's Requiem Mass.

"I think so," I smiled, navigating the curving mountain roads.

"Do you know where we are going?"

"No idea where." She leaned over to kiss me as we drove. For a second there, it was almost as if the trust that happened before all the breakups, the warmth before the past wrongs, it was all there. Everything was right. The connection was back.

On Sunday, we finally opened the shades, and the light shone in on the dark blue sheets. While eating breakfast, we looked at the papers. Jasmin asked me about the Balkan War that was still raging.

"What is the U.S. going to do?"

"I think I heard something about a man who played his cello right in the middle of Sarajevo, as a local theater performed *Waiting for Godot*," I replied.

"Godot ain't coming," Jasmin retorted. "No one is rescuing anyone. They are being slaughtered as the world looks away; Clinton is paralyzed and you are talking about the cello."

I was taken aback by her change in tone. She asked another question about San Francisco and the Bohemian Society, mentioning something about a former lover of hers who had been a part of the old 1872 society. I had no idea, except what I had read about in *Tales of the City*.

The mood in the room was changing. I felt like I was being quizzed. She asked a third riddle about what women liked, what they wanted. I answered, trying to say something about women wanting honesty, but it wasn't to her satisfaction. She squinted her eyes. And then she ushered me out the door.

"Please do not call again," she said. "I knew you weren't for me."

I stumbled out into the day, and the sun glared at me. I put my hands up against my eyes, wandering into the street, stumbling into the path as a trolley zoomed my way. As I turned around, I saw the front of the train heading at me and then it was over.

Waking from the dream in my dingy room in the Haight, I pulled out the blue notebook and wrote down what had happened. I was ignoring something out there. There was something I was not seeing, looming. But I didn't know what. Still, the dream was not uncommon. I had a variation of it several days a week. I grabbed the newspaper and a cup of coffee. Reading, I noticed that "*Turandot*" really was playing at the San Francisco opera that season. And that ACT UP really had disrupted the opening. Maybe I had made a mistake not sticking it out with ACT UP and my community at the opera? But who was my community—the woman I was chasing or the activists? Why had I walked out in the dream? What was I chasing? All I knew was that there was more romance in the dream than anything I had experienced in a very long time. I looked at that dusty old copy of *Love in the Ruins* from senior year with its homage to Dante and the "death-dealing Western world." I was lost in San Francisco. The ruins, the smell of smoke from the fire on my street still in the air.

Tessa was still around. We talked all the time. I wasn't really sure why. We rarely understood each other. But we still got together all the time. She was a familiar sympathetic friend. A few days after I got back from Princeton, we sat listening to music at Cleo's on Pierce and Haight. She told me about a friend of hers in the Mission.

"She tends to be really masculine, you know, she works on cars, has grease all over her jeans and stuff, wears boots," she explained, describing her neighbor.

"Very butch."

"I don't like to use that word," Tessa said, scolding me. The admonitions seemed to just roll from her lips.

"Everyone I know uses the word at work to describe lesbians with masculine mannerisms. It's a term of endearment," I tried to explain.

"It's also a mean stereotype," declared Tessa, ever an adherent of the second wave feminism in which she grew up. Sex wars were always raging between us.

"One of my friends suggested we have butch days at the apartment for my roommate who just came out."

"Cab, what about the Rilke I got you? In between your adventures, have you gotten to take a look?"

"I like the term 'sexual generosity.'"

"That's a good way of putting it," she smiled.

"I love the book, love it. Thank you."

"I knew you would."

"He says that romance shouldn't be a substitute for other things missing within us. We just have to sit with the feelings about all those things that are absent."

"Exactly Cab."

"But it's easier said than done. He says it's about the questions, filling life with them, getting to them, giving them space."

"So what questions are you asking?"

"I'm trying to figure out why so many people are dying. What happens when they die? What happens when I dream and I see them or when I die in a dream? Are we ever going to get out of this? What do we do about Sarajevo, the civil war in Rwanda? Am I ever going to have a girlfriend again?"

"That's why I went to Nepal, just to ask a few of those questions."

"Any answers?"

"Yeah, lots."

"Like what?"

"Seeing good people out there trying to be a part of a solution."

"But what holds so many of us off from that?"

"I don't know."

"I guess, it's getting beyond old grudges, letting go of old things," I confessed, as if trying to convince myself. "I no longer care about what happened before. It is good to be here."

"I thought you missed the South."

"I do. I completely miss the South. That's why I still read all the Walker Percy stories. In *Thanatos Syndrome*, he describes Lucy who drinks whisky like the best of them. I still hope for someone who will at least drink Shiner Bock beer with me. But we have to live in the here and now, looking at life as it really is, making our choices to act when we can, or at least to 'make friends with her terror... the depths' Percy describes."

"That's where the gold is," Tessa chimed in, "lurking in those shadows."

Eventually, Tessa and I started walking. Bulldozers were clearing the rubble from the remnants of the final Victorian houses that had been damaged from the fire over Thanksgiving weekend. It took what felt like forever for the fire trucks to arrive. By now, most of the corner was gone, a remnant of 1960s counter culture turned to rubble. It smelled of urine. Crack vials were still on the corner, like a hangover of the dreams from the neighborhood. Inside the garbage, a magazine was sitting there with the headline: "The '60s San Francisco—Get Over It!" Tessa was trying. We were all trying. I could talk with her for hours. But it wasn't always comfortable. Still, she was helping me make sense of it all. Sharing and commiserating as I collected more and more stories, talking with residents in the building, busing around town, conducting oral histories, drafting more and more notes in the blue notebook.

Later at work, Willy stood with his friend, signing out of the building.

"Cab's gonna know we're crazy," his friend Mark said.

"Cab already knows I'm crazy," he smiled, looked at Mark and then at me. "I find it endearing."

"Not that I admire everyone's forthrightness," Mark followed.

"Forthright or bold?" Willy asked. "Everyone here is pretty honest about where they are at, that no one here lives with piety. We're honest about the indulgences we enjoy."

"But why do you think people can be so honest here, as opposed to the East?" I asked.

"Well, when you face your mortality every day, you get that way," Willy said as he walked out.

2:24 AM at Work

"I think he just loved being with the bears because they didn't make him feel bad. I get it too. When he was with the bears, they didn't care that he was kind of weird, or that he'd gotten into trouble for drinking too much and using drugs... They didn't ask him a bunch of stupid questions about how he felt, or why he did what he did. They just let him be who he was."

-Michael Thomas Ford, *Suicide Notes*

After everyone else at 1994 Market went to sleep, I spent the evening watching two and a half hours of Watergate hearings, and reading the annual sex readers poll in *Details* magazine. I didn't want to face what had happened when Willy had walked to the edge. The call came at about 2:24 a.m.

"Cab, Mark is coming over."

"But Willy, you know I can't..." I responded, looking at a memo stating that Mark had been banned from visiting because of multiple infractions of building rules.

Residents saw the building rules as controlling and patronizing. Everyone hated them. My job was to serve as a mediator between those who made them and those who abhorred them.

"Cab, my window is open. I'm looking at it. I'm thinking about jumping."

"Can I come up?" I asked.

"Yeah."

"Okay. I'll be there in a second." I hung up the phone, called my supervisors, and went up to the sixth floor, where I knocked on Willy's door.

"Can I come in?" I asked.

"The door's open."

Madonna was blasting as I walked into the dark, cluttered apartment. Row after row of art books lined the walls. Willy sat low behind his table full of ashtrays, cigarettes, and a beat up typewriter.

His face was red, with a half grown moustache complimenting his distinct short spiky blond hair. He was wearing his standard blue warm-ups, Reebok high tops, and smoking. The window was open wide. There were no bars on it, and it offered a clear view of Market Street, six floors below. Willy sat in his low chair, about eighteen inches off the ground, crossed his leg, and ashed his cigarette. He had had a lot to drink. His words slurred, his eyes dotting from left to right behind his steel-rimmed glasses.

It was hard to believe that he had been in gay porno movies. But it was something everyone knew about him.

"Was that fun?" I had asked.

"It was never work if the guys were cute," he had told me with a smile, revealing his crooked teeth. In previous weeks, he had told me he was getting his life together. He was giving up on men. He was going to concentrate on art. And when he did, the results were often astonishing. Tom, who had been one of the organizers of the positive art shows, told me, "Willy's work displays a powerful rawness, which I can simply admire. He really is in touch with that and I don't know where that comes from."

I could see that rawness now. In his room on the sixth floor, it was beginning to fly out of control.

"He's really been unraveling lately," one of the case managers had explained earlier in the week.

I pushed aside a photo from a magazine of a nude man holding his erect penis.

"Cab, this isn't working for me here anymore. You know."

He was sobbing and his voice was getting deeper.

"Jim asked my friend for an ID when he came in here the other day. He didn't have one," Willy explained. "I said 'it wasn't part of the policy here.'"

"'It was as of two weeks ago,' Jim said. And he didn't let him into the building, humiliating both of us. I was boiling. It isn't working for me. But I have nowhere else to go. They treat me like an animal here," Willy lamented. "I know I am just an AIDS patient, but ...." He was crying and smoking a cigarette. "But I'm still a human and I have rights. I can't live here anymore. I have to go."

He emphasized the word "go" and began sobbing even harder. Madonna was still playing. "*You must be my lucky star....*"

"Mark is my lover, yes, my lover. He's been 86'd so he can't come into the building. I was thinking about throwing myself out of the building earlier, actually thinking about jumping for the first time in my life. I just don't feel worth anything. I have no dignity here. Cab, I got so drunk tonight. It's the only thing that takes away all the pain."

His pack of cigarettes was lying on the table. I asked if I could have one.

"Take one. This is serious shit," Willy said and then chuckled.

I struggled for words as I lit the cigarette.

"Thanks for calling downstairs. You're an amazing person." I didn't want to sound trite. But I did not know what to say. He smiled again. And we talked for a while.

Eventually, my supervisors Raoul and Jim showed up. They knocked on the door and entered with condescending looks, like they were dealing with a child. A cop came in and asked if Willy was still thinking about hurting himself or if he wanted to go to the hospital to talk with a counselor. I immediately regretted telling them what had happened. They both stayed for a while, and left ten minutes later. Willy stayed in his room. I went downstairs.

After everyone went to bed, Raoul and I talked for the next thirty minutes.

"You do begin to get better at this stuff," he said to me. "You really do. It gets easier... but there's a point when you enter the mentality of the client. That becomes unhealthy. You know that sick feeling you have in your stomach now? It's like being slimed. These people have no exclusive right to pain. It was around before we all got here and it will be here long after we leave."

"Lepers have been around forever and the more I look at this, the more I think it sounds familiar. I sometimes worry we're treating the residents here in a similar way," I said.

"You're coming to a crossing point here."

"Huh?"

"All your stuff with the clients, death and with the policies. I think it's wonderful that you bring to us a consideration of humanity vs. policies. But your job is just to follow them."

"I agree. Well, I just wanted to let you know I'm finding a place for their memory," I lied, wanting him to hear that I was okay with all this.

"Thank you for letting me know," he said.

"It's not that I'm not angry. But I am letting go of it, and beginning to be grateful to have known a few people who worked so hard just trying to take advantage of living."

We talked a while longer before saying goodnight. When he left, I paced the lobby and watched the Watergate hearings to keep myself from falling asleep. I hoped Willy was okay. I looked out into the street, feeling alone all through that long, cold night.

A Morning Bus Ride

"Last night... I dreamt of a stranger... Only with him could I be alone... "
-Marion, *Wings of Desire*.
Wim Wenders, Peter Handke, and Richard Reitinger, 1987

The bus routes in San Francisco extended from the beach to the Financial District and back, picking up people going to and from, making their way through the lively streets of this wide-open town. I rode for hours. People poured inside, some on acid in the morning, others meditating or passing out, listening to music for long, quiet distances, trying to get somewhere or find something. Much like the angel Damiel in *Wings of Desire* who looked into the internal monologues of people in the subways, I always wondered who they were, what their internal struggles were, how we were joined and separated. "Why am I me and why not you? Why am I here and why not there?" Damiel thought, looking at them.

Rick from high school dropped into town for work. He only had one day in the city, so we planned to meet for breakfast. My roommate and I took the #6 bus into the Financial District with all the people on their way to work, jumping on at the corner of Pierce and Haight. Rick was staying at the Mandarin Oriental Hotel.

I hadn't had any action in weeks, and I was looking for contact with every girl I saw on the street, at work, in cafes and buses—everywhere there were people.

It seemed like every temp employee in the Haight was on the #6 bus that morning, wearing their crumpled best professional gear, recovering from their hangovers. Some held huge paper cups of coffee, red the paper or novels, such as *The Crying of Lot 49* or stared into nothingness as they made their way to their copy room jobs, where they'd spend all day in the basement. A few read the *Wall Street Journal*; everyone carried a backpack, and only some had showered. One man sat cutting his toenails, with his sandals in his lap. Most of the guys wore wrinkled khaki's; the women read novels by Marquez or Vintage classics with splendid covers. Holding onto the straps hanging, my roommate, Raymond told me about coming clean with his completely self-absorbed workmate, Steve. We bantered and my eyes turned to the woman sitting directly behind him. She had black hair pulled up behind her head, a fine cream-colored cotton shirt, her suit jacket on her lap, and was wearing a coy expression. She looked directly at me. I locked eyes with her for a brief moment and turned back to continue my conversation with Louis. By the time we crossed Laguna Street at the projects, I caught her looking at me again and turned away nervously, taken aback. At Franklin Street, our eyes locked again.

"Hmm," I thought as Raymond went on, talking and talking as I schemed.

"Do you have a pen?" I asked him.

"Sure," he handed me one and went on.

Five minutes later, Raymond got off at Sixth Street. The bus had cleared out a bit and I sat down, contemplating how I could get her number. I turned my head and she was sitting right beside me.

I was going to initiate chitchat. But she beat me to it.

"What prep school did you go to?" she asked.

"Greenhill in Dallas," I replied, somewhat taken aback.

"I knew it. You can always tell people from prep school. I could hear it in your voice and see it in your clothes."

"What about you?"

"I didn't go to prep school. I just went to high school in Davis, and a small college in New England."

"What school?"

"Wesleyan, in Connecticut."

"You're kidding. The person I'm going to meet right now actually went to Wesleyan. I used to visit there all the time."

It turned out she even knew Rick and Grant. When we got to the Financial District, she walked me over to the Mandarin Oriental across Market Street to meet Rick. And we said goodbye.

"Neat," Rick said when I told him about the encounter. He was standing in front of a gargantuan window, with the Pacific Ocean right behind him.

"This makes my day."

"Makes my day as well," I said.

We trekked out on Geary to have Bloody Mary's at the Boat House right on the beach. After many smokes and refreshing gin and tonics, we had concocted a plan for the big date to follow.

"Don't expect too much from the first date. A little dinner, wine—not beer. Then go to a noisy bar so you can sit really close to her. Have a few drinks and get a little contact."

"What happens if she doesn't drink?"

"If she doesn't drink, then you better brush up on what's going on in Sarajevo. You're a charming guy. You can handle it."

"That's right."

"Look Cab. I was reading something the other day about San Francisco. This writer, I think he's Michael Porfirio, he says there are two kinds of San Francisco women, the 'Sophisticates' and the 'Fly' girls. The Sophisto's are the posh, highbrow types. They have gone to good schools and know more about art, culture and haute cuisine than you ever imagined. The Fly girls, on the other hand, they have no idea about porchetta and polenta or crudo on the half shell, but they can do somersaults, and dance on tables. You have to figure out who you are dealing with here and play to that. If I had to guess, I'd say Gina's a Sophisticate."

"I think so. My last girlfriend Sue was more of a Fly type, amazing. But she left me feeling empty."

"Well, watch for what you're wishing for."

"What do you mean?"

"I mean watch out. She may not be as cool as Sue was."

"I'm just trying to make a new friend."

After a final cigarette on the steps of the Pacific Stock Exchange on Sansome and Pine Street, we said goodbye.

"Not much money goes through here," he said, sounding philosophical.

"This thing has so many possibilities. You've already got so much to talk about—Wesleyan, hometowns, the East Coast versus California, college, and what a small world it is. You're set."

Or so I thought.

My day ended with Rick just in time for my 5:30 workout at Pinnacle Fitness. On the way up to the gym, a younger woman in worn jeans with a short brunette bob walked into the building with me. We took the same elevator. I was immediately taken. She looked down. I looked down and then at her. She looked up again, straight at me.

"Hello."

"Hello."

We got off the elevators and went our respective ways. I wouldn't see her again for months. But there was something about her. I was taken aback. I loved a girl with a bob.

Two nights later, my friend Ann and I went out for gumbo before my date. She vented about the sad scenario she had found herself in with her boyfriend from London. "He was such a horndog. I used to fuck him every night I'd see him."

"So what happened?"

"And then he dumps me the second he leaves town," she moaned before ordering another beer.

"Oh Ann!"

"It's ok. I'm going to see the Kronus Quartet. They're performing 'Purple Haze' tonight," she announced. "You wanna come?"

"No, I'm off to see Gina, the woman I met on the bus."

"Have fun," Ann said, looking at me with a sense of warning. She seemed to have a hunch about where things might go. "And be careful."

Gina was a mixed bag of personality traits, and I could tell we were off balance from the start. It was as if she was a different person from the one I met on the bus. She was wearing oversized overalls and a black one piece. Her eyes were dynamic.

"I've got a huge amount of work to do later so I can only stay for a bit," she announced when I arrived. She wanted to go support a female friend at a reading. So we went to hear monologues in progress at a performance space in the Mission.

"I'm going to say hi to her quickly," she said when we walked in, leaving me to my own devices, as she greeted her friend.

Everyone sat down, crowding onto the floor, and waited for the readings to start. One woman read about crystal meth. Another rambled on about a trip to the beach and her inner explorations, sounding like an old Patti Smith monologue. As the readers shared their stories, a woman in a motorcycle jacket with a sticker that said, 'Cunt Licker' sat eating on a burrito, the aluminum foil wrapping crinkling. A younger man read about sitting up at 3:00 a.m. and staring at a brick wall. "With no fear, I can go through with no hesitation," he read, but it was not so simple. Sometimes he could not make it through. He recalled a friend who found a line of rushing traffic not to be transcended either, killing himself. Now he was gone. Gina sat listening intently, not looking at or acknowledging me. I hated this. When he finished his story, I clapped intently. I was relieved he was done.

After the show, we strolled down to 16th and Valencia to get a bite.

"What did you think of the show?" she asked.

"I liked some of them. But I felt like they should have been paying me to listen to their stories."

"Really, I loved it."

"I liked your friend's monologue. But there is a fine line between art and therapy."

Between crepes and wine, we talked about our lives and families. She told me about her immigrant background and her family escaping the Holocaust. I told her about my family from the South.

"Your family have not suffered the tragedies other people have, hence the weaknesses," she replied condescendingly.

"I didn't realize we were having a competition."

"It's not. But I know a lot of horrible stuff happened in the South."

"Like everywhere, like here. There's nothing I can do about where I come from. But I can try to be different. That's what I'm doing here."

"So you moved to this island of misfit toys?"

"Yes. My dad went to law school with future Supreme Court justices, the best and brightest and their raw ambition. I could have done the same. But wanted to be something different."

"But we carry our histories wherever we go," she continued.

Pivoting to what was usually smoother terrain, I brought up the movies.

"Have you seen *Schindler's List?*" she asked.

"I don't want to see it. Just seems like Spielberg's ploy to get an Oscar. Now all of a sudden the man who gave us *Goonies* cares about the Holocaust? I don't buy it."

"Well he is Jewish," she continued.

"In publishing they say books about the Kennedy assassination, the Civil War and the Holocaust always sell. It's not that they are not great topics but it is hard for me to look beyond the source."

She looked at me with a sense of disgust.

"You're being closed minded," she scolded me with righteous indignation. "That movie is revolutionary."

"Have you seen *Man Facing Southeast?*" I asked, trying to change the subject. "It's a story about an alien who ends up in a psychiatric hospital in Argentina."

"Nope. But I would have seen it if I knew about it. You're refusing to see this film. That's wrong," she lectured me.

"I saw enough of those movies in college," I said trying to make my case. "He wants people to take him seriously and to create a hit. Plus it just sounds like all the stories from Krakow Ghetto pulled together." She was glaring at me. "I'm more of a *Wings of Desire* person anyways. The angel's struggle with who he is, with history, with Berlin, feels very resonant."

"Well, we are all of our history, all that came before us. I am and you are. That's why I was curious about you. I heard something in your voice."

"But why did you talk with me?"

"I had a hunch."

"What was the hunch?"

"It's not what you think."

"What was it?"

"You sounded like people I know who went to prep school."

"That's true. But I'm starting to think you have the wrong impression about me."

"I'm not sure. You're cute. But it's time for you to learn a little about history and maybe even women."

"Really. Don't we all? Aren't we just people?"

"Yes, but there is more to it. I mean you seem like a nice enough guy Cab. But you represent privilege. Your Southern family represents that. Your ignorance represents that. And now you're here. It's like entitlement coming to San Francisco. You need to open your eyes to what that represents. Women are still being killed by men, Black men are still dying because of the vestiges of slavery."

"I see that every day at work. I saw it in the LA Riots."

"Then connect the dots Cab. All these things—the racism, slavery, homophobia, and sexism—they are all the tools of patriarchy. They are still here. Patriarchy uses these tools to control."

"I see it. But I can't control all that. I don't."

"Don't be so sure Cab."

Now I was glaring at her.

"Well, you can learn from it. You can learn from history. And act on it."

"Isn't that what I'm doing?"

"As a social worker?"

"Yes. And as a writer, as a person."

"All those Holocaust movies—did they scare you?"

"Yes, I found them brutal and haunting. But also fascinating. Plus the uniforms in *The Damned* were super sexy. Those Gestapo SS leather jackets were fabulous. I think Hugo Boss designed some of them."

"Wearing Hugo Boss to kill people." She didn't like the Hugo Boss point. "He also designed the clothes for the Hitler Youth and used prison labor in his factories. To this day the company has never apologized."

"We all have history to learn from," I replied. But she was not having it. We went our separate ways. I was still interested in her, ever ready to chase someone whose club I could not be a member of, to try to win her over. She agreed to brunch the following Saturday and then didn't show up. I was lost in the chase, meeting people and not quite connecting. That's what my dream was about with Jasmin. She was talking about Sarajevo. Willy was talking about not feeling welcomed, that he feels like an animal because the government treats him like that. He's at the building to die, not to get better. Everyone was telling me parts of a bigger story. Gina was talking about the Holocaust. Tessa saying don't be cavalier. Learn a little about history and the world. Learn about yourself. They were all trying to tell me something about me that I could not see. I felt like the angel in *Wings of Desire*, desperate, but unable to touch anyone.

The problem was history. The same thing was happening here. History was suffocating me. It's never easy becoming an active subject in history. I was the walking representation of a kind of American masculinity that people like Gina could not abide by, whether I meant to or not. I had to learn to be something else. I had to acknowledge her subjectivity, to learn about the struggles all around me. History lulls and tugs. But how have we become who we are going to be? What is our becoming? What becomes of those fragments of our past lives? Can they come back together? Can we? How do we make the most of our time in history, I wondered as I watched people walking in and out of the bars, going to see shows, performances, my clients moving to and from, in and out of this world. I thought of an old tape I had lost in high school, wondering if I was ever going to find it again. Looking around I knew there was another story I was writing. I knew it. I just didn't know what it was I was writing. History was still beyond knowing. "Something is terribly wrong," I wrote in the old blue notebook before going to work.

A Tragic Sense of ...

"Laws that have fallen into desuetude are the most terrible of all laws."
-Miguel de Unamuno's *Tragic Sense of Life*

Pedro rode a skateboard to work, carrying a rocking chair on his back. "I'm not into no tricks, I'm just trying to skate it," he told me, smiling. It was a relief to see him. But the good feeling soon turned. "I'm planning on a filing a grievance against one of the staff members," he continued, dragging the chair across the lobby.

"Why?" I asked, wondering if it might be me.

There were moments when he looked vibrant and alive. Other times, I didn't know.

"Did you hear about what happened to the lady who runs the restaurant next door?"

"No."

"She was shot. The place is coming apart at the seams," he said and skated away.

Richard walked in. He looked rattled. He said he had just been mugged while walking up Ninth Street, between Folsom and Howard.

"I've been walking that walk for 15 years," he said, shaking his head. "He put that knife up against me and I thought it was over. I thought he was going to push it into my stomach."

We talked, just unpacking the day. "This place is like a snake pit where they put the mentally ill. All through the history of mankind, people have exploited the poor. I heard during the earthquake in LA that that people were charging everyone one dollar for a glass of water. Raoul and everyone here, they should all be working in Auschwitz or Dachau. They're all a part of this history. When Louis was so scared about intruders that he called the cops, he got kicked out of the building. The cops came up to his room and he said, 'There they are,' and pointed to an empty closet. Within a couple of minutes, the cops began to understand what was going on. The next day Raoul went up to his room and told him he had to get out of here by the end of the day."

After Richard went upstairs, Pedro came down and offered me a plate of food.

"Thank you, but you know I can't take this. I really appreciate it, though," I said and gave him back the plate of beans and sausage he'd brought down for me. He took the plate and went back upstairs. When he came down again, he said, "It's attitudes like that that make me want to move out of this place. I know this place is full of rules. But it's up to you how you follow them."

I joined him outside later to talk. "It just hurts. All I know is it hurts," he mumbled with a quiver, alone, tears of grief welling up in his eyes. He said he felt like he was being treated like a child. I listened and went back inside. He stood by himself in the cold, before coming back inside and passing out on the couch. I couldn't wake him. I finally got him up after countless attempts. He stumbled straight toward the wall, his eyes still barely open.

At the end of my shift, I had to write an incident report.

When I got back the next day, Pedro said he was furious with me. He said he had been humiliated by Raoul's treatment after reading the report.

"It's just not right," he said over and over.

Bruce, another resident and former therapist, commented, "He's got to keep up with helping people out in the building. He has a lot of family betrayal history. His work in the building helps him feel attached."

I was beginning to feel like another one of Pedro's bureaucratic tormenters.

Reading Miguel de Unamuno's *Tragic Sense of Life* during the late hours of the shift, I could not but help thinking of the Raouls's rules. "There is always a way of obeying an order ... a way of carrying out what one believes to be an absurd operation while correcting its absurdity," wrote Unamuno. I wasn't as good at "correcting" the "absurdity" of the rules as Unamuno was, but I felt like I needed to do something.

When Pedro walked down again, I tried to talk with him. I told him I was sorry. He seemed to be over it. But he still looked upset.

"What's wrong?" I asked.

"It's Hank. I just found out."

"What?"

"You didn't hear? Jim found him in his room."

He looked out into space.

"I'm sorry, Pedro." I never knew what to say in moments like these. "I remember you telling me about going out one afternoon and having a great day together. At least you got that great day together."

"We didn't actually go," Pedro said and looked up. "That was the problem. We never got out. We coulda had a really nice day, gone for a drive through Marin, getting high."

"He just never had any strength left. I saw him walking in and out of the building with a pillow. He lost so much from wasting-syndrome. I always had this image of you guys driving through Marin, laughing. I'm sorry you missed that."

"Me too..."

"The last time I saw him was in the Civic Center. I asked him how he takes it. He said he was living now, but he was soon going to be leaving. 'I've already accepted what's going to happen to me,' he told me, recalling the riots from 1979."

"You're lucky you had that talk with him. Last time I saw him, he was too sick to talk. I wish we'd been able to at least share a smoke together."

I couldn't help but think there are few warmer people than Pedro. He always saw the fullest of these characters.

"No one else better die. Not another one of my friends. Thirty-seven people I have known have died in here. With every person who dies it gets harder for me to watch people here who are passing. Hank died of the same thing as me. I have neuropathy. The fevers don't bother me anymore. But the headaches and neuropathy do," he paused, reaching down to pull his pants up to his knees, running his hands along his legs. "The neuropathy really hurts," he explained. "Hank taught me to die. But I'm not gonna be able to get a second chance. I told Raoul that the whole thing choked me up a bit. And he said he agreed."

211

As I listened, I thought of what Raoul had said during Christmas. "Most of them won't be here next year." *Dear God, help us out of this one*, I thought, looking at Pedro wander up the stairs with his cat BooBoo. I thought about Juan who gave his friend a party the last month he was alive. Maybe this will be everyone's last year. Why is time running out for them? I couldn't begin to know.

"I'm gonna take a bus ride tomorrow," Pedro told me as he went up.

"Where?"

"I don't know. To the beach, to take acid. I don't know. Fuck this world."

Conversations with Toby

"AIDS research is reeling and in serious need of detoxification,"
-Project Inform, San Francisco, #14, June 1994

Work offered a glimpse of a world I had had no idea about just a year prior. Every day, I witnessed a cavalcade of disjointed lives, reeling from the unanticipated accumulation of losses and misdirection of the first months of the epidemic's third presidential administration. With little in treatment advances, those impacted were left to cope as best they could. Some, like Mark, resigned themselves to it all; others such as Pedro despaired. A small group of those, such as Toby, gambled with what little they had left.

One of the younger men in the building, Toby walked out of the hospital earlier in the day. He was in his mid-thirties, and his young face seemed to display all the emotions of the ordeal—fear, hope, and the creeping anxiety. I noticed him beginning to look frail a month prior. He was losing weight. His baseball cap hid eyes that betrayed a sad awareness of what was happening. Toby always wore a turtleneck, leather motorcycle jacket, jeans, and white sneakers. Sitting in a chair in the lobby, hunched over in the chair, he looked pale.

"Hi Toby. What's going on?" I asked him.

"I walked out."

"Of where?"

"The hospital."

"What happened?"

"They were killing me in there. I was just laying naked in my own shit."

We sat there, not talking, for a while. He looked down, breathing heavily, winded from the walk into the lobby.

"Are you in pain?" I asked.

"The problem is that I have an infection in my lung," he told me, his voice raspy. "They don't know what it is, so they'll probably go in again tomorrow. The doctor plans to put a tube through my chest cavity to drain the lung. The problem is that if he goes in, the infection could spread that much quicker through my body. But he needs to know what the infection is so he can treat it. If I don't have the procedure, I'll have about three months to live. But they say if it's treated, I could have another two or three years. So I think I'm going to go for the big money." He paused for a moment. "I wish I had never gambled," he said.

"Gambled?"

"With my life," Toby followed. "Ten years ago, they called this the Gay Cancer or Kaposi's Sarcoma. I thought it was such a joke. I thought only the really hardcore guys on Christopher Street got it. That wasn't my scene. I was hanging out with artists and people like that in New York at the time."

"How could you know? No one knew what was going on." At the time, much of the world seemed to want a split between the good gays from the leather guys. The respectable crowd was thought to be safe and innocent.

"But HIV did not pick or choose. It went after everyone, including me," Toby lamented. "They say homosexuality marked the beginning of the fall of the Roman Empire, that the decadence and debauchery brought about the end," he continued.

"So did income inequality," I responded, having a hard time listening to him blame himself for having sex. "Everyone has their theories. Lots of people blame themselves. But it's a disease. That's it."

"Well, Reagan was pretty good at letting us die. But we're not the only ones. Look what they did to black people with the syphilis experiment? They infected people and just let them get worse for science's sake. They just watched them die."

At some point, the conversation turned to Terry Gilliam's film of Kafkaesque bureaucratic hell, *Brazil*.

"I laughed and laughed at that movie," noted Toby. "'This is my receipt for your receipt.' But that's really what it's like," Toby said.

"My favorite was Robert De Niro, declaring, 'We're all in it together.' That's all we have, I replied."

"Well, I'm not keeping my fingers crossed. Buddhism teaches us not to become attached to things. Those desires cause pain. Without these desires for material things, we are free."

We sat quietly for a while before Toby said he was going to bed.

"When are you having the procedure?" I asked.

"I'm going to New York for it. I hope I come back," he said, with a strained voice.

"In a few days, you could be in Central Park."

"That would be nice."

He entered the elevator after a pause.

"Goodnight."

"Goodnight."

Up he went. I didn't know if I would ever see him again. I never knew how to handle such situations. I didn't want to say, "You're coming back." I didn't quite believe it and neither did he.

Dark and Light City

"San Francisco is a breathtakingly beautiful city, with lots of great contrasts between dark and light, often overlapping each other. It's a great setting for a horror story."

-Christopher Moore

I read the obits every week, usually when I was out, stopping to read the *Bay Area Reporter* whenever a fresh edition hit the streets. It wasn't long before the obits of most of the people in the building made their way into the paper. Most of the time, they didn't come as a surprise. They certainly did not at the Trash Disco after work. Madonna's "Lucky Star" played as I looked through the paper at the bar and sipped a vodka tonic. It was the first time I had heard the song since sitting in Willy's room a month prior when he was thinking of jumping. I didn't know a soul at the bar. But I kept on dancing with myself.

Work remained as a twisted whirlwind. All anyone wanted to talk about was sex or death. Everyone was dying or getting laid or hoping to avoid the former, or enjoy the latter.

It was a rough shift at work. Early on, Richard walked in.

"It happened again," he said, sounding jittery.

"What happened?"

"I got mugged again."

"What happened?" I asked.

"Just walking home from the club again. When he put his knife into my back and asked for the money, a part of me hoped he would push it in. And then when I bled on him, he would die too."

"But he didn't. You must be doing something right?"

When people died, the residents in the building took to speculating when they had last gotten laid. The common hypothesis was that when the sex died, so did everything else.

"I know so many people who gave up when their erections ended," said Juan in a caustic moment.

After a particularly rough Friday, when Richard had confessed to having lost most of his strength, I decided to go to New Wave City to dance. It was better than going to bed with my thoughts. Dancing was a good enough diversion.

Watching the Jam play "Boy About Town" on the video monitor, I looked out at the bodies on the dance floor, teenage angst oozing all over the place. I just sat drinking and watching. Somewhere between "The Safety Dance" and "Hit Me with Your Rhythm Stick", a young woman with short black hair and an intense side part came up to me.

"Did I meet you last weekend at Enrico's?" she asked, smiling coyly.

"I don't think so... Did you?"

"You look *just* like a guy I met last weekend."

She walked off. I danced for a bit and talked with a few of the others at the bar before going to the bathroom. The line was endless.

The girl with the black hair was standing in line in front of me. And gradually, we got to chatting about therapy, work, sex, and college. She looked at me and asked what I was doing.

"Hanging out. What's on your mind?"

"What's on *your* mind?"

"Late night diner food?" I suggested.

"I gotta go. I'll be back in a minute," she said and ran off. I had no idea if I was going to see her again.

When she came back, she said, "I've made a decision. I'm going home. Good night."

She walked off only to talk with another guy. I walked back to the bathroom. When I got back to the now desolate dance floor, she was gone, but he was still there. I walked outside as she was hailing a cab.

I looked at her, smiled and said, "You sure?"

She smiled back and gestured for me to join her. Her place was in Cole Valley, above the Haight, secluded by the university. I should have just gone home, because I could see she was getting sad as we rode back to her place.

Her home was austere with almost no decorations. She put on The Velvet Underground on the CD player.

"I've been meaning to read this," I said, picking up her copy of *All the President's Men.*

"You can keep it," she said. "It's the sort of thing every used bookstore in town has for a dime."

I set the book down and moved in for an embrace.

"I was thinking you were playing hard to get," she whispered.

We fooled around. It was awkward. We were both self-conscious.

"What do you feel like?" I asked her.

"I like to be done so hard that I don't know what I'm thinking, and not to be asked halfway through. That's a drag. It has to be animalistic. That's the real turn on."

We stumbled through things, a little of this and that, her on me, me on her, clothes off, but nothing was really going.

"Do you want to go?" she asked. "I'm just letting you off the hook."

I wandered out into the cold in the valley at 5:15 AM, fog everywhere. Footsteps followed me, while I walked through the pitch-black street to the intersection. "Oh god just let me get home. Get me out of here." The city was completely quiet and the sun hadn't risen yet. A cab zoomed through the fog and stopped, like a guardian angel. Someone is watching over me, I thought as I got inside.

I told Bobby and Charles about it later that week, talking at Vesuvio.

"People are strange. I had a girlfriend who always wanted me to punch her," Charles told me.

"What?"

"Yes, every time we fooled around."

"Did you do as she asked?"

"Yeah, but not too hard."

"Was that ok?"

216

"No. She always said 'harder, harder.' She said, 'hit my boobs.' I didn't want to. At one point, I told her I didn't feel like punching her harder and the sex slowed down. Later, I found out she had been divorced. I asked why. 'Domestic violence,' she confessed."

"I can't tell if any of it is worth it," I said. "It takes hours of chatting, scheming, buying beers, cabs, banter. I'm not sure it's worth it."

"Of course it is," Bobby said. "Look at all the stories you are racking up."

"I don't know how to read those situations."

"What's there to read? She wanted something, but she didn't want everything. She wanted you to come over and maybe to force something and then for you to leave. So you left."

"You think I blew it?" I replied.

"You got to see her world, her life. Isn't that the most fun part?"

"Just like in college, getting into the Scripps Dorms," I added. "Being invited to someone's house is like being allowed to undress their secrets."

"Their inner life, revealing something magic, like the grail."

"There is an exquisite beauty we're looking for. It's out there. But there is a lot of treachery to get to it. It's the story that keeps revolving around me. I write and rewrite it. But I still can't shape the story."

"And are you still doing your oral history interviews?" he asked.

"With people all over town. Every day I'm off work. I find secrets about the city. When I was walking home the other day, I saw an old journal in the trash. Some woman had left all her stories out there. Take a look," I said, and handed it to him.

"'I wish I was one of those few who were born with a purpose,'" Bobby read from the journal. He flipped through the pages of maps, pictures, and old poems. "'A person who knew what they wanted and knew what to do. But I am not. I'm doing what I'm doing. Getting by, struggling. Learning. Some call it water...' Looks like you found something here, Cab."

"I know. I'm just not sure what. I love her longing and optimism, even as she doesn't know. And then she threw this journal away, in the trash. I can't imagine it's meant for the trash. There's got to be more to it. You see a picture of her whole life in there. Notes from her friends, her roommates. Long notes about friends."

"Maybe it was for you?"

"Maybe it was? I feel like she was leaving a clue for someone," I said. "Like Boo Radley leaving the kids toys in the tree in *To Kill a Mockingbird*. The clues are everywhere. When I was a kid I used to go through the Uffizi Gallery with my mom all the time, sketching pictures and taking notes. And then one day, I left the journal in the bathroom. Mom was furious with me. It was gone. I always wondered if anyone found the journal."

"What would someone learn from your old journal? What could we learn if we found that old journal? What would you ask her if you saw her? Do you think the universe is trying to get you your old lost journal, that thing you lost?"

"I have no idea. I didn't ask the right questions the other night."

"It didn't hurt to ask, though. Your questions got you pretty far. You had to ask them then, even if you didn't get the answer you wanted."

I went home, crawled into bed, and took a short nap before my graveyard shift. There was a strange feeling of awareness in the almost-asleep space, fading in and out, looking at the world and losing a grip as I slipped down before rising again and wandering back through the night to Market Street.

It was often quiet at the beginning of the shift. I let a few people into the building. A few guys had been at parties or they were coming back from visiting friends. The night gradually became silent. From my perch, I watched Market Street, and the seconds dragged. I became aware of a foreboding feeling that had joined me as I went through the evening tasks of sweeping, greeting, and doing the rounds of the building. The eerie presence lurked, accompanying me while I wrote reports, and completed tasks.

Walking through the halls, I caught a glimpse of a silhouette of an emaciated body wasted close to death, forcing me to do a double take. It was a resident I hadn't seen in weeks, like one of those horrible pictures of the Jews in Auschwitz from 1945 after liberation, eerie almost dead skeletal bodies. I caught his eye. And he acknowledged me with a warm smile.

"Goodnight, Cab," Carlos said before letting himself into his room.

"Goodnight," I said.

He was alive. How, I was not sure. Kindness remained inside his body. He looked like he had returned from the underworld. But still, there was a beauty in his face.

When I got back downstairs, street people walked by the building, looking into the lobby. Some were only stopping to linger and look at the light. One walked up to rattle the doors. I clutched the chain with all the keys. I continued my rounds, not sure what form loomed in the distance, what body might appear laying crumbled dead on the floor of the elevator; who night might crawl in, or might I find sneaking up the stairs, having only broken in minutes before. A man was outside digging through the trash can, looking for food or cigarette butts.

The door buzzed. It was Pete, one of the residents, still healthy but obviously scared.

"I'm so glad you're here, Cab."

"What happened?" I asked him.

"There were a bunch of teenage boys making fun of this kid who was obviously a little delayed." He paused, clearly rattled. "And he just went along, laughing too, not quite knowing it was about him. It was sad and humiliating."

I groaned.

"People are cruel."

"Sometimes I just have to get off the street," Pete explained, sounding as if he was about to cry.

"I know. The streets are rough tonight. People are desperate."

"A dozen years into this thing, AIDS and poverty are gripping each other," Pete said. "The first generation is dying or dead and a new one is getting exposed to this and most of the people out there have little to no idea what is going on. More and more it's people who are really poor. It's exposing something in all of us. Something that is really ugly."

"Extending everywhere."

The morning edition of *The Examiner* arrived just a bit before 5:00 AM. The bakery dropped off a bag of bread for the restaurant and a small bag for the late-night counselors. It was fresh and energizing. By 5:30, the morning sky had begun to brighten.

After work, I walked back up Page Street into the Haight-Ashbury, and picked up a copy of the *Bay Area Reporter*. I had barely slept the night before. This morning, I was going to sleep, I thought. But my head had other ideas.

I sat to read the *BAR*. Flipping through the pages, there was Toby's obit. A picture of his young, handsome face, his stare seemed to leap from the page.

He had died the week before at the age of 36 during that trip to the East Coast he'd told me about the night before he left.

"Thanks to the staff at 1994 Market," he had written. "Dear Fred, I'll be seeking you in all the old familiar places. I love you very much," the obit concluded. The procedure in New York didn't work. Looking at the picture, I couldn't believe how young he looked. Young people were supposed to live. Young people didn't die. I thought of seeing Toby in the Mission last summer. And then talking with him about the procedure he was going to have during the holidays. He told me about the danger he was putting himself in, going in for such work, but that it was worth it, because the procedure opened the possibility for something.

"I'm going for the big money," he told me at the time.

"Are you scared?"

"Yeah."

And he had reason to be. The procedure didn't work.

I lay in bed on my back with my eyes closed, staring into the infinite. Toby, are you out there? Will I see you if I cruise around here? Are you still carrying a pack of Marlboro 100 Lights in your right vest pocket? Wanna share one? Is anybody out there? I wondered. I still felt compelled to ask. The questions felt urgent. Toby, where are you now? You certainly are not going to be walking in through the front door any time or ever again. Are you in some other place or are merely becoming acquainted with the worms? Are you reading that old journal of mine at the Uffizi Gallery?"

Physical decomposition is, of course, inevitable. Ashes to ashes, dust to dust. But metaphysical decomposition seems impossible. I was half asleep, daydreaming of flying through endless clouds, hoping I might run into him. Could you climb up through a pothole, the words Heaven painted on the inside of the sewer cap, only to share a smoke on a park bench on a foggy afternoon in this living theater? The saddest imaginable idea would be that it really was over. I couldn't imagine everything ending with that last heartbeat. The heart was not a strong enough muscle to explain every thought, will, and dream. But I, like everyone else, had no idea. Having spent the last two nights prowling amidst whores and strippers, I probably wasn't the one to ask. I remembered what Juan had said about death coming after sex ended. I reached down between my legs, reminding myself of the basic element of my being present and desiring. When I watched *Angels in America* a few months prior, I thought of Toby, who reminded me so much of Prior, whose lover left him because of his illness. Daydreaming, I joined Prior and Toby in the clouds, dreaming the morning away. When I awoke, I cut out Toby's obit, and posted it in my old blue notebook, along with the other obits, putting the journal away sitting right by my old porn stash, just on top of Tip O'Neil's obit.

I thought of Sue doing what she used to do with me. It was more fun in my mind than with her, well sort of. Somehow, the sex memories offered a feeling of acceptance. It was the only such feeling I knew. And I was craving it. I'd be back at work in just a few hours for the 4 PM shift.

Word about Toby's death flew around the building now that the obituary was out. Brian was carrying a suitcase out of the building when I arrived.

"I'm going away for a while," he said. He'd been getting sicker and sicker. "Toby was one of my best friends. I adored him. Intellect is the best aphrodisiac, you know. Rose died yesterday. But it was of natural causes. She died on heroin. At least it wasn't HIV. Isn't that refreshing?" Brian smiled with a forced sarcastic grin, revealing a Kaposi's Sarcoma lesion on his neck.

Willy nodded, making a comment about his kidney stone.

Throughout the shift, the homeless man I had been hearing the night before was sneaking from room to room, knocking on people's doors, in search of a place to hide away.

When Brian left, Willy stayed to chat.

"I remember sitting with my friend at a party," he said, "I was telling him some stories. And he looked at me and said, 'You fuck a lot don't you?'" Willy laughed. "The old days in this city were a wild ride. Wilder than any of the *Tales of the City* on TV". He continued. "I used to go to the bars every night, to No Name across from what is now Lonestar Saloon," he continued. "Pot was really cheap. I would primp myself up, twirl my moustache. I'd roll nine or ten joints and take them to the bar. And we'd share them with everyone. The bartender used to take us in back, lock the door and share 'em with everyone. We'd share acid, speed, whatever. It was a great way to get to know people. We all got to know each other really well. I'm glad I had that. I'd do that every night here. I'm glad we had that together, in those years before this nightmare. *Tales of the City* captures a bit of that feeling, of people coming here and coming out as who they were. It really was an open space where no one cared where you were from or what you did. It was a different experience."

"But we grew up Reagan, conservative," Brian joined in, walking back down the stairs. "This is a different city, affecting us in neurotic, crazy ways. But I'm glad that world was created for us, even if that oppositional culture is starting to disappear."

"There are still pieces."

"Maybe so.

"I love it here. It helps me remember the world of experimentation what came before this, some of which is still out there for us. After Stonewall, we created a whole world for ourselves, new families of choice, public sexual spaces, and organizing. It all overlapped into something extraordinary," Willy continued.

"*Tales of the City* reminds me of that jovial daydream," I chimed in, tapping my paperback copy. "Of people and history in Northern California, old movies, thousands of coffees and people washing up on these shores, having arrived from points unknown, of people coming out and being able to be who we really are without being arrested or condemned."

220

"But it's hard to feel it now. Today, it feels like this extended eulogy," Brian continued. "Something else has to come out of this at some point."

"I just read this line from *Tales of the City*. I love it," pulling out my book.

"'Oh, Mona....'" I read. "'Loosen up, dear! Don't be so afraid to cry . . . or laugh, for that matter. Laugh all you want and cry all you want and whistle at pretty men in the street...!'"

Brian smiled and paused. "That feels like a long time ago."

"Something is happening now too," I replied. "I can just tell, even in this dark place. Something will come out of this. That happened with the Renaissance in Italy. It came after the Plague."

"Yeah, tell that to everyone who died."

Brian was right, of course. Great art is rarely a consolation. But life here was teaching me something. I was finding something else here. The requiem of these moments offered a deeper way of looking than I'd ever seen. Somehow, even in all the pain, the San Francisco of all the people I was meeting revealed something, even if it was falling apart.

On Tweekers, Famines, and Femme Fatales

"Her eyes change like the sunlight,"
-Walker Percy, *Thanatos Syndrome*

"This city is a point upon a map of fog...
a city unknown. Like us, it doesn't quite exist."
-Ambrose Bierce

On free days, I took the bus all over town for coffee dates and meetings for oral history interviews with anyone who wanted to talk. There was a story out there but it was always eluding me. I knew I could find it. The looking was my everything. People say San Francisco is a small town, but those walks up the hills after the bus dropped me off, through the park, into the woods, back downtown, and throughout the avenues—they felt endless. I spoke with artists, conspiracy theorists, writers, and the leather folk on Folsom Street; the guys who cruised at Lands End beach, looking at the waves, the surfers at Mavericks, the organizers and sex club goers, story upon story. Along the way, a world of sex radicals and hustlers revealed itself, amidst the tales of those who never returned home after WWII or Vietnam, who built a world here. In the meantime, there was my story, which didn't seem to have any direction.

At work, things were almost quiet.

Juan came in late. I commented that the space was feeling almost calm.

"But this disease is still moving through us," he said, "Even if you can't see it." He looked around the room with his baby face and glasses. "I'm like a shiny apple with worms running through it. You can't see the worms, but they're working their way through my insides, consuming me. The same thing is happening out there." He gestured to the streets. "The city is nuts. People are tweaking up and down Market Street. Earlier in the week, I was scared to go to the bank machine to cash my check. There were too many tweekers who had been running around high with no sleep. I stayed away for a couple of days."

"How long does it take to use up a whole check on speed?" I asked.

"A few days. But during that time people stop sleeping or eating, gradually losing themselves in the hallucination."

"Like zombies."

"You see 'em out there, walking after the high and the month's check has run out, scratching and wondering, no food or water for days, and then they crash."

"Have you ever done it?" I asked.

"Yeah, it was fun," Juan confessed, smiling. "But I got some sleep afterwards."

"Me too, in New Orleans. I bought it from some guy trying to hustle me when I was 16. It was so much fun. We were up all night, walking the Quarter looking at strippers, making new friends, taking in all the city had to offer."

"The other day I was with a guy, who insisted on sticking it up his ass, before sex."

"Really? I've heard of poppers during sex. But crystal?"

"I tried the poppers once during sex. But that wasn't too fun."

"I love them. But why wasn't it fun during sex? What happened?"

"You don't want to know."

"I do."

Juan paused and smiled. "When I was about to orgasm, I reached for the little yellow and orange Rush bottle on the table, pulling in to my nose, and I spilled it all over myself and the sheets."

"Oh no. Could you breathe?" I laughed, covering my mouth, knowing the ammonia-like smell of the amyl nitrite could be overwhelming. "I'm sorry."

"Barely," he said. "It was awful. The chemical smell filled the room. I lost my erection. I had to keep the windows open for days. So I stayed in Gabriel's room until the smell went away," Juan confessed.

"Some of the clubs used to pump them into the air vents so the whole place smelled like them," I said.

"I'm not that good at that stuff," Juan continued. "It's not something I can play with any more. I'm becoming more and more absent-minded as the disease is progressing. I left the building the other day without a check in my pocket. I returned from the bank, went back to my room for the check, left again, and still forgot the check. When I went back, I had locked myself out of the building. Tell me it doesn't sound like I'm crazy. People tell me I look fine but I'm wearing down."

"Juan, you look fine."

"Yes, but this is still running through me." He became serious, changing topics, as he was prone to do. The residents of 1994 were acutely aware of the feeling of being left behind. The epidemic had been raging for years now. And few officials seemed to care. They felt like they were being left on the remainder bins. And they wondered why. "America's disease is not AIDS. It's too much hate," Juan concluded.

"I know."

It was hard to disagree.

Juan was not alone. Everything felt like it was deteriorating, including Pedro's mental state. "Those in his life, they begin as friends. Then once in his sphere, he begins to distrust them," Jim had warned me. "He gives meals to staff and others to gain favors or to get around the rules," Jim continued. "It's a paranoid personality disorder. He assumes we are all deceiving. We're housing him. That's all we can do. But now, Pedro fears leaving the building because he thinks Miguel, the old desk clerk, has a key to his apartment that he could use to get into his room. He thinks Miguel has already gotten into his room and stolen things from him. They started as friends. But now Miguel is out of the building."

When I finished my talk with Jim, I walked home, thinking about all the meals Pedro brought me. Were they gestures of friendship or something else? Everything felt off especially, my attempts at romance. Lingering memories of Sue walking up to the door in boxers glad to see me, or staying overnight with Chloe were hard to shake.

Before my 4:00-midnight shift the next day, I found myself sitting in the Church of the Advent, a small Episcopalian church on Fell Street. AIDS quilts hung on the walls. Incense wafted through the air of the half full space. The old songs and liturgy felt comforting. But I wondered about what to do. "Prophets are always the bearers of bad news," Father Marc preached in his sermon on the Gospel of St. John. "At some point, we are all lost in the woods." Midway through the sermon he disclosed that he was HIV positive. He was going through what everyone seemed to be going through. "In the disasters of life, we find God in so many ways," he preached, seemingly trying to convince himself. Emotions welled up as I realized I was not sure I could believe what he was saying. The distance between where I was and those days when I believed felt vexing. But I was right there with his anguish. Others were better at finding peace in all this than I was. People I knew in the AIDS world talked about Shanti, or peace within us. But I was having none of it.

"Read *Facing an Abusing God* by Blumenthal," Dad had advised on a recent phone call. "It's about the Holocaust and child abuse survivors and their relationship with a god that allows people to suffer."

"It's a cruel story, Dad."

"You're tearing off the layers of your old faith and finding something knew," he insisted.

After church, I made my way to North Beach, to do some writing upstairs at Vesuvio. Across the street from City Lights—Lawrence Ferlinghetti's old beat bookstore—I made my way up the curling stairs to the second floor of the old Vesuvio bar, where I bought a coffee and opened my notebook to write. Photos of old writers hung from the walls, college buddies from Columbia, literary heroes leaning off each other in Tangiers, laughing, looking like they belonged here. That was not a feeling I had. A sense of morality in the air, I was rattled. My assumptions were shaken.

My friend Kelly came over to meet me. I was reading the paper when she arrived. The horoscope page flipped open.

"Let's read them," she said, and sat right beside me. "Oh you're a Scorpio too. That must be why we're friends," she declared.

We chatted over coffee and fries. And somehow the conversation made its way back to the Holocaust. Another date about the Holocaust. Groan. Her dad had survived it. She was an expert. This wasn't going anywhere. She wanted to know about my work. I told her about the death saturated building and the lack of progress for treatment.

"But there's so much progress. The spirit of humanity is stronger, and yes, we are a strong spirit," she insisted, looking at me.

"But we're not so good at living together," I lamented, feeling like she was a little out of touch.

When we finished our food, she told me she had other plans for the day and had to go after a bit. She walked down the curly steps. Looking down, I watched her walk outside, stepping around a few homeless people sleeping. *So much for humanity being stronger*, I thought to myself as I got back to my work. The homeless guys were still down there, looking lost. Juan was right. Neglect was everywhere. I kept on looking around the second floor of the old coffee shop, Jack Kerouac Alley below, glimpsing at a black and white photo of Dostoyevsky across the room, just by the window. People were sitting solitary, some reading, some writing. Light shone into the old café filled with cigarette smoke. I thought of the Underground Man in *Notes from the Underground*. He spent half the book contemplating bumping into an adversary who did not know he existed. I was obsessing on reconnecting with ghosts and phantasms, writing about what was no longer there. I looked out the window at the people walking on Columbus Ave. Two of the homeless guys had disappeared. A group of people stood outside smoking. They seemed happy, unlike myself. I felt like I was in an entirely different place. Existential longings grasped at me as I made my way through a life away from the person I cared about more than anything. Everyone was a substitute. But there was nothing I could do. So I tried to write away the feeling, waiting for the feeling to pass. The mood dragged and clung. The hours clicked along, haunting the minutes passed before I wandered down Market to Van Ness for my 4:00-midnight shift.

"Cab, can you work the midnight shift tonight?" Jim asked when I arrived. "Everyone is out sick."

"No problem Jim," I replied, sitting, looking down the sixteen hours I had ahead of me. All afternoon, motorcyclists in black leather zoomed down Market Street, cruising to and from through eternal returns.

By nine p.m., no one seemed to be around. I went to get a coffee in the back. When I walked out, I thought I saw something outside in the lobby. Nothing but a shadow. I started reading a paperback at the desk in the empty lobby. It has been said that we read to know we are not alone. Giuseppe walked with his wife every night for the last years of his life, which he spent in a prison cell. John Donne wrote poems about metaphysical connections with the dead. The Sandinistas carried inhuman weights of food through the mountains in order to be close with the new man of their utopian future, in a communion between what was and what they hoped would be. Here and now all was still.

Pedro walked down.

"What's up Pedro?" I asked.

"I'm devastated," he replied.

"Why, what happened?"

"We're all looking for something in this life," he remarked. "You are looking for a plot for your story. Well, I'm looking for my Luke from *Beverly Hills 90210*."

"Really?" I asked. "I love that show. We watch every Wednesday. We read the *I Hate Brenda Newsletter* every month. I never would have pegged you as a *90210* fan."

"Well, I have been from the very beginning. You get attached to these characters. And I just found out."

"About what?"

"That Luke left."

"Yeah, that was last Wednesday."

"I know but I missed it. I just saw Luke's last episode."

"It was amazing," I replied.

"In his last scene, he drove down the dirt road on his motorbike, without even waving goodbye, disappearing into the distance. It was over. He was gone."

"Devastating," I replied.

I was smiling at Pedro. And a strange absence filled the room.

"Oh Luke, take me with you," he swooned. "I'm shattered," he gushed and walked outside, visibly upset, looking at the cyclists still zooming.

A half hour later, he came back and walked upstairs.

"Night, Cab," he said.

"Get some sleep buddy."

It had been a long day already. Between Luke leaving on *90210* and sleep eluding me most of the week, daydreaming followed, my mind slipping here and there, in and out of consciousness, not quite awake, not quite asleep, a panorama of images of this surrealist left coast passing by, people surfing, writing poems, wearing bikinis, following bands, racing from Oregon to Mexico, one end of the coast to the other.

"It's too dark in this town," said Jasmin, driving with me, in the midst of a dream of escaping the city, making our way through the Redwoods.

"Lets get out of here."

We drove and drove, south past Santa Cruz through Big Sur, listening to the laser-light-illuminated AM/FM radio, singing along. The mountains bursting up through the skyline as the dawn made its way into distance, the night gone. We drank coffee and looked around as the California day unfolded on the road. None of it felt real, just outward in front of us.

While we were driving, I thought of Frederic Forrest's advice to his daughter in *Valley Girl*: "Don't worry honey, buy the more expensive one."

Could there be more to life than that, we all wondered. We knew there had to be more. There had to be more to our lives than just growing up and stumbling into default career choices, choosing things we knew we could do instead of doing what we should do.

This was why we did all the drugs we did, to find something else out there, following Ken Kesey on the *Electric Kool-Aid Acid Test*. We were all looking for something, when Phil, Becky and I had taken our first tabs of LSD in high school. That was a part of all the experiments before we all said goodbye and the shimmer disappeared from so many of my friends' eyes.

They say acid creates flashbacks but I was never really sure. We took so much acid, getting lost in ourselves, sometimes unable to make our way out. Sometimes, we just needed help from friends to make it back. It was all a matter of traveling as far out there as we could and then returning without losing too much of ourselves on the way. You knew, you hoped a friend could pull you back if you needed. We all had to feel something, be part of something. We had to feel it, to consume it, to know it, to have those feelings, to allow ourselves. I used to think about Syd Barret of Pink Floyd, who had a break from reality after an acid trip, never to return. Few of us had ever really made it back from there. But maybe that was ok?

Looking at my life, I imagined looking at myself, greeting everyone, and me sleeping in the quiet night in the building on Market Street. We are all half dead. But even with our half-lives, Juan's stories, Pedro's despair, it all felt more alive than anything I had seen, full of solidarity, smiles, jokes, hugs, nudges, winks and half connections within a tragicomedy. Everyone was a diseased pariah. History had brought the ugliest of scourges to a cohort weaned on dance music, most of whom were disappearing, a generation passing in front of my eyes. Most of us had nothing much else to lose. There was a strength in the desperation, the vulnerability.

All this flashed through my mind as Jasmin and I drove through the woods.

"You want a smoke?" she asked.

"Please."

226

"If There's a Heaven Above" by Love and Rockets started playing on the mix tape.

"Oh, I love this song," I said.

"Me too."

"Life is a mess here."

"But it's also beautiful."

We kept on driving.

"Hey wait, wasn't that a sign for a castle?" Jasmin smiled, the soundtrack for *The Rocky Horror Picture Show* playing on the mix tape, thunder and rain dropping from the sky. Eventually, the rain stopped.

"We're near the beach. Should we stop?"

"Let's do it...."

We parked, grabbed a few towels, a bottle of wine and cigarettes, and wandered out to look at the waves. The morning sun shone on the waves. Rocks stretched out of the water in the distance. It was a moody, crisp Northern California morning. We found a place near the water and lit a fire.

"Cab, you're not talking. You're being. You're sitting."

"I know."

"I know. At a certain point, here you are. I know you love *Le Grand Meaulnes* and all King Arthur Percival stories. We're all wandering. But eventually you realize it's not out there."

"I know. I know. I'm not against sitting. I sit all the time."

"There is a lot of the world to see."

"But I stayed in the U.S. after college. I didn't go wander like junior year in college. I didn't go chasing refugees and political crises elsewhere. I stayed right here in this rickety, crumbling U.S.A., where we arrest the homeless and neglect the sick."

"And see, you're finding something magic here."

"I think you are right," I replied taking in the morning along the beach.

She reached over, grabbed my hands, and looked at me.

"Just listen to me," she looked earnestly. "What would you rather have right now? Is there anywhere you'd rather be than right here?" She paused and started to turn on the small tape player she brought from the car.

"Come on, Cab. Just listen. Take it all in. This could be a moment you have for the rest of your life. Just you and me, the trees, the beach, the sun rising and the crazy moon fading in the distance."

"And the waves...."

"And the whole world," she elaborated. I had an image of people living on small boats in Vietnam and Hong Kong. "Tomorrow will come soon enough," she continued. "I know everyone is dying around you, but you have time, even if those around you don't. That's beyond us."

"I know. But I think I am losing my mind watching. You know that scene Kurt Vonnegut's novel, when he says he can't imagine orbiting the earth in space, lost, in a world without a god?"

"We're in that world now, on our own here. It's up to us."

"I know. But the eternal silences of those infinite spaces frighten me."

"Me too."

"And back on earth, it just takes so long for us to fix everything and get it right. I know I have time. But..." I trailed off.

"Cab, look around. Look at all we have." The waves were rolling over the water between the rocks. It was a line Chloe used to say, looking out at the field in the domain.

"Sometimes, I can see a world opening up," I said, looking out at the water. "Other times, I have this image of everyone on the way to a party and I'm just watching."

"Cab, come on. Life's here, right now, not elsewhere. Is that what is happening to you?"

"No, but it feels like that sometimes, like all I've known is slipping away."

"That's hard."

"I get it all the time."

"It's playing the cello for hours and hours as a kid, by yourself, trying to find the notes."

Jasmin held my hands. "Look around. What do you see?"

"I see a sky that goes on forever. But when I look around—everyone takes everyone for granted. Everyone angles and competes, looking for the bigger, better deal. We walk over each other."

"I know, Cab. But it's a choice. We don't have to play that game. We can choose not to."

"But it gets messy. I remember in 8th grade with Sarah, how upset she got at the end of the year camp out when all the girls in the group ostracized her."

"Yeah, that was sad," Jasmin confirmed knowingly. "Sarah and Grant had been going out all year long until Grant dumped her for Susan. Sarah was so upset that she told all the rest of the girls that Susan had been giving Trey head while she was cheering at the football games, cheating behind Grant's back. Susan heard about it and went to all the girls. She got the idea into her head that none of them should talk to Sarah for the rest of the year. And they followed along, effectively ostracizing her."

"Wow, I don't believe that. What a scene. I knew they were mean, but had no idea they were destroying each other. How did you know about that?"

"I was there."

"You were?" I wondered. "I met you here."

"No, I was there...."

Things were getting eerie. I looked at her and her complexion was shifting, changing. Her eyes were like sunshine, glimmering. I heard her, but in a blur: "The femme fatales that you covet, the sirens lure. Sailors far and wide chase us to their deaths. But can you say no?"

I was looking at the waves on the beach and started to feel tired, painfully tired, unable to keep my eyes open. I looked at her, the sun dancing in her eyes.

"Do you mind if I sleep for a bit?" I asked.

"Sleep. Just sleep, Cab." I lay back into the sand, falling deep.

Hours later, I woke up. Jasmin was gone. It was the afternoon. I was alone on the beach. The car was gone. I had no idea how long I had been there or if I was ever going to leave.

"Cab," I heard Pedro say, laughing. "I know they don't pay you much. But at least try not to snore." I woke up.

228

"Just closing my eyes for a minute," I said. "Thanks Pedro." I rubbed my face.

"And snoring," Pedro laughed. "There's a sleep mark on your cheek from your notebook. You'd better clean your face."

It was 5:30 AM. I had been out for a while. And no one seemed to have buzzed. The day was starting, and my shift was almost over.

Later, I told Dad about the dream.

"It sounds like you were having an anima projection," he said. He was fascinated with Carl Jung and the collective unconscious.

"Huh?"

"It's the feminine archetype. You have it in you, just as you have an animus, a male archetype. But they're painfully separated in our world and consciousness. Some people fixate on one at the expense of the other. It sounds like that's what was happening in your dream."

I didn't know. He went on.

"It was amazing. She was taking me places I have never been here, luring me further out. And then she turned on me."

"Well, then you turned on yourself.

"How?"

"You left yourself behind. It's all you in the dream, every character."

"Yeah, I left Sue behind, treating her like dirt and letting her go."

"And a part of you knows it. Maybe everyone knows it but you can't see it. And Jasmin was reminding you."

"I guess so."

"There are a lot of feelings rummaging through our unconscious minds."

"I know."

"You are obsessing on the femme fatale who takes you on a wild ride through the San Francisco night, just like one of the film noir Lauren Bacall movies. 'You know how to whistle, don't you, Steve? You just put your lips together and blow....'"

"But it's my life, Dad," I said, "Well, sort of."

"A dream is a wish. And in this case a reminder about conflicts churning through your mind you are trying to work out."

"A world of hopes and fears and conflicts I can't seem to shake."

"None of us can really," Dad continued.

"You think so?"

"It's just becoming something, learning from the dialogue in your head, the surreal images telling you something about yourself."

"The dreams happen every few nights. I find someone again. The trust is back. And then there is a betrayal."

"Who is betraying who?"

229

"I guess I'm betraying myself, over and over again." I could imagine Dad nodding. He did not say anything for a minute.

"That's for you to figure out," he replied, pausing. "It's also a cultural history," he elaborated. "Think of Plato's *Symposium*."

"Not the *Symposium* again."

"Yeah, the whole work is about love and separation. The gods were worried humans were too powerful, so they had our male parts cut off from our female selves. From then on, we were lost, the two parts of ourselves eternally estranged from each other. Wholeness eludes us. We miss the other, eternally hoping for resolution. We spend our lives separated from our true selves, unwhole."

"Obsessing about others, eternally looking to reconnect, trying to resolve our separateness."

"The gods wanted it that way," Dad laughed.

The Loss Exercise

"...by 1990, more San Franciscans had died of AIDS than died in the four wars of the 20th century, combined and tripled... It should be clear to any psychotherapist that the psychological tasks of survivors of such a situation could not be simple... Psychological denial, without accompanying survival guilt, may include denial of the personal and social impact of the HIV epidemic on the gay community in general, denial about the complexity of feelings connected to "safer" (more properly protected) and unsafe (unprotected) sex, and denial of the likelihood that the epidemic may take on irreparable psychological toll from many survivors especially those with multiple losses..."

-Walt Odetts, 1994

"Everyone here has to do the training. It's part of the job," Jim told me, reminding me I had to attend two full weekends of sessions on loss and AIDS caregiving training at our offices South of Market.

A little training might not be a bad thing, I thought. And I certainly did not have anything else better to do.

"Please do not have sex with each other," the tattooed facilitator began our workshop inside a funky office near the sex clubs in San Francisco's SOMA district. She had a septum piercing with a circular barbell through her nose. We sat in a small, hot room full of people. "Or at least not till we're done with this training."

"It's all about feelings," Karen said. She was our nervous, middle-aged group facilitator. "What were our feelings at this moment?" she asked, exhorting us to open up, even when we did not feel like it. Each of us was there because we were interested in becoming caregivers or buddies to people with HIV/AIDS. My group included Richard, a handsome, confident gentleman from Ireland; Robert, who appeared reticent and ready to bolt at any minute; Charlie, a funny man without much hair; and Dan, who reminded everyone he had HIV over and over again. Karen looked anxious and asked everyone to check in. No one was really sure what to say.

Silence.

"I resent being here," said Robert. "It's been thirteen years of this and I'm kicking and screaming with my heels in the ground."

Charlie was next in the circle. "I'm scared of talking, working, or learning in front of others," he explained, echoing the growing sentiment.

"People with AIDS are always being used. I'm terrified about that," Robert said. "I think the HIV resents me."

I was happy to be at the training. It was a break from the usual routine of writing and existential ennui. The whole weekend felt like a cultural event. Stories seemed to flow from all corners. I jotted down everyone else's reactions all weekend long. Karen scolded me a few times, but I kept writing, seeing our work as a part of a large social movement.

Following our check-in, Dr. Charles Garfield, recalled the history of the Shanti model of peer support. "There are no simple answers," he explained. "I worked the Apollo moon trip, putting in eight years of work for the flight to the moon. Humans can do amazing things when we work together for a common goal."

He had a PhD in psychotherapy. He assumed they could do the same thing with cancer as they did with the moon landing. After all, here was another goal, something a lot of people were working on to stay alive. Garfield started caregiving, developing a model, which became useful when something weird came up in San Francisco in 1981.

"Caregiving is about stories," Garfield said.

"I walked up to a client's room and he was dressed as Jesus painting a pink cross. He asked if pink was the right look," Charles said, reflecting on HIV and mental health. "I started to laugh. It's ok to laugh. It really is." For the first time in the day, everyone laughed.

"The work is a spiritual path," Garfield continued. "What is the message? Learn that life is not a rehearsal. Be authentic. It unlocked in me the capacity to be my true self. The heart is where the intelligence is."

"The ability to reverse roles is of serious importance," Garfield continued, describing a model of mutuality. "Show up, pay attention, and care, because a lot of others do not. Most conversations involve monologues, while the other person is rehearsing his response. But we're here to build partnership. We're in this together. If my end of the boat sinks, so does yours."

I was thinking of the women I had been seeing, rarely investing anything emotionally.

"Some of the people you work with may have never been accepted on an unconscious level. We do that for them," explained Garfield. "It's entirely appropriate to love. You have Shanti clearance for this."

We talked about ways to make face-to-face encounters work. Some might even change someone's life.

"Walk in the world for me. Take something I have shown you or taught you, and show it to the rest of the world, for another man to teach people to walk joyfully through the world of disorder," Garfield concluded. Listening, I felt invited to be a part of a vast movement of ideas.

In the late morning, we turned to the politics of AIDS. Paul was the policy director. He had short hair, a buttoned up blue shirt, and a pencil in his pocket. "Politics must be mentioned," he said. "Instead of a physical problem, it has been looked at as a sociological problem. As of January 1, 1994, in San Francisco, there have been 13,503 cases and 9,968 deaths. There were 242,000 cases in the U.S., and One hundred sixty thousand deaths, which we blame on Reagan for saying nothing for the first seven years. It started in 1981 with a cancer, Kaposi Sarcoma. In LA and New York, there were a lot of men with failing immune systems. At this time, there was no response from the government. By 1985, $300,000 was allocated—four years too late—unlike toxic shock syndrome, which got a quick response. The problem here was that this disease had to do with elements that our society is not good at talking about: sex, drugs, death, and illness. The people who society disregards were impacted first—the disenfranchised, the dispossessed. There were no real treatments until AZT in 1987 and then DDI and some new developments in 1989. Since then we have seen no new developments. Instead, we have gained in the ability to take care of people with HIV. Unfortunately, there has been a sense that there is no problem. Education and treatment are behind. 160,000 deaths later, and we can mention a condom, but we can't say what fluids

232

we want to contain. We have done so much more in publicity and education for other diseases. At some point, it appears that someone will get sick at some time with HIV. Some live 16 years and others two years. We don't know why—is it good vibes or solid differences among viral tracks? We started being able to test for the disease in 1985. In 1981, a lot of people died of pneumocystis pneumonia. The problem now is that there is no nontoxic approved method for treating this. We do know how to treat certain opportunistic infections such as pneumocystis pneumonia. But we don't know enough about how to treat this thing. And a lot of this has to do with early response. Early on, it was called Gay Related Immune Disorder or GRID. This misreading was both inaccurate and it stigmatized people. This has changed, but the damage has been set into our consciousness. And it's part of why there was no funding for the disease at the beginning: because it was affecting homosexuals. So the research was not up to par with the need for a decade. You had wasting syndrome with weight loss and lack of capacity to take nutrients, dementia, and a lot of women's issues that were not counted as diagnostic indicators. So people just died of untreated immune related complications. The numbers have been permanently skewed so who knows how many have died of AIDS. Today, we have finally developed prophylaxis to prevent these conditions. But the poor and disenfranchised are not given preventative medicine or the right kind of support to stay alive. And the treatments we have are highly toxic. They prevent the development of the virus, but also other antibodies and cells the body needs to defend itself. This puts the body into jeopardy. Sometimes the body can no longer stand the damage. AIDS research helps us understand the immune system. The breakthrough we need is nowhere in sight. So the deaths continue. Last year, we witnessed the highest number of AIDS deaths yet, and it looks like this year is on track to beat that."

Listening, I jotted down notes. The racism that always lurks beneath the surface, rearing itself in the failed early inaction toward people getting sick—queers and sex workers—those who were seen as disposable, the poor being ignored.

Loss comes in stages with the multiple deaths, Paul continued. With each death everything flows again. There isn't a caregiver who is not impacted. He recalled walking down the street and seeing a friend who he started to walk up to to say hello. Then he realized that his friend, Thomas, had been dead for five years. The person walking by was a memory, a ghost walking down Castro Street.

By the first afternoon, we moved into group exercises. Sixty of us sat for the afternoon session.

"I want you all to come here and pick up one of the pads of paper," asked Moonear. He was an affable Buddha-like black man, with a gentle expression, his shirt buttoned all the way to the top. His beard extended from his sideburns all the way down to his chin, his eyes betrayed a weariness with this experience.

"More than anything, HIV is a disease of loss," Moonear explained, as he began. "I would like you to write down the names of the four people you love the most in the world; four things you love to do; you four favorite material things; and four things about yourself you most appreciate," he instructed as he passed out red, yellow, blue, and pink sheets of paper.

"Writer, friend, social worker, athlete," I was writing as Moonear walked through the crowd with a trash can.

"Throw one of each category in the trash can," he instructed. I looked at the cards, and threw out "athlete" for my favorite things about myself, along with a random group of cards; Grant, running, and records. Fuck.

That was hard. Moonear walked by again, and instructed me to throw three more people cards into the trash. I was breathing harder. Charlie started to clutch his cards; Richard was weeping, Robert wouldn't look.

"People with HIV are often forced to contend with losing whole groups of friends, many friends from years and years prior," Moonear explained, insisting we throw another batch of cards into the trash can.

Several were clutching the cards tightly, refusing to throw anything else into the trash can.

"Fuck it," mumbled Robert, and he threw everything he had into the trash can.

Moonear walked through the room and grabbed all of some peoples' cards. He left others, myself included, with most of our cards. Some had a choice; others had none.

Charles had no cards left, just himself.

Some had written their kids on their cards and lost all of them.

"Feel free to reflect on what just happened," Moonear said in a quiet voice as he looked around.

The room was quiet.

"I used to love skiing," Dan, a young surfer type, started to weep. "This is fucking enlightenment at gunpoint."

I was thinking about the scene from *Sophie's Choice* when the Nazi told Meryl Streep she had to choose which child would die or he would take both.

Moonear asked us all to talk about what it brought up. Debriefing, a younger woman talked about her grandmother; quiet weeping filled the room. Several of us had red swelling eyes. But we made it through the day.

"See you next week," I said to Charlie. "You ok?"

"I guess so," he chuckled to himself strolling off.

Over the next few days, things were anything but quiet at work. It felt like the gates holding in the crazy unshackled. Discontent flooded from the building into my life. One of the residents overdosed, triggering a panic in the building, everyone fearing they were next. I listened to stories for hours. Raoul lashed out at me for not being sterner. Pedro spent a full evening crying and telling me he did not want to die on his own. And when I got home after working a double shift, one of my clients was sitting in my bedroom.

"You gotta go home," I told Ed, a disheveled, elderly African American man of unsound mental footing, who'd just moved into the building, sitting in my room in my writing chair, having followed me home on the bus. He looked surprised, shrugged and walked out.

"Why'd you let him inside?" I asked my roommate Pete, once Ed had left.

"You were doing your oral histories. I thought he was one of your interviewees," he replied.

"Now he knows exactly where I live. People get killed by their clients. And you confirmed my address."

Everything felt unhinged.

I jotted some notes in my journal later that night: "The virus has entered my dreams and my home, bringing uncertainty to an already disheveled, mental landscape." I was supposed to be the one who had everything together. But the virus was shaking at my foundations. All through the week, I thought about the loss exercise. Its implications reverberated everywhere, dislodging thoughts about my old life, this life and the one I was trying to create, unleashing a panorama of images of hellos, goodbyes, departures, and memories.

"You leave high school for college in a new town, saying goodbye, to go to a new place for a job," lamented Kirk, after he moved to Washington, DC, after graduating from Vassar. "It's what life is all about." When Mom and my brothers moved out before my freshman year in high school, Dad and I went to the movies, unable to think of a better thing to do. The family as we knew it was disappearing. I came to idolize the upperclassmen at the school who drove me to and from football practice, telling me the score on things. And then they left. Soon enough, I was one of those seniors, leaving never really to come back. At 1994 Market, when people left, they departed this world. I still had no idea how to handle the cycle. You meet new people and you lose them. The cycle goes on and on. You can't go home again argued Thomas Wolfe. That's what modern living is all about in America.

"I miss my friends so much," noted Charlie, reflecting on the epidemic's first decade of losses. "Every day. That doesn't go away."

A week after the first training, we met again for the follow up weekend to do more counseling exercises and work through any issues that might have come up after the loss exercise the week prior. I was rattled for putting Grant's name in the trash can in the loss exercise. It was my own choice. But how could I have put this person's name in a trash can? Still, he felt lost to me, especially since his dad died.

We talked all weekend, finishing Sunday afternoon with a ritual. The facilitators asked us to form circles, leading us by each other in opposing intersecting directions, so everyone eventually passed everyone.

"See the person who needs love, who needs to be loved. See an old and faded friend in the eyes of the person in front of you," said Moonear, as everyone walked by holding hands, looking into each other's eyes, zigzagging past each other through the Sufi dance. I stared at a guy from Santa Cruz who looked just like one of my old football linebacker buddies from years earlier. And it all blurred, all the lives.

When we finished, Dr. Garfield produced a photo of his father to begin our final exercise. "For a man who was one of the greatest pacifists, who was the most gentle man, I wonder what he thought of a century with so much war," he said as he lit a candle for his father. He asked us to tell stories about people who were important to us.

Ali, a black lesbian, told us about her father.

"He was a party dude. I remember a trip he told me about when he said he ate way too much, but had so much fun. I miss him so much. He loved me and embraced me as a lesbian," she said. She also told everyone about being in recovery.

"I want to tell you about the first person I met with HIV. He was my dad's best friend from 1956," I shared with the group. "They were best friends for decades. He travelled across the East with Mom and Dad in the sixties. He was part of some of the best years they ever had. For a while, he lived with Dad and

235

me after the family moved out. We'd go to get Indian food and go to the movies every week. He told me about his life, getting lost in the desert, reflecting on who he was and where he came from. His father had lived through the underground of Weimar Berlin. Thomas showed me that world, in the movies, a life that I would not have known without him. I never really knew what to make of his life or memories. But they are not going away. I think of him every day I do this work. And I feel like he's with us now."

As soon as I was done, another one of the counselors stood up with a picture of her son. She spoke with a British accent.

"This was Max," she said. "He died last year after his 18th birthday. He is gone. But when I look out at you, I see parts of him in so many of you. I see his hair, his eyes, his smile in so many of your faces."

Listening to her talk about her lost son, I was in awe of this mother's beautiful dignity. Tears welled up in my eyes. I could not take any more of this and I put my hands on my face.

Later after we were done, I talked with the English woman about her son.

"Your story killed me," I confessed. "I'm sorry."

"You know I said I saw so many parts of him in so many faces here. But more than anyone else, you carry his face, eyes and smile." She gave me a hug.

All the volunteers sat in a circle with people with whom we had commiserated and who understood. I cheered for everyone who had participated in the training. "You have all been amazing," I told them. "Actions speak louder than words and your actions speak volumes."

That foxhole camaraderie, like nothing I had experienced since high school football, lasted through the night. After we finished the formal training, a few of us went out. Half the staff was there for beer and pizza. Work hard, grieve and dance as much as possible. Unlike college activism in which people seemed to compete to see who had been the most oppressed, this was a movement I could be a part of, I thought. Later on, we went to Café San Marcos on Market Street. The disco erupted when "It's Raining Men" came on. We were all still at it, surviving and thriving, the song thumping. Everyone put their hands in the air; "Hallelujah," we sang, connected for a brief moment, dancing like the years before this dark cloud descended on Castro Street. We stayed at the club till closing time.

But as quickly as it started, we all went our separate ways. Throughout the weekend, I felt like I was losing one way of seeing the world where I grew up. It was a perspective on the US as a place with a government that took care of us. Like those who watched the Vietnam war unfold in front of them, I was seeing a system that left people behind, deeming certain populations of people expendable. I was also finding a different kind of people willing to step up and be there for each other, expanding what democracy could include, what it could mean for everyone. For a few days, we had all felt a bit of togetherness.

During the workshops, I found myself thinking about the loss exercises that were part of living, greeting and letting go, and embracing what's around. This was just part of living. I thought of Charlie who talked about his friends who were gone. For many, remembering was the most pressing of endeavors. These thoughts churned through my mind. But when we were done with the training, we still had to face the epidemic on our own terms. And we all walked out of the club into the world, back to our own individual lives and struggles.

To Lose the Earth You Know

"Something has spoken to me in the night...and told me that I shall die, I know not where. Saying: '[Death is] to lose the earth you know for greater knowing; to lose the life you have, for greater life; to leave the friends you loved, for greater loving; to find a land more kind than home, more large than earth.'"

-Thomas Wolfe, *You Can't Go Home Again*

Early in my shift the next day, two men from the emergency medical services walked up and slammed the door.

"We have an emergency in room 509!" they yelled. They went upstairs in a rush. A few minutes later they carried Julio, one of Juan's best friends, out in a stretcher. He lay in his pajamas, with an oxygen mask over his face. He put his hand up, two fingers for peace, a V for victory and defiance.

Juan walked in wearing a cross a friend had given him. "He is here now." He pointed at his heart, seemingly also referring to Julio, his neighbor down the hall. Juan had a sad peaceful look. That friend had passed long ago. "I had one week in which fifteen friends died," he told me. "I went into a severe depression. Over 150 of my friends and acquaintances have died of this." He walked upstairs.

It wasn't fifteen minutes later when he called me, telling me the paramedics were coming for Jose, his other neighbor. He had refused surgery a week earlier and came home from the hospital too early. He wore a painful grimace as he hobbled out of the lobby with Juan to wait for the paramedics. Once he was gone, Juan told me he was used to it. He said he had no more tears to cry.

With a smile, he told me he had something to show me. He pulled up his pants exposing three spots where KS lesions were growing on his legs. This was it, the first signs of the lethal AIDS-related skin cancer that no one knew how to treat. Early images of people with HIV/AIDS were filled with them, people covered in them just before they passed. It was a sign. The beginning of the end——he broke out laughing. "I knew it was going to happen sometime. I have aged forty years in these last six. I am a sixty-year-old in a twenty-seven-year-old's body. I have grown to see life for its fragilities."

Buddy, Alvin, Benjamin, and Paul all died in the building within the week. Richard told me Paul's funeral was devastating. Two days later, he had to go to the hospital. I was there when he got back.

"I got really nervous and my heart started beating harder and harder and it got irregular and the pains started," he told me in the lobby. We talked and I checked in on him later.

Everyone seemed rattled. A feeling like something was lurking, chasing us——pervaded everything. I felt it all shift. It only intensified as the night continued, ebbing and lulling, through the dark, quiet hours, rolling back at 5:00 in the morning. Noises startled me. I thought I saw a resident or a visitor, passing before my eyes. Pedro, who had been nodding off on the couch, jolted his head, alert to the noises of the garbage trucks, graffiti painters, bums, rats, and other early morning noises that reached us inside, awake. Who knows what old triggers pass through his mind? He had conditioned himself within his condition. He rarely slept. He would stand out all night in the street, just watching. I didn't know what he might be waiting for.

People were desperate. Burt, a resident I almost never talked with, came up to me early in an afternoon shift. "I'm going back to rehab," he announced. "If I don't get out of here, I'm going to kill myself. I can't stay in control. I can't resist. I've made some big mistakes. I just have to get out of here. There isn't enough love here. Nobody will lend a hand. Not a single time have I had a person come up to me and say, 'Do you want to go to a movie? I've seen you've had some problems lately.' But no one cares and I don't think I can make it by myself." He told me about weeklong binges and getting mugged in the middle of Golden Gate Park. "As he was talking, I was thinking, I will only give him $60.00, not the $160 I have with me and then I ran. It felt as though I had jets under me, as though something else had taken over. And I made it to the clearing and to the police station. There really is someone watching over me. Walking, I was thinking that really I am an angel. But my kindness is also a form of vulnerability."

Everyone coped with HIV and life in their own ways.

I told Dad about the week. "Watching everyone here coping with all this, this mostly feels like a tragedy." I tried to sound like I had a grip on things. "But people are navigating the darkness as best they can."

"They will be stronger and more prepared for the next lives," Dad responded. "It wasn't at the church in North Dallas where we went for years, it was among the prostitutes and queers that you've found real spirituality.... They are not too fat to forget about god and spirit, like so many of us are."

"It's a weird space here, Dad. I don't know whether I should start thinking of everyone in the past tense. So many keep on going, but they're living between two worlds, with one foot in the here and now, another in another place."

"One foot in the gutter and the other in the sublime."

"Everyone copes. Some go upstairs and just get loaded. Others are compulsive 12-step goers."

"Like Thomas. That's how he spent his last days. He loved the grittiest of the 12-step meetings in Monahans."

"One of the residents, Pedro, said I'm on his will for his cat. He may be half gone, but he's still here."

"That's good, Cab. It means you mean something. I should tell you about Thomas's last days some time. It was a mess, just like what your folks are going through there."

"What happened?"

"He lost his mind, and stabbed himself in front of his family. He really lost his mind. Dementia consumed him."

I could never shake that memory. The image of him as grotesque and beautiful at the same time. Cruel and caring, his partner almost seemed glad when he was finally gone, the virus no longer running through him. Sometimes death really was a gift, when living was too much. Sister death or a rip off, none of us seemed to know. But some did.

Back at work, Carlos was looking gaunt.

"You look tired," I said to him. He was sitting in the chair by the elevator where Toby used to sit, with his head down.

"It's not that I'm tired because I never go anywhere. It's that my muscles ache. It's hard for me to lift my legs...." he said. "I hope better times come."

238

"Okay," he followed with a shrug of his shoulders. "Goodnight" he said, walking to the elevator.

In the middle of the shift, I closed my eyes for a few minutes. A snap hit the building, as if a plane had crashed into it, leaving it shuttering. My neck snapped, as the 4.2 Richter earthquake cracked from North Berkeley, ripping and shaking San Francisco. Dust fell from the ceiling. There wasn't any damage to San Francisco but the memories of the 1989 Lomo Prieta earthquake left many of us shaky.

"Did you feel that?" Michelle, a trans resident yelled, running downstairs in nothing but a bathrobe. "It's too shocking," she said histrionically.

"Was that an earthquake?" she asked, answering: "It's too hysterical for the masses to know what is really happening."

"Well, I'm not hysterical or the masses, so tell me," I responded.

"We're going back into the ocean this year."

"Really?"

"Cab, we are going back home. I can't tell you how many people just like myself I have met who have said the same thing. We are going back into the ocean, back to Atlantis."

I loved Michelle. She was a five-foot, very lispy, small transgender person. I usually had no idea what she was talking about, but at other times I understood her perfectly. Her favorite movie was *Wizard of Oz*. Some days, it was like we were all on the yellow brick road going back to Oz, she explained, at least she was. "It's been a long road," she said, sounding tired but open to sharing bits and pieces of what she had seen. We often talked about her life as a trans person, hustling, working at the Motherlode. "We are the least understood people in the world," she said, reflecting on living a life in between this space and that. "We are all going back to Atlantis." She ran back upstairs. Everyone had their own way of coping.

Ernie walked in. He had spent the night with Julio in the hospital.

"I don't know what he's talking about. Julio is getting really weird," Ernie lamented. Julio and Ernie had been together for years. "It's beginning to scare me." Ernie's voice began to break, and he trailed off. "The nurse says it's the dementia and it's part of the dying. He's saying really strange things about cats and most of the time I don't know what he's talking about. He keeps telling me he wants to make some soup. He thinks he's home. I asked him if he knew where he was and he says he knows."

"Does he know what's going on? I know my godfather used to make lots of lentil soup and play Chopin on the piano long after he had lost his mind."

"How long did he last?"

"He died three years ago. But the dementia robbed much of who he was. Does Julio know what is going on?"

"He knows he's dying and he's at peace with it. It just scares me. They say that the AIDS is taking over and he's losing his brain. I just want to be there with him. I hope they let me stay tonight." Ernie was carrying a McDonald's bag and wearing an old gray sweatshirt under the black leather jacket he always wore. "A lot is on my plate." He went upstairs.

"You ok, Ernie?" I asked.

He looked at me and paused for a second. "I'm ok. One thing this horrible disease has taught me is if you can be ok when things are hard, you really can be a happy person. I'm trying to live up to that." He walked upstairs.

Something about the McDonald's bag as comfort food he was going to eat by himself felt terribly sad, and noble. The quiet bravery of the place moved and surprised me. As he was walking up, Keith ambled out of the elevator.

"I don't even know how I got AIDS," Keith said. He was an elderly African American man from Oakland with a grey beard. It was the first time he had broached the subject and it seemed to come out of nowhere. But everyone's feelings were out there, shaken up to the surface. "It sure has ruined my plans. I was gonna go back to school. I knew that when I was smoking crack, it sometimes really hit me. Once I passed out on the bus after smoking all night with an Elvis impersonator," he paused, shaking his head, laughing. "AIDS is like the polishing of our souls," he continued. "Rocks pressing against each other, creating diamonds. That's what's happening here."

I walked up to the roof for the sunrise where I could look out over the city, the trees in the distance, in between the buildings and the sunlight of the early morning, surrounding and welcoming. There were moments when it all looked clear and bright. One of the old stories from Sunday school—of Jesus taking Peter and the apostles up to a mountain top—came to mind. For a second everything became clear, as a simple light made its way through the morning, making its way across the sky, between the buildings, through the streets, the homeless down below, the ancient trees, and the water in the distance. Like one of the Blake poems, Terri, Hank, Charlie, Ernie, Allen, Willy, and Keith were all the bards, whose past, and future see; Keith was right I thought looking out.

When I got back downstairs, a group of people stood at the door for Terri, who had just shuffled off. They had given his memorial the night before. Michelle brought them in. Sistara was with them. She was the trans queen of Haight Street, she told me when I first met her. They were Terri's sisters. Pastel makeup all over their bodies, they reminded me of the Cockettes Kaliflower Commune on Sutter Street. Their most famous member, George Harris III, was transformed by his experience there. Constantly on LSD, his reality ebbed between 1970s sex magic and 1940s black and white celluloid. He grew a beard, threw out his khakis, strung beads in his hair, pierced his nose, and referred to himself as Hibiscus. He walked the streets of San Francisco without shoes, clad in skirts he'd picked up from garbage bags, remainder bins, and leftover piles—"waste of a culture"—Hibiscus aspired to live the life of an angel. Several in the commune whispered that he looked like, "Jesus Christ with lipstick." He died a decade later, an early casualty of the AIDS crisis. That spirit from the Kaliflower Commune seemed to resonate with Terri's sisters.

Sistara told me about the memorial.

"It was wonderful," Sistara gushed. "Everyone had a story about Terri. So many to make you cry or make you laugh, many from people who I hadn't even seen before." Sistara and the others looked at peace with it all.

"Did anyone talk about Frankie?" I asked.

"We all did. She was part of Terri's magic."

240

I had met Sistara the previous fall as she popped in and out of the building, never missing a step, or falling out of stride, even as Terri got sicker and sicker. She always saw the color in Terri's life, reveling in it. Shortly before Terri passed, she took her to a huge party for her at her friend's house. They dressed her up and wheeled her out in her wheelchair—with her ever-present entourage. She even took Terri to the Castro Halloween, wearing five-inch heels and a striped mini skirt. Now, her family was upstairs grabbing the rest of her belongings, including the old toaster she dubbed Frankie. And Terri was somewhere else, walking Frankie.

Pedro walked downstairs, holding a plate of food.

"What a weekend," I said.

"What a weekend," he agreed. "What's wrong?"

"It's been a rough one."

"Yeah."

"You know how much I respect your ways of helping everyone here?"

"Why do you say that?"

"I say it because I don't want you to think your compassion goes unnoticed."

"Well, God notices and that's all that really counts," Pedro said. "I wasn't put here for nothing. I wasn't put here to have a shitty childhood, to have my Dad put cigarettes out on my arms, get sent to Bellevue and then to die. I was put here for more than that."

"What are you doing with the food?" I asked.

"I give it to the guys outside on the street. No one here wants it. But they do."

Pedro walked out the door with a plate of hot cooked food. I saw him give it to one of the guys who usually dug through the trash cans, one of the invisible people on the streets, in the shadows.

I sat down to write in the journal. Josh, another resident, walked downstairs.

"I was sold as a child!" he said, startling me. I looked up at him.

"I found out from the TV."

I just looked at him nodding, not knowing what to say.

"I could show you," he said.

His eyes were glassy.

"If I had money I would buy myself an encyclopedia set so I can educate myself."

As I was listening to him, I started to feel very tired, the kind of fatigue you feel when your mind is giving way to madness. It was a feeling that seemed to be expanding.

"I was sold when I was 14-years-old. I'm a Hebrew Israelite," he went on. He showed me a picture. "I had sex with her when I was lost and lonely in the city. But that didn't help. I want to avenge myself for what happened, for the conspiracy against me."

"I gotta go, Josh. Lets continue next time," I said, pointing to my watch, letting the story go. "Shift is over."

"Okay," he said, wandering off, mumbling.

I signed out and went home. My next shift wasn't for another sixteen hours. It was time to go home and sleep. It would be good to sleep. Back at work, Ed called at a quarter past 4 AM. We had thought he wasn't going to make it. He'd been in the hospital for two weeks. His condition felt precarious. Either he was going to take his medication or he wasn't. I had only ever known Ed as being very sleepy, as if he was on Quaaludes.

But today, in a calm, sober and alert voice he called to ask if there was any mail for him. I guess the medicine had taken.

While I was looking down and writing, a man came downstairs in a dress and a huge orange wig that covered his eyes. He leaned over the counter.

"Hi Cab," he greeted me, hair falling into his eyes. I couldn't tell who it was. He wouldn't uncover his eyes. A shiver ran down my back.

"Who is this?" I finally asked.

"It's Josh, see" he pulled the wig up, smiled and strolled off.

Then Brian walked downstairs.

"Have you met the wicked witch of the west?" he asked me.

"Who is that?"

"Anna, the new case manager. She has an Eastern European accent."

"Oh yeah, I met her. Yes."

"She said 'We are all in this together,' to me the other day, to which I replied, 'No honey, you can go home and get married, whereas I'm going to die.'"

Everyone was lashing out at everyone.

"People are angry because we've watched too many good people die," Juan told me later in the shift. "We're being crippled by this disease. There is a cure out there. But the government is sitting on it because of all the money it is making on this. Plus, the government wants to see homosexuality die."

I looked at him and nodded.

"I have no concrete information," Juan conceded. "God did not kill Sodom and Gomorrah out of anger, but out of compassion, a desire to cure. I didn't choose to be gay. I was born this way."

"Juan, what are you talking about? That's awful. You sound like a televangelist."

"I know. But sometimes I think that."

Juan, looked at me and then at the chair by me. He was sitting across from me.

"Who's in the third chair?"

"Huh?"

He gestured to the empty chair at the desk.

"No one."

"Really?" he smiled.

I looked at him and his smile got wider.

"Who's in the third chair?"

"There's you, me, and an empty chair..."

"You, me, and an empty chair, or father, son and the holy ghost in the third chair. She moves through everyone, in every smile here, every homeless person. Her big energy moves through all of us."

242

Juan was smiling. I began to as well. He pointed out to the people outside, digging through the trash cans. "What we do to the least of his brethren, we do to him. You see that don't you?"

I just sat listening to Juan. He continued: "Jesus was buddies with Mary Magdalene and the hookers. He would have been with us right here."

"I'm not sure I believe in god these days, but I do miss him."

"Just because you don't see god doesn't mean he isn't there," Juan followed.

We talked for a bit. He'd go back upstairs, come back down. For hours, we talked about the people on the edges of this city, as he elaborated on his own guerilla theology.

As he went up, Keith came down. He wore his hearing aid and a black tweed hat. He had been getting weaker and weaker. But he was always up for telling stories about his years bouncing around from military service in Germany, from hustling to homelessness before he got here. He hobbled more than he walked and usually he sat.

"When you get kicked out on your ass, you gotta just let go, and get centered. You see, I talk with my guardian angel about things. Sometimes they kick open the way to lead me through. You gotta just keep talking to the man upstairs. Maybe that's why I'm still around with AIDS and cancer and everything. I mean, I woke up that morning in front of the Acropolis and I was pinching myself, trying to see if I wasn't dreaming. But it was real, and hours earlier I was scared shitless. I sometimes forget all this fantastic stuff has happened to me. We hung out with the members of the Stuttgart Ballet. They lived down the street. That was when I served in the military in the Sudetenland in Czechoslovakia. This is why sometimes I'm compelled to write, just to allow the rest of the world to see what I've done as a gay black man."

He had made a living in the army as a houseboy and a hustler. "You can sell your ass but you never sell your soul. That, my friend, is key," he said. "Keep talking to the man upstairs, stay in touch with the guardian angel. You have to allow it the space to take care of you....This is why I've stayed alive so long, through cancer, through radiation all week, without losing my hair."

Dad was right. These were different, fuller kinds of people, dancing between this and something other. In so many ways, many were already there. They were showing me how to be ok being lost. Between Keith and Juan and Pedro and all the people I found, a new world of stories had opened I could find myself in, the line between us and them blurring every day.

After work, I sat to write at the corner of 16th and Valencia. Looking out at the street as it started to rain, the smell of the rain filled the café. I was early to meet Tessa and Anne, who were going to see *A Streetcar Named Desire* with me at the Castro. Walking over, I picked up the new *Bay Area Reporter* and turned to the obits. And there was Julio's obit. He'd died in the hospital. I thought about Ernie and Juan looking at the picture. My thoughts raced from despair, to nostalgia, to ennui. Could he really be gone? It felt like my whole life in San Francisco was consumed with loss. After a minute, I left to go to the bathroom. When I passed by the popcorn and concession stand, I looked at the old photos of the Castro from the 1920s, everyone in elegant black tie dress from a premiere.

"I love thinking of this place from the '20s and '30s when people sought solace in the movies," I said to Tessa when I sat back down.

"It was a way to get away from the problems they saw all around them," she said.

"One of the guys at the training last week told me about going to see a double feature here in 1981. Before he arrived, he went to get some rolling papers at the pharmacy. Someone had posted a photo of the KS lesions on his body, and erosion on his teeth. The note said, 'Hey Guys, watch out, there is something going around.' That was the first time he heard about AIDS. His life would never be the same after that."

The theater was packed. An organ player began to play a majestic symphony of movie music. The black and white film commenced. Brando screamed for Stella in the misty New Orleans night, not unlike the foggy evening we were having. The two guys sitting next to me chuckled during some of Brando's particularly frank moments with Blanche. The film ended with her transcendental line, "I have depended my whole life on the kindness of strangers." We had all felt that way at one point or another. They escorted her off to the asylum.

"Whew, Blanche was nuts," I said. "I adore her," I smiled at Tessa as we walked out along with the crowd.

"Me too," Tessa replied as we walked back to her bike.

"Thanks for going with me."

"Any time."

The rain began again. People were strolling about. The evening felt alive and my thoughts turned back to the organ player at the theater. Walking, I was enormously grateful for him for taking us away to Oz, back to a technicolor dream somewhere far from the everyday.

244

First Glances

"San Francisco itself is art.... Every block is a short story, every hill a novel. Every home a poem, every dweller within immortal."
-William Saroyan

Most of the afternoons when I didn't have to work, I took the bus downtown to Pinnacle Fitness at the corner of Kearny and Post Streets in the old Gumps Building for an aerobics class. Running into the building, I waited for the elevator. It opened, people pouring out. It had been weeks. When I heard the steps entering the hallway around the corner, I held the elevator door. In ran a college-aged woman in black bellbottoms, slick brown Spanish shoes, a blue silk blouse wrapped around her waist, and a denim Levi's jacket. Carrying a suede backpack and a department store bag, she looked tired.

"Thanks a lot," she said and smiled as she entered. She had a bashful grin that wasn't quite hidden beneath her frizzy hair. She looked at me, then down at her toes and her expression changed. I was intrigued. She leaned against the elevator wall and grinned to herself.

"Long day? You look tired."

"I am," she said.

"Me too." I feigned exhaustion from a day of work I hadn't had.

"I can't believe I'm actually motivated to work out this afternoon."

"I know. Me too."

"Wait, have I see you before?"

There are limitations to an elevator interaction. But for that brief moment, she offered a glance that lingered. As soon as the moment had begun, it ended, and her eyelids closed. She had told all she was willing or comfortable to. And then, an epiphany, her eyelids peeled back, allowing me, with the focus of a pair of eyes, a possibility, a hello. The elevator stopped at the fifth floor and we both got out.

"Have a great workout," she said.

"You too."

"Maybe the tide is turning," I told Charles as we chatted at his apartment on Polk Street after the workout.

"Dates are weird here," he said. "Its kind of like single-issue voting. They test you."

Charles and I had had a few adventures of our own of late. The previous week, on the way home from the gym, he'd grabbed someone else's bag by mistake.

"It's got coke in it," he said, smiling at me, as he rummaged through it when we got back to his place. We made plans to get the bag back to its owner, but not before ingesting everything in it, up our noses. We stayed up all night, talking on the roof with his roommate, Scudder, drinking bourbon and coke, listening to old Heaven 17, '80s dance music.

"Your point of differentiation is how you handle this stuff," Scudder smiled, taking another sip of his bourbon and coke, as the sun rose.

"Sometimes San Francisco isn't too bad," I said. "And sometimes you stumble." "But sometimes you don't," Charles said.

"Maybe luck is coming my way?"

"You met someone?"

"Yeah, the girl on the elevator. She gave me her number."

But there was still some karma to contend with. The following Sunday, I went out with a woman I had met the week before with my *Melrose Place, 90210* buddies, Mimi and Chris. She had been sitting with this awkward guy she had come with and was obviously not dating. Mimi helped me with the plan of action.

"Cab, he went to go play pool—go talk with her now!" Off I went to chat with her. A beer and a couple of ruminations about the future of the Golden State Warriors later, I had her number.

The date didn't go well.

"My timing had been off and I let my catty North Dallas side take over," I told Mimi the next time I saw her.

"What really happened?"

"Remember when we met and were sitting at the barstool and drinking?"

"Yeah."

"She never got up the whole evening when I met her, so I never got to check her fully out. Not until last Sunday night when we were playing pool. She was taking a shot and I walked around to go get my beer when I noticed her leaning over the pool table. She was more bodacious than I could handle. I can't believe I hadn't seen that before I invited her out. It wasn't going anywhere anyway."

"Cab, I can't believe you," Mimi screamed, grabbing her stomach laughing. "I'd hate to go out with you."

She was right. I would have hated to go out with me too. Between Chloe and San Francisco, I was a mess, with femme fatales tormenting me in my sleep. For a bit there, all I cared about was the inner person. The trappings did not matter. I'd had enough excessive makeup in Dallas for a lifetime. By the time Tessa and I got together, all I cared about was the person, whether she showered or not. Over time, that got a little old. Her mix of patchouli oil and dour politics did not make for a very refreshing mix. Still beggars could not be choosers. Over time, when I thought about our lack of compatibility, I came to see that other forces were at work. Insecurity and lack of ease came to characterize the post-Chloe period. Chloe and I had had a blast for much of our time together. But as things cooled, Chloe confessed to longing for the intrigue of anonymous encounters, dangerous places, and bisexual explorations over the regularity of a conventional relationship.

After that, every new relationship became an opportunity to show Chloe I could be different. I always had to prove something. But my crusade to prove there were guys who actually cared about female orgasms was too much to take on every time we went to bed. Everyone brings something to a relationship, which connects with all the old places in our lives. I could not shake them loose.

Two years after school ended, Tessa was still my friend, leaving the old baggage behind, at least for the most part. We hung out all the time, rarely mentioning anything about our past. But when we went

246

to see a play called *Somebody Else's House,* those old memories came pouring back. At one point in the play, the lead actress recalled being in bed with a much younger boy who was not very experienced. "It was taking so long for him to come that I was beginning to feel as though I was in the dentist's chair," she explained. "I just lay back and watched as he squeezed his eyes shut and writhed on top of me until finally he made a sound as if he had been shot in the leg. 'Oh, he's having his little eruption,'" she realized. It was going to be her last time with him.

"That line really stuck with me," I told Tessa after the show.

"Why?"

"I guess it said more about how women see us than I wanted to hear. I felt slightly embarrassed for him," I confessed. "And myself."

On the Stroll

"I have never gone to bed with a woman I didn't pay."
-Gabriel Garcia Marquez, *Memories of My Melancholy Whores*, 2005

My friend David was a super-preppy black gay man with a Brooklyn accent. He wore Brooks Brothers suits and worked in the accounting department at the law firm where I temped those first few months after I moved to town. He focused on the numbers for hours at end, even after evenings tied up as "a sex pig" in South of Market, the night before.

"The numbers keep me honest," he confessed. Long after I was let go by the firm, we stayed in touch, going to get coffee, running around town, going out for drinks with the other legal aids, trying to get laid. He always had an eye out for young associates who worked too hard and needed some stress relief. Mostly, we were buddies, but he tried to fool around every time we went out. The rejections never offended him.

"David, I'm done scamming except for this Southern California girl I met at the gym. It's been too much. Gina and that crazy bus ride into the city and then that horrible, horrible date. I'm done for now," I said over brunch on Racing Day at Jumping Java, a café off Market Street.

"That's good. You were beginning to look like a wolf. The 1:30 in the morning sort——you know the type. A little too persistent. Just one more Mack the Knife character that the world doesn't need. Women read lack of assurance. That's the problem."

"Then what do I do about it?"

"Nothing, beyond being aware of it."

"After this girl from the gym, I'm done for a bit."

"Tell me about her."

"I just met her on the elevator at the gym."

"Does she know about you?"

"What about me?"

"What a lone wolf you are?"

"No. Not really. I'm trying to keep it in check."

"You shouldn't have to try, Cab. She's either into it or she isn't."

"Well, she doesn't know that part of me yet."

"Oh, she knows. She doesn't know, but a part of her does. That's the thing, Cab. They always know."

"How do you know?"

"I just know. We all know. That's part of why we don't deal with women. In New York, we used to call them fish," he said, laughing. "We were awful."

"Okay, no more lone wolfing."

"Let all that go. Those old fantasies are very powerful, but you have to let them go or they will hold you back, keep you from moving ahead."

Later that afternoon I met Anne and Tessa for a beer before going to see Kronus Quartet. Anne's new boyfriend and Anne had had a fight. She cried to us as we drank at Mad Dog in the Fog on Haight and Fillmore Streets.

"I can't believe this guy," Anna kvetched.

"I can't either. What happened?" I said.

"And you guys were doing so good," Tessa said.

"He always masturbated during the day," Anne followed. "And at first, we'd do it at night when I got home. But then, he stopped being able to sleep with me."

"Really, he couldn't handle two a day?"

"At first yes, then no."

"Couldn't he just wait for you and hold off during the day?"

"I guess not."

"That's like most guys."

"All guys?"

"It was just too hard to feel that all day long without acting on it, just too much. He had to sit around all day thinking of you after you left for work. He probably couldn't get anything done without clearing things out first."

"But we did it the night before."

Tessa was watching Anne and me discuss.

"I can't write a word without a little one first," I replied.

"Are all guys like that?

"Most. I guess."

"That's exhausting."

"It's awful. We get sick if it stays in there too long. Just too much. But when the fantasy is more intriguing than the real thing then you are in trouble."

"Yeah. I guess that's what happened."

We all went to the show, listening intently as the four musicians filled the room with dissonant sounds that seemed to tap into a dark, caffeine-infused anxiety churning through the city. Tearing at the quartet format their sound evoked an otherworldly, raw, sometimes beautiful, angry imagery. Afterwards, Anne and Tessa went home. I went to meet some of my old friends from Vassar who were all in town for the weekend.

They'd all moved to D.C. to live the post-college dream after college. That hadn't quite worked out. We chatted for hours, up till 3:00 AM, drinking bourbon and Cokes. Buck hadn't changed. D.C. was not for him, so he moved back home to Dallas to work for his father, doing bookkeeping for the family company. Scudder couldn't handle D.C., either, so he moved back to his parents' house in Oregon City, which was not a good move for a very queer boy. That did not last long. Eventually, he made his way to San Francisco, where he worked in retail, and lived with Charles. Kirk was in law school at the University of Michigan, and feared he was being boxed into the system. With his student loans, he knew he would have to take a corporate job just to pay them off. We all had our respective fears; Kirk was afraid to screw it all up; Buck, of failure; and myself, a world without intimacy.

My fear lasted through the next day, through house cleaning, dinner, and going out again with the guys in North Beach. It would have been simple enough if I had just grabbed a cab home and been done with it. But I didn't. It wasn't to be. I said goodnight to the guys shortly after midnight. Steam was rising from the wet streets and there was not a cab in sight. Charles lived at Hyde and Clay. That put me precariously close to Polk Street. I walked down into the city's Tenderloin district, curiously exploring the red lights and rainy streets. Ahead of me, there was a sign for the "Paradise Spa Open 24 Hours a Day." I rang the bell, looking at the life-size photo of two people at the beach, smiling—a boy and a girl, nude, holding hands, selling the world's oldest commodity, always, always available for a sale.

"You want a massage?" a bald man, of Chinese descent, asked.

"Yeah," I said.

"Come on up."

There were men playing pool and cards. I had been wondering how legitimate these places were. *Massage*—" A woman in a black mini skirt walked up, and took me by the arm to a bedroom.

"Do you want a massage?"

"Yes."

I just stared at the bed, wondering.

"How much?"

"Forty."

"I only have twenty. Is that enough?"

She looked at me and went to talk with the bald man again in Chinese. He ushered me to the door. She wasn't as friendly anymore like she had been. *Tsk, tsk, tsk* the man snickered at me as I walked back down the steps to the street.

"Speed?" a couple of men asked me, walking down the street. Everyone was on something. It was the drug of choice for the tricks of the town, along Polk Street. Everyone had bulging pupils, a deal to make, loans pending, people to meet, debts to pay.

I took a left at the corner of Ferrell, across from the Playboy Club, one of the city's sleaziest corridors. Under a hotel awning, a woman asked, "You got somewhere to go?"

"Yeah," I responded, and smiled at her.

"You're coming with me." She must have been forty-years-old and was missing a tooth. She was grinding her chattering teeth as she ushered me inside. A greasy looking man, the kind of person you seem to only see in places like this, opened the door for her and she led me into another door into a bedroom. She unbuttoned my pants and put on a condom.

"Let me show you... Can't wait for you to see..." she slurred, starting to pull down her flowery pants as she sat in the La-Z-Boy chair.

"Don't worry about it," I said. I needed to get out of there, fumbling around and turning for the door.

"You dick. Fucking frat boy asshole," she started to scream, as things turned for the psychic worst. The five-foot-tall woman walked out into the street in her high heels and stretch pants, out and away, and I left, walking in the other direction.

"I don't know what's going on," the guy who let us in said, with a sympathetic glance. Neon lights from the hotel were blinking and shined in his eyes.

"Neither do I," I said as I hit the streets again, definitely still on the prowl.

Cruising could be the loneliest activity in the world. I could have gone to the Triangle on Filmore but I had absolutely no interest in meeting and greeting, in the feast and famine world in which I found myself. Basta! It was time for the dry spell to end. I strolled down past the apartments on Sacramento with my hands in the pockets of my tweed coat. I turned up my collar as it started to drizzle. And then I saw a blonde woman under just a little roof cover. Her breasts pushed as far outside of her shirt as possible, while still remaining partially hidden. I walked past her and then back.

"Hey baby, you want a date?"

"Yeah. How much?" I asked, having learned my lesson to negotiate early.

"How much you got?"

"Twenty."

"Fine."

"You got a place to go?"

"Sure. Let's go."

I flashed back to a scene from an old movie with a sex worker explaining that either her customers pay for it with marriage or they pay for it in the street, but we always pay for sex. At least her clients got what they wanted, hopefully. Off we went to another million-dollar renovated luxury suite, with concierge. This hotel was no better than the first I'd seen earlier on. Between the smells of urine, cum, and sweat, with a mix of crack and rotten Project Open hand food, a putrefied smell seemed to linger from a party last summer. We walked past stained red carpets and dirty gray walls. We didn't say much. This place of last resort was full of people, writers, and hangers-on. I had no idea who they were. A man with long hair, horn-rimmed glasses, and high tops stood talking, with some other glossy eyed, under-showered, street boys. She led me up a few flights until we finally reached a back wall, near the roof and she stopped. It wasn't even a room, just the last stop of desolate empty hotel staircase. Exasperated and winded, she said, "Well, pull your pants down."

So I did.

"You pay first."

I gave her my twenty.

She looked at her watch. And the rush was on. She put on a condom and started working her mouth and then her hand. And a minute or so into it, she said, "You gotta finish. I gotta get outta here." She gave it one more effort, someone screamed down the stairwell, and she began hobbling down the stairs.

"You're gonna have to finish that on your own," she explained, she told me already down a few steps. That I did, humiliated, having given a lot more of myself away than the twenty dollar bill. This was a new low in a town of lows; watching her hobble down the steps, toward the elevator as I stood there with my pants down. I avoided following her speed-induced instinct to get the hell out of there fast. "[S]trangers who were more or less forced on each other rarely made a good team..." posits András Vajda in a scene in *In Praise of Older Women*. The protagonist translating for patrons at a brothel in World War II saw that most of the guys walk in in one mood, but they looked miserable when they were done. Now I was one of those sad souls. Instead of taking the elevator down past floor after floor, I weaved through dozens of floors, seemingly endless steps, past rows of corridors, of room after room of lives I'd never know, arguments inside, screaming behind the doors, all those people moving in circles, converging, occasionally touching, usually missing each other. On the street, I saw her back at the corner when I finally finished making my way out.

Something was terribly wrong; a threshold had been crossed over. At least that's how I felt walking home, a sense of uselessness accompanying me. Thinking about the Underground Man who did "not know for certain what ail[ed]" himself, I walked down to Market and then up the long route. A bunch of guys were smiling in line at Eros. One was talking about going to Blow Buddies, the iconic blow club.

"Let's go to church" he suggested, referring to the sex club.

"Right now," they laughed.

"The line is too long here."

At least someone knew what they were doing. I was filled with disgust, and these guys were sharing a space where they laughed and got off without apology. Public sexual culture was everywhere in San Francisco, more than anywhere I'd ever been or known. There were bath houses and jack off parties, where guys got off. The women had their parties. Safe sex signs were all over the spaces. "Come together!" had become a sort of mantra. You saw the words on subway ads. Each seemed to thrive as spaces where magic things happened and people supported each other. All the while, the straight people created shame-based rituals. And queers turned these spaces into works of art.

That summer, I had interviewed Buzz Bense, the owner of the Eros for a story for *SOMA Magazine*. He had suggested to me that public sexual spaces are places to revel in human connections and kindness. "There can be extraordinary moments where people have heartfelt connections," he explained, "Where people feel like they are the recipients of random acts of kindness, where the beauty and humanity of people is evident because they are treating each other so well. To me it all relates to the spirit." I did not have too much of that feeling of the spirit as I walked. I wondered if the next time I was walking by with a full load, I'd drop by Eros, where Buzz had given me a free pass for something probably more fulfilling. But I'd tried with guys before and it never worked. I thought of my lunch with David, when he'd said I was starting to look like a wolf. I was lower than I thought I'd ever get. It was a long cold walk back to the Haight. Part of the reason I had made a point of not going home earlier in the night was the party at my apartment that my roommates were having. I was not in the mood for it. Back on my street close to the house, that unshakable 1975 feeling was starting to grasp at me again, to envelop me. At out apartment, I opened the door to my roommates up hanging out with a half dozen friends, their pupils bulging, sitting around in a circle after dosing tabs of acid.

"Cab!" everyone welcomed me with a cheer. I went to the bathroom to clean up a little. When I returned, Ray was standing there with a cold beer for me, his pupils dilated, and a strange smile on his face. I felt a sense of relief.

"Good to see you," he smiled.

"Thanks!"

"What happened tonight, Cab? You look like a hot mess," Raymond teased.

"You wouldn't believe it."

"Try me, fuck-star."

I told him about the half misses across the tenderloin. "I hate myself," I confessed.

Raymond looked at me. "Take it easy. Everyone needs to release some steam, when we see too many corpses. Get over those bourgeois mores. As long as everyone is having fun, getting what they need, and playing safe, who cares? Isn't that the point of all this? Let go of all those Sunday school thoughts. They are for the closets. It's all a mess out there. In capitalism we're all prostitutes. Moralizing about sex isn't going to get us anywhere. There are enough sex panics raging out there. But next time, save your load for Blow Buddies."

"I tried that in high school. Didn't do it for me. That's how one of the boys got me in bed. He said guys know how to give the best head. They know what other guys need."

"We do."

"But the hairy face and tough stubbly skin was a mess."

"Who said anything about kissing?"

"I could use that."

"We all depend on the kindness of strangers, right?"

Finishing our chat, we all hung out, got even higher, and went bowling in South San Francisco until 6:00.

I slept in through church, woke up with a grimace and memory burn. Had the night before really happened, I thought. Charles called and I had one last lunch with my Vassar buddies at Zuni Café and tried to put distance between the current moment and the slimy memories of the night before. Charles helped me with a story I was working on for *SOMA Magazine*.

"There are two stories I'm working on. One is about sex in San Francisco and the other is about things we have issues with," I explained.

"Well, the sex story sounds great. Keep on doing your research and I'm sure there's a lot to explore. There are lots of things I have issues with here. I was on the train today and a guy took off his sandals and started to cut his toenails. I have issues with personal hygiene maintenance on trains."

"Excellent. I'll add that to my list."

"Don't forget about the sex story. That's where you are going to make your mark, my friend," said Charles.

Former governor Jerry Brown was sitting right by us at the next table eating a salad and drinking a martini. He'd lost to Clinton in the primary two years before.

"Is that Jerry Brown?" I whispered to Kirk.

"I think so."

"Governor Brown?" I asked smiling. He looked up. "I voted for you for president last year. I love your radio show. You are the only radio commentator who paraphrases Foucault."

"Every day, guys. Don't forget about freedom in your story. It all overlaps within this experiment in living we're creating out there. That dream is still strong. Just make it part of your larger life, your journey. We're doing a lot in Oakland. Stay involved, guys. We need you. We need everyone." He wrote down his number for the office. "Drop by sometime."

Charles and I talked long into the afternoon before work. Somehow, the tone of the world was lifting and lightening. Another story was out there. I just knew it.

"The present moment feels like I've stumbled into a place between the trials of Job and the penance of Heracles, every day walking through a revolving door, crossing the same Rubicon, with the same problems, names and faces changed, repeating itself over and over," I kvetched to Charles, killing time before my 4 PM shift.

"I know you took the philosophy classes at Vassar," he replied. "With all the others in their black turtlenecks and cigarettes. I even saw you there, reading Nietzsche."

"I was one of the hungover ones."

"Remember the myth of eternal return?"

"Yeah?"

"What should we do if our lives repeated themselves over and over again? 'Everything becomes and recurs eternally—escape is impossible!'" Charles said, quoting from *Will to Power*.

"And he died of syphilis from prostitutes," I replied. "Just like I'm probably going to."

"I heard it was dementia. People want to moralize about the life of the philosopher. But we don't really know what happened. He's punished by history for pointing to a space away from the puritans, pain mixed with sex breeding uncertainty—that was his whole point."

"Yeah, but there was a lot of uncertainty. And some syphilis. I guess that's what we're doing here—crawling through the wreckage. I gotta go, Charles. Work starts in a few."

We settled up and I walked down the street to work. When I got there, Ernie was walking out. He'd buried Julio earlier in the day.

"Is he okay?" I asked Jim.

"I don't think so. I just talked to him for an hour."

"Good man, Jim."

"It breaks my heart."

"Me too. You'd think some sort of divine providence would shine down on us." He was smoking a cigarette. "I'm driving Bette Middler this week so maybe it is possible?"

"I loved *Beaches*."

"Me too."

"Did you ever know that you're my hero?"

Jim went to bed and I sat down. Fifteen minutes later, the buzzer at the door began again. Someone was holding it down. I walked up to the door to open it. Jerry, one of our residents, ran in screaming, hobbling in with his crutches, trying to get to the bathroom.

"Oh no, oh no, oh no! It's coming out. Diarrhea is coming out! Oh no! Oh no!" he moaned, desperate and humiliated. "I can't stop it."

The lobby filled with the smell of defecation. I sprayed deodorizer and pulled out the mop to clean up. It was the only thing we could do to kill the smell. Jerry was a long-time member of the Gay Men's Chorus. He still went to rehearsal every Sunday, including this one. He used to travel with the chorus. But with increasing irregularity HIV-related incidents left him unable to go very far.

"Oh, life can be so cruel," he said, hobbling out of the bathroom with the towel I had given him wrapped around his waist a few minutes later. "If only I had been able to hold it for thirty more seconds. But what's the point in crying over a little shit?" he said and shrugged.

My admiration for him and everyone else coping with this grew every day.

After cleaning up, I sat back down at the desk and flipped through the channels. *The Big Sleep* was on. Walking through the city, Philip Marlowe dug through the lives of everyone around him. All the while, he became more detached. I was becoming the opposite, internalizing the stories around me and becoming more and more a part of everything here, looking for tricks like my clients did, feeling suicidal, trying to reconnect with feelings, as I walked through the city. I was looking for clues to a crime, only to discover that I was the one who had committed it. Consumed with sex and tricks, illness and pain, compensating for the latter with the former, always eluding the difficulty of one with the other, the throes everywhere. But no one seemed to hear any of us shouting at the top of our lungs for help, spreading the ashes of our dead friends at the halls of power in Sacramento, waiting for a date in the rain. There's always someone being left out and dehumanized. After he wrote *Life in Auschwitz*, Primo Levi threw himself down an elevator shaft. It was one thing to survive the camp; the guilt of surviving, that was more than he could bear. It was that kind of a week.

Orgasm Addict in an Urban Brawl

"After a while I had to face the fact that a person isn't just a body, a person is a thinking, feeling, confused, worried, nervous, fearful being..."
-Vito Acconci, 2006

On Friday, I got off work at 8:00 in the morning and tried to sleep for a bit before heading out to see a psychoanalyst Dad had helped me find. The previous week's descent into that space between attraction and the abyss had been a little more on the self-destructive side than I cared to repeat.

I took the bus up Fillmore to find his office. There, in a room full of Egyptian objects, totems, an oriental rug, and a few degrees on the wall, Dr. Carl, and I talked.

"Tell me about yourself," he asked, cheerfully.

"Well, I love music," I replied.

"Like what? What are you listening to now?"

"*The Age of Anxiety* by Leonard Bernstein. But that's not why I'm here." Becoming jittery and emotional, I divulged the details about the previous week and how confused I was feeling. He just listened. "I'm not sure it's the best way..." I explained. "But I felt compelled to chase that feeling, that sensation, looking for life and feeling like I'm disappearing, losing myself as I walk and walk, like one of the detectives in the French movies who don't realize they're the criminals they are chasing," I said. "The city seems to be consuming me. I'm chasing a feeling I might have had, that I can't seem to grasp again," I tried to explain. "It's not like I want to get married or have kids. It's unethical to bring kids into this mess," I said. I hadn't figured out how to laugh yet, but I knew I needed to. He gave me a sympathetic look. "I just pray for the down moods to pass." I paused and looked around the office. "I feel like I am becoming addicted to the search, to the compulsion. Every night, traipsing around, chasing people, paying, people letting me watch..." I told him asking for a referral to a meeting or something.

"I can call and make you an appointment at one of the 12-step groups, but I'm really not too concerned," he said.

"It's been like this for years now."

"Like what?"

"Like hoping for someone. I'm always looking for that feeling, for that sense of being accepted. But I can't get it."

"Sounds like you think you are never going to get that feeling again."

"I don't. Walking it's like I can't find my way home, even when my apartment is just across town. But I'm weary of going back to the empty room. I feel like everything is caving in on the way, the sea pulling, the city grasping me. I can't get away from it; the stories of the mass slaughter of the Tutsi in Rwanda, the sense of no one being around to help, or being in space without a god able to do anything." We talked about work and whores, the patterns of isolation. I talked and talked and talked and talked, about dreams and work and music. It felt good to confess, to have someone bear witness. The catharsis left me feeling lighter.

When I left his office, I took the bus to Noe Valley to hang with Mimi and Chris. When I arrived, they were busy chatting about the difference between successful and unsuccessful dates. Mimi was wearing a miniskirt, ruminating about her struggle to be creative and successful at the same time. All I could do was look at her lips.

"So what about the date with the girl from the want ad?" asked Mimi.

"Don't ask," I groaned.

"What happened?"

"I bailed when I saw her."

"What?"

"I walked into the bar, saw her, got terrified and beelined for the door without saying a word," I said.

"Awful, you are awful," she said and laughed. We both laughed at my cache of bad dates they'd heard about over the months.

I had to agree; I was awful, laughing for the first time in a long time.

The next day, I went to the 12-step meeting Dr. Carl had found for me. It was in a dark room on Cesar Chavez St in the Mission. Eight other guys were there sitting in a circle, most of them a little older than me, but not by much. I think I was the only straight person in the room. Hearing the stories of guys hooking up on the buses, at sex arcades, just walking to get the paper, I was a little envious. This was the city everyone loved, of everyone connecting. But perhaps it was not making them happy? That's why we were all there. There was no leader, so we facilitated the meeting ourselves.

"I find myself walking out of work to go to the backroom down the street," one man confessed.

"I do that all the time. What's the problem?" someone asked him. "What's to worry about?"

"Do you get back to work on time?"

"Yes."

"So what's the problem?"

I was thinking the same thing.

"I am wasting hours and hours and hours of my life on sex and porn," another man said.

I felt the same way. I loved sex and felt compelled to get off every day. I certainly did not enjoy holding it all in. My brain got constipated. No writing or ideas could flow without movement. But was it addiction? I couldn't really tell. The meeting droned on. Everyone there was looking for love and trying to make sense of their desires. Many were getting something. But it wasn't clear anyone was getting what they wanted.

"I was in a club last night, with a guy doing me in the front, while another was doing me in the back," another man explained. "It felt so kinky. I usually love those spaces. But as the years go on, I am starting to feel like my soul is being drained out of me, disappearing."

Finally, we circled up, said a little prayer and everyone split.

As I was leaving the meeting, a part of me felt envious of all the guys who could just walk into the backroom of a club, or go to the park and get some. I had to spend all night trying.

"I don't want to even hear about your depraved heterosexual ways," my friend Cleve used to say when I'd tell him about these struggles.

On my walk home, I overheard music coming from one of the bars on Mission Street. It was from an old Buzzcocks album of my youth, I walked by just in time to hear the first lines: "Well you tried it just for once found it all right for kicks but now you found out that it's a habit that sticks....you're an orgasm addict!" It was a habit that stuck, but I had never worried about it. I started to smile. I was sick of worrying about it now. "Come on, Cab," I thought to myself. "Lighten up."

Walking past Guerrero Street, I looked at a sign in the window of a bar, noticing a flyer with the words, "URBAN BRAWL!" I looked closer. The flyer was for a writing workshop. It started the following week before my midnight shift. It fit into my schedule. I decided right then and there I was going. I walked into the coffee shop across the street, ordered a coffee, pulled out my notebook, and started drafting notes for the workshop.

"Put your pen on the paper and keep on writing. I don't care about what, but keep on writing," Sarah, a brown-haired, funny lesbian explained to the six of us the following week, there the first day of the workshop. "Plant the seeds of your story. Let it flow." We all sat together in a group and work-shopped ideas with each other, created collages, visual markers, and histories of our stories. Something was opening up. "A combination of the sublime and the apocalyptic sufficient to sharpen anyone's sense of an ending...." I wrote the words I had seen somewhere, glued the letters cut from newspapers and magazines to a map of the city, a montage. My story started to have geography; a time, a place, a world, a life, and storyline running through it. "Keep on writing..." Sarah implored. "... Let it go where it needs to go." In the battle between Eros and Thanatos, a new storyline was taking shape.

Three Dates

Julie, the girl from the elevator, and I had our first date that Thursday night. We had been smiling and winking for days, chatting between workouts. The day she walked by in that yellow and orange, skin-tight lycra outfit, I knew I had to make something happen. So, I asked her for her number. She answered when I called. We were supposed to go see *Alphabet Soup*. But first, we'd meet at her place. On the way to her place, I passed Polk Street, wondering what she had been doing two Saturdays prior as I was trolling about down the street.

She was smiling when she opened the door. I was immediately taken with her olive skin and frizzy brown hair. Wearing a flannel shirt and torn, worn-out jeans, revealing just a bit of underwear in the behind, it wasn't so much grunge as a San Francisco Russian Hill vibe. She offered me an Anchor Steam beer when I arrived.

"It's my favorite beer. I named my cat after it," she said, opening the beer and pointing at her cat.

I loved the way she smelled. She had one roommate who was out. Fashion magazines were stacked all over a coffee table. A Nirvana CD was playing. I sat flipping through her magazines as we talked fashion; I read some of the sex advice columns. We chatted about college in Southern California, where we had both gone to school. Dostoyevsky's *Crime and Punishment* was her favorite book. She was currently reading *House of the Spirits* by Isabel Allende. At some point, I turned off the CD player and put on the radio, scrolling to a '70s station. Somewhere between "Too Much Heaven" by the Bee Gees and "More Than a Feeling" by Boston, she asked me to come take a look at the view outside her living room. She opened the window and we crawled out on the ledge, where she had some plants assembled, and a small sitting area to look at the city from Russian Hill down through Chinatown.

"I love this view," she whispered, leaning against me. Our jeans rubbed and then we were at it. There would be no bands or dancing. We wouldn't make it much past the couch, where we made out and talked for hours. I meandered home sometime in the middle of the night.

The next day Chris came over and we went out for drinks at the Casa Loma, a grimy dive bar on Fillmore Street. Charles came to meet us. Inevitably, we kvetched about politics. Charles was wearing white buck shoes, khakis, and a polo shirt.

"I love the shoes, Charles," I said.

"Just a part of the preppy handbook. Every good Republican needs a pair," he said.

"What?"

"You're a what?" Chris' jaw dropped.

"Yeah, I thought Buck told you that."

"Well, I knew about it at Vassar."

"Everyone was a Democrat there. The only way to make inroads or get anything going in D.C. was to be a Republican. I started the Young Republicans Club there in a sea of patchouli oil."

"Do you believe any of that crap?"

"Not really, but the Republican parties in D.C. always had more free drinks. The Democratic parties could never compare."

"But you're not there anymore. You're in San Francisco. Are you sure you want to be out about that here? Did you see what they did to Dan Quayle during the election?"

"No."

"When politicians come, they usually think they can just walk the streets and be safe. But when he came, he traveled to North Beach. A crowd of people saw him and started to scream, 'Kick his ass!' and basically chased him out of the neighborhood, pelting him with eggs. He pretty much got back into the motorcade and left. I wouldn't advise coming out of the closet about this one. Not here."

"There are a few ideologues here, single issue voters, whatever. I don't care what people do with themselves, the drugs they take, the abortions they have, whatever, I just want to be left alone. But a lot of this mess does go back to LBJ."

"LBJ was the best, the War on Poverty, everything, the best programs since Roosevelt. Except for foreign policy."

"And now, we have Clinton. What an asshole," Chris said.

"Come on, Chris. Don't forget the Motor Voter bill," I replied.

"Guys, may I introduce a new topic?" Charles jumped in, lighting a cigarette.

"Please."

"Fashion."

"Guys the new *I Hate Brenda Newsletter* just arrived. Check it out," I noted, pulling out a copy of the fanzine about the TV star. "I love this thing. Seven thousand subscribers nationwide." We all looked at it, looking at pictures of her reciting the Pledge of Allegiance at the Republican National Convention, flipping through. "She says her band is like a combination between U2 and Pearl Jam. What a twat!" Chris paused.

"I just love that people are obsessed enough about things to make this," I commented.

Chris looked up. "You should write for them."

"I don't know what I could add."

"Send them something."

"I don't know what I would write. All I think about these days is San Francisco and AIDS." I paused, adding, "and sex and romance and my lack thereof."

"Is that what your novel is about?"

"It's about this, us, me, sex and San Francisco. But I don't know where it's going."

"That seems like plenty," Chris said.

"But I have no plot."

"My Dad's biggest book was all about going to New York and finding a therapist, who he fell in love with and the memories he shared," Chris replied. "That was enough for him too. Just write about your dark and light point, your it, your world, your us, our bad temp jobs, the dinner parties at our apartments, the scenes we are part of, the beer we drink too much of, the bad dates, the gossip, our unemployment, the total scene, our San Francisco. Go back to the scene of the crime and tell us about it."

"But I don't know what that is."

"Not yet."

"Walter Benjamin aspired to write a story out of thousands of other people's lines," I followed. "I want to do that."

"From all your dates and your clients, everyone here," gushed Chris.

"With no beginning or end. The story goes on forever. That could be my illumination."

"You've done lots of good research. Speaking of which, any new adventures with dating? Personal ads?" she inquired, raising her eyebrow. Midway through the conversation, an older woman with frizzy brown hair came up to me and asked, "Did you go to Michigan? I know I have met you somewhere."

"I don't know," I replied. "I sure did not go to Michigan."

"But I know you from somewhere." I looked at her and recalled that day we chatted on the street.

"Like two years ago? We met in the Tenderloin. You were talking about your research."

"Yes, that's it. You were so shady there. I thought you were a john."

"No?"

"I really did. But also a little cute." We bantered about, playing the name game. We both knew similar people at 1994 Market Street, where she'd seen me at the training. She was buddies with Raoul from work. We both had the same trouble with him.

"He's a bit catty," she acknowledged.

"A bit," I nodded, smiling. She went to talk with her friends, but I got her number.

"What's her name?" Charles asked as we walked out of the pub, on our way to get late night food.

"Elizabeth."

"She looks like Stockard Channing in *Grease*."

"I know. I love it."

"So, now you have this cute Julie who's cool, and a new friend who seems to be channeling the wiser sassier ingénue. Quite a choice."

"I know. But we just met."

"I saw the way she was looking at you. Watch out, Cab," Chris continued. Charles nodded in agreement.

"What do you mean?"

"Remember when I was with the girl I met on the bus?" asked Charles.

"Yeah."

"I thought everything was great. She was wild, into constant sex. And then she started asking me to slap her."

"A little fun and games between safe, sane, and consenting adults. No problem," I replied.

"But it wasn't that clear. I slapped her a few times and she asked for more. And then she wanted me to pee on her."

261

"What's wrong with that?"

"Nothing. But it didn't stop there."

"What happened?"

"She kept asking me to hit her harder."

"So what happened?"

"It was just too much. Sometimes in San Francisco you tap into something dark. Watch out."

We talked for a long time and went home.

The phone rang at 9:00 AM the next morning.

"What's up Cab Calloway?" Dad asked, sounding chipper.

"Oh, just reentering, wading back from a sea of dreams and oblivion," I replied. Dad told me he was separating from his second wife.

"At the age of 57, I'm still a dirty billy goat," he said. "Are you finding any poetry? Tell me about the scene?" he asked, reminding me about his time here after college. Almost every time we talked, he bragged about going to the seminal October 7, 1955, reading of *Howl* at Six Gallery with Allen Ginsberg.

"That's not it anymore Dad. It's a lot more spoken word, drag kings, and lesbian stand up comedians regaling us with stories," I replied.

"How are you handling the hippies and feminists?" he asked.

"You know, Dad, San Francisco is chock full of sex positive feminism," I explained, trying to beat back his litany of complaints about deconstruction and the cultural revolution, without acknowledging the old dour, puritanical currents of the sex wars he was referring to.

"I'm sure there are. You know, Cab, when your old man has disappeared having gone climbing in the Himalayas looking for a medicine man, you can toast the Women's Movement of the 1990s. I feel the same way about the ancient Red movement. I miss it."

Later that night, Tessa and I went out for a few pints of beer at a dark pub in the Mission. Some days we really clicked, others the conversation felt like a job. The conversation usually fit into the same pattern of me talking, her listening, and not too much in between.

"Tessa, what about you? What's going on?" I asked after a while.

"I'm just a little frustrated with the world. It's too much about men who dominate and women who caretake."

"What do you mean?" I asked, not wondering if she was talking about us.

"It's a whole world of men who control and women who console," she replied, as if telling something about us. Since we stopped going out, she'd done a lot of commiserating about my struggles at work, with AIDS and other things, perhaps without reciprocity.

"Can't we throw out that script and find a new one?" I asked, feeling irked about her generalizations without seeing what they were pointing towards.

"Easier said than done, Cab."

"I think its already happening. Tessa, a lot of guys like to be topped and there are plenty of women with little interest in consoling. Look around you. We are in San Francisco."

"Gay guys, not hetero guys."

262

"How do you know?"

"What do you mean?"

"The most popular rental at Good Vibes is 'Bend Over Boyfriend,' a movie about guys who get fucked by their girlfriends. Guys love butt plugs. The script is changing every day. It's a whole new world out there."

"Butt plugs how did we get to butt plugs?"

"It's all part of the conversation. It's all part of the research."

"Ah, the research," she replied.

"The prostate is too good a secret for just gay guys to enjoy. You know?"

She nodded. There had been sex wars in San Francisco for ages. We did our part to add to the clash.

"Well, there's a little homo in all of us, as Leo Bersani says."

"I guess so. But old imbalances have not quite disappeared."

"Everyone falls somewhere on the range," I replied, ignoring what she was saying. "It's all fluid. These categories are not so hard or fast."

"I know," she replied looking sad. "But that's not what I was talking about."

"But Tessa," I replied, caught up in my thinking still not hearing her. "It's more than just sex. I'm finding something else here. Something so much more open to human messiness, much more honest. Our lives are fragile. People are pushing back against shaming each other. They are building movements around pleasure, motivated by love, not competing oppressions like it was in college, where people seemed to try to win by showing they had been through more than the next person. Remember the Rodney King march the night we heard about the verdict when we were all on Highway Ten?" I asked. Tessa nodded. "We were all marching and one of the campus activists walked up to me and said, 'Who invited you to our march?' Who was she? Who made her in charge?" I started to rant. "She had no divine right to anger."

"Dahlia, I remember that. I know. She thought of herself as the spokesman."

"Self-appointed."

"Do you think I'm like that?"

"Not now," I confessed. "That's what Hank told me about you. He said you once made someone cry on the Nepal trip in college because of all this stuff."

"That was three years ago."

"Yes, but all generalizing about men and women. Isn't there a way to move beyond this?"

"Sure. Of course. But your being defensive doesn't help."

"I'm not." I looked around. "Well, maybe a little bit."

"But why, Cab? Don't be too hasty to condemn, Cab. You sound cavalier, not an admirable trait. All I'm saying is there are other perspectives and experiences that might not be yours that you could do well to try to understand."

"Fair enough. I hear you."

The air was clearing. No one seemed too mad. We should have stopped, but that was not the case.

"It's kind of frustrating," I continued.

"For me too," she said.

"I feel like I talk a lot. But I don't hear from you," I said.

"But when I talk you don't try to hear me. You take the contrarian position."

"I know."

"But here we are. We're talking. We're listening. I'm trying. We never talked like this when I was growing up. Is this why we stopped going out?" she asked broaching a topic we almost never discussed.

There was a long pause.

"There are things I could say but I shouldn't. Or I'd rather not say. But I thought I was ready for someone new, and unfortunately I wasn't. I tried. But I was caught."

It was silent again and I recalled her clothes coming off. It was great at the beginning. But then after a while my feelings changed and I was not able to make it work. It was one of those subjects we did not broach, that always went unsaid.

"But I'm glad to know what you're thinking," she finally said. "Anne and I were talking about you last week, about a good number of things, about how we both had observed a quality of you making a short point that had much deeper roots and ideas extending far beyond the surface. I'm kind of surprised to realize the person you see in me."

We finally got the bill and started to walk through the Mission.

"I don't see my friends that way," Tessa continued.

"I see them all as parts of my life."

"But we can't ever really know what anyone really thinks." She started to tell me a story about her work.

"It's hard," I finally commented.

"What is?"

"We're talking and then you changed the subject."

"Well, I change the conversation when I see its gone as far as it's gonna go. I don't tend to interject if you make a point I take issue with. I think I know what you would say and see no point in taking on your argument."

We stopped for a dessert at a café.

"It's all a bit of a dance. I guess we both do it. But I'm tired of trying to convince you that I am something. The other night on the phone when you called me crass I felt as though we were at square one all over again. After two years, I have no interest in trying to convince you." I didn't know what I was doing. But in one outburst, all the conversations we'd had for a year were being wiped away.

"Cab, you know I admire you."

"And I you. I'm sorry. I guess we are all a bit fragile." I looked around the coffee shop, at all the books, the people reading, and writing poetry, and the line of people waiting for a couple in the bathroom to finish whatever they were doing, faint noises.

"You think they're ok?" I smiled. The sounds continued and we cracked up laughing.

"More than anyone, you are in touch with your baseness of it all," she gushed.

"That space between street and the sublime."

"All the sex, the grime of it all."

"The city is full of people trying to find something amidst it all. Instead of being consumed by shame, they are trying to make sense of it all. Last week, at church, the reverend talked about being HIV-positive, and putting himself at risk when he lived in seminary, going to a bathroom and having anonymous sex that left him exposed and eventually becoming sick. During his sermon, he read from Romans. '[I]n my flesh. I can will what is right, but I cannot do it. For I do not do the good I want, but the evil I do not want is what I do... I serve the law of God with my mind, but with my flesh I ....' That conflict sounded very familiar."

"You know, we never went to church when I was growing up."

"You guys were doing other things. How many languages do you speak?" I asked her.

She looked at me. "Three, four...." She moved her hands on the table. I slowly pulled back. "Honestly, I never know where to draw the lines in terms of showing interest or affection. I'm just not sure."

The whole conversation started to feel sad. We walked in silence back to her bike. I didn't want to say anything else. She stopped in a bodega and came out with a pack of cigarettes.

"I didn't know you smoked," I replied.

"I grew up in Paris."

"I find out new things every day," I said watching her taking a drag of a cigarette. "But I still do not really know you."

We both smoked a few.

"I guess not. But does that really matter?" she asked.

"Well, yes."

"You lose a sense of mystery between people," she continued, looking at me, as if talking about it all. She'd tried to be a friend, accepting me as I was, as we moved from college to San Francisco, while pointing out that it would help to try to hear people, to really try to understand them. But I had missed what she was saying. What I did know was that I drove people away. Still, I'd grown tired of stumbling along through the obfuscations. It all felt like drifting along without a rudder.

"So many people are ontologically challenged," I blurted out, seemingly channeling Dad, who used to repeat the phrase over and over again. "I'd rather not waste my time with them."

"Yeah, I agree, but that doesn't mean ripping everyone to shreds."

"I hope I'm not doing that. But I would rather move beyond the surfaces...."

She looked at me. "To the skeleton," Tessa replied, as she took a last drag and put out her cigarette. She looked around at the old Victorians. "Goodnight, Cab. Goodbye."

The long evening finally ended. As I watched Tessa riding off on her bike, I was not sure if I was going to see her again.

I walked back home and inside, feeling a little upset. I didn't know how to shake the mood. Italo Calvino's *If on a Winter's Night a Traveler* was sitting on the old wine box that served as a side table in my room. A book about a man losing the end of a story he was reading, only to chance upon instructions calling for him to write the ending himself, I started to read. "How long are you going to let yourself be dragged passively by the plot?" the text seemed to ask me. "You had flung yourself into the action, filled with adventurous impulses: and then?" Drifting in and out, I still read. "If you continue lending yourself to this game, it means that you, too, are an accomplice of the general mystification," the book warned. Was I an accomplice? There had to be a different ending. There had to be. The book dropped onto the floor and I slipped into sleep.

Writing, Remembering, and Perfect Laughter

> "You will ride life straight to perfect laughter. It's the only good fight there is."
> -Charles Bukowski, *Factotum*

At work, a news report after midnight declared, "Pneumonia claims poet Charles Bukowski." Sitting there, I had a flashback to Marchello and my Dad talking about the drunk bard almost a decade prior.

"You're the first person I've met who actually likes him," gushed Dad. "And you're Italian!"

"I met him and he was completely drunk," Marchello bragged. "He's always drunk." We all became the best of friends, that connection beginning a conversation that lasted for almost a year together. Over and over, he brought us together in that perfect laughter. His novels were companions on lonely train rides, his writing ennobling some of my longest, best by myself hours traveling through Europe a few years later. When I finally met up with my buddies in Siena, they all ended up reading my beaten-up copy of *Factotum*. I remembered walking through Siena, Italy, those friends, after a late night in the bar, singing Louis Armstrong songs, talking about one of Bukowski's old stories; the medieval streets of Siena glimmering. We all knew we'd have to come home some time. But none of us were in a rush. This was too magical. We broke out in song, as Bukowski had in his silly story we'd been reading.

Right there at work, I started writing notes of my associations, drafting a story about Bukowski and me, not just Bukowski, not just an obituary. I wrote straight through my shift and made my way back home, calling all the weeklies all over town, telling them what had happened and asking if anyone wanted my obit. Sometime around 2:00 in the afternoon, I got a call from the *Bay Guardian*.

"Is Cab Callaway there?"

"Yes, this is he."

"This is the *Bay Guardian*. Are you a writer?"

"Yes, I am a contributing writer at *SOMA* and the *Bay Area Reporter*."

"Can you get me 300-350 words for the obit by tomorrow?"

"What time?"

"I'll start worrying if I don't have anything by 11:00 a.m."

"Then I'll get it to you by 10:00."

I put on Tom Waits and started writing my first draft of the story. When I finished, I met Charles for a beer and pool.

"That was what all the tough guys at Vassar used to carry around when they weren't reading Nietzsche," recalled Charles.

"Very macho. It's true," I conceded. "Some of it was terrible. Now everyone wants to write like him. But he could write a story. Despite the chaos, it was beautiful. Being a writer here is not that easy. I told the editor at the *Bay Guardian* I was a writer for *SOMA*. I hope they don't call to check my references. After they stopped paying us, a group of us filed a grievance with the San Francisco Writers Union. The owner finally shelled over the $50 bucks for the story I wrote. Afterwards he told me to get lost, that I was done with the magazine. I'm not sure it was worth it."

"Was it?"

"I don't know. It was a lot of work. It's just fun to write it all out, like Bukowski used to in his dingy hotel rooms in Hollywood."

"Not really."

"'When I was sitting holding my balls, I saw this woman, but I had one hand on my balls and one on my beer, so I didn't move,' declared Chloe back in the day, doing her best impression.

"Pretty good," Charles applauded. "I'm impressed. Good Bukowski."

"Chloe was the best at imitating Bukowski. But she didn't like him."

"I know. I remember that."

"Despite the crassness, he was also fragile. In my favorite story of his, he fretted every day on the bus to work, fearful that the bus driver was going to drive off the bridge. And every day, he took the bus over the bridge. The fear was always there."

"So, tell me about Julie," Charles said.

"We both work out at the same gym. She went to San Diego State. She's Catholic. And very cute."

"Very hot, lots of whips and chains. The Catholic girls are always the quickest to rebel from the power structures and become libertines."

"Chloe was. But I'm not sure how reactionary she is."

"Less whips and chains. You sure she can handle you, Cab?"

On the way back from drinks, Charles and I took the bus. Out of nowhere Julie walked on, with a cute expression. She walked by Charles and me, without noticing us, in her own thoughts.

"Hey, Julie," I called out to her. "We were just talking about you."

She looked up and came over to sit by us.

"I just got back from the Adrienne Rich reading."

"Everyone is reading Adrienne Rich these days," I replied. "This is Charles."

We chatted for a bit. She only had one stop to go.

"This is my stop," she said.

"See you soon?"

She nodded and got off.

"You're writing about Bukowski and she's going to see Adrienne Rich. That pretty much says it all," Charles laughed.

"I guess so. But she's cool. At least I think she is. I can't stand Adrienne Rich."

"Really? I would've thought you'd love her."

"I know. I should like Adrienne Rich. But Chloe quoted Adrienne Rich in her Dear John letter to me."

"Charming."

"Yeah, she loved me. What can I say?"

"Another Catholic girl into Adrienne Rich? Are you sure this is a good idea?"

"I know. Good drinks tonight. I'll see you later."

"Julie's cute," Charles replied as he was getting off the bus.

"I know. I adore her."

When I got home, I called Julie and we planned our next date. "You two seemed so queer together," she laughed. "Is there something you're not telling me?"

"Well, Charles is quite a dandy. I'm a little envious."

Feeling the buzz of something new, I started reviewing the obituary, flipping through the pages of my old copy of *Factotum.*

"Outside somebody honked their automobile horn. They were very loud and persistent. I set the bottle down and screamed out: "GOD DAMN IT YOU SON OF A BITCH, SHUT UP!" Bukowski wrote. I had underlined the passage when I was in Italy. It seemed like San Francisco. "The night coming on in and there was nothing I could do..." he lamented in another archetypal night in the life Charles Bukowski's Henry Chachinski. "He championed the art of boozing alone because there didn't seem to be anyone better to be with," I wrote in the obituary. "He wrote about isolation as a gift. 'And, you'll do it...There is no other feeling like that. You will be alone with the gods, and the nights will flame with fire.' That flame touched a lot of us, the perfect laughter reminding us of something. Thanks, Chuckie. For now, those interminable nights have subsided," I concluded. The next morning, I reread the obituary, ran a copy over to the paper and met up with Julie.

Pictures of Lily and Marcel Proust

"And suddenly the memory returns....The taste was that of the little crumb of madeleine which on Sunday mornings at Combray.... But when from a long-distant past nothing subsists, after the people are dead, after the things are broken and scattered, still, alone, more fragile, but with more vitality, more unsubstantial, more persistent, more faithful, the smell and taste of things remain poised a long time, like souls, ready to remind us, waiting and hoping for their moment, amid the ruins of all the rest..."

-Marcel Proust *Swann's Way*

"Please accept my resignation. I don't care to belong to any club that will have me as a member."

-Groucho Marx, telegram to the Friar's Club of Beverly Hills

To get to Julie's place, I rode the #22 bus to Union Square, and switched for the bus to Jones Street, where I scaled upward toward Broadway and Jones, one of the highest peaks in the city. Standing up there, I could see Broadway stretch across the city from Chinatown through North Beach straight to the old Bay Bridge. The view from her window was everything I needed.

For date two, we made out and listened to Nirvana. I read her fashion magazines, and flipped through an old copy of *Time* covering the health care debate going on in Washington.

"Dan better call in all his favors and get that health care bill passed," I said in passing.

"Who is Dan?"

"Dan Rostenkowski, a corrupt old Chicago politician who heads the House Ways and Means Committee. If the health care bill gets through his committee, it can get through the House. But he has to make it move."

"Cab, you amaze me," she said, surprised I knew who these people were.

She pulled out an old Woody Allen movie, which we watched, laughing and making out all night. I stayed over.

The following Monday, I was planning Julie date number three when the phone rang. Of all people, Elizabeth was on the other end of the line. I was going to meet Julie at eight so I could easily meet Elizabeth a few hours before for drinks.

We met at the Mad Dog in the Fog, an Irish pub in the Lower Haight. Between a couple of pilsners, we talked compulsively. After a beer, she asked me what I wanted.

"I crave satisfaction," I told her.

"What do you mean?"

"The lover and friend and companion to illuminate and satiate, someone who listens and actually does understand."

"Oh, I know I made the right choice in giving you my number," she said with a smile, while taking hold of my hand. I walked her outside, where I sat in her car buzzed out of my mind from our talk, sensuous KD Lang singing her lesbian folk anthems on the tape deck. I was going to see Julie in five minutes.

270

Needless to say, conversation topics did not flow as they should or could have with Julie the whole evening. All I knew was complete distraction and focus on what Julie was not, an outgoing outrageous city person. I spent the night and became perplexed and confused. She wasn't shy about taking her pants off but wouldn't take her shirt off. We slept together but the morning ended with a blush, without really connecting. We walked to work, through the morning rush, saying goodbye as we parted with a strange, not knowing what to say to make it right, glance at California Street, in the financial district.

"Let's get a coffee at Vesuvio after work, okay?" I asked.

She agreed.

Later, we talked. "I have no sense of this stuff—no comprehension," I confessed.

"Well, don't look at me. I am terrible at this stuff," she said.

Getting back on track, we walked back to the winding stairs, and up Broadway through Chinatown for dinner, more conversation, a nap. By 11 p.m., I'd have to make my way back to my work for the midnight shift.

The next day, I skipped *90210* night for coffee with David at Café Flore, our usual meeting spot on Market and Noe. It seemed like everyone in the neighborhood was cavorting, bantering about, taking in the springtime in the outdoor café. I showed up about thirty minutes before he did. Guys were prancing around, vying for trade, camp, oregano, and huge doses of caffeine coursing through the wide-open place. Some guys were sitting and drinking by themselves, looking like they were reading the paper or their books, while furtively glancing around the room.

"I love the place," I said when David arrived, looking very dapper, still in his dark blue Brooks Brothers suit after his day of accounting at the firm.

"Me too, although the guys can be a little pushy, you know," David followed.

"Oh, I know. And sometimes misogynist," I added. "My friend Rebecca was here and a guy said to her, 'Cute sweater, too bad there are tits in it.'"

"What's wrong with that," David followed. "I know. But we love you being here. I miss you." David always said he missed me when we met. "Weeks with no cards, no calls, no messages, or invitations to go out. You must be up to something."

"I just don't like the dick-heavy Crowbar."

"That's my favorite spot."

"Perhaps. But there are places with a more androgynous atmosphere."

"Maybe in prewar Berlin. But we don't need that pretense here. This is the town of the ever-evolving clone. Plus you always have me. Okay, so what about romance? Are you still a lone wolf or are you up to something? I smell something."

"Oh, David. I'm a mess, an over-caffeinated, excitable mess."

"Why? What's going on?"

"For the last few months, it's been all famine. Months and months of famine. And then in a few days, two women have come my way. One who is gorgeous and older who's into politics and HIV work, very queer and smart, always talking about safe sex as hot sex; the other very Catholic and cute and into

271

cooking and aerobics, who likes Adrienne Rich. But she's not as reactionary in the virgin-whore way that I adored."

"Is she into sex?"

"I'm not sure. I jerked off after leaving her yesterday. It was too much for me."

"Cab... What are you doing? It doesn't sound like much of a choice."

"Well, I don't want to rush. She's adorable. I just hope I am not projecting too much into this."

"Well, that's the challenge, isn't it? The other girl sounds great. It's fun to feel abundant for a while. Why not put your energy into her?"

"Well, she's way smart and savvy, but also a little into herself. I'm not sure."

"So, go from there and find your way. You can handle it."

I always loved chatting through it all with David.

Later that night, Julie and I were chatting on the phone. I was in my room in the Haight. She was on Jones Street. An awful sound, like a metallic science fiction movie, screeched from the line, interrupting the connection. She didn't pick up when I called back. First five minutes passed, and then ten and fifteen, at which point horrible ideas started to cross through my mind. All I remembered was the machine like sound and Julie screaming "Ow!" and the dial tone. What was going on? Was she okay? I threw on some sneakers and grabbed a cab for her side of town, practically shaking. I told the cabby. He listened without saying anything, driving me across the majestic city, assuming I was completely crazy or at least stoned.

Arriving, I knocked on her door. Silence. At first, Julie did not answer. And then she opened and gave me a big hug. "I don't know what happened on the phone," she confessed. She was wearing a brown one-piece long john.

"Come in. Do you want to stay over?" she smiled. I did. And we had another ecstatic night of making out, touching, talking, touching a little more, getting off in a glorious crescendo. The next day, the euphoria remained; the sun shone over the water below the bridge. My life felt as vital as it could be in the city. We strolled through Chinatown and North Beach in the early morning on the way to Julie's work. We'd have other nights, but not many more like that one.

Back at home, I picked up a copy of *Tropic of Cancer*, reading Miller's musings on sex as a route toward a new world. "Close together... to have her here in bed with me, breathing on me, her hair on my mouth—I count that something of a miracle."

And I thought about Julie. She was there with me. But didn't feel the same way about it. Some nights shame grasped her; on others a freer spirit moved through. But I could never tell who was going to show up. As soon as she opened up, a sense of regret drew back at her, just like the scene in the elevator, over and over again. She looked down. But then she invited me over.

On Saturday, she cooked for me. It was so nice to just sit with her, chatting, eating, and hanging out. Afterwards, we went to see a play called *12 Steps to a More Dysfunctional You*. It was so bad, we dubbed it ten minutes till we got the hell out of there. Close to her place, we sat in the park by Gracie Cathedral, talking politics and sadness. I was not connecting with her.

"I'm cold. Let's go in," she said.

"I wonder why we continue to do certain things over and over and over again, which make us unhappy," I said.

"Men are feral," she followed. "It's the basic element of what kind of creatures men are." I wasn't hearing what she was saying. All I felt was a desire for connection, however elusive it might have been. As sleepiness grasped us; we crawled into her bed. She took off her pants, revealing a black negligee. She was breathtaking. But we were not in the same space as Thursday night. She wasn't really with me the whole night, although she tried, muddled along, touching and fumbling away as she seemed to get off, but I was nowhere. She turned away and pushed up against me. She put on some Calvin Klein boxers and was even sexier. But we were even further apart.

Chloe and I used to fight when it came to defining the space between us, before reconnecting for brief moments. The space between Julie and I felt tenuous. We were trying to share it. I was trying to know Julie. But I was not that sure what I was finding. We slept in and said goodbye for the week the next afternoon. I hated saying goodbye to her, hoping to get a chance to maybe spend the night in her apartment again. I wondered if I'd get another chance, not sure I would.

I was off on Monday so I went to meet Elizabeth in the Mission.

"Lets go for tapas," she suggested.

"Topless," I laughed. "Sure we can go for topless. That's a great idea."

"*Tapas*, the Spanish food," she corrected, laughing.

I needed to go get cigarettes. Every minor discussion was pregnant with possibilities for bickering or sex, conflict or lust. The banter all added to a growing rapport. We drove around looking for the right restaurant. I felt like I was in second grade on a date with worldly wise, Stockard Channing in *Grease*. When she commented about my choices of foods, I told her I was beginning to feel self-conscious. I don't know how things got so frank.

"I noticed the first time we went out that you could be a little obnoxious," I retorted.

"I can be," she smiled, looking sensuous. She did not seem to mind me being confrontational. So the conversation went on and we got back to the college conversation. I mentioned Vassar.

"Yeah, I heard that the other night when you mentioned it. I just filed it away for future reference," she said.

"My friend Lisa, who works at the AIDS Foundation, told my roommate to tell me to keep an eye out for you, that you had issues."

Now Elizabeth was feeling defensive.

"Then what are you doing?" she asked me.

I looked at her and shrugged.

"What are *we* doing?" she followed.

"I don't know."

"Well, I know you're interested in me," she said and smiled.

I shrugged, agreeing with her.

"When you suggested we go somewhere else for beers the other night at Mad Dog in the Fog, I knew it."

On the conversation proceeded. We chatted about lesbians, sex, role-play, gender, performances in the masculine, feminine, tops or bottoms, the politics of submission. I could talk with her all night. She told me about a weekend of wild-eyed people she used to get together with blowing each other off; one of the women she used to sleep with told a present girlfriend of hers how much she wanted to get together with her again.

"It's tough being popular," I replied.

"Wow." She looked at the pitcher of sangria. "I can't drink any more of this."

"What do you want to do now?" I asked. "I mean, we could go to get a coffee or go back to my place. I have a great record collection you know, or go back to your place."

"I do have an awful good CD collection myself," she smiled.

"Then there we are."

And off to her apartment we cruised. She put on a Dead Can Dance album. We talked about theology and social work, ethics and activism. She was going to apply for a PhD program at Johns Hopkins. I was applying to social work and theology programs. I had my feet on the wall when I moved over and put my feet closer to her instead. Next thing you know, we were fooling around. Over the sheets, under the sheets, futon up, futon down. It wasn't long before I started to feel really guilty.

"I want you to be here with me," Elizabeth whispered, noticing my absence. "Here in my bed, not somewhere else."

"I can't help but think of tomorrow."

"Just stay right here, in this moment. Tomorrow is not going to happen till tomorrow. There's no way to know what it will be like or whether we will see each other again."

I took this as my cue. My hand sat between her legs.

"It's time to get the gloves out."

"Are you sure?"

"Of course."

Julie's eyes danced through my head, but this was a moment. I loved chatting with Elizabeth, but. She put her tongue in my mouth and just left it there, with little to no intrigue. Stingo recalled a date prodigiously bobbing her tongue in his mouth in *Sophie's Choice*. I felt the same way. But I was curious about all the latex she had been alluding to. I wanted to play. Safe sex is hot sex, that was the San Francisco mantra. I wanted to see how true that was.

"Okay, I'm going to get my box of supplies. I don't even want you to see how much stuff I have in there," she cautioned, rummaging through a cigar box full of safe sex supplies. When she finally pulled out a couple of gloves, I could not stop laughing at this world of rubbers. Cheers to the modern era of protection, plastics, and prophylactics.

While Elizabeth was an abundant person, with a wildly expansive mind, I could not connect with her body.

"The mind is the biggest sex organ in the body," David had reminded me at Café Flore.

"Really?"

"Well maybe second biggest."

We joked and slowly worked each other, with our gloves on.

"Like Bill Clinton and universal health care. I don't care how I cum."

"Keep your day job," Elizabeth groaned. With gloves on, she showed me exactly what needed stimulation. She climbed the mountain with my hand, and turned to me and she gave me head with a condom on. Of course, I could not feel a thing. So I sat up in bed and started on myself. She watched as I told her a bit about what I was recalling from an old pin-up fantasy about a girl, sitting up arching her back, wearing a miniskirt. I was thinking of a layout from a 1983 *Penthouse* spread and Chloe in her bathroom, sitting on the sink in front of the mirror with her dad passed out on the couch in the other room. Elizabeth sat masturbating, looking at me, as I looked at her, imagining.

"And what is she doing to you?" she asked.

"She is in the shower," I replied, my fantasy shifting. "You are in the bathroom sitting on the sink and you invite me to come to you," I explained, recalling that old moment long past. "I watch your back in the mirror as you sit up on the sink. I can see you spread your legs, and your back in the mirror as we begin." Elizabeth was busy with her hands and so was I, now fantasizing about Winona Rider in *Heathers*. Anyone but Elizabeth. I never got off.

"Were those fantasies me or just in general?" she asked while we were lying in bed.

"They were you," I lied. I hadn't been able to finish, which felt strange. She consoled me.

"It's okay. I think it's hard to share your sexuality with someone."

"The problem is the old fantasies are losing their appeal. But I have no new ones. The turns-ons are the old adolescent fantasies."

"It's okay. You'll let go of them when you need to let go of them, when you're ready." She paused. "That fantasy was still over the top. Christ, your hand was like my vibrator. I've never felt it like that before."

"I know people who can't get off without them," I said, immediately regretting my words.

"You're telling me I'm going to have to get on a 12-step plan because of my vibrator?"

"No, no," I stammered. Feeling bad I leaned over to her.

"Julie," I said looking at her, the word now out of my mouth, lingering in the air. As Dan Quayle had famously observed during the presidential race two-year prior, Words are like toothpaste—once they come out, you can never put them back again.

"What? You were thinking of her," Elizabeth gasped.

"If I hadn't saturated the 'I'm sorry' earlier tonight, I would say it now."

"You're right. You have," she went on. "That's so lame."

"It is. What a day. I felt guilty on Sunday about being with Julie knowing what was going to happen on Monday with you."

"You knew this was going to happen."

"Yeah...But it wasn't that I wasn't thinking of you in bed. I was looking at you in bed and reconnecting my past with my present."

"We all have relations with the past, which are part of being alive. It's poetry. But it shouldn't keep us from being here now."

"This isn't. But every guy has a relationship to the first time they felt a certain way. For me, it's the old magazines I've been carrying around since 7th grade, the 'Pictures of Lily,' like the Who song. They set the scene for the theater of the bathroom that I told you about, setting up the stage, triggering a feeling every time."

"Those are powerful feelings."

"That 'past life' tells us who we are, connecting older days and futures into an ever-flowing now."

"But you're letting yours get in the way of this one. I asked you to be here now with me and I don't think you were honest."

"It's hard to shake, taking me from this world to some other place, arousing and reminding the scene."

"But Cab, you are not an old man. You are here now"

"I know. I know."

We kept talking and I finally fell asleep, having set the course and thrown us off track. A part of me knew we were birds of the same feather. All night, I felt repulsed with myself, not about the sex as much as the mix-up. Freud said there are no accidents. Even with the flub up over the name, I was still chasing something, the elusive feeling with Julie. The feeling only lingered the next couple of days. I woke up in a blur of emotions. I had to sit and pause. This was not my usual misery. I pulled out my blue notebook and started to write:

"... you know about the wheel of fortune. The feasts and famine, the dry spell of the coldest winter I ever spent was the summer in San Francisco, the frigid Baghdad by the Bay, the wheel spinning, between the Julie character, the young lady, more autonomously driven than choosing to let on, smart, hot body, great apartment, and lots of tricks. But Southern California seems to have bleached some of her capacity to see the larger world. She's a little cold, but I can't help the constant compulsion to spend more time with her. And then there's the experienced one, Elizabeth, the southern sensualist crossing the line between roles, fantasy, bisexual, open and experimental. She studies the anthropology of sex work, HIV prevention, safer sex, latex, lube, and cultural attitudes. She's a little obnoxious and problematic, a little outrageous and ready to chat. I could talk with her all night long."

Wednesday night, I was writing when Elizabeth popped by. We sat in my room chatting. Before long she tried to pull me back into bed. I had to pull away. She was not pleased when I told her it couldn't happen again, bruised and inflated egos everywhere. Still, no one wants to just be friends.

"I can't imagine hanging with you now," she said. "Flirting has so much to do with our relationship. I know I don't want to hear about her. She sounds like she is caught in something too. When you told me about her seeing you and your friend Charles on the bus, she thought you guys were gay, that's so odd. Cab, can't you see that as a reflection of a culture of people who are so uncomfortable about intimacy that when they see two guys sitting together on the bus, they must be gay then? I also know I can be quite a bitch and I don't want to be catty with you. We just went really deep, all the way down to that fantasy. I didn't realize how many issues you have tied up with sex."

"Well, I told you."

"I know, but that seemed more like your Woody Allen shtick."

"Yeah, I'm sorry. But it was still kind of fun, right?"

"Yeah, but I was your experiment. You were dishonest with me."

"Really, we just had two dates. We hadn't talked about being exclusive."

"That's true. But you were being emotionally loyal to her."

"I knew one third through the sex that it wasn't going to happen again, but went on anyways, which might have been a mistake."

"Well, now you've lost a great companion and compatriot."

"Can't we just shuck this whole thing off to things that went too fast and far—no harm, no foul?"

"No, we can't. I know what you mean, but we can't."

"I know you've slept with people and blown them off afterward."

"Yes, I have. But having taken it to that level, I know it won't work."

"I guess the chemistry was wrong," I said, trying to tap dance around the issue of no longer being attracted to her.

"I understand. It's just that that's never happened to me before—that the other person doesn't come back for more. Christ, I thought I was done with this shit. This won't work."

"I know, but this is San Francisco where we all use sex to get to know each other...."

"Charming, Cab."

"I know. But there is such a thing as taking the sex and mixing it with friendship."

"Oh, it's all so sad. You are amazingly in touch with your feelings, especially for your age. I got your messages last night and they were so cute. You were so Woody Allen-ish. You even told me you were going to talk my ear off before going to sleep. But then you had the chutzpah to call me her name before you went to sleep. I knew you must have been thinking of her."

Elizabeth left. I wouldn't see her again for a long time.

I pulled out the journal and started writing:

"Maybe she was right? I don't know. The whole thing, which initially appeared exciting, struck me as cruel. There was also a bit of an ego wound. Elizabeth would have been happier if she could have been the one doing the dumping or maybe she really wanted to be with me? Or maybe we should not have gone that far? When our egos hurt, few of us feel like libertines. Monogamy doesn't work and non-monogamy doesn't work. Everyone in this town is into non-monogamy. But it wasn't that simple—even with the manifestos on safer sex, promiscuity, and ethical polyamory, vulnerability was still part of being human. Everyone has wounds, sad stories of their partners being more turned on by others, or catching them at parties with other people, even if they were in open relationships. Jealousy is still part of the equation. None of us wants to feel used or taken for granted. She knew the dance well. If we couldn't be buddies, then we couldn't be anything. And she made sure to let me know it. And why didn't I want to be with her? The old Groucho Marx remained vexing. We could talk and play around for hours. But I wasn't attracted to her."

Much of what had happened felt like an odd reconciling of the hangover of the 1970s Sexual Liberation. Sex was still intimate, associated with opening ourselves up to each other. Certainly, we were creating something new here, as sex and desire intermingled with questions about life, liberty, and the pursuit

277

of happiness. But the contradictions of the struggle over pleasure were also many, each leading to a sort of creative destruction. New relations were opening. But the pain was everywhere, much of it self-inflicted.

Julie and I had spent the weekend together, creating a fellow feeling of comradeship, despite the confusion. I didn't want to deal with the sex or neuroses. Who knew how long it would last? But for now, getting to know her felt delicious. It was a relief to avoid the neuroses that I'd gotten so used to, if even for a brief moment. The obsessions with sex and connection, and the quest for security, were everywhere. But few could find them.

On Betrayal

"Tomorrow, there might be a revolution, a plague, an earthquake, tomorrow there might not be left a single soul to whom one could turn for sympathy, for aid, for faith. It seemed to me that the great calamity had already manifested itself, that I could be no more alone than in this very moment."

-Henry Miller, *Tropic of Cancer*

"It's not the disease that is killing me. It's the loneliness," Juan told me toward the end of a long talk at work.

"I'll be there for you, Juan," I replied, not really knowing what I was saying. Certainly, I was not hearing Juan. I didn't know what to say so I grasped at the sort of answer that Charles Garfield warned us about in Shanti Training. "Just listen. That's enough," he advised. I pretty much ignored Raoul's admonitions about boundaries with clients at work. Instead the residents of the building and I shared cigarettes and confidences in that blurry space in between desperation, laughter and despair. Desolation and confusion were everywhere. We did what we could.

There was a lot going on for everyone. Friday I spent the night at Julie's, and left on Saturday to go to the Visual AIDS Arts show. Almost all of the art was from the people in the building. Knowing everyone who put the material up, seeing their day-to-day lives, coming home from parties, hospital visits, their support groups, twelve-step meetings, weekends of sex, the jokes and gallows humor; I saw their appearances and heard their stories. The show was glimpse into their interior worlds as well as their resistance to regimes of control or oblivion. One of our clients drew a comic book sketch of himself, in a bed in the hospital, with rotten Chinatown groceries on the table by him, sitting by him along with a non-descript orderly, cosmetics rendered useless at covering his KS lesions, a TV with no cable, and demon seed teens mocking his demise. The piece seemed to laugh at the mess that his world had become, highlighting the absurdity of it all and lampooning it.

Another made a photomontage of a traffic jam of angels carrying bodies up to the heavens. Willy's self-portrait included layers of color, obfuscating his face, with jagged strokes that seemed to cut and pull, inflicting pain like his neuropathy. Ernie displayed photos of the Mexico where Julio, his lover grew up. The show also featured Julio's post humus images of his San Francisco. Josh needed a wheel chair to get around. His black self-portrait of himself as a trans prophet reflected an otherworldly engagement, one foot between this material world and some place different. With each picture, I saw a part of these people I had rarely seen, honest glimpses of their thoughts during their last days. In their own way, each spoke to a dichotomy between the physical and the spiritual, as the body eroded, while the spirit flourished, eventually to be liberated from the failing body.

Ernie displayed a print of water under ice, the water below the surface like the HIV moving through the system. We talked about his work. "One of the difficult things about AIDS is the look of the disease, which frightens and scares most people," he explained. "You know the legions and the gaunt look and the pneumonia complications. I think people do have an inner life. When people become so sick, they go look at themselves in the mirror in the bathroom and they have a lot less esteem simply because of the way they look, but their inner life is still with them and that's their core. I think people have to make a real effort to get beyond the look of AIDS and to think about the value of people inside. That hasn't changed... That is what I want to try to get across, that you can have an inner life, that you have value and work."

It was hard to feel that optimism. Few of us felt like we had any value at all.

Tuesday, I began to attend a support group for caregivers. The facilitator asked everyone how we cope with the work, just getting through our day-to-day tasks.

"Let's remember the love we have for all of this," said Moonear, facilitating. "The love we all feel as part of this, between friends and clients and everyone in this city as we do our best to take care of ourselves."

"I'm pissed. I'm so fucking pissed off," said Mary, a middle-aged participant. She was working on her masters degree in social work and her best friend was dying. It was taking a toll on her. I listened intently.

"Cab, are you angry?" Moonear asked me after the social worker was done talking.

I was feeling like I wanted to put my hand through the wall, I replied, surprised with my answer. "Yes, I'm angry. I'm tired of hearing we don't have the cash. I have a hard time accepting that we can't do more. I'm pissed at the agencies and their rules and the social workers that don't seem to acknowledge that we might be just as fucked up as our clients. That we all need each other, all of us." As I was talking, I felt a great relief in acknowledging the frustration, to be heard and to listen.

The next man talked about an event at work. "Today, I met a man whose antibody test came back positive during a counseling session." He sat shaking his head. "These were the most fortuitous 45-minutes of his life," he confessed, still looking down. He had been abused, run away from his parents, shot at by the police, tried, failed, and eventually succeeded in making it across the river from Mexico. "I guess it's another border to cross," he told me. HIV was another in life of struggles.

"We learn a lot from this," another woman acknowledged.

Later at work, I pulled out the blue notebook to write. It was 3:57 in the morning and the smell of rain on asphalt made its way into the building, reminding me we can all be invisible and infinite; life can still seem limitless. The buses passed by in the morning, leaving a trail of fumes. We are all fearfully and wonderfully made. We are all part of this big frail abundance. The flaws and aspirations, limitations and courage were everywhere, even when we strived to do better, even as we floundered.

Pedro walked in and out of the building all night long. In between, we talked.

"You look relaxed today," I told him.

"Yeah, well I have accepted that I am going to die and all that shit."

"The Buddhists say when we accept the biggest fear of our life—that we are going to die—then we can be happy."

"Really? But I still want to have another lover, even though my last lover was in 1990. I want to spend three months in Israel, to go by myself to see all the temples."

280

He went back upstairs and then came back, sat down on the couch, and looked out into the rain, in a somber moment.

"You don't look so good. Did something happen?"

"No, it just hits me. Cab, I don't know if I'm going to make it," he confessed with tears welling up in his eyes. "If I'm going to die, I am going to die. I don't want to do this by myself. That's the part I can't adjust to or accept." I sat with him as he kept on talking about self-medicating or ending it all.

When he left, I wrote a case note for the file.

Later in the afternoon, at the 4:00 p.m. shift, Pedro came up to me, this time very angry.

"If I can't trust you who can I trust? Why did you do that?"

"The case note," I said, realizing.

He nodded his head.

"I had to. We have to write up everything that goes on here, so everyone knows what's going on the next shift."

"I had Raoul going through my refrigerator earlier today after that note you wrote. I would have done anything for you," Pedro said. "I cooked for you. I let you in the building when you were locked out. I was here when you were scared and you didn't know whether you would have this or any other job."

"But I didn't ask for your help," I explained. "I didn't ask for you to bring me meals." He looked angry and betrayed. "I have done my best with you, Pedro."

"No, you have not. I know you can do better. You ought to think about that for a while."

As Pedro walked up to the elevator, Juan was coming down. He stopped to talk.

"Last week, you said something to me that I have thought about a lot." He looked somber. "I don't think you thought about it, Cab. Because I do know that you would not take care of me when I get sick. Circumstances are circumstances. You won't give up your job for me. I know that. I don't say this to guilt you. I know you've been there to support me like not many people have during my whole life. I love you too much to ask you to endure the pain involved with really being there for me."

He was right. "You know, I've been looking around a lot lately and I realize nothing much has changed for man," he continued. "Peter said to Jesus, 'I'll be there fighting by your side' and Christ said, 'Before the cock crows, you will have betrayed me three times.' The ones who were eating with him would do the betraying."

"Is your time coming?" I asked, after thanking him for his candor.

"Coming? It's here. I've never had time. My triumph over AIDS is that I don't care when it takes me." He paused and smiled. "But the bottom line is, we are all going to die. We all have AIDS. And it wants is our T Cells. It wants 'em bad."

Dancing with Robert and Oblivion

"I remembered the line from the Hindu scripture, the Bhagavad-Gita; Vishnu is trying to persuade the Prince that he should do his duty and, to impress him, takes on his multi-armed form and says, "Now I am become Death, the destroyer of worlds." I suppose we all thought that, one way or another."
-Robert Oppenheimer, on watching the atomic bomb explode

"... we had always imagined death. Some of the dead were among us, just like us, just trying to survive. Others were more in the distance, the elders we barely got to know except as we lost them. We went crazy and cried a lot, or went crazy and stopped crying...."
-Mattilda Bernstein *The End of San Francisco*, 2013

Every Tuesday night, Julie and I went out swing dancing at Café Du Norde, an old speakeasy, turned underground jazz club, on Market Street. Our teacher had a spitting resemblance to Robert Oppenheimer, as if his doppelganger was teaching tango classes in San Francisco. He was handsome, with charming stare, exactly like the old newsreels of the physicist reflecting on the destruction unleashed by the bomb, same sad eyes. Such feelings tenuously connected me with the pulse of the city, holding us together, albeit precariously. The room filled with moving bodies, silky dresses, drums, brass music, beer and sweat. While Henry Miller wrote about a world falling apart and a Paris shuddering with bright shiny orgasms, I thought of San Francisco, its inhabitants dancing, as some perished, making their way from here to somewhere else while others shared the same kinds of sensations Miller described.

But it was hard to keep my worlds separated. One Tuesday after the show, Pedro stepped on the same bus Julie and I were taking home from dancing. He smiled at Julie and me, and went to sit in the back. We went back to her place and fooled around some more. "It's where I want you to be," she said, smiling. Later, we read the *Times* on her roof and looked out at the city.

The next day at work Pedro came downstairs.

"Cab, I think I'm losing it," he said, crying. "It's not just you. I can't trust my mother. I can't trust anyone. I'm losing my stuff. I left my keys in Julio's care in a jacket, remember? Well, now my coat is gone."

"Julio is gone."

"I thought I gave my keys to him?"

"You can't find 'em now?"

"They were in my coat. I put them there after I went to get them from Julio's."

"It's not easy holding onto all the pieces."

"Holding onto reality. I'm not even sure what's real anymore."

After work, Julie and I went out dancing at the 181 Club. When we got back to my house, we listened to the radio. An old Barbara Streisand song came on: "

"You don't bring me flowers," Barbara sang.

"*You don't keep me up all night talking anymore,*" Julie sang along. "Are you a player?" she asked, lying in bed.

"How do I answer that?"

"Well, are you?"

"No," I said and smiled, looking at her, not knowing what to say, so we lay there snuggling, enjoying the feel of each other's bodies, and the fellow feeling. When we started fooling around, the usual dry grind ensued, she said, "You don't have to do that by yourself." For a second, it was a little scary to be in bed with someone who I adored. I eventually grabbed the box of condoms under the futon and she started to laugh.

"You sure you want to?" I asked her. "People often lose interest once they finally do it."

"That's why I didn't want to sleep with you at first," she said. "But now I do. Are you sure you won't lose interest in me?"

"I won't."

For some reason, I started getting emotional, breathing hard, telling her about the feelings I had after Chloe. "I haven't been the same since. For the last three years, letting myself care was tricky; those sensations felt elusive. I've been the one to get over the relationship first, always knowing I was the one who wasn't going to get hurt again; dealing in my own needs was the most important part. It's been very weird. For a while I thought that if you like someone, that's enough for a relationship. So I got together with some people who were friends and it didn't work. The personal and the sensual chemistry has been wrong until you." That night everything was right.

Afterward, we lay in bed laughing. The next morning, we got dressed and went out for breakfast. All she had was her blue party dress from the night before.

"She's got it going on," Ray noted, when she was in the bathroom.

We went out to Bagdad Café. After brunch, she went home and I met David at Café De Flore before work. Then I went to see Mimi and Chris for cocktails and slept a few hours before my next shift at 8:00 a.m. Sunday morning. It was one of those adrenaline-fueled weekends, running on very little sleep, lots of coffee, and cigarettes.

When I got to work, Jim took me into the back room with a serious look on his face and told me.

"Cab."

"What?" I got worried.

Jim paused, looked down and back at me. He sighed.

"...Ernie died."

I felt like the world was imploding.

"But I just saw him at the Visual AIDS show, showing his pictures and Julio's."

"I know. Me too. He came home, crawled into bed and never got out. They took him to Davies Medical Center a few days ago and he never recovered." I looked at him, crumbling. "That's how it goes," he said, patting my shoulder and left.

My stomach turned to knots. I flashed to night after night of talking to him about his life, his move from New York five years prior, his fortieth birthday, his plans for his birthday this spring, and all our

283

talks as Julio was getting sicker. That was the hard part of it, I thought. He said we have to be ok when it's hard. That way we can be happy. If you can be ok in the hard parts then you can be a happy person, he told me. But there were limits. The image of him going up to his room by himself with a McDonalds bag to eat by himself when Julio was sick stuck with me. Despair still ate at even the most Tao of us.

When I returned to my desk, Michelle standing there talking to what looked like the air, holding a full conversation. I rubbed my eyes.

"I've been misunderstood and stomped on when I've told the truth, especially when the guy got me with the rock in the head," she said without greeting me. She turned her head toward me.

"Center yourself," she said, looking at me, recognizing the anguish on my face, before running off.

Betsy, the woman from Project Open Hand, walked in. I hadn't seen her for ages. She was there to deliver a few meals and stopped to talk, reporting on a few of the residents in the building. Over the next four hours, I did not get a minute to myself. I listened to everyone, words colliding with thoughts of Ernie's mortality fading into oblivion, beneath the surface, moving from this existence into the next like the diver in Paestum jumping from a cliff into the water, from this life into the next.

Always in glasses, jeans, and his leather jacket, one of the kindest people in the building, images of Ernie were with me all day. I didn't know how to deal with all the sensations running through my body; the grief, terror, loss of control, sadness, shakes, and nausea. Unlike usual, I was unable to cover up all the rumblings. An ocean seemed to move through my stomach, water crashing, rushing up to the cliffs and back out into a vast abyss, cutting back and forth, leaving me to shudder.

Ernie's dad and his friends came by to take some of Ernie's stuff, carrying it out to his car in milk cartons. There was Ernie's old leather jacket, his Castro Clone signature piece that he used to wear every day, now without Ernie's body to fill it, an empty, inanimate object, that had once been connected with everything in his world, his sweat, desire, warmth, art and security. I remembered the leather convention the previous July, when Ernie told me about all the men from all over the country who came to visit, five thousand leather wearing bikers all outside the building. Ernie could barely handle it. He was going to three or four meetings a day, that week, anything to stay sober, away from narcotics, leather, alcohol, even sex. All the bikers seemed to remind him of some old part of himself. They tempted him, bringing out his extreme quirkiness, which I always saw as a great oddball center of his personality.

Life was a series of challenges—AIDS and addiction, which stressed him out. This was a challenge he knew he could handle, even as his days waned. When Ernie's old demons hovered, he found himself stepping outside himself, seeing just exactly how absurd everything looked. He could look at himself and the city, even as his life was fleeting. That day, the leather jacket felt like all that was left of him, being packed away. Julio had gone and Ernie followed, leaving this life for parts unknown. That desolate feeling of eating by himself with his lover dying in the hospital was over. Sometimes the losses were more than people could endure. Parts of ourselves died, bit by bit until there was nothing left.

My mind wandered watching them take his stuff out of the building. Mom and Dad made a go at being there for Thomas that final weekend when we were all caught off guard by how quickly Thomas's tailspin had accelerated. The night Thomas went into the hospital again Dad went to church and lit a candle for him, knowing he was gone. Back at the hotel that night, Mom came up to him. She had only just moved out of the house where we had lived. He held her as she wept.

Thomas's death marked the true commencement of their divorce. It was a reminder of happier days, a brilliant first year in college in 1956, trips around the world, to Iran, Afghanistan, India, Mexico; from Cambridge to Texas, comrades making friends not war together over four decades, there was little to nothing left for them together once he was gone.

It was strange thinking of Thomas's departure years later. Ernie was the one who had just died. But Thomas's rapid decline, losing his mind first, then his body, still rattled me. Even after seeing so many others, I had no greater solace, understanding, or philosophy for coping with the losses that were everywhere. Thomas was the first I knew to go down in such a fashion. And he always came back, his memory clung to me. Absolute goodbyes were hard to come to grips with. Every person who passed reminded me that they were they were someone else's best friend.

Looking at all these darting to and fro, it seemed strange, the value we put on certain people in our culture. Part of the reason I so appreciated Thomas was his imagination, his lusty desire to know. He had received a PhD from Harvard as he hustled in Hollywood, drank compulsively, before embracing a twelve-step program. All the while, he kept on chasing stories and shadows in the desert until AIDS consumed him. Regardless of his intellect, with the onset of the disease, he become dispensable, like his other comrades in the military discharged for conduct unbecoming and humiliated as he was, like the other drug dealers and immigrants, sex workers and homos—just another outsider left to flounder, to hustle for mediations he could use to treat the AIDS running through his body.

Now, we were trying to support those coping with the carnage. Jim called Juan to ask him to help out when he heard about Ernie. Juan was signing out his guest Scott, and Michelle started asking questions, sensing something was wrong and digging for information.

"You look terrific. How are you doing?" she asked.

"Could be better," Scott replied.

"Why, what's wrong?"

Scott fumbled with his words and Michelle pushed him.

"Someone on Juan's floor died."

Michelle became grave.

"Who?"

"Ernie," Juan said, sounding very tired.

"Ernie?" Michelle exclaimed, literally jumping back in disbelief. "Oh god, oh god. I've got to go tell other people in the building. This is the problem with this building. I didn't even know he was in the hospital. I would have gone to see him."

"Over the last few days he wasn't himself anyway," Juan said patiently. "Going to see him wouldn't have done any good."

He left. Michelle looked at me in a panic.

"I gotta go," she declared and ran up the stairs into her own night world of dementia, deep in her own thoughts, memories and fears that she might be next. Everyone worried: *Am I next?*

For once, I know where Michelle is coming from. I jotted notes in my notebook. I wish I could have seen him again to talk to him. Tomorrow Jim would have to retype the building roster one more time. Less than twenty of the original sixty-four residents are here. All the death becomes normalized. Every week lists of friends' names and obituaries were printed in the local paper, all from the same disease. Certainly, Sarajevo and Belfast and South Central LA had their death tolls. But this I felt and saw. We rarely heard about those deaths, just as the world knew little of these, just the celebrities, Rock Hudson or Freddie Mercury. All was quiet and separate as we endured the "hell" of parting Emily Dickenson felt.

I looked up from writing and Brian was standing there, but without his usual grin or sarcastic crack.

"I'm going crazy," he confessed, looking at me blankly from behind his round glasses. Ernie was Brian's best friend.

"I tried to see him just to say goodbye. Oh hell, just to say a few things, one last decent chat instead of the brief hellos, which were all he had energy for these last few days. This is beyond anything that most of us can imagine."

Later that afternoon, I went over to Julie's place.

"What happened?" she asked, looking at me.

"One of my clients didn't make it."

"What do you mean?"

"I mean he died. His lover died a few weeks ago. He was fine. But then after the art show, he crawled into bed and never woke up. His dad came to pick up his stuff. It was okay until I saw his dad taking his stuff away." I started trembling.

"Oh, Cab." She said quietly.

We lay on the couch gazing at the view of the city.

"Tell me about him," she said.

I began breathing harder and harder, grasping my hair, and pulling my head down.

"Well, he was the kindest man around. He always smiled walking through the building. He used to go to meetings every day, trying to stay sober after he tested positive, trying to live as best he could. But..." It was starting to be hard to talk. "He's gone," I kept saying over and over, hating the very idea of how hard he worked just to live a normal life, twice as hard as anyone else I know, breathing hard. "Fuck" I said to myself, between tears, as I gasped for air. "I'm sorry."

"It's ok," she soothed, holding me, running her hands through my hair.

"You are there by chance and I am here by chance," she said as she looked at me in the eyes. "You are a person who can't hide from these feelings and I can't help but notice them."

"It's so many goodbyes. My head is spinning."

"But we're a hello. Remember that."

"We're a hello."

All the death clutched me. Julie wrapped her arms around me, as if protecting me from the illness that seemed to be seeping the life from all of us.

Good Friday in the Castro

"I have to leave you now. I'm going to that corner there and turn. You must stay in the car and drive away. Promise not to watch me go beyond the corner. Just drive away and leave me as I leave you."
-Audrey Hepburn from *Roman Holiday*

On Good Friday, Julie and I strolled through the Castro after seeing *Breakfast at Tiffany's* at the theater. She was the Audrey of my world; her energy, olive skin and brown hair thrilled me. Neither of us knew what we wanted. But that was ok.

"It's kind of a sad movie," I said as we walked home.

"But she is fabulous," Julie said. "'Any gentleman with the slightest chic will give a girl a fifty-dollar bill for the powder room.' Words of wisdom."

"There are a lot fewer gentleman today."

"Yeah, she's a little lonelier than I remember."

I spent a lot of time at her house that week, eluding the world as best I could. But there were limits to escapism. That Sunday after work, Julie started kissing my neck and my mind wandered to Chloe. I didn't want it to. But it did. Julie was being affectionate. But I couldn't help thinking about Ernie and then of Julie and back to Chloe. The feelings I'd had of being with her, of trying to connect, to bridge the gap of separateness. Her roommate came home and we stopped. It wasn't working anyways. Chloe used to always joke about how bad the sex was. It was a sort of an invitation. Chloe feelings were coming up, sensations of separateness, of being together and apart.

In between dates and work, I bused around town interviewing whoever would talk for my San Francisco AIDS oral history. The interviews added intensity to life and work. After each, I'd go over the answers, looking for patterns in the stories of people coming here, reinventing themselves over and over, generation after generation, through the travails of letting go and finding something new.

After a week of interviews, I went over to Julie's. It had been a taxing day of handling both toilets not working. Half the guys had either neuropathy or some other physical disability. Everyone wanted to let me know that the elevators were down. I had gotten almost no sleep, going to bed at 1 AM after work, only to wake six hours later to go back to work the following day.

Julie didn't feel up for a movie, so we stayed home, having fun listening to one of the new mixes and cooking. I pulled her into her room and we enthusiastically started fooling around and I smiled and whispered how much fun it had been to fool around with her, to hang with her, and how fun that was.

"We must really like each other because our sex is terrible," I whispered, as Chloe had with me, with endearment and acknowledgement. It was one of those statements that had brought us together. But I hadn't really thought about what it meant. Not until I saw the expression on Julie's face. While I was trying to tell her how much I appreciated her, she heard the statement as an affront. She stopped kissing me and became silent.

"Well, maybe we shouldn't be doing that anymore then."

"Huh? What do you mean by that?" I asked.

"Exactly what I said."

"I didn't mean it like that. I didn't mean anything. It was a stupid joke Chloe and I used to say to each other."

"Well, I'm not Chloe. I'm not your job. I'm not any of those things."

She walked out of the room. I knew I'd blown it and I couldn't get the words back. A whirlwind of work pressure and relationship anxiety began to spin through my head. Julie and I got distracted and had to run back to the kitchen for the rice. We ate a bit and we got ready for bed. She guarded herself all night, covering and distancing herself.

"I just don't want you to lose interest," she whispered in bed.

"Do I look like I'm losing interest?"

I told her that it was a silly joke and a term of endearment. She was not convinced. I gave her a backrub, and listened to her talk about her weekend with her parents. "I barely gave Dad a hug," she confessed. The same thing was happening with me. Warmth was disappearing. Eventually, she went to sleep. I lay in bed looking at her, and wondered about the new separation coming between us. You are never so isolated as when you lay in bed with someone having not been able to communicate.

In the next few days, the miscommunications would only continue, as misunderstandings grew exponentially. She forgot to meet me at the museum, thinking I was coming to her house instead; same thing Sunday night when she was too tired for the movie. I ate the taxi money and went to her house. But we were missing something.

Boundaries were no clearer with work. I woke after dreaming about Ernie enticing me into bed with himself and his dead partner, Julio, lying there feeling repulsed. When one of the other counselors quit without notice, I had to work graveyard shifts all week long.

The only thing that was working was the writing project, interview after interview with people who moved here decades ago after World War II or Vietnam, hustled, who campaigned with Harvey Milk, acted up, had heard about HIV in its first days, developed buyers' clubs, or became treatment activists. With each interview, the stories become more and more interconnected. And over time, I started to find myself woven within this culture tale, observing myself making my way through the city. Listening to stories of chance encounters, conversations, Sue's old roommate who worked with Harry Britt, who took over Harvey's seat on the San Francisco Board of Supervisors. Writing, I found myself thinking of Dante taking on heroes and villains, creating an alternate reality in eternal exile.

As it all crumbled, I thought about Jaromil, who longed "for a girl's face lighted by the nudity" of her body, about Dante and Beatrice. Julie was drifting away like Audrey in *Roman Holiday*. But I couldn't walk away as she seemed to want me to.

"How can I make it up to you?" I asked as she became colder and more and more distant. She did not respond.

Instead I talked with my friends about it, the residents, everyone but her. I conferred with everyone I knew about the situation.

"Men focus on sex," David said at Café Flore.

"It's one of my favorite subjects. I could talk about it for hours," I said.

"I know but that's because you're a guy. The sex *is* the relationship for us. Whereas for them, it's something they do to keep the guy."

"Some actually like it."

"I wouldn't know," he said.

"But I wanted to talk about it. And that killed something. One of my old girlfriends once said I killed the mystery between people by over-talking things. I think she may be right."

"You try to communicate. But that's not always easy."

"Try and run a card to her. Tell her what you are thinking."

"Good idea."

I brought her my card at 8:30 the next morning, catching her at the beginning of her shift.

"How are you?" she asked, smiling enthusiastically. I got out of there fast, not wanting to distract her at work. "I'm sorry," I wrote. ".... You mean the world to me... Let's hang out." Later in the afternoon, I called her after she got home from work. She said she was happy to hear from me and invited me over.

An hour to get to her place, with slow bus after slow bus, when I arrived, I kissed her, hoping for more. She kissed me and then pulled away. The reality that this was not going to happen started to set in. I knew I'd miss her, but which deprivation tormented me more? When I saw Julie, I went crazy, in delight and frustration.

"You have to be around at least until April to go to that game with me," she smiled, referring to the San Francisco Giants season about to start.

"At *least* April?" I asked.

She turned away to cook.

So I worked and drafted notes about the cycles of feasts and famines, trying to figure it out. When I was wasn't writing I was interviewing people, as all the stories blurred into each other. There was the big San Francisco story and then there was my story. After turning in an article, I chatted with my friend Rebecca, my editor at *SOMA* Magazine. We were strolling along Valencia Street. I explained the situation to her. She had her dramas with her girlfriends as well.

"I'm so impressed with all this intrigue," I said, bantering away. "I had no idea."

I told her about things with Julie.

"I can't believe you said that. You can never make a woman feel like she is inadequate."

"I know. I know. I apologized and apologized. I sent her flowers and letters and mix tapes. She didn't let me kiss her or spend the night with her for three weeks."

"That's harsh."

"Becca, I am completely attracted to her aloofness, transfixed by her otherworldliness. Like the lesbians you see walking, talking, with no interest in you. They have another life."

"Well, elusiveness is hot. But Cab, I know this could be taken the wrong way. But the gay men you see here, they are born gay. They are gay in mind and body. But a lower percentage of lesbians are gay in mind. Many have just had bad experiences with guys. If you ever wonder about why the ladies are walking in another direction, you have to realize that women are involved in a mass reckoning with assault. Many are turning away from men. Men may not know that but it's part of the conversation."

"Guys have a lot to account for," I replied.

"Many do. My friend got an abortion when her boyfriend's condom broke. He said it was not him. He walked away because he could. A lot of women are doing the same thing."

"It's sort of the history of the world, repeating itself over and over again. One of the women in our building told me that she was exposed to HIV when she was raped. She started shooting up after that. It took her a long time to see the connection between the assault she experienced and what she was doing to herself banging the needle into her arm over and over again."

"Women are becoming active subjects in history here Cab, not objects of the male gaze. We are remapping our lives. Sometimes guys are part of it. But more often than not, we're leaving you behind. Guys are good to play with if we want. But not to depend upon."

"I know so I leave them alone. I have to. But another part of me wants to be the one who is different."

"Take your time, Cab."

"I know."

"Give her some space."

As I walked home, I looked at the city and thought of the people who'd come and gone, of Ernie's smile when he came in the door. I thought of Pedro, who shat in his pants at work the other day, of Julie recoiling, and the other residents who had crossed my path, the strangers out and about, half here, half elsewhere. The man selling flowers on the corner, the kids on skate boards, men looking for a glance, everyone strolling, talking, greeting each other, looking down, walking their dogs and living their lives as the sun went down at the corner of Castro and Market Street.

Made My Bed

"I've made my bed, I'll die in it"
-Hole, "Miss World". 1994

Kinship danced with aloneness all spring long. Julie and I saw each other every once in a while, briefly together, and always drifting apart. Eating Chinese food with Charles, my fortune cookie read, "A handful of patience is worth more than a bushel of brains." Few of us had much the spring of 1994.

Clinton's healthcare bill was floundering. Prop 187, demonizing immigrants was gaining support. Governor Wilson was running TV ads featuring Latinos crossing the border, blaming immigrants for unemployment. Walls were going up everywhere. Retrograde ideas about punishing the poor were gaining currency. And the Republicans looked like they might retake congress.

The recession might have been over, but few felt any of the gains.

"When is the economy going to get better?" Richard asked at work. "I check for prices. Everything's going up." Like almost everyone else in the building, Richard lived on a fixed income.

"I'm still devastated by what happened to River," bemoaned Lucy over beers at Casa Loma bar later that night. Since college, she had aced her LSATs, been accepted, enrolled, and dropped out of law school.

"I drove back down to LA and placed flowers at the Viper Room for River," she said, referring to the teen heart-throb who had died of a drug overuse the previous fall.

"Really? That seems like so long ago." I followed. "I'm still haven't gotten over Ian Curtis killing himself."

"I know. At least I'm not crying about Freddie anymore. I'm getting tickets for Hole at the Fillmore. Do you wanna go?"

"I'd love to. I love that album."

"Kurt wrote the whole thing."

"Really?"

"That's why it's so good."

"She drove him to kill himself, right?" I asked.

She shrugged her shoulders.

"As Courtney said, 'I gave that man a cup of coffee and a blow job every morning.' She loved him."

"I'm sure he was a piece of work to live with. Okay, let's go."

That night, we went to the newly opened Fillmore West on Geary, full of old Rock 'n' Roll posters from the 1960s and '70s and ephemera. But this was a new moment. I bought a dayglo colored poster, featuring a surreal purple donut, for the show. The place was teeming with people, music ratcheting from wall to wall.

"Someday you will ache like I ache," belted Courtney Love, screaming as if news of her husband's suicide was still fresh. We all seemed to feel that way. But instead of crying, our bodies slammed, grasping each other. Waves of sound and emotions thundered throughout the room. Courtney leaned off stage, backwards into a sea of hands. The crowd held her. Lucy and I jumped up and down, lunging with the crowd in a collective sweaty convulsion, my clothes were drenched, arm pits wet, oozing with teen spirit. I pulled myself up on the stage, hurled up and off the stage into the air, flipping backward, a gesture of hope for our collective future, landing on a pile of hands, the whole group catching me, lightly dropping me through the crowd of grunge kids, all of us linked together, at least for that moment. We all needed each other. I flashed back to doing the same thing at Husker Du shows in Dallas years prior, bodies moving in a montage of ideas, colors blurring, movements ebbing from the Beats to the Factory, poetry uptown, pop downtown. Punk was the first movement I felt like I was a part of, lunging back and forth as the Dead Kennedys played "Holiday in Cambodia" in Dallas in 1983. Bouncing up and down, from the stage into the crowd that grasped me, a new community seemed to invite me into a way of being. Seeing our lives as connected to something larger, it was a way of looking at the city, its streets, aesthetics, and bodies of ideas in space, shelved between the Beats and ACT UP. Kenny Scharf's surrealistic graffiti, the movement's burning ambitions, evolving shapes, images and sensations felt like a collective longing for something. Between graffiti and HIV, this space was ever flowing, tragedy overlapping with comedy. Looking at the bodies flying off the stage, like the Ramones blitzkrieg, the Avengers tales of cheap tragedies I listened to years ago, I wondered if their singer Penelope was still around, reading poetry somewhere. Sweating with countless others in this high-octane climax of lunging, hormonal bodies, our passions filled the old Fillmore, Courtney's grief, and all of our collective mourning.

"I'm Miss World, somebody kill me," sang Courtney.

The music lulled and pushed as the tempo changed, slowly building up to a crescendo of feelings, mixed with sound, the crowd throbbing, almost out of breath, elbows hurling to the violent, albeit lustful music, sexy and angry.

After the show, Lucy and I stood outside smoking, taking in the cold spring air.

"I want to tell Courtney how sorry I am," she told me.

"About what?"

"About Kurt."

"Don't you think everybody says that to her?"

"We'll see. Let's ask her."

She gestured over to Courtney Love walking straight over. There was Courtney, stumbling.

"Courtney, you were amazing tonight. I am so sorry about Kurt," Lucy said weeping, in a crazy empathic, star-worshipping display of emotion. It felt odd, moving and surprisingly real.

"Me too," Courtney wept in response, slurring her words, but sounding authentic and anything but annoyed with Lucy's sentiments. Completely high, she smelled like a few of the ladies I had made friends with in the Tenderloin. The three of us made our way around the Fillmore, talking about Kurt and music, fucked up and searching, stumbling and mumbling. She asked us if we wanted to get high with her. We demurred; she started to head back to the venue, turning left up an alley, red neon lights and the smell of crack emanating from the distance.

We kept walking back to the Haight.

"I loved the way she smelled," gushed Lucy.

"Me too."

"I thought she wasn't getting high anymore."

"I guess not."

"She smelled like whore," noted Lucy in envy, without a hint of judgement.

"I know."

"I just love that smell."

"We are too sensitive for this world. You know that, Cab?"

"I know."

We kept walking back, through the graffiti lined streets, broken glass everywhere.

"I have been seeing a lot of Bobby lately," Lucy said, changing the subject, referring to our old college friend.

"I haven't seen him as much. He drove up here a month or so ago. I love seeing him.... But he's nuts."

"I know. I adore him. He was working as a waiter. Now he's working as a personal assistant. He sits in the office watching the OJ trial all day."

"Have you followed that?"

"Yes, a bit. Everyone in LA follows it."

"Not, here. I can't stand it. People are dying every day and all anyone is talking about on TV is OJ. No one seems to give a shit about it here. Bobby and I talk for hours. But not about that trial. There is too much to hash through of the joys and the petty humiliations of past and future girlfriends. It's all pretty abundant for him."

"But what about your friend? Is that still happening?"

"I'm not really sure."

"That doesn't sound like it's going. I'm sorry."

"What about you?"

"Between Bobby, Freddie, and River I've got my hands full."

"I miss Freddie too."

"I miss him now more than ever. And Bobby just wants to be friends."

"Ah, I thought that ended in college."

"Maybe for Bobby, but not for me. I've been in love with him."

"Aw Lucy, I didn't know that. I'm sorry. You're right. I guess we're all going through it."

"Even Courtney, out there high and reaching out, telling tales like Blanche DuBois."

But for a second there, we were all together.

"I wonder if she found what she was looking for in that alley?"

In Ourselves

"The fault, dear Brutus, is not in our stars, but in ourselves."
-Cassius, in William Shakespeare's *Julius Caesar*

That spring an interplay between togetherness and isolation seemed to ease its way into most every interaction. Pedro hated the bureaucratic confines of the building on Market Street. Still we were inexplicably linked, ever dependent and repelling each other. Staff members documented the drama every shift. The daily log traced the ups and downs and goings-on from one shift to the next.

"What's up, Pedro?" I asked as Pedro sat on the couch in the lobby.

"Why should I tell you? If I tell you the truth, you'll write a memo." I looked at him as he stood at the elevator getting inside. It was going to be another long one. He came down shortly afterward.

"I don't need help from you or anyone else," Pedro declared. He was up and down all night. Usually he sat the couch. "I don't come down here to sleep. I come down here to hang out till the sun comes up," he confessed, in between dozing. "I hate to sleep at night cause I'm afraid of the night." He put Visine drops into his puffy, red, half open eyes. After a pause, he dropped his Visine. The noise of the bottle hitting the ground woke him again. He walked to the elevator. "I am going to take a bath and have something to eat. Maybe I'll be back down. Goodnight."

Later, he came back down, telling me he did not want to sleep. He was afraid of not being able to move. "I am scared to go that way. It's my worst fear to die and not be able to breathe. I woke this morning and could barely bring air into my lungs because of all the fluid and phlegm. My biggest fear is suffocating after being buried alive." He was back on the couch looking out the window to Market Street. "I don't know what to do with Boo Boo," he said, talking about his cat. I looked at him and saw a tear in his eye. "I spent the night in the hospital the other night and have to go again. But I don't know what to do about Boo Boo. She has to get food." He was looking out again and started to scratch his head. "Was it last night? I don't know. I need to get some stuff for my fish tank."

Romance did not make any more sense.

David and I met at Café Flore with two new friends, Paul and Mark. Paul and Mark were snuggling and chatting. They were asking about me about my life with roommates in San Francisco.

"Two roommates in the Haight sounds a little tight," Paul said, with an effected, almost British accent. He had been a college professor, but that didn't work out. So he made his way here.

"And my roommate Ray just came out, so there's a little high drama several days a week. He's becoming more and more precious."

"Can you just ask for a butch day to get yourself a break?"

"I'm not sure that would work but it's worth a try."

Paul always gossiped about his days at Princeton, where he seemed to imply everyone was queer. He gave lots of suggestions for my plight as a heterosexual man in queer San Francisco.

Gradually, the topic moved to sex and romance.

"So who holds out on who first?" I asked looking at Paul and Mark.

"You mean using sex as leverage, a way of making a point or hurting another person?" asked Mark, sitting up. "That's the worst. I would never do that. And if someone did that to me I would hit the road. I would say, you know hon, you aren't the only ass in the city. You think I'm going to sit around and wait? I'll be back in a few hours. And I would leave, even if I was just walking around for a little."

"Guys don't pull that shit on each other," Paul added.

"No, girls are taught all their lives to use sex for that, to use sex to control the people they are with," Mark followed.

"My sister controls her boyfriend back home, giving him blowjobs if he's good, withholding to make a point. I kind of feel sorry for him," David commiserated. "But it's his choice."

"Not to mention, usually by the time that goes on in a relationship, things are terribly, terribly wrong," Paul said. "You know what?" he continued, as if he had just had an epiphany. "Maybe you should go out with a dyke."

"I'd love that. But, what's in it for them?"

"The problem would be finding the right one."

Things were getting nonsensical.

As I was walking out, I thought about the story, "Trying to Know Julie" wondering if I would ever figure out an ending.

I sat at the barbershop on Haight Street. One of Mimi's friends from Atlanta was there. We chatted about haircuts and the number trim to get. He had a sharp buzz cut. I wanted one, but had never had it quite so short.

"Tell him to use the number three and you'll look great," he advised, before walking out.

"Your friend was smart," noted the older Italian barber.

"It's true," I replied.

"I don't run into too many dumb people around here anymore. You can't be. You just can't be naïve in this world anymore."

"It's true," I agreed.

"I have been here since 1949. You have no idea how much I have seen change over these years."

"What was the craziest time you ever saw out here?"

"Oh the 1960s—they were wild. But I don't know how you kids survive now. These streets through here used to be very active. Well, they are still. But now everyone looks dead out in the streets." He gestured outside, where a few crusty punks with dreads sat with a dog and guitar, nodding off by a tip jar. "Then the drugs, the acid, and the speed and now the crack. Back then, the streets were full of people going out dancing and enjoying their lives. They all smoked, but they were happy on the insides. Today, people look unhappy on the inside. And then there's AIDS. It's gotta make you crazy."

"Believe me, it does."

"When I was young, I used to be able to put a needle in my arm—get high—no problem. Share a needle—no problem. Fuck a girl without a condom when she is on her period and all bloody. Now I don't know how you kids do it."

The number three buzz cut did look pretty good.

"Do you mind if I give you a number two buzz on the sides?" he asked.

"Go for it."

"See, it looks great."

"Thanks."

I thanked the old barber, paid up, and left.

I walked through the neighborhood. It had been weeks since the gaffe and it seemed like it was over but I could not admit it.

I called Julie just to see what she was thinking. She didn't pick up, but she called me back a few hours later.

"When I got home, I didn't hear your message and I went to do my laundry and just got back," she explained.

I thought of Mark's sentiment at Café Flore.

Mimi and Chris concurred between episodes of *90210* and *Melrose Place* later that night.

"Just act like you don't like her," they advised. "It's the best way to make a woman like a guy."

"Such games."

"Always. Look women find their power in countless ways."

On *Melrose Place*, Allison told her hot therapist that she didn't think he was doing her any good.

"You don't see," he told her. "But you run from every man who cares about you. You have not loved Billy since the day you got engaged."

"Its such a soap opera," gushed Mimi.

"I love it. Some of my favorite stories are soap operas. There is a kernel of truth in them. Mario Vargas Llosa says we're at our best when we separate sex and love."

"Really. I don't believe that," Chris chimed in.

"Do you believe that?" asked Mimi.

"I'm not sure. I love sex. I adore it. I also want the body and the spirit. But I'm starting to wonder if it's possible. Maybe growing up means we do away with the soap opera of romantic love?"

"No," they both replied.

"It makes us crazy," argued Chris. "But..."

"Makes me crazy," Mimi interrupted. "But I wouldn't live without it, especially when the two overlap. The combination is rare but lovely. But it's not always necessary."

"It is also the source of our pain," I conceded. "It makes us miserable."

"Getting dumped is hard. But it opens up something," Chris added.

"I just don't know. I'm starting to wonder if it's possible to merge it all. It can't just be pleasure, can it?"

"Why not?" Mimi chimed in. "Maybe it doesn't have to be connected to anything?"

"Well, I usually would agree with that. But even then it leaves me wanting."

"Well, maybe that wanting is what you could write about."

"Sex is about freedom—from convention and repression," I replied. "But I feel like I'm losing something chasing it."

Dr. Carl

The next morning, I took the bus to see Dr. Carl. I told him about my week—the interviews I was doing, the women, the barber, a dream I'd had about a guy I had fooled around with in high school, and Ernie's dad carrying out his leather jacket.

"Cab, you describe this overburdened self. Do you realize how powerful some of this stuff is?" He'd suggested I start writing down my dreams.

"I had a dream this morning. I was in bed at my grandparents' house in the late 1970s with my brother. I was nine and he was twelve. I had been listening to the Bee Gees on the radio and fell asleep. Half-awake in the middle of the night, there was a sensation. I felt something below my waist. I looked down and my older brother, who had been asleep beside me, was under the sheets giving me head." I started becoming very emotional.

"What's going on?" asked Dr. Carl. "Tell me where you are at now?"

"I'm not sure." I started weeping. "I'm not sure if it was a dream or if it really happened."

"How can you tell?"

"I could never really tell. I'm not sure what happened. It was a rattled feeling of being very little in the same bedroom where my uncle stayed after the war. Grandad used to scold him for peeing in the middle of the night and waking him up. My uncle went to Vietnam, but said staying with Grandad was scarier. Grandad came home from the war and beat all the love out of everyone for him. He scolded dad for masturbating. So there I was in that room with the radio, the Bee Gees playing 'How Deep is Your Love.' It was so icky. The memory seemed so real. I went right back to sleep. But I just don't know what was real or not. I just don't know what to do with those feelings."

"That sounds very real. Did it happen?"

"I think so," I responded, feeling emotional, tears trickling down my cheeks. "I always remembered it that way. But it's just becoming something I'm becoming aware of only now. I'm just beginning to see how fucked up that was. We never talked about it. It was just kids growing up. We all felt embarrassed and ashamed for mom and dad fighting and screaming so much, scared to say anything for fear of dad or grandad beating us even more. If we ever questioned what was going on, the belt came out. And dad cried and ranted; Mom ran away, and grandad terrified us."

"Cab, do you know the difference between embarrassment and shame?"

"I guess."

"One is feeling awkward about something and another is feeling like you did something wrong. Now you sound like you did something wrong. But you were a kid."

"I know. But it was all part of being a kid, my parents and grandparents, drunk and violent, all the screams, they still ring in my head, dad screaming at me, the ever-present violence, my mother checking out, driving her crazy until she moved away, looking for tenderness, my brother, my mother, me..."

"Cab, you didn't do anything wrong."

"Well, I've done something wrong now."

"What have you done wrong?"

"I've blown off so many, so many of my girlfriends, haven't been as present when I heard their stories about the pain, the violence they've gone though. Chloe was raped by the janitor at school and they had to sew her up afterwards. Marsha had a guy force himself on her at a party. Sue, where lines got blurred. Julie, where something happened with her father. I didn't try to understand. As long as I got laid everything was fine. There are so many women with so much pain, trying to grapple with the violence they've endured."

"You didn't let them all go?"

"Well, Chloe blew me off, like Julie is doing now. I feel like I'm living through some weird Greek drama, that bad movie that keeps on repeating and repeating itself. The furies are out there, laughing. I blew everyone off and now I'm on my own. But I feel like the underground man in *Notes from the Underground*, ruminating about his nemesis. And now I troll around San Francisco, wandering the Tenderloin, making friends in the tranny bars, finding dates in the dark corners."

"You sound like you regret some of that. But you don't need to go through the world like this."

"It all just feels very large, with each piece connected to something else—violence, assault, HIV, drugs, sex. Just this spring, something like a quarter million people died in Burundi and Rwanda—a quarter million people, slaughtered." Tears started pouring down my cheeks. "That's the same number of people who have died of AIDS here in thirteen years. It's overwhelming."

"Cab, your tears are not going to stop anyone from dying. They really are not."

"I know. You're right. But everything out there—the poverty, the hate, whatever is going on in Rwanda, AIDS, and all these women I know who have been raped. There is so much pain. And I feel, in a way, a part of it."

"You are a part of it. We all are. It's a big feeling."

"There is so much betrayal out there. All the guys in the building, left behind by the world, to perish. The women enduring on their own. I can see why they no longer seem to have an interest in guys like me."

"Cab, there is your life, with all its rights and wrongs and then there is the larger world out there. You don't have to carry all that weight."

"It's hard to see them as separate."

"They are not necessarily separate, but you have your life to live."

"But I've got my own culpabilities in some of this."

"At some point, all these stories intersect. We carry the weight of our histories with us. You just told me a story about a kid enduring something very hard, feeling responsible and burdened, without being able to move past it, so he repeats it, and passes on the feeling."

"The feeling has been inside me so long, I don't know what to do with it. How do I learn from it?"

"Be aware of it. Tell your story. Let go of the shame. Don't just act it out. You're growing up, seeing the world as it is, in all its yin and yang. And you're starting to see your life as part of this. The weight of your childhood might be a little heavy. You don't have to carry it with you. Learn from it instead of repeating it. Learn from those you are with. A part of empathizing is really hearing the stories of others. And look at your own life, your own story. Tracing our own shadows, we become more attuned to the lives of others. Jung described this as knowing our full selves. It's a way of bringing light into the darkness."

"Peeling the layers off ..."

"So to speak."

When we finished the session, the sun was out. I wandered across town, past Polk Street, looking at everyone strolling about. Some guys were spray-painting, shaking their spray cans. A few others were skateboarding by. The city was in motion, lights and colors, shadows and murals on the wall—all blurring together.

Grace

"Seemed to me that drumming was the best way to get close to god."
-Lionel Hampton

At work, Jim was worried about Pedro.

"You haven't seen Pedro all day, have you?"

"No. I know he was going to and from Juan's apartment. He was upset about something."

Jim went upstairs to let himself into Pedro's room. He came down five minutes later in a fury.

"Cab, please call the ambulance," Jim told me as he ran down.

"Is Pedro okay?"

"I found him lying, unclothed, face down on the bed."

"Is he breathing?"

"Barely."

The ambulance came and took Pedro away in a stretcher. His body looked limp; his eyes rolled up into head.

As Pedro left, Roz, the sister of one of the residents, came in. "Keith just died," she notified me, referring to her brother. She looked sad, but relieved. In an odd way, I was as well. I enjoyed talking with Keith until the very end. But the last few times I talked with him, he hacked his lungs out, just asking if his meal had arrived from Open Hand. The last time I'd seen him, Roz was pushing him in his wheel chair. He looked out as if beyond this world, then back at me, smiled, and said, "Hey you, how are you doing?" A light-hearted greeting, the guy had pretty much accepted where he was going and what was happening to him. "You gotta be happy and comfortable letting it all just happen, allowing the spirit to watch over you," he'd said earlier in the year. "I found myself in some incredible places by just allowing things to happen. Once, I woke up in front of the Acropolis."

Thinking about Keith traveling the world and ending up in a last stop in San Francisco reminded me of all that I loved about the place. Keith used to forget his sister was coming to see him. She'd wait in the lobby for Keith to pick up the phone. Roz was old school—a southerner who had moved to Chicago during the Great Migration in the 1950s. She took it to herself to educate me about the importance of jazz as cultural sustenance and spiritual uplift. We spent hours talking jazz while waiting for Keith to pick up the phone. In a simple little way, our conversations may have helped distract her from ugly realities of her brother's deteriorating condition.

"To know a person, sometimes you never know who your best friends are, who your friends are. They might be right here in front of your face," Keith explained that last time we talked. "If I had the strength, I'd write some of this down, you know." But he never did write it down. Instead, those memories seemed to fade away, floating in a never never space, making their way into the lines in my blue notebook.

"Cab, this is something from Keith and I," Roz said, offering me a package as she was leaving. I unpacked it to find a biography of Lionel Hampton, a jazz musician. Inscribed inside she had written, "To

Cab, a wonderfully refreshing polite, caring, and compassionate human being. Keith and I thank you for your sincere concern and kindness... more than you can ever know. Unfortunately, today, it is rare. And how great it is to know someone who appreciates and enjoys exploring history in so many varied areas and who know that the future will only be as successful as our understanding and knowledge of it. Enjoy! Roz an Keith, '94."

Everything slowed down the next few weeks. Without Pedro around, the building felt quiet. Nothing really happened. No Julie. No Mimi, No Chris. No Juan. It just stood still. We just stood.

I walked out to clean the sidewalk in front of the building.

Pedro walked by. At first I thought he was an apparition.

"I was afraid you left the door locked," he said and smiled, holding the door open.

"You're back," I walked up to greet him. "I'm so relieved. I wasn't sure you were coming back."

"Neither was I."

We were both beaming.

"I lost 40 pounds. Thirty in the last three weeks. That was scary. The hospital helped me stabilize. And I'm back to the way I should be. I never thought I would want to gain weight. I gained two pounds and it was a good week. I have ten more pounds to go and I'll be happy."

"I'm glad to be talking with you. I was worried. You seemed pretty upset."

"I was. I'm sorry for that the other day. Cab, I wouldn't do that to you. I know how much this job means to you, after all we've been through."

"It's okay, I'm just glad you are here."

"I'm in a state of grace. I have done so many crazy things and I'm still here. I heard about Keith. How can he be gone and I am still here?"

"I know. But it's out of our hands."

"I saw him that last week before I went into the hospital and he mumbled to me that he had all the gratitude in the world. He pointed to his heart and smiled."

"'Gratitude is when memory is stored in the heart and not in the mind.'"

"Who said that?"

"Lionel Hampton."

"He liked to smoke weed," laughed Pedro, with a cough.

It was good to see Pedro out again. We wouldn't fight any more. I wouldn't write any more memos about him and he wouldn't try to bring me meals.

We talked most of my shift.

302

Last Dates

"...now we're done with sex, where we gonna go?"
-Kathy Acker *Blood and Guts in High School*

"I don't know what to do," I said on the phone with Rick.

"Well, let's talk. Let me help you out."

"Julie wants to go out again."

"What? I thought you were going out."

"Not really. I thought she had blown me off."

"What happened?"

"Well, I got back into town after our trip to LA, I called her. The next day she returned my call. I asked her what we were doing. 'I don't know,' she responded and added 'I don't feel like talking about things now.' She got off the phone to answer another call and didn't call me back."

"She sounds like she's done or at least on the fence."

"Really on the fence. Sounds like I'm the idiot still chasing her."

"Why?"

"Well, nothing else to do."

"Ok, so then have fun with it."

"And then she said lets get dinner."

"What are you two doing?"

"I'm making her dinner and taking her to a movie."

"If she doesn't want any tonight, then I would say you're going to have two options. You can either tell her you need to talk or you can keep on letting her test you the way she is."

"I know, but I can't stand that she has one up on me the way she does. That's the problem. She has the carrot. She owns all the cards. She can do without me longer than I can do without her."

"But she's really hot so..."

"I don't know. I have no idea how much longer this can last. I walk around wondering what I'm going to say if she dumps me. I have it all planned out."

"So you have nothing to fear? What are you cooking?"

"I was thinking of making burritos."

"Ok, just keep it light and control yourself. She's testing you."

"She's testing me and I'll never understand."

"We all get insecure. So be good to her. Romance her. Tell her how beautiful she is."

"I do all the time but it doesn't work. She doesn't care. These women are enigmas."

"So do this. Learn as much as you can from Julie and start something else on the side."

"That's what everyone was saying on the chat-rooms on the Well. Keep things open."

"What's the Well?" asked Rick.

303

"It's a San Francisco online community. It's only getting started. The whole world is changing here, including dating."

"Then get hip, Cab. But if you sleep with her again, don't tell her how bad she is."

"If..."

I got off the phone and started planning the evening. I looked up jazz clubs to go to after dinner. I bought groceries and a little Pinot Noir, to take to Julie's house after work. And went to work.

The residents had another art show in the lobby, where everyone was gathered for the reception. Halfway through, Carlos called an ambulance. It showed up about 15 minutes later. Everyone was busy munching on burgers, gabbing and listening to music when the paramedics brought Carlos through the lobby in a stretcher. He had been vomiting profusely all day. The room was silent as they carried him through. We wished him the best.

"Everyone has been through so much for so long," Richard said matter-of-factly on his way out for cigarettes. At the end of my shift, several of the guys left in drag to go cheer up Carlos.

"Go get yourself some ice cream after work and don't worry about any of this," Al told me as he was leaving.

I left for Julie's. When I got there, she was already cooking in the kitchen.

"Do you think this will be enough pasta for my lunch?" she asked. "I just love having lunch packed from home for work." She sang "Revival" by Mi Phi Me to herself while moving around the kitchen. She was in her own world. Her eyes turned to me and became self-conscious. I recalled the first time I talked to her on the phone, when we talked about the movie *Reality Bites*. Her enthusiasm filled my ears with an endearing charm. "I've thought so much about that movie," she chimed in, her voice high and sometimes silly. She had sounded young and childish but I was won over. Now when I looked at her eyes, I saw the ocean, an abyss, not sure anything was there. Like swimming in dark water, I had no idea what was there.

She made cappuccinos and we sat in the living room.

Sipping the foam, I gazed around the room—the view outside her window toward the city, the goofy CD's, her cat named Anchor Steam, the coffee table with copies of *Details Magazine, the J Crew Catalogue*, the old *Time* magazine we'd talked about, and Julie sitting on the floor right in front of me. It had become a sanctuary of sorts over the last couple of months.

"How was your day in the wine country with your mom?" I asked her.

"We tried a few wines, had a group discussion about when to have sex and just hung out."

"You know I become incredibly charming at wine tastings."

"I'm sure you do," she said.

"So, what did you guys conclude?"

"That we shouldn't, no one should have sex if they don't want to."

"No course not," I replied, recognizing she was probably talking about us. I changed the subject. "I love your outfit," I told her.

"Even the t-shirt? I thought it was too big."

"I like it too big. No seriously, it kind of looks like a uniform from a show like space *1999* to *Star Trek: Next Generation*. You know how they all wear matching adult contemporary casual uniforms that are also utilitarian? Like they could go from a big meeting with a general to beam down to another planet or something. You know what I mean?

"Cab Callaway, you are a real piece of work," she laughed while shaking her head. "What do you want to listen to? I want to listen to a CD."

"How about a little *In Utero*?'"

"I refuse to put that on for you. It was only a couple of weeks ago that you were saying you hated that cd."

"Not me. It must have been someone else," I lied, bantering along. "Not me. I have always loved that song."

"Yes, you. You made me turn off the CD."

"Okay, I have to admit it. His music sounds better now that he killed himself."

We listened to the CD and tried to talk, cooked a bit. The conversation eventually trailed into nothingness and we both started reading. When she went to go brush her teeth, I stopped reading and started pacing up and down the hall of her house while waiting for her to be done with the bathroom. The tension about the bathroom wait seemed worse than usual. Our last few nights had ended badly. I wished we had just finished it on the phone so we didn't have to go through this tonight. I thought of the last time met.

"I'm feeling super exhausted," she told me at the same point in that evening. "We should stay home and watch a movie instead of go out," she said. There seemed to be little I could do to settle the situation. I leaned over to kiss her and she pushed me away.

"You don't want me."

"Right now, I'm totally not feeling sexual and you're just going to have to bear with me on this one." She started to cry. I asked what was going on and she pushed me away.

"Don't interview me."

There was a long, silent pause.

"I can't take this..." I mumbled to myself. I got up and put on *Harold and Maude*, a movie that I usually adored. But I couldn't help but dwell on how bad things had become, not knowing if I should cut it off. I really liked her. I knew I'd miss her. Still, the two of us lay on the couch, awkward and angry. Harold was busy planning his own death. I admired him for it, laughing at each prank. Julie was not laughing. I spent twenty minutes with the words on my lips, imagining the consequences, and fearing saying what I needed to say.

"I think you should go home," I finally blurted out.

"What?"

"I think you should go home. I can call you a cab."

"I think you're being unfair."

She sat there on the couch in our makeshift living room, not moving, not getting up, not putting on her shoes, just looking at me. She was not leaving.

"Okay, well I'm going to bed. You can come if you want."

She came into the bedroom and we lay there, estranged.

"I still believe I have a lot of love to share," she whispered.

"You do, Julie. You helped me with Ernie, that really helped. But you haven't been here since then. I don't know what that was about. I feel like I'm chasing you now."

"I'm chasing myself too Cab," she confessed. "When I was a kid people always made fun of me. My parents used to tease me for being bashful. When I was a teenager, the other girls used to tease about sex stuff. And I used to freeze. Now when I hear something like that, I freeze."

We tossed about, half asleep all night. But I was still glad to see her and be with her, gradually accepting where she was, and that I ought to be better at just accepting things. Looking at her asleep in bed, my mind trailed back to my younger self when sex had something to do with two people sharing something and mutually wanting each other. To be without clothes meant trust, an exposure, a joy of youth—not something to be ashamed of. We made it through the night. Julie was in a hopeful mood when she awoke. And we'd made plans for tonight. But now the door was locked in the bathroom. I thought of how even when things were really bad between Chloe and me, we still brushed our teeth together. But Julie was in the bathroom by herself with the door locked. Eventually she finished and I went to brush my teeth.

She was sitting and looking disgruntled when I finally walked out of the bathroom into her bedroom. "Cab, I don't know what's going on," she said, shaking her brown hair and looking down, not knowing what to say. This was it.

"What's up, hot stuff? You need some time on your own?"

She nodded in agreement. "I feel really bad. Like I've been taking you for granted for the last few weeks."

"Don't worry about that, Julie. We just need to give each other a break."

"I just don't know what I'm doing."

"It hasn't worked the last few weeks and we might as well nip it in the bud. Ever since I said that stupid thing I said, things have not worked at all. And I sent you that card which really did not work."

"I know, it was sweet but it made me feel really weird."

"Well, I feel bad that you showed me yourself and that I made light of it."

"Yeah, but I hate to think I am so fragile. I know I cannot deal with being in a sexual relationship right now."

"We should stop seeing each other, then."

"Cab, but I know no matter what that I will keep seeing you and you will stay in my life."

"But we won't being going out anymore," I said looking at her. I knew we would not see each other again.

She just looked at me in an odd sort of way.

"That all sounds very defeatist."

"It's reality. We should just cut our losses and move on. If we're having problems at this point then..."

"Oh, Cab. I don't know what to say. I just need to sleep and figure this whole thing out."

"Julie, this hurts. We had such a good run and then it switched like a whiplash. It makes me so sad." Feelings started to well up, but then they stopped. I got up, picked up my shoes, and had a final look at that old window with a view of the city. I put on my jacket, walked back to Julie, leaner over the bed, gave her a hug without looking at her, pulled away quickly, said goodbye and left. The finality of the whole thing was a lot faster than I would have expected.

Outside, my eyes trailed down Broadway, through Chinatown, past the Transamerica Building, out to the water, and beyond the bridge. I thought about where this tale of the city had taken me, in between walks to work with Julie over the last few months.

Walking downstairs, I remembered lying in bed with Chloe at Vassar just a few weeks before I left for Italy. "I'm only going to say this once Cab, but we've been through a lot together," Chloe noted reflectively. We knew it was about over then, just as it was with Julie. There were other stories to be explored. Toward the end of high school I wrote, "I've got the blues all over, it's time to leave some of them behind" in my notebooks over and over again. But why had I had the blues so long? I knew there were others out there. There would be other stories, of course. I knew that.

A Raymond Chandler Evening

It's a Raymond Chandler evening
At the end of someone's day
It's a Raymond Chandler evening
And the pavements are all wet
And I'm lurking in the shadows
Because it hasn't happened...yet.
-Robyn Hitchcock and the Egyptians, "A Raymond Chandler Evening," 1986

Leaving Julie's I walked down Polk Street, found a pay phone and called Charles.

"Hello?"

"Charles, this is Cab. Is it too late for me to be calling?"

"No, not at all."

"I'm in your neighborhood. I was with Julie."

"Do you want to come over?"

"That would be great. Do you have smokes and stuff?"

"I'm just about out. Wait—did you break up with her?"

"I'll pick up some cigs," I said, not answering his question.

I stepped into a cafe where I used to go with Mimi and Chris when they lived in the neighborhood to buy a pack of smokes. The rain was picking up, creating a slick colorful shimmer. The city lights reflected on the puddles on the sidewalk. It took me a little longer than I expected to get to Charles's apartment up on Hyde and Clay.

I was in the mood for a drink. Standing outside, Charles buzzed me in. When I got to his floor, the door was open. Heaven 17's dance anthem "Please Don't Go" was playing, and Charles was sitting there with a book in his hands.

"I love this line." He smiled, looking at me, pushing his reading glasses down and reading from *The Long Goodbye* by Raymond Chandler:

"...The first quiet drink of the evening in a quiet bar—that's wonderful."

"That would be wonderful," I said.

Charles stopped reading, looked at me and asked,

"Do you want some coke?"

"Sure."

"Coke first then bourbon and Coke, OK?"

"Perfect."

"First more Chandler," Charles insisted. "'The queer is the artistic arbiter of our age. The pervert is the top guy now,'" Charles read some more. "What do you think Cab? Do you agree?"

"Absolutely he is. He has to be. Certainly, the aesthetic arbiter. That's what the city is all about."

"Here's to that," Charles replied taking a big snort of coke, through a rolled-up dollar bill. He offered it to me. "Bump?"

"Thank you very much," I replied, putting the dollar bill to my nose, leaning over to the table, where the coke was lined up, and taking a line up my nose "The people perverted will never be converted," I declared when I was done, scratching my nose. "Everything is changing. And staying the same, as my saga with Julie attests to."

"Yes, well these stories dart back and forth, taking us places we could never imagine."

"Yes they do," I replied, holding one nostril then the other, breathing in, the cocaine making its way up my nasal passages. I looked around the cozy room, the high ceilings, windows, lights and views of the rooftops across the city. "This place looks great," I said, starting to feel very high.

"This is going to be the early 1980s room with the TV, and all black steel furniture," Charles said, mixing a consolation bourbon-and-Coke and handing it to me. "I'm glad you came," he said, scratching his nose. "There is a chance for us," he continued.

"I hope you're right."

"I'm sure. It's all opening up for you.'"

"Is it?"

"You don't sound so optimistic."

"I'm just relieved. My world does feel better. It feels lighter. I'm so relieved. I kind of feel high."

"Me too. I've been toasting to Nixon. Can we toast to Nixon?" he asked, rubbing coke on his teeth.

"No Charles!" I looked at him. "I can't toast Nixon. Plus, I thought Republicans were against drugs?"

"Only the losers," Charles smiled. "So what happened with Julie?" he continued putting his finger to my teeth with a little coke for my gums. "Nummy?"

I rubbed the coke on my gums.

"It's nice right?" Charles continued.

"Yes," I replied, pausing and thinking. "I feel like the conversation ended. We ran out of things to say or feel."

"Damn, she was cute." He paused. "But I think there was more to it. She was a part of something in the city that you were attracted to, the new place you were trying to know..."

"While letting go of the old," I interrupted Charles.

"She was lovely."

"Julie was a feeling and a mirage I could never hold. The real beauty was everywhere else, the people around me, the quiet heroes."

"Why did it all slow?" asked Charles.

"My gaffe."

"Well, maybe?"

"What do you mean?"

"I'm not sure she could handle you."

"I guess. I mean, I think it was after I cried my eyes out about my client with her. I brought AIDS into our world. Before that, we were just flirting and hanging out."

"I know. But it shouldn't have mattered. She could not handle the sensation, the sex and stigma, survival guilt that you seemed to carry," posited Charles. "Even the dark humor of it, of living."

"Huh?"

"Your whole story, the activism, the breakups, the search, the trauma, this was all part of navigating the line between Eros and Thanatos that HIV brought up in your life, into the world around you."

"I never talked about that with her."

"But she felt it. She saw you. She sensed the rawness of your feelings. Everyone in this town is reconciling something about sex and their histories, the violence, the disease killing the guys here, the bashers who come in from the East Bay. People gravitate to the generative, life affirming feeling. Even if it gets addictive."

"I kind of followed it. When my clients went into those places, I followed them. I felt like I had to follow those experiences. I had to have those sensations. I had to cover up the bad stuff. She was a hiding place. And maybe that wasn't necessary. She was a life force."

"Yea, her story was in a different place than yours. What year did she get out of school?"

"1993."

"Well that explains a lot," he said.

"What do you mean?"

"We graduated into the recession after taking ecstasy in college," noted Charles.

"And maybe, imagining that there were some ideas for another way to live."

"There's still a little 1960s in us. We come from the 1960s directly. She missed that wave completely."

"I was only in the 1960s for a few months."

"That's enough. These guys got out of school with an agenda, looking to ride the next economic wave. What does Julie do?"

"She works as admin person in an internet startup," I replied.

"Well, that's it. Her mind was on other things."

"Makes sense. My friend Leather Tongue Lisa is making her own internet server."

"Lisa, who runs the video store on Valencia?"

"Yeah."

"I love that place."

"They're all on the Well, looking to do something else, to make money. They're different from us. But they're onto the zeitgeist in a way we may not be. This is a new world opening up, connecting people."

"Well most of it is right on. But it can miss a beat too. My friend said the other day that he wanted to help kids in Africa by getting them all computers. I was like, that's bad anthropology."

"Right. I know."

"It's weird. Maybe you're right."

"The Julies of this world are on a different trajectory. There's already a new dynamic out there."

"It's not just the internet. Nelson Mandela is going to be the president of South Africa. I never thought he'd get out of jail."

"I know. Let's drink to him," Charles poured me another drink and rubbed more coke on his teeth.

"To a free Nelson Mandela," I chimed in.

"And here's is to Nixon. Can we also toast to Nixon now?" asked Charles. "He's gone."

"Charles!"

"Come on Cab. He's dead."

"Ok, ok, he actually had some good domestic policies—Clean Water, Clean Skies Acts. Not quite LBJ, but he would have won without the break in. His ideas are still with us, the Southern Strategy, that unhinged racism, the War on Drugs, not poverty."

"To Dick going and Nelson coming."

"And Julie going...and new things coming." I paused, munching an ice cube. "The thing about Julie is, unlike Chloe, she was consumed with shame. But I have got to let go of that," I continued. "I don't know why I stayed so long. Do you know *On Our Backs* magazine?"

"Every issue. Lots of great fisting tips. Who knew?"

"And political commentary. It's full of people creating something else, gender fuck, drag kings... Julie didn't laugh. But she inspired me to write it all out. She was my muse."

"You don't need her now."

"You're right. But her scent, her skin..." I sighed. "It made her feel real. But maybe she was just an illusion, a reminder of something. An illumination..."

"Yes she was."

"But there's still a little to learn from SF. There are so many stories, so much longing, so many people finding their own pleasure, instead of waiting for the repressed."

"That's right."

"All right. Okay, I have another toast."

"To what?"

"To the Zapatistas."

"Who are the Zapatistas?"

"There was an article in *Z Magazine*. The Zapatistas are from Southern Mexico, blasting out dispatches about NAFTA on the internet. Anyone with a computer, any mom in Toledo, can be a Zapatista."

"A virtual movement?"

"In January, they issued their first declaration from the jungle, calling for subversive revolution with poetry."

"Do you mind if I changed the subject?" Charles asked, grinding his teeth. "Did I ever tell you about Josey—my old girlfriend?"

"No."

"She was amazing. Well, amazing when she wasn't writing bad checks from my checkbook. But she was black and she really liked that I am a dandy. The more dandy, the better. At Vassar, she loved the most fay guys. That was always her look. She didn't want macho. She wanted femme guys. She wanted men who she could dominate."

"Including you?" I asked.

"Well, we're not together, but I liked being dominated."

"How?"

"My favorite thing was being tied up with the red ball gag in my mouth."

"Teeth marks all over it. The pervert is the top guy, right?"

"Exactly."

"Pleasure turns to energy," I concurred. "Einstein's law. This is the New Jerusalem one of my clients declared the other day. A new city."

"Like the Catacombs, Temple of the Butthole."

"I know. I love Gayle Rubin's stories about it. She was popular because she had small wrists."

"Very talented."

"But then they had to close it because of AIDS."

Charles shook his head, "Gay liberation really only had a decade and then AIDS."

"But what of us?"

"Guys like me chasing girls like Julie?"

"Girls like Josey chasing and dominating guys like me."

"We're hopeless."

"Well, we might be the future?"

"I'm probably leaving at some point. I'm going to apply for social work school. Somewhere with less rules and more freedom."

"But don't move too fast. There's a lot to your story here," Charles said. "You don't want to leave it without figuring out what this meant or what's the ending."

"I know. You're right. But I can't find it. My oral histories are one book that makes sense. But the Julie thing hit a nerve. So did all the deaths. That's what I'm trying to figure out. They both happened at the same time. There's another book there in the other half of the story, in between feasts, famines and plagues. The same thing with all these women, my screwed-up repetition, it's all a part of a story. I'm just not sure what it means."

"That's what you should be writing about."

"I am. I've already started taking notes about what's happened. I want to make sense of our time here. The story of Chloe at Vassar and Tessa and LBJ Lucy at college, and Lili and company in high school and every girl I was ever dumped by or who I dumped, and why I turned away from the willing and sexy ones for the elusive ones I could never hold onto. All the sex panics that left us reeling. But we still run away. Why did Alvy turn down Allison Portchnik? She was lovely and more than willing."

"That's the million dollar question."

"But it all happened here in this wide-open town. One of my clients said the other day that Gay Liberation meant coming out as who you really are."

"Maybe it's better to be unhappy and be who you are. You learned a lot from them. Its also a little *Sophie's Choice*—the southern protagonist, and the encounter with the sexual 'other'—tainted by death."

"And the weight of history." I looked around the room, out into the fog night outside the window. "And we have a rainy San Francisco night and a city in front of us," I said. "Well, the first draft of my first novel was all about a grail sighting, what happens when we touch the sublime and then have to come back down to earth. We chase and chase and chase, grasp the grail and then we don't know what it means. We fail to ask the right questions, just like Percival, always chasing the grail, and leaving unchanged. Bobby and I were talking about the feeling of being with the girl who is supposed to be everything. She's smart. She's sexy and you still don't feel anything. And you realize there's still a long way to go to make sense of any of this."

"But Cab, you are. We are. You always are."

"I hope so."

"Thanks for being here tonight, man."

"It makes it fun, even if I never really got to know Julie."

"But Cab, you did. She's everywhere here."

Clueless

"I never dreamed I'd like any city as well as London. San Francisco is exciting, moody, exhilarating. I even love the muted fogs."
-Julie Christie

In 1903, Jack London published *The Call of the Wild*, about his adventures in the Yukon during the Gold Rush of the late 1890s. His journey brought him from California to some of the coldest places on earth. Along the way, he stumbled upon "a path blazed through the forest, an ancient path... The path seemed to begin nowhere and ended nowhere, and it remained a mystery, as the man who made it and the reason he made it remained a mystery."

I'd stay in San Francisco for another year, before leaving for graduate school out East. There would be other girls, adventures, an incident involving someone's head being shaved before make up sex, and lots more interviews that would make up the basis for my first book, hoping to make sense of it all, praying somehow that the carnage would slow, or reveal a secret meaning. None ever appeared. I wasn't sure what path brought me there during the peak plague years, four decades after my father had lived down the street. But the road showed me something larger, helping me connect my experience with countless others. For a while, it felt as if everything was disappearing, yet countless apparitions appeared along the road, as the clash between connection and separation revealed a new way of walk among them.

In the summer of 1995, I quit my job and travelled to Mexico. Deg and I got lost on the way, somewhere between New Orleans and Guanajuato. It wasn't the first or last time. We stumbled between Austin and Mexico, just about got arrested with Willy Nelson in Luckenbach, on Independence Day, before I drifted back to San Francisco to pick up my stuff. It was okay being lost. San Francisco had taught me that.

"It's okay getting dumped, Cab," Chris counseled me while we talked over a beer that summer. "You learn to be compassionate, to actually feel what other people feel. I know this sounds cheesy, but it's good you learned to feel and maybe even care."

"A part of me is glad it happened" I replied.

"Why?"

"It forced me to see beyond myself and my childhood, to see all of this city, its stories, other peoples' lives, and the movements to create something with them. If I hadn't gotten dumped, I wouldn't have had to move beyond myself and my little world, the life I had in high school, the private sphere of personal concerns. This forced me to see something larger."

Shortly before I left town, I met with Cleve Jones, the founder of the AIDS Quilt, for a brief interview. He was sick, having lived with HIV/AIDS for well over a decade. He recalled his friend Bobbi Cambell, one of the first people to die of HIV in San Francisco.

"There's been so many like him," he said. "I would like so much to be able to survive this and to tell these stories of how incredibly courageous we were. I know we made mistakes... terrible mistakes.

And I guess you have to say that we failed in so many respects. But I still think it's amazing what we have achieved. If the world could see it, I think the world could learn a lot about courage and dignity, what's important and what's not important. I have. My friends all have. It's been an indescribable horror to face, to continue to live and to continue to fight. It's pretty amazing. If Bobbi could do what he did, when he did, at a time when there was such fear and ignorance and hate, that's a real inspiration for me."

He continued, talking about other friends of his who suffered through horrible pain, who refused to give up easily, holding on to their last breaths.

"I consider myself a Quaker and Quakers worship in silence," he told me. "You can speak at meetings, only if you are moved by God to do so. In my whole life, I've only spoken at a meeting twice and once was after coming back from saying good-bye to Marvin before he died. When I watched Marvin, and all my friends, I would wonder where these people got the courage and the strength and the endurance to keep on going? But watching Marvin die, it was very simple. As long as Marvin was alive, he was being loved and loving back. That really was what kept him going. All of his family was there and all of his friends. He just really did not want to leave us. There are a lot of lessons of this experience that go way beyond boundaries of sexuality, way beyond anything about gay people. I hope our whole experience isn't lost. I don't think it will be."

I didn't think it would be either. Cleve wasn't sure he was going to live much longer than his interview with me. But he still missed his friends who were gone. This did not stop him from living. We went out for margaritas and smoked a joint driving through the woods.

"I've reached my perfect equilibrium of buzz," he said as we drove, passing me the joint. I had a bit of a crush on him. The whole life here was about these kinds of moments. It was all about the connections.

Jones would live for decades after that interview. He's still around today.

After leaving work, Pedro and I met up outside the building. There was more to his story than I knew. I wanted to figure some of that out, as well as honor the time we had put in together at the building. Sitting at a bar off Market Street, he pulled out a wad of cash and bought me a beer.

"Where did you get all this cash?" I asked laughing.

"You know," Pedro smiled. Without saying a word, we both understood what he was doing outside the building all those nights, all night long.

"Are you still seeing that girl from the bus?

"Nah. But I adored her."

"I'm sorry. You guys were so cute together."

"Enough to spin my head. I'm still spinning."

"Me too."

"She touched something in me, Pedro. Something deep."

"Oh Cab, she was a heartbreaker. But so are you. We all loved you in the building."

"Well, not everyone," I said.

"Okay, not everyone," Pedro concurred.

"Not Ted."

"Yeah, he used to call you the 'Iron Sphincter.'"

"Look at him. Maybe it's good I'm a little tight here."

"Too much."

"Really?"

"Nah."

"Remember Dave?"

"Who used to sit on that cart outside the building?"

"Yeah, Raoul hated that."

"Really? Little prick. No heart," grimaced Pedro. "A little Eichmann."

"He's the first one who died in the building on my job. So many deaths. It still moves me. I was so overwhelmed when I heard."

"Me too, Cab."

"The hardest was Terri and Frankie."

Pedro looked at me like I was nuts, paused and laughed.

"I thought you were bananas there. It was a toaster. She was dragging a toaster."

"Are you sure Pedro? Who's to say?"

"That was a lot of deaths ago."

"Too many. Way too many."

"I promise not to be a social worker like Raoul. I promise."

"You better not."

"There are other ways to be. You don't have to just go along."

"I promise not to be another Raoul."

"Caesar Chavez just died. Try to be more like him. Try to be kind. When I was a kid and my parents died, I ended up in Bellevue. And there was this orderly—not a social worker or nurse or anything. But he smiled, brought me food, and checked in on me every day. I was so down. I didn't think I could move. I didn't want to live. But he was so cute, his smile so sweet. And he wasn't the only one. My nurse used to give me a hug every day. I started to come back to life, until I got this."

"You seem like you are back," I said and smiled. "I promise to be like them."

"You better. So am I in your book?"

"You are my book. You really are."

We drank and laughed and talked about life in the building and San Francisco. He seemed to have forgotten or forgiven all those the memos. I called him to say goodbye before I left. But I didn't hear back from him. He didn't need me now. But we'd seen a lot of morning sunrises, illuminations on Market Street, had a lot of conversations through the past two years. He was still alive. I'd miss him most. He was the one who showed me connection like few others.

I wouldn't see too many of the rest of the gang again. Juan sat down for an interview for the book. So did a few others.

Over that time, several of the older friends from Texas made their way through town. I tried to write and make amends as much as I could. Becky even called me when she came to town. We went for coffee and a die-in with ACT UP at the Civic Center. She seemed to have forgiven the past.

Chloe called when she was passing through. We drank a lot of beer. I told her about my work and the loss exercise. She had recently had an abortion and seemed raw. We had a good cry together. She'd keep on moving down the same path. I lost touch with her as the years passed.

By this point, San Francisco was home. The openings and closings were everywhere. A couple of days before moving east, Jerry Garcia of the Grateful Dead, finally shuffled off, dying at the age of 53. The Deadheads had long been part of the landscape. I went to Golden Gate Park worried about his followers. When I got there some guys were playing hacky sack in front of a makeshift memorial. There was no apocalyptic death dance. He was just gone. The fans moved on to Phish. Jerry had famously turned away from playing at the Altamont concert of 1969, embracing life instead of conflict. His fans seemed to be doing the same thing.

A couple of days later, Charles and I got stoned and went to see *Clueless*, seeing it as a playful call to engagement. We enjoyed the final days in the city and I moved back east for graduate school, a copy of that old blue notebook in my bag. I wouldn't open it again for a long time. I'd only return rarely. In the summer of 1996, I walked down Castro Street and everyone looked alive again. My former clients who'd looked gaunt had flesh on their bones. People described the phenomena as Lazarus Syndrome after the new medications came out for AIDS. The near-dead were coming back to life again.

"1993-'95, were the worst years," recalled David Barr, of ACT UP, years later. "It was a really terrifying time. Then we got lucky."

They were the hardest years. Those of us who survived would carry the scars for the rest of our days. The executive director of the agency where I worked, Shanti Project, quit after having a breakdown. AIDS left wounds that lingered, even for those who were HIV-negative; survival guilt, and trauma seeped life out of the survivors. Conversely, resiliency and community regeneration were everywhere. So were the old wounds, that never really got better. I never stopped thinking about Thomas.

I was excited but had mixed feelings about the lessons of what had happened.

I wouldn't go back too many times. But I stayed in touch with Bobby and Charles, visiting them in Europe where they both eventually moved. I never saw Tessa again. Julie reached out on Facebook years later. I found Marsha there. At some point, she confessed she'd lived in a car and a tent drifting between homes with her daughter.

"I am reminded to embrace where we are rather than fear the unknown," she told me. "I would have to land somewhere, eventually. But I'm reminded to be grateful for this journey we are on and the love and support of family and friends. I am reminded not to become so attached to anything in life that we compromise our spirits. Without that journey, I would not know these things."

Chris stayed in San Francisco, while Mimi moved to New York, where I ended up. But we drifted apart. I saw Elizabeth at harm reduction conferences. But she was right. We were never going to be buddies. The sex panics we all endured would only accelerate nationally, triggering more conservative reactions, which I fought with all my being. As the years passed, I thought more about Thomas and became an AIDS activist, dancing to remember everyone I met in San Francisco. Those feelings kept me involved in the AIDS movement for the better part of the next quarter century, working in AIDS housing and harm reduction settings from Chicago to New York. At the syringe exchange program where I worked in the

317

Bronx, the losses continued. One of my transgender clients was thrown out of her single room occupancy hotel room window; another stopped taking his Hepatitis C medications which induced clinical depression, and he died; another OD'd; another went on a drug run only to return home to find her husband had died of a heart attack and her infant son had starved to death; another was shot to death. The police used to arrest my clients going to the program on drug possession charges, despite public health law stating they had the right to carry used syringes. There was no cure for the racism, for the violence, and the sexism that afflicted U.S. culture; instead it just fueled the epidemic and its related carnage.

Even years after quitting AIDS work and becoming a professor, I never quite stopped thinking about San Francisco. I carried that old blue notebook through moves from San Francisco to Chicago to New York, from apartment to apartment, where it sat on bookshelf after bookshelf, looking at me. But I didn't know what to do with it.

When I traveled, whenever I looked west, I remembered what had happened there. Driving from Austin, the memories screamed from the sky. When a client or friend died, I remembered everyone, as the new deaths opened all the old graves.

I'd often walk up to someone, who reminded me of someone who had once been with us, to say hello. Then I'd realize the silhouette in the distance was not my friend. My friends were in some other place. It was like a ghost, a good one, a sad one, a memory of a connection changing shape, within the fade in's and fade outs of this time.

And finally, two years after Dad died, a quarter century later, I pulled out the dusty old blue notebook, full of ACT UP stickers, and started rereading those stories that I had written during the graveyard shifts between Bush presidencies, daily notes, what had happened when I was trying to know Julie. And there it was. The story I was missing, that I had been looking for all those years, between oral histories and bad dates, was right here. It had always been there. Looking, I was able to see it for the very first time. So I started writing.

Acknowledgements and gratitude

While I believe good artists borrow and great artists steal, I humbly acknowledge the following works from which I borrowed ideas, inspiration, a few lines between friends in a much larger dialog about writing and living.

My and Greg Smithsimon's *The Beach Beneath the Streets*. *My White Nights* and *Ascending Shadows: An Oral History of the San Francisco AIDS Epidemic*. Rob Magnuson Smith's *The Scorper*. Jorge-Luis Borges' story "The Garden of Forking Paths." Erich Maria Remarque's, *All Quiet on the Western Front*. Elizabeth Bernstein's *Temporarily Yours: Intimacy, Authenticity, and the Commerce of Sex*. Milan Kundera's *Life is Elsewhere* and *The Unbearable Lightness of Being*. James Baldwin's *Giovanni's Room*. Michel Houellebecq's *Whatever*. Pat Califia's *Public Sex*, Arthur Koestler's *Darkness at Noon*. F Scott Fitzgerald's *This Side of Paradise*. Herbert Marcuse's *Eros and Civilization: A Philosophical Inquiry in Freud*. Project Inform's PI Perspective, issue #14, from June 1994. Leah Raeder. Isabel Allende's *The House of Spirits*. Armistead Maupin's *Tales of the City*. Spitz and Mullen's *We Got the Neutron Bomb: The Untold Story of L.A. Punk*. Terry Gilliam's *Brazil*. The Avengers "Cheap Tragedies." The Smiths' "Boy about Town." The Jam's "Boy About Town." The Buzzcocks' "Orgasm Addict." X's "We're Desperate." Herb Caen. Don Snowden's *Make the Music Go Bang: The Early LA Scene*. Pam Tent's *Midnight at the Palace: My Life as a Fabulous Cockette*. Wim Wenders, Peter Handke and Richard Reitinger's 1987 film *Wings of Desire*. Michael Mason (@MichaelPorfirio). Albert Camus' *Exile and the Kingdom*. Psalm 139:14. Walt Odetts' "Survival Guilt in HIV-Negative Gay Men," in Hatherleigh's Continuing Education for Psychologists, Vol. 4, #15. Tom Hallman Jr's 1986 piece, "Mount Hood Climbing Disaster Never Ended for One Father Until Now: Tom Hallman at large," *Portland News*, 5 September 2014. William Blake's *Songs of Experience*. Stephen Vizinczey's *In Praise of Older Women*. Thomas Wolfe's *You Can't Go Home Again*. Mattilda Bernstein's *The End of San Francisco*. Kathy Acker's *Blood and Guts in High School*. Gayle Rubin's *The Catacombs: A Temple of the Butthole*. Roman Holiday written by John Dighton and Dalton Trumbo. Shelley Jackson's talks with Vito Acconci, published in *The Believer*, 2007. Simon Critchley's *Bowie*. Joel Schumacher & Carl Kurlander's 1985 film. *St Elmo's Fire*. Fyodor Dostoevsky's *Notes from the Underground*. Nietzsche's *The Will to Power*. Ten Hands' song, "Old Eyes." The Last Poets song, "This is Madness." Italo Calvino's, *If on a Winter's Night a Traveler*. Joseph Cambell. Charles Bukowski's *Factotum*. Woody Allen's *Annie Hall*. Groucho Marx. Lone Justice's song, "Dixie Storms." Harry Chapin's song, "Taxi." Legs McNeil and Gillian McCain's *Please Kill Me: The Uncensored Oral History of Punk*. Hole's *Live Through This*. Julie Christie. Jack Kerouac's *On the Road*. Henry Miller's, *Tropic of Cancer*. Pat Conroy's *The Prince of Tides*. Mark 14:1-72. The Stoned Roses' song, "Bye Bye Badman." Poi Dog Pondering's; "Living with the Dreaming Body." Grateful Dead's, "Deep Elem Blues." Grace Jones', "Pull Up to My Bumper Baby." Billie Holiday's "I'll Be Seeing You." Clary Bundy's, "Killing Me Softly." Dylan's "Subterranean Homesick Blues." Alain-Fournier's *The Wanderer of the end of Youth (Le Grand Meaulnes)*. Franz Kafka's Letters to Milena. Jack London's *The Call of the Wild*. Doris Lessing's, *The Golden Notebook*. David Bowie's *Rock n Roll Suicide* and *Heroes*.

Bowie and Queen's *Under Pressure*. Adrian Drover and Jimmy Webb. T.S. Eliot's "The Wasteland," "Little Gidding," and "The Love Song of J Alfred Prufrock." Richard Harris', "MacArthur Park." Rilke's *Letters to a Young Poet*, as well as countless quotes from movies including, *Throw Mama from the Train*, *Princess Bride*, etc. William Butler Yeats' "When You are Old." Robyn Hitchcock and the Egyptians, "A Raymond Chandler Evening." Hole's 1994 record *Live Through This*. Love and Rockets song, "If There is a Heaven Above." And thanks to Jim Swanson, Gary Pantor, Tim Barkow, and Jamie Jenson for their iconic images of the art and culture of this majestic city.

Poetry advise courtesy of Scarlett Shepard; base lessons from Dodi Shepard. Thanks to Hannah Carl, Ian Landau and Craig Hughes for their careful edits, suggestions, and encouragement. Gratitude to Rob and Jamesy for inspiring, remembering, and chatting about the craft from San Francisco to Estonia to Honk Kong. Thanks for supporting the novel Jakob Horstmann.

And most of all Caroline for always being there to talk it through, even when this story was just notes in that old blue notebook. Reading chapters in the morning with you was always my illumination.

About the Author

Benjamin Heim Shepard is an activist living in Brooklyn and the author of *White Nights and Ascending Shadows: An Oral History of the San Francisco AIDS Epidemic* and several other books. This is his first novel.

***ibidem*-Verlag / *ibidem* Press**
Melchiorstr. 15
70439 Stuttgart
Germany

ibidem@ibidem.eu
ibidem.eu